SHE WRITHED WITHIN HIS GRASP, SOBBING AND CURSING HIM WITH all the swear words she could remember from the *arrieros*, but his mouth relentlessly continued its assault, his tongue teasing, flicking, at the soft peak of her breast, finally his lips covering, pulling gently, insistently at the nipple until he felt its softness grow taut in his mouth. His one hand had been resting lightly, fingers spread, on the slight swell of her abdomen, and when he heard her give a soft, startled cry of pleasure, his hand moved downward to add its gentle persuasion, stroking lightly the satin soft thighs, tightly pressed together, until they parted instinctively beneath the seeking, questing hand. . . .

Fawcett Gold Medal Books
by Marcella Thum:

MARGARITE

Marcella Thum

FAWCETT GOLD MEDAL • NEW YORK

A Fawcett Gold Medal Book
Published by Ballantine Books
Copyright © 1987 by Marcella Thum

Library of Congress Catalog Card Number: 86-91300

ISBN 0-449-12999-3

Manufactured in the United States of America

First Edition: February 1987

For Sharon McCaffree, fellow romance writer and friend

Chapter 1

"IT isn't fair, Mama! The dressmaker has just brought Margarite's gown for the carnival ball. If Margarite has a ball gown, why can't I have one too?"

The door had swung open so abruptly that the woman and man seated thigh to thigh at the tea table were too startled to pull apart. Then, hastily patting at her disheveled hair, Countess Elissa Ludwiga Von Melk gave her daughter a flustered, furious glance. Another moment, and she was sure Baron Von Friedrich would have invited her to accompany him to one of the balls being given by the imperial family at Hofburg Palace during the carnival season. Now the intimate mood she had so carefully created was not only shattered, she could no longer conceal from the baron the highly embarrassing presence of an almost fully grown daughter.

She laughed, a light, brittle sound, then turned with an amused shrug to her companion. "May I present my daughter, Paula, Baron Von Friedrich. I must apologize for her manners. I'm afraid she's a silly chit of a child who still belongs in the nursery."

Hardly a child, the Baron Karl Gustaf Von Friedrich decided after one sharp glance at the girl who had burst into the room. An overly plump fourteen or fifteen years old, at least. The baron prided himself on being something of an authority on young girls. After all, there was hardly a brothel keeper in Vienna who wasn't aware of Baron Von Friedrich's penchant for very young untouched girls. Not that he didn't occasionally amuse himself, and fulfill his necessary social obligations, by arousing the expectations of more experienced women like the count-

1

ess Von Melk, even though he hadn't the slightest interest or inclination to satisfy that expectation.

Now his gaze slid past the flushed Paula to the girl who hesitated in the doorway behind her. The baron felt a frisson of pleasure. The girl was unfortunately a few years older than he preferred his bed partners to be, but there was still a look of childish vulnerability, of dewy innocence in the beautiful oval face, a soft, unfinished face for all the budding breasts he could easily imagine beneath the simple white muslin ball gown she wore. The full crinoline skirt descended in flounces from a tiny waist which was encircled by a green velvet sash, almost the same shade as the girl's brilliant emerald eyes.

The baron rose to his feet, staring at the girl as he asked, "And is this another daughter, my dear Countess?"

Elissa frowned as she noticed the way the baron's gaze lingered on Margarite. She had been startled herself when she had first seen the girl in the doorway. Of course, she spent very little time with the children, but hadn't Margarite been a gawky all-arms-and-legs hoyden dressed in a middy blouse just yesterday? Elissa felt a sharp stab of jealousy. How was it possible that her first ball gown could change a young girl into a tearing beauty, one who could compete even with Elissa's own more mature charms?

"Margarite is my stepdaughter," she said stiffly, "the daughter of my late husband, Count Johann Von Melk."

So that explained the faintly foreign look about the girl, the baron decided, the lustrous sable black hair and fine-textured skin that was not milky-white but a bisque shade, the delicate cheekbones with an exotic slant to them. He remembered hearing that Count Von Melk, while in the Austrian diplomatic service in Mexico in the late 1840s, had married a wealthy Mexican beauty who had died several years after the marriage, leaving the count with a young daughter.

"What a charming name—Margarite," the baron said, crossing the room to bow over the girl's outstretched hand, his lips not quite touching the downy skin. "It's the name of a flower, is it not?" He smiled engagingly. "You will forgive my saying so, Countess, but you are much too lovely to have been named for such an ordinary little flower."

Paula, who was never happy being left out of a conversation for long, said proudly, "Margarite traveled all over the world with her father. She can speak four languages: Spanish, English, French, and German." She giggled. "Although Frau Lerner says Margarite's German accent is atrocious, not properly Viennese at all."

Paula's mother stirred, annoyed, gazing at her stepdaughter. "It's too bad your tutor didn't spend more time on your manners, Margarite. Or do you always enter rooms without knocking?"

"I'm sorry, *Madame Mère*," Margarite said, deliberately choosing the form of address that she knew Elissa disliked. In the beginning, she had reluctantly called her stepmother "Mother," only to please her father. After his death two years before, she had continued, because she suspected Elissa hated to be reminded that she was old enough to be her mother.

"And why are you wearing that ridiculous gown in the middle of the afternoon?" Elissa demanded irritably.

"On the contrary," the baron said, smiling easily at the girl, amused at the friction he could almost feel in the air between Margarite and her stepmother. "I think the gown is most attractive." He half-turned to his hostess, lifting a questioning eyebrow. "I can't imagine why I haven't seen your lovely stepdaughter introduced at a court ball, Countess."

Elissa bit back the angry retort that sprang to her lips. When her husband was alive, Johann and she had received invitations to the court balls at Hofburg Palace, but now that she was the Widow Von Melk, she was sure that the baron was aware that such invitations no longer came her way.

"Margarite is much too young to be attending balls," she said coldly.

"I'm almost seventeen," Margarite said, her chin setting rebelliously as she gazed at her stepmother. "The empress Elizabeth was only sixteen when she married the emperor."

And look how that marriage had turned out, Elissa

thought spitefully, as if all Vienna didn't whisper about the kaiserin's frequent long absences from her husband.

Still, it would never do to criticize the empress in front of the baron, who was still gazing at Margarite with an expression on his face that dismayed Elissa. Wasn't it bad enough, she thought indignantly, that Johann should not only die but leave her with his impossible child to raise, and precious little money to do it with too. And now this child she had nourished to her bosom had turned into a serpent that could destroy Elissa's chances of finding a new husband in the baron. Or any other man, for that matter, she thought, suddenly appalled. Elissa was vain but not stupid. What man would look at her twice with a nubile young beauty like Margarite in her home?

It was then she remembered the letter. She was sure it was somewhere amid the jumble of papers Johann had left. A perfect solution to her dilemma. She smiled sweetly at Margarite as she said, "You're right, my dear. I must confess I hadn't realized that you are almost a young woman. Certainly old enough that I see that I must, reluctantly, of course, agree to the urgent request that I have recently received from your mother's relatives. They are most eager that you be allowed to visit them."

Margarite's eyes widened, startled. "Mexico? I'm to go to Mexico?"

"No!" Paula cried, her voice anguished. "You can't go, Margarite. You mustn't leave me. What will I do without you?"

Elissa twitched her fan irritably. "Come now, darling. We mustn't be selfish. The Ortiz family is one of the oldest and wealthiest families in Mexico. No doubt they even have entrée to the imperial court of the emperor Maximilian and the empress Carlota."

Seeing the hesitation in her stepdaughter's face, she skillfully played her trump card. "It's what your father always wanted, Margarite. He told me time and time again how much he wanted you to know your mother's family. It was almost my darling husband's last request. . . ."

She patted her eyes with a lacy wisp of handkerchief.

It wasn't a complete lie, she thought complacently. Of course, when the letter requesting Margarite's presence in Mexico had arrived two years before, her husband had tossed it to one side immediately. "Do they think I'll ship my daughter halfway across the world, especially with the unsettled conditions in Mexico these days? Perhaps later, when Margarite is older and I can travel with her. . . ."

Smiling archly, Elissa turned to her companion for support. "Don't you agree, Baron, that it's a wonderful opportunity for Margarite?"

The baron tugged at a corner of his waxed, skewerlike mustache. His bland, handsome face, the smiling amber eyes, did not alter in the slightest despite his irritation. He had already observed that the countess Elissa was wearing too much rouge, and the overly tight corseting did not completely hide the embonpoint around her waist and hips, the result of too many rich Viennese pastries. Obviously, the countess didn't want a fresh young beauty around to contrast with her own fading charms.

He gazed coldly at the widow, outraged that she should attempt to enlist his aid in her sordid little plot to ship her stepdaughter off to Mexico. "I've spent very little time in Mexico, but in my opinion it is a country filled with brigands and bloodthirsty half-castes, combining the vices of the white man with the savagery of Indians." He turned, with a gracious bow to Margarite. "There are, of course, exceptions, like the Ortiz family, descendants of the original Spanish conquistadors, who for a while managed to bring some civilization to a country that still lives in the dark ages."

Elissa fluttered her fan, more annoyed than alarmed at the baron's description of the country to which she was sending her stepdaughter. "I'm sure that has all changed now that the French Army has been so successful in Mexico. The newspapers have been filled with how enthusiastically the Mexican people welcomed Emperor Maximilian, how grateful they are to him for freeing them from the tyranny of the Juarista government. And I understand the empress Eugénie herself has said that the empress Carlota's letters to her have been filled with glowing reports of the Mexican people and the beauty of the countryside.''

"Oh, I've no doubt that French troops can easily defeat the Juaristas, who are little more than bandits and outlaws living in the hills,'' the baron agreed, and thought, amused, how stupid women were. As if Napoleon III had sent his French legionnaires to Mexico to bring liberty to that country. It was a bondsman's war, pure and simple. President Benito Juárez had defaulted on the loans he owed France, loans backed up by bonds owned by Napoleon's own half brother. To recover the money, Napoleon had dispatched French troops, who had deposed Juárez, then set the puppet archduke Maximilian on a nonexistent Mexican throne in his place. Since the baron himself owned some of the Mexican bonds, he was quite in agreement with Napoleon's decision.

He added thoughtfully, "What is unfortunate is that Napoleon followed his wife's advice and offered the Mexican crown to the archduke Maximilian. The archduke simply hasn't the ability to govern anything, despite his Belgian wife's overweening desire to be an empress like her sister-in-law Elizabeth.''

"How dare you speak so disrespectfully of the emperor Maximilian!'' Margarite exploded angrily.

"Margarite!'' Elissa said, shocked. "I must apologize for my stepdaughter, Baron. I'm afraid she has the manners of a *lazzarone*.'' She gave the girl an annoyed glance. "You will apologize to the baron at once, Margarite.''

The girl's chin lifted obstinately, and the baron said, smiling, "There's no need, Countess.'' The amber eyes twinkled as he gazed at Margarite. "So we have another one of Maximilian's 'little countesses.' ''

At the girl's bewilderment, he shrugged mentally. No doubt the girl was too young to know of the embarrassing number of young and not so young countesses who had mooned after the golden-haired Maximilian, before his strong-willed mother, the archduchess Sophia, had finally managed to marry her son off to the daughter of King Leopold of Belgium. The reason for Maximilian's mesmerizing effect upon women had always eluded the baron, but there was no doubting the man's considerable charm.

And it was a charm that affected not only women. Many Austrian men found the good-natured Maximilian preferable to his stiff-necked, henpecked brother, Franz Josef. The baron wondered if perhaps that was why the emperor had swallowed his pride at having to accept anything from that upstart Corsican in Paris and allowed his brother to accept the Mexican throne. Not only had the emperor rid himself of a popular rival, but with the agreement that he had forced his brother to sign before he sailed off for Mexico made very sure that Maximilian could never inherit the Hapsburg dynasty.

The baron's heavy-lidded eyes studied the girl in the demure muslin ball gown, the softly rounded flesh beneath the short puff sleeves, the angry warmth in the luminous green eyes that he was sure indicated a yet unaroused passionate nature. He could feel in his loins what pleasure it would bring him to be the first to bed the girl, to know that he was the first to possess that softly trembling body, hear her first cries of pain and fear, and finally, under his practiced ministrations, wipe away every trace of pride and innocence from that child-like face as if she were a wax doll that he could mold exactly as he wished.

Ah, well, he sighed regretfully to himself, turning his gaze away from the girl. Her leaving for Mexico was probably for the best. It was one thing to indulge himself with young girls brought in from the countryside with no family or friends to protest their treatment at his hands. But even the emperor Franz Josef, who had a habit of overlooking the outrageous, often licentious, behavior of his own brothers, would frown upon a member of his aristocracy seducing an overly young countess, even if she were only minor nobility.

Margarite took a deep breath and felt the muscles in her stomach relax. Although the baron couldn't have been kinder, considering her rudeness, she still felt vaguely relieved when that smiling gaze left her face. By that evening, however, as she and Paula prepared for bed, she had already forgotten the baron.

"Oh, look, it's snowing!" Paula said. The two girls in their voluminous flannel nightgowns had been trying to warm themselves in a corner of the room at the white porcelain stove shaped like an oversized inkstand. Now they both rushed to the window.

The snow fell lazily in thick feathery flakes past the spire of St. Stephen's Cathedral into the narrow streets, where carnival revelers still gathered for one last merry fling before Lent began.

"They'll be sleigh riding in the Prater woods tomorrow," Paula said eagerly. "Perhaps even ice skating." Then, remembering, she said forlornly, "I don't suppose it snows in Mexico, does it?"

Margarite wasn't sure. She had only dim recollections of her childhood years in Mexico, bright sunlight and dark faces, a walled courtyard in which she played, a beautiful woman holding her tight, smelling of some delicious scent, and a voice like music, lulling her to sleep.

Paula flung her arms around her stepsister. "I'll miss you so, Margarite," she wailed. For a moment the two girls clung together, their tears mingling. How could I have ever lived through these last two years without Papa, Margarite thought, if it hadn't been for Paula.

She drew back finally, aware that the chill creeping through the window was causing goose bumps to rise on her flesh beneath the nightgown. "I'll race you to the bed!"

It was a dead heat, with both girls leaping into the enormous four-poster at almost the same moment. The maid had taken the chill off with hot water bottles, and the feather-stuffed, billowy counterpane engulfed Margarite as if she were falling into a warm snowbank.

For a moment she luxuriated in the warmth, then heard Paula sniffling softly on her side of the bed. She reached out and found her stepsister's hand, squeezing it gently. "I won't be gone forever. I'll come back to see you. I promise."

"You'll be old and married," Paula protested. "I won't even know you. It won't be the same."

No, Margarite thought unhappily. It wouldn't be the

same. Forcing her voice to a cheerfulness she was far from feeling, she said, "Well, you'll probably be married too."

The thought silenced Paula for a moment, her voice not quite so despairing when she spoke again. "I plan to marry a Hussar like my papa was," she said firmly. "I think men in uniform are so handsome, don't you?" then, curiously, "What sort of man do you want to marry?"

When her bedmate did not answer, Paula giggled. "Oh, I forgot. You still have that awful crush on Emperor Maximilian, don't you?"

Margarite felt her body grow warm, wishing she had never told Paula about that summer's day, almost five years ago now, when she had been presented to the then Archduke Maximilian on the parterre in front of Schönbrunn Palace, the Hapsburg country home a few miles outside of Vienna.

As a high-ranking member of the diplomatic service, Count Von Melk had been allowed in the enclosure near the archduke Maximilian and his wife, who were on a family visit to Vienna from their home in Trieste. Margarite, only eleven years old at the time, had been so awestruck by the military band playing, the fashionably dressed women, and her first view of the magnificence of Schönbrunn that she hadn't even heard her father's introduction until she looked straight up into a pair of the bluest eyes she had ever seen.

The archduke was tall, slim, and even more handsome in his white and gold-braided uniform than her father. His golden beard, divided in the middle, did not completely conceal a slight deformity, the protruding Hapsburg underlip. But Margarite soon forgot that minor disfigurement when Maximilian smiled at her. It was a dazzling smile, as warming as sunshine as he reached down and took Margarite's hand and pulled her erect from her hastily dropped curtsy. The blue eyes fastened upon her face, and for one heartstopping second Margarite felt as if no one else existed in the world but this man and her.

"What a charming child, Count Von Melk," he said.

"She will be setting aflutter the hearts of every man in Vienna one of these days."

Then someone else was waiting for his royal attention, and he turned away. Margarite felt bereft. Her father must have seen the stunned look in his daughter's eyes, for he laughed teasingly and said, "It seems the archduke has made another conquest."

He reached, smiling, for his daughter's hand. "Come along, *Liebchen*. I'll buy you a lemon ice, and you'll soon forget all about the archduke Maximilian."

Curled up in a ball on the far side of the bed, Paula murmured drowsily. "Did you notice the way Baron Von Friedrich looked at you? I think he likes you. Mama was furious. The baron is handsome for an older man. Mama says every woman in Vienna has been chasing him for years. . . ." Her voice trailed off, soon to be replaced by light snores.

Making sure that Paula was asleep, Margarite slipped out of bed and, going to the armoire, took down a hatbox. The lithograph hidden within the box was a much reproduced, overly colored picture of Maximilian, made just before he left for Mexico. Margarite took the lithograph over to the lamp, cupping it tenderly in her hands. It was not a very good likeness, she decided. Maximilian was much more handsome in real life, and no lithograph could catch the spirited blueness of his eyes, the warmth in his face.

A flutter of excitement caught in her throat. Was it possible, she wondered, that when she went to Mexico, she would meet Maximilian again? Only this time, no longer a gawky child but a young woman. Would he think she was beautiful, she wondered wistfully, staring at herself in the dressing table mirror. If only she were inches taller! And her eyes were not that odd green color, but dark and mysterious.

Sighing, she put the lithograph back into the hatbox and, turning out the lamp, returned to bed. When she finally fell asleep, it was to dream of a tall slim man with golden hair and laughing blue eyes, beckoning to her, but always tantalizingly just out of reach.

Chapter Two

𝒯HE *Louisiane* was an old dark hulk of a ship, only recently converted from sails to steam. She had been hastily and optimistically put into service by the French shipping line, *Compagnie Transatlantique*, to transport what they expected to be thousands of eager French citizens transplanting themselves to the new French colony of Mexico.

When Margarite boarded the ship at St. Nazaire in mid-April, however, along with her chaperone and traveling companion, Frau Luise Hundt, the only French aboard were government officials and military surgeons. The remaining passengers, aside from a few German and English travelers, were a small cadre of Austrian and Belgian troops recruited by their respective governments under an agreement with Maximilian, but who had somehow managed to miss the earlier shipment of their colleagues to Mexico.

Frau Hundt was an impoverished middle-aged gentlewoman with a round, simple-appearing face but a shrewd eye. She took one look at the young, handsome Austrian and Belgian officers lined up on deck watching Margarite board and whisked her charge immediately off to their small cabin. Not that the countess Elissa Von Melk was paying her anywhere near a decent sum for accompanying her stepdaughter to Mexico, Frau Hundt thought grumpily, but she was not a woman to shirk her responsibilities.

It wasn't feasible, of course, to keep the girl imprisoned in the cabin for the whole six weeks of the voyage, but whenever Margarite appeared on deck, Frau Hundt was never far away from her young charge and the half-dozen young Belgian and Austrian officers who immediately buzzed around her. There was safety in numbers, the chaperone decided, and as far as she could tell, Margarite smiled with equal and devastating effect upon each of the young officers without picking any special favorite.

Frau Hundt had accepted her post as chaperone to the young countess Von Melk only because she was, as usual, desperate for money. As the weeks passed, though, she began to develop a reluctant, almost maternal affection for the girl. Very quickly it became obvious to her that Margarite, despite her beauty and social position, had had no experience or training in how to behave toward the opposite sex, how to manage discreet flirtations from beneath lowered eyelashes and behind a fluttering fan as every well-born young Austrian girl was taught at her mother's knee. The countess was entirely too bold in looking directly into a man's face, too quick to lively laughter, too argumentative and outspoken in her conversations. Not to mention her overly hearty appetite!

"A young lady should eat like a bird, and hasn't anyone taught you it's impolite to contradict a gentleman?" she scolded Margarite in their cabin after watching the girl eat a sailorlike breakfast and then argue with Lieutenant Franz Schiller as they had promenaded on deck afterward.

"I can't help it if the sea air makes me hungry," the girl protested. "And Lieutenant Schiller insists that the Army of the Confederate States will win the Civil War in America and my father always said that the Union Army was sure to win."

Her chaperone lifted her hands in dismay. "Do you suppose any gentleman wants a wife who eats more than he does and argues politics with him?"

The girl's chin set with a regrettable stubbornness that Frau Hundt had already noticed. "Papa always taught me that a woman has as much right as a man to speak her mind," then, laughing, she dropped a kiss on her chaperone's unhappy face. "Don't worry. You'll see. I'll manage to get a husband someday."

No doubt she would, her companion thought, gazing with a sharp twinge of apprehension into that lovely young face. The fresh sea air and sunshine had brought a faint pink alabaster glow to the pale skin, made the green eyes even more luminous beneath the dark, arched brows. Did the child even realize how dangerous it was to be so beautiful, she thought. One thing Frau Hundt had learned in a long and full life. More tears stained the cheeks of a beautiful woman than a plain one.

Margarite tied a gray moiré bonnet trimmed with pink ribbons over her dark hair. The colors of the bonnet exactly matched her gown, with its inset pink panels in the bodice and the narrow pink cords along the flounces of her crinoline skirt. She reached for her cabin mate's hand. "Come along," she said eagerly. "The officers are drilling their troops on the main deck. We don't want to be late."

The drill had already commenced by the time they made their way above deck, their crinoline skirts having to be discreetly handled going up the narrow companionways. The young officers had donned their dress uniforms for the drill. Watching them putting the enlisted men smartly through their paces, Margarite whispered to Frau Hundt, "I think the Austrian uniform is the most attractive, don't you?"

Frau Hundt sniffed. "Pretty uniforms don't win wars," she said.

Frau Hundt was Austrian by marriage, but Hungarian by birth, and therefore had little love for the Hapsburgs. Her first husband had been killed in the Hungarian Revolution against Austria in 1848; her second husband, a member of Emperor Franz Josef's much vaunted Hussars, had been slaughtered at the Battle of Magenta in 1859. Despite the gallant charges of the Austrian cavalry, the old-fashioned muzzle-loading rifles the Austrian infantry carried had not stood a chance against the modern weapons of the French. By the end of that steamy hot June day, the blood that covered the battlefield and stained the beautifully tailored Austrian uniforms a magenta red had given the dressmakers a new fashion shade.

"I'm sure Lieutenant Schiller will be valorous in battle in Mexico," Margarite protested.

Frau Hundt had little knowledge, and less understanding, of the war in Mexico. No, not war, she thought dourly. Napoleon III never called his military adventures war. In Algeria it had been pacification; in Mexico the fighting was called intervention.

"Anyway, you must admit Franz is very handsome," Margarite said dreamily, her eyes lingering on the young lieutenant in a way that instantly set her companion on guard. When had the lieutenant and her charge advanced to first names? she wondered, alarmed.

Margarite's chaperone had already made discreet inquiries into Lieutenant Schiller's background. Although several of the young officers aboard had aristocratic connections, Lieutenant Schiller had none. His family was bourgeois, his future in the Austrian Army therefore limited, Frau Hundt knew, from having been an officer's wife herself. Certainly the lieutenant was not suitable husband material for a Von Melk.

And although the girl might protest that she had no interest in marrying the young man, her chaperone knew that romances had a way of blossoming on shipboard. From that moment on she stuck to Margarite's side like an oversized limpet, until Franz, in despair, was sure he would never manage to get a moment alone with the girl.

It wasn't until their last night on board, as the ship lay off the harbor of Vera Cruz, that fate intervened, causing Frau Hundt to retire hastily to her cabin after indulging too freely in the rich late-night dinner. Margarite brought her cabin mate soothing stomach powders and cold damp cloths for her head, but after her companion finally fell asleep, she couldn't resist the opportunity to slip up on deck one last time.

It was a clear, moonlit night and she could see faintly the dark coastline of Mexico. Her new home, she thought, and a sudden feeling of desolation swept over her. She had been so busy the last two months preparing for her trip, she hadn't had time to wonder what it would be like living in a Mexico that she hardly remembered, with relatives who were complete strangers. Although she and her stepmother had never been close, at least Elissa was a known quantity.

She had felt the same sadness, she remembered, when she and her father had sailed from the United States, leaving behind the friends she had made there. Tears had burned behind her eyes that day, too, and her father had tilted her chin in his hand and said sternly, *"Kopf hoch, Liebchen.* A Von Melk always holds his head high."* As if she could still hear her father's words in her ears, Margarite swallowed hard, her chin rising determinedly.

"I was hoping I'd find you here, Margarite."

Even with her dark hair pulled loose and whipping in satin streamers across her pale face, the countess Von Melk presented a picture more ravishing than Lieutenant Franz Schiller had ever seen. In the moonlight her creamy skin was the color of his mother's fine Rosenthal china, and her mouth curving softly upward at the corners, he decided, begged to be kissed.

He could not resist reaching out and covering one small hand that rested invitingly on the railing. "As soon as we reach Mexico City, I plan to ask permission of your uncle to call upon you."

"Won't your military duties keep you too busy?"

"Oh, the Juaristas won't hold out much longer," Franz said confidently. "I understand there are still pockets of rebel resistance, but I wouldn't be surprised if General Thun's Austrian troops, along with Marshal Bazaine's French legions, haven't already chased Benito Juárez across the border into Texas."

"And what if the Union Army wins its war?" Margarite asked teasingly. "Papa always said that President Lincoln would never allow the French to maintain a monarchy on the American continent. It had something to do with, I think he called it the Monroe Doctrine."

Franz shrugged impatiently. "A piece of paper won't stop Napoleon or Emperor Maximilian." If his companion weren't so achingly beautiful, Franz might have felt a flicker of annoyance at his lady love's irritating habit of contradicting him. Then he reproached himself for a fool. Here he was, at last, alone with Margarite, and he was talking about warfare, hardly a romantic subject!

Franz whispered huskily, "You do want to see me again, don't you? You surely have guessed my feelings toward you. Can I hope that you care a little?"

Did she? Margarite wondered guiltily. She liked the young lieutenant, with his boyishly handsome face, the carefully tended mustache above a mouth as soft as a woman's, the way his shoulders filled out the white, gold-braided tunic. But then, she liked all the young officers. They were fun to be with and charming. She had enjoyed the attention they had showered upon her. But, of course, none of them were as tall and blond and handsome as the emperor Maximilian.

Emboldened by the fact that she had not withdrawn her hand from his, Franz pulled the girl gently toward him. Her face lifted to his held a sweet shyness, but her enormous green eyes gazed openly into his, her lips half-parted. Franz groaned softly and covered that inviting mouth with his own. It was not done, he knew. A gentleman didn't even kiss the hand of a young unmarried woman. But there was no way the lieutenant could have resisted such a temptation. The fragrance of Margarite's hair filled his nostrils as his arms tightened around the slim figure, pulling her closer into his arms.

At first Margarite did not find the kiss unpleasant. Then the pressure on her mouth became bolder, as if the lieutenant were trying to force her lips apart, to insert his tongue shockingly into her mouth, and, affronted, she struggled to break free.

Instantly the arms fell away, Franz's voice boyishly apologetic. "I'm sorry, Margarite. I had no right. Please forgive me."

It was her fault, too, Margarite realized. Having never been kissed by a man before, except, of course, her father, she had been curious how it would feel. All the romantic novels she had read clandestinely when her governess wasn't watching had made it sound so exciting, a man's embrace. What a lot of fuss over nothing, she thought.

When Franz reached out to capture the small hand

again and press it to his lips, he was startled at the
transformation in the girl's face from a sweet, shy uncertainty into a cool, haughty remoteness as she pulled her
hand free and murmured, her voice polite but distant,
"It's late. And I've still packing to finish before we
disembark in the morning."

Much to the passengers' annoyance, however, they
were not allowed to disembark in the morning. The
Louisiane lay at anchor in the harbor all morning and
into the afternoon. The captain had a meeting with the
quarantine officials but had yet to receive clearance
from the custom house. Early in the morning, the passengers had crowded the rail for their first glimpse of
Mexico, but after a while, disappointed at the sight of
desolate sand dunes and scrub palms, the monotonous
flat adobe buildings that made up the town of Vera
Cruz, most of them returned below.

Margarite stayed behind with Frau Luise, her eyes
straining to catch a clearer picture of her new home. She
noticed a harbor island near the ship and shaded her
eyes with her hand against the tropical sun to study it
more closely.

"That's the *Isla de Sacrificios,* Countess. It's a military cemetery now, the Frenchman's graveyard, it's called
these days."

The crisp voice belonged to James Marsh, one of the
English passengers. He and his fellow English passenger
had spent almost the whole trip playing whist with each
other in the saloon, hardly bothering to speak two words
to the other passengers.

"You know Mexico?" Margarite asked, too curious
to resent the man's sudden friendliness.

The older man nodded. "I've lived in Mexico for
twenty years. I manage a silver mine near Real del
Monte, not far from the Ortiz silver mine, which your
uncle owns, Countess."

He spoke of owning a silver mine as casually as another man might speak of owning a plot of ground, Frau
Hundt noticed, but Margarite wasn't interested in hearing of the Ortiz wealth. "You've met my uncle?" she
asked eagerly.

James Marsh shook his head, a look of faint amusement in his eyes at the question. "The Ortiz family and I don't move in the same social circles. But then, the Ortiz family haven't been seen in society much lately, what with Don Manuel's youngest son turning against his father, siding with the Liberals, and the oldest son killed in an accident last year." He gave Margarite a quizzical glance. "You knew about your cousin's death, of course?"

"No." Margarite shook her head. "I didn't know." She did vaguely remember her father's mentioning that she had cousins in Mexico. How odd that her uncle hadn't mentioned his son's death in his letter to Elissa inviting Margarite to Mexico.

"I'm afraid I don't spend much time in Mexico anyway," Mr. Marsh said.

At Margarite's puzzled stare, he laughed, a brusque, little laugh. "I mean Mexico City. The Mexican people always call their capital, Mexico, not Mexico City."

Frau Hundt, who was growing warm in the afternoon heat that hung over the ship like a suffocating wool blanket, said, exasperated, "Do you suppose we'll be delayed much longer before being allowed to go ashore?"

"It's hard to say. You'll find in Mexico there's standard time and Mexican time." He gave that little rasping laugh again. "Your emperor Maximilian found that out the day he arrived at Vera Cruz and discovered there was no one to greet the imperial party. The official reception committee was late in getting to Vera Cruz. The emperor took the late reception in stride but they say the empress Carlota was considerably upset."

"You've met the emperor?" Margarite asked, her eyes widening, fascinated.

The Englishman shrugged. "Oh, yes, many times. He's very democratic, invites all sorts of people to his receptions and parties at Chapultapec."

"Chapultapec?" Margarite repeated the word slowly. "The emperor doesn't live in Mexico City?" Then, smiling, correcting herself, "I mean, Mexico?"

"Oh, he maintains the imperial offices at the National Palace in Mexico, but the first night he and his wife spent in the National Palace, they were attacked by bedbugs and were forced to sleep on billiard tables. After that, the emperor renovated the old viceroy's palace at Chapultapec, about an hour's drive from Mexico, and moved his living quarters there.''

If Frau Hundt hadn't been so miserable in the oppressive heat, she would have heard the suspicious warmth in Margarite's voice when she spoke of the emperor Maximilian, a warmth she had never heard there before. As it was, Margarite's chaperone was too busy holding her parasol with one hand and fanning herself with the other to give more than cursory attention to the conversation going on around her.

"The newspapers in Vienna were filled with stories of how well received the emperor was by the Mexican people," Margarite said. "Maximilian and Carlota were cheered all the way from Vera Cruz to the capital."

The English mine manager had lived too long in Mexico to allow himself to be pulled into political discussions. He said carefully, "The emperor is very popular in certain quarters, I believe." Then he added dryly, "It's unfortunate that Maximilian has little popularity in the United States, especially now that the American government has won its war and President Johnson can turn his attention to Mexico."

He had the startled attention of both women now as he said, "I forget, you probably hadn't heard. The captain received the news only an hour ago from the quarantine officials. The Confederate Army surrendered a week after we left St. Nazaire and President Lincoln was assassinated five days later." He glanced downward over the railing, nodding, pleased. "Ah, I see the customs cutter has arrived. It shouldn't be long now until we're cleared. If you ladies will excuse me, I'll finish my packing."

Margarite glanced toward the aft deck, where the Austrian and Belgian officers were assembling the enlisted men and their gear, wondering if they had heard the news about the Union victory. But there was no time to ask Lieutenant Schiller in the last-minute rush of packing her dressing bag and making sure all her trunks and portmanteaus were carried off the ship.

The passengers who disembarked, finally, at Vera Cruz did not linger in the town. "The *vomito*," Mr. Marsh warned. "What we call the yellow jack. It's particularly bad in Vera Cruz this time of the year. And Europeans are highly susceptible to the disease."

He had secured a carriage to drive Margarite and Frau Hundt, his friend and himself, to the railroad station and urged the driver to make haste. Margarite was not unhappy to hurry through the town, which was one of the most dismal she had ever seen. She kept her handkerchief to her face, trying to blot out the noisome smells from the streets that were little more than open sewers, and averting her eyes from the ugly black birds that clustered everywhere she looked. They circled in the sky, squatted on the roofs of the crumbling buildings, and waddled in the streets.

"The *zopilotes* are the Vera Cruz sanitation department," the Englishman said, nodding wryly toward the birds. "The law protects them or the town would be even more of a cesspool."

When they reached the tiny railway station, he hurried Margarite and Frau Hundt onto a dingy train with plaited straw benches. The railroad track, he explained, had been built by the French and ran only for 50 miles to Paso del Macho. At the railhead, the passengers would have to take a mule-driven coach, or *diligencia,* the remaining 250 miles across the mountains to reach the high plateau where the capital of Mexico had been built on a drained lake bed.

Margarite twisted on the hard bench, trying to see out of the Venetian blinds drawn against the sun, worried that the train might leave without Lieutenant Schiller and the other officers and men. At the last minute, though, the Austrians and Belgians arrived, flinging themselves aboard a second car almost as the train was pulling out of the station.

The railroad car was hot and stuffy, with the sun beating down upon its flat roof. There was no drinking water to be had, and the view from the windows of bare sand hills, scorched bushes, and an occasional cactus made Margarite's throat feel even more parched.

At the railhead at Paso del Macho, the passengers spent the night in a tin-roofed posada, both of the women sleeping sitting up in chairs rather than chancing the filthy-looking bed. Before daybreak, teams of eight mules were backed between the shafts of high boxlike carriages and the passengers' cowhide trunks and leather portmanteaus strapped to the roofs.

The passengers were served a breakfast of stale bread, bitter chocolate, and warmed-over tamales from the dinner the night before. Yet, after all preparations had been made and the breakfast finished, the coaches still did not move.

An irritated Frau Hundt, who had a crick in her neck from sleeping on the chair, asked impatiently of Mr. Marsh, "Now why the delay?"

"We're waiting for the French patrol that will escort us on the first leg of our journey," he replied. "No *diligencia* would travel the highway to Mexico without an armed escort."

Frau Hundt paled beneath the circles of rouge on her cheeks. "The Juaristas would dare to attack us this close to Mexico City?"

The Englishman shrugged. "Juaristas, guerrillas, just plain bandits, call them what you want. They infect the countryside like fleas. The French crush one band and another springs up to take its place."

"Mr. Marsh, you're frightening the ladies!" Lieutenant Schiller said sharply. "I'm sure the situation is nowhere near as desperate as you make out."

James Marsh smiled thinly. The lieutenant would soon learn, he thought. Anywhere in Mexico outside artillery range of a French garrison was guerrilla country.

The sound of a bugle and hoofbeats interrupted any further conversation as a detachment of cavalry carrying the French tricolor rode up to the cluster of huts. A man wearing a kepi, red trousers, and with a sergeant's chevrons on the sleeve of his dark blue tunic detached himself from the rest of the group and rode up to Lieutenant Schiller, his hand touching his kepi in a quick salute.

"Robert Marcel, Sergeant, First Regiment, the Foreign Legion, on detached duty from Saltillo to escort you and the other passengers to Orizaba."

Lieutenant Schiller introduced himself and his fellow Austrian officers. "Our orders are to report to General Thun at Mexico City as soon as possible." He gestured toward the Belgian lieutenant standing beside him. "Lieutenant Chazal is to report to Major Tigdal under the command of Colonel Van der Smissen of the Belgian Legion."

The French sergeant's face stiffened. "I'm afraid that's not possible, Lieutenant. Major Tigdal and three hundred of the Belgian Legion were killed more than a week ago at Tacambaro."

Margarite thought she had misunderstood the man's French, until she saw the blood drain from Lieutenant Chazal's narrow face, the horror in the Belgian officer's voice when he asked, "All . . . all killed? How could that happen?"

"Major Tigdal's command was outnumbered, surrounded on all sides by Republican forces. They barricaded themselves inside a church. More than a hundred had died, including Major Tigdal, when the enemy set fire to the church and the remaining troops were forced to surrender. The surviving Belgian troops were lined up against the church wall by the Juaristas and shot."

Frau Hundt whispered, "*Herr Gott!*" and crossed herself.

Lieutenant Schiller, remembering then that there were women present, turned to Margarite and said hastily, "Perhaps you and Frau Hundt would wait in the carriage. We should be under way very shortly."

Obediently, the two women climbed into the carriage and sat silently, waiting. From the window Margarite could see Lieutenant Schiller talking to the French sergeant. She could not hear what they were saying, but it was clear the sergeant was making some sort of protest, finally shrugging with Gallic resignation. The two men disappeared from view. A few minutes later, Lieutenants Schiller and Chazal returned on horseback.

Franz rode over to the carriage, leaning down to speak

to Margarite. "Sorry to make you wait in this heat, but we'll get started now."

The carriage driver, a grizzled individual who spoke English with what Margarite recognized at once as an American accent, asked gruffly, "Where are the red trousers? Ain't they coming with us?"

"Sergeant Marcel has other, more pressing, duties," the lieutenant said briskly. "Lieutenant Chazal and myself, along with the other officers and men, are quite capable of protecting this caravan, if the need arises."

The two Englishmen had joined the women in the carriage. Now James Marsh asked quietly, "Do you think that's wise, Lieutenant?"

A faint flush stained the young lieutenant's cheeks at the implied censure in the man's words. "I can assure you, Mr. Marsh, you'll be quite safe under our protection. We have twice as many men as the French troop had, more than sufficient guns and ammunition, and"—he smiled grimly, looking down at his dusty mount, sweat running down the animal's flanks—"horses which the sergeant was persuaded to lend us."

Only the officers had been given horses, though, Margarite noticed. The enlisted men were crowded into and on top of the coaches before and behind the one in which the regular passengers rode.

Evidently deciding it was useless to argue with the lieutenant, the driver, grumbling beneath his breath and cursing loudly and profanely at the mules, cracked his long whip with a terrifying sound like a pistol shot. Several Indian urchins trotting alongside threw rocks at the lead mules at the same time, and the *diligencia* started with a lurch, almost throwing Margarite onto the floor.

The next four days the coach raced along, jolting over roads which were often nothing more than dried-up, rocky streambeds, or bounced up and down dry gullies called barrancas. Margarite clung to the side of the window to keep her head from bumping the ceiling, her arms and legs black and blue from being flung against the other passengers.

The mules were changed at relay stations, where more

French troops could be seen. Each night there was a brief stop at a posada, fortunately with beds cleaner than the first one, then another start at daybreak.

If the coach ride had not been so uncomfortable, Margarite would have been fascinated by the brief pictures of Mexico she caught from her snatched glances out the *diligencia* windows. As the carriage left the dry plains and climbed steadily upward, she had her first glimpse of wild tropical foliage, vine-garlanded giant trees loaded with fruits she didn't recognize, flowers of every color filling the air with fragrance, and, finally, a snow-covered mountain peak in the distance as they approached Orizaba.

Although talking was difficult with the coach lurching and bumping over the miserable road, Mr. Marsh answered Margarite's questions about the countryside as best he could. The odd-looking plants like swords stuck into the ground were maguey, he explained. "The Indians couldn't survive without the maguey. The plant provides both food and drink." He laughed shortly. "Though pulque's not a drink to everyone's taste."

"Are they very fierce, these Indians?" Frau Hundt asked, clutching at her hat with one hand and at the side of the coach with the other as the wheels struck a rock and the carriage seemed to leap into the air, descending with a thump.

"Fierce? Not at all. They're a very docile race," he assured her. "We've had Indian workers at the silver mine for years, and you couldn't ask for a more contented lot as long as they are given their weekly supply of pulque."

The *diligencia* slowed a little as it passed a long string of *arrieros,* swarthy-faced men driving loaded mules, then slowed even more as the mules toiled through a mountain pass so high that clouds floated below them. Finally, to spare the exhausted animals, the passengers got out and walked.

Franz swung off his horse and walked a short distance beside Margarite. "Is it much longer before we reach Mexico?" she asked, hoping she didn't look as exhausted as she felt. Her ribs ached from the constant jouncing and she was sure her once jaunty feathered hat was dust-covered.

"We'll stop at Puebla tonight, then Rio Frio for our midday meal. We should be in Mexico City by tomorrow night."

He glanced down at the girl beside him, then said in a low voice, "That last night aboard the ship, I'll never forget, Margarite. Whatever happens . . ."

She knew he was thinking of the massacre of the Belgian soldiers and she gave him a frightened glance. "Nothing's going to happen to you, Franz."

His mouth jerked at the corner and she saw for a moment her fear reflected in his eyes. Then he straightened and said quickly, "Of course not. I'll turn up at your uncle's house, you'll see. You won't be able to get rid of me so easily."

Behind them, they could hear Frau Hundt come puffing up the road, groaning and complaining, John Marsh supporting her with his arm. "Barbaric land! Are we expected to walk to Mexico City?"

When they reached Puebla and the comfortable posada awaiting them, she was still grumbling. But by the next morning she had sufficiently recovered to eat a hearty breakfast of fresh eggs and butter, coffee and fried chicken. As the coach left Puebla, Mr. Marsh pointed out to Margarite the shattered ruins of the fort and convent, destroyed in the French siege of the town in '63 to avenge their embarrassing defeat the year before at the same place.

After a short stop at Rio Frio, the coaches rushed forward. The mountain peaks in the distance seemed closer now, the air amazingly crystal-clear. Then the woods alongside the road began to close in, dark, somehow menacing, lofty oaks, pines, and cedar. Margarite found herself nodding, falling at last into a cold, jolting sort of uncomfortable sleep.

She wasn't sure how long she slept; she only knew what awakened her, the terrifying sound of Frau Hundt screaming in her ear, "Bandits! *Herr Gott!* Bandits!"

Chapter Three

STILL half asleep, Margarite could hear their driver cursing, the squeal of metal against metal as he tried to brake the cumbersome vehicle. The *diligencia* swayed, its wooden wheels dropping off the road. Margarite was flung against John Marsh as the carriage dipped dangerously, at the last moment finding solid ground and pulling to a shuddering stop.

Margarite let down the window which had been drawn shut against the dust, and peered out. Through shifting clouds of dust, she could see past the lead carriage, which had also stopped at a drunken angle, to a narrow bridge ahead. There was a cluster of at least a half-dozen men on horseback at one end of the bridge, effectively blocking the road. She had only a brief glimpse of sombreros, kerchief-wrapped faces, and the glint of sunlight on the carbines the men held almost carelessly in their hands, when John Marsh jerked her unceremoniously away from the window.

"Stay inside the coach," he ordered. "There's no need to let them know we've women with us."

Then he thrust open the coach door and stepped outside. Margarite could hear Franz, sounding very close to the carriage door, as he shouted for his men to take their positions, make ready to fire, and the Englishman's voice, low but loud enough so that his words carried clearly inside the coach.

"Don't be a fool, lieutenant. Can't you see you're outnumbered?"

"Stand aside, sir. There's only a half-dozen. . . ."

"And another two dozen in the trees on either side of

26

the road," Mr. Marsh pointed out grimly. "Do you want the women caught in a crossfire?"

There was a short, bitter silence. Margarite could imagine what Franz was feeling, his frustration at having to surrender his first command in Mexico to a group of brigands.

Then, his voice harsh, the lieutenant gave the order for his men to hold their fire.

"We'll all be murdered," Frau Hundt wailed. She gave Margarite a sudden, terrified glance. "Or worse!"

"Try to be calm, madame," the second Englishman, a small, fussy man, said irritably. He was taking a small pouch of coins from his suit coat and pushing it down behind the seat cushion. "I suggest you hide what jewelry you can. . . ."

The words had no sooner left his lips when the door to the carriage was jerked open. A swarthy man with a pistol in his hand gestured them out of the carriage. "Quick! Quick, *Señores!*" he ordered, then seeing the two women, stepped back, his teeth flashing as he doffed his sombrero and added, smiling, "And *señoras.*"

The passengers climbed out onto the road. For a moment Margarite was only aware of the smell of sweating horseflesh and saddle leather, the saddles oddly small and high, the silver spurs unusually large, wicked-looking, and flecked with blood. The bandits milled around the coaches, yet she sensed there was a practiced discipline to the disorder. Guns were being ripped from the hands of the enlisted men, and officers were being pulled off their horses. When Lieutenant Chazal resisted, he was struck almost offhandedly but with enough force to send him sprawling into the dust-covered road almost at Margarite's feet.

The bandit holding a pistol on the passengers from the coach had coolly removed watches and money pouches from the two Englishmen. Then he gestured toward Frau Hundt. She clutched her hands to her breast, her terror for the moment forgotten at the thought of losing her jewelry. "You'd steal from a woman? What sort of barbarians are you?"

Since she spoke in German, the man misunderstood.

His glance roved politely over the outraged middle-aged woman, arms crossed over her breasts as he answered in Spanish. "Your virtue is in no danger, *Señora*. It is only your jewelry we require." His hand snaked out and jerked the enamel and gold necklace from around the plump neck.

When he turned to Margarite, she stepped back, her head rising haughtily. She would not have those dirty fingers touching her! Quickly she unclasped the matched strand of pearls that was the last present her father had given her and dropped them contemptuously into the man's hand.

The bandit's eyes glowed with pleasure as he gazed at the girl. So engrossed was he in her beauty that he didn't notice Lieutenant Chazel's hand reaching stealthily for his pistol. Another of his compatriots did, however, and yelled out a warning. With a swift, vicious movement, the bandit's heel ground down upon the lieutenant's wrist, then slowly, very slowly, he pointed his pistol down at the lieutenant.

Margarite heard, disbelievingly, the hammer being pulled back on the gun, saw the almost indifferent amusement in the man's eyes, and knew the bandit would kill the young lieutenant with as little regret as if he were swatting an insect.

Without thinking, too shocked by the man's savagery to even realize what she was doing, Margarite flung herself into the dust of the road, shielding the lieutenant's body with her own. Her eyes flashed angrily as she spit out in Spanish, "*Canalla!* Would you shoot down a defenseless man?"

It had been two years, ever since her father's death, that she had spoken her mother's language, and she was startled at how the words sprang naturally to her lips.

The bandit, surprised at hearing Spanish coming from this young European woman, gazed admiringly down into the girl's furious face. Then his eyes drifted downward to the sweet swell of breast and tiny waist, the flesh, pale and gleaming above the dark stuff of her gown. "You have too much fire, *dulcita*, for a beardless boy like that," he said, grinning lewdly.

His hand was gripping her shoulder to pull her to her feet, when a man on a sorrel horse edged his mount closer to the carriage. Unlike the other bandits, whose clothes ranged from torn trousers and shirts to silver-buttoned jackets and polished boots, he wore a straw sombrero, unadorned black trousers and shirt, with a black serape flung over his shoulders.

For all his plain garments, there was an air of authority about the man. Still crouched beside the fallen Chazal, Margarite looked up into the man's face. The features were almost completely hidden by the sombrero and a black silk kerchief, but she caught the icy glitter of eyes, of which color she could not tell, fastened upon her. For a moment she had the paralyzed sensation that there was no way she could wrench her own gaze away from that assessing stare that held her helpless in its grip.

Then, his voice muffled by the kerchief, the bandit chief turned that glittering gaze upon the bandit with the pistol and said only one word, *"Basta!"* The man, scowling, reluctantly released Margarite and turned away.

Beside her, Margarite heard a soft, urgent whisper. *"Ma'm'selle!* The pistol. Give me the pistol."

Looking down, Margarite saw, appalled, that the Belgian lieutenant's hand was creeping toward his pistol lying in the dust of the road. He'll be killed, she thought. And for what? It won't bring back those poor Belgian boys butchered at Tacambaro. Instinctively her own hand reached for the pistol to pull it away. She had never held a gun before in her life and she was surprised at the weight. She wasn't even aware that the gun's hammer was already lifted, or that as the young officer tried to snatch the gun from her grasp, her finger had fastened on the trigger. But she was aware of the sudden, deafening explosion in her ears, and the sharp pain shooting through her wrist and arm from the recoil of the weapon in her hand.

She saw the man on the sorrel horse sway.

At the gunshot, the bandit on foot turned swiftly, muttering a low curse. His pistol flashed downward toward Margarite. As swiftly as he moved, the man

moved faster, putting the sorrel between Margarite and
the pistol.

Once again the low, muffled voice, repeated, "*Basta!*"
Then, raising his right arm, holding a carbine, the man
gave a signal. To Margarite, watching, hardly daring to
breathe, it was as if one minute the road was crowded
with men, the next, the bandits had disappeared, fading
into the surrounding forest, becoming part of the darkness.

"Is it bad, Patricio?"

The pain was like a mist blurring before Patrick's
eyes, so that he hadn't even been aware that the rest of
the men had gone, drifting off one by one, scattering, as
usual, after a raid, in a dozen different directions.

How long had he and his second in command been
riding into the dark pine forest? At least an hour, he
guessed, although the jolting pain in his shoulder made it
seem much longer. Far enough into the forest, hopefully, to keep ahead of the French legionnaires who
would surely be informed of the robbery as soon as the
diligencia reached the next French outpost.

Carefully now he slid out of the saddle, clutching at
the horn, when the pain jabbed like a red hot iron from
his shoulder down his spine. Gabriel quickly built a
small fire, then was beside Patrick, gently removing the
stiffened serape to which the blood had long since dried,
using his knife to cut away the shirt beneath.

Then he gently probed the wound with his fingers, the
flesh hot and swollen beneath his hands. "The bullet's
still there," he said, frowning. "*Gracias Dios,* not far
beneath the skin. It'll have to come out."

He fetched a bottle of tequila from the saddlebag.
While Patrick lifted the bottle to his lips for several long
swallows, Gabriel heated the blade of his knife at the
fire. He worked swiftly, efficiently, ignoring Patrick's
muttered curses as he cut at the flesh, at last applying
deft pressure with his hand to squeeze the bullet free.

"Be grateful it was not one of our guns that shot
you," he said, blood dripping from the bullet he held

finally in his hand for a moment before tossing it into the trees. "A Colt at such close range, you'd have no shoulder left."

"I wouldn't have been shot at all if that fool Diego could keep his hands away from a woman," Patrick growled, perspiration beading his face so that the skin shone with a faint coppery gleam, his dark eyes narrowed against the pain throbbing through his body.

Gabriel found a clean cotton shirt, tore it into strips, and made a rude bandage which quickly stained a deep red as the wound began bleeding again. "It wasn't Diego who shot you, Captain," he said mildly. "It was the *señora*."

Gabriel was right, Patrick thought irritably. It was the woman who had shot him, protecting that young puppy of an officer, who was undoubtedly her lover, or why would she foolishly risk her life for him? Carefully, gritting his teeth against the pain, he pulled on his bloodstained, torn shirt. His pain wasn't helped any by the knowledge that he should never have attacked the caravan of *diligences* in the first place. His orders included only carrying guns across the border, but his men needed fresh horses, and he had been unable to resist the temptation when he had seen the caravan so easily within his grasp. Anyway, how could he have known that that little hellion would actually shoot him?

Unbidden, the young woman's face suddenly floated before him, the way she had looked in those brief seconds before she had shot him, the emerald green eyes flaring wide and almost childishly defiant in the small, oval face. She hardly looked old enough to know what to do with a man in her bed, he thought annoyed, trying to blot the face from his mind. But the more he tried to push the face from his thoughts, the sharper and clearer it became.

Gabriel touched his shoulder gently. "Are you all right, Captain?"

Patrick scowled. "Of course, I'm not all right. You just dug a bullet out of my shoulder, didn't you?"

Sergeant Gabriel Valdez's broad *mestizo* face, more Indian than Spanish, did not show the relief he felt. The captain's temper was returning. That was a healthy sign. He said placidly, "After we've eaten, I'll put some cactus pulp and cobwebs on the wound. You'll feel better in the morning."

The next morning, however, it was clear that the wound had not improved. Despite the dressing of cactus pulp and cobwebs to staunch the bleeding, the flesh around the wound was streaked red and puffy. Patrick himself, the color high in his face, as if with fever, had spent a restless night. When Gabriel suggested they should spend the day resting, Patrick snapped, "With the French swarming all over the forest? And we have to be at Brownsville in three weeks to pick up the new shipment of guns."

He bit his lower lip until it bled as Gabriel helped him onto the sorrel, but gradually, as he learned to brace his body in the saddle against the jolting, the pain became duller, endurable. It was the cold that bothered him the most, the bone-wrenching cold and then the waves of heat until perspiration ran down his face, blinding him. And even worse was the dizziness. The world spun wildly around him and he swayed and almost fell from the saddle.

Patrick was vaguely aware that Gabriel had stopped and was tying him to his saddle. The sergeant's face swam before his eyes, but the tequila the man poured down his throat shot a swift warmth through his body, driving back the cold and bringing the world into focus for a moment. Something was wrong, Patrick thought, gazing around him feverishly, as he felt the sorrel once more moving between his thighs. The sun! The sun was wrong. They were heading south, not north to the border.

He sawed weakly at the reins, and roared loudly, but his voice sounded as if it came from a great distance, "Damn it, Sergeant! Where are you taking me?"

It was the last thing he remembered before the darkness completely engulfed him.

When Patrick became conscious again, he knew at once where he was, even before he opened his eyes. He recognized the sounds and smells: caged birds singing in the patio below his grilled window, the rhythmic patting of hands as *tijoles* were formed in the kitchen off the patio, the heavy sweet scent of jasmine and tuberoses from the garden. Within the room, close to the bed on which he lay, there was another, even more familiar fragrance—the scent of lily of the valley perfume that he always associated with his foster mother, Star McFarland Kelly.

One part of him raged: How had he come here? Yet another part of him, the small, ragged boy who years before had found love and safety within the walls of this house, felt a rush of joy at this homecoming.

"Patrick. Patrick, darling." The woman's voice urging him to wakefulness spoke Spanish, but there was nothing Mexican about the gray-eyed auburn-haired woman smiling down at him anxiously when he opened his eyes. How long had it been? Patrick wondered. At least six years, the two years away at school, the four years of the war. Yet she hadn't changed. The auburn hair flaming in the sunlight that spilled through the window, the slim, erect figure, and the smile that had so easily made a willing slave of a prickly, defensive boy, were the same.

"Thank God, Michael, he's awake." The woman leaned down and kissed Patrick, smiling tremulously. "We've been so worried about you, darling."

Behind her, Patrick saw his foster father, not pure Mexican either for all the black hair, the high-cheekboned face and swarthy skin, not with those striking dark green eyes.

Michael Cordoba Kelly came to stand at the foot of Patrick's bed, frowning darkly in a way that Patrick remembered only too well. Don Miguel hadn't changed either, Patrick thought, using automatically the name by which the vaqueros and peons on the Cordoba rancho called the *patrón*. He could already sense the old familiar friction that had always existed between Don Miguel and himself.

"How do you feel, Patricio?" Don Miguel asked.

Patrick had already made a quick inventory. His shoulder still throbbed, but his head was clear, and the annoying chills and fever seemed to have disappeared. He struggled to sit upright. "I'm fine." Then, abruptly, "Where is Gab . . . ?" He broke off quickly. "How did I get here?"

His foster father gave him a long, thoughtful look. "A man brought you three days ago, a *mestizo* by the look of him, dumped you at our front door, then disappeared."

How had his sergeant known about the Cordoba rancho? Patrick thought, annoyed. All these months he had deliberately stayed as far away from the ranch as possible, kept his own name and identity secret even from his closest associates, so that there would be no way that his foster parents could be involved in his own dangerous undertaking. He had seen it happen too often before, whole Mexican families, women and children, executed by the French authorities because it had been discovered that one member of the family was a guerrilla, a fighter in Juárez's Republican Army.

Then he frowned, remembering. Shortly after he had accepted his present military duties and had been assigned Sergeant Valdez from the Republican Army to assist him, he had had a conversation with Gabriel. Both men were well aware that they faced the very strong possibility of being stood up against a wall and shot if they were caught smuggling United States guns and ammunition to Juarista's scattered forces in Mexico. He had made Gabriel promise that if he should be killed, and Gabriel survive, that the sergeant would send word to the Cordoba hacienda near Cuernavaca.

Well, so the damage was done, Patrick thought, a devil-may-care glint in the indigo blue eyes that he had inherited from his Irish father. All he had to do now was keep Don Miguel and Star from learning the truth about what he was doing in Mexico and slip away from the ranch as quickly as possible.

"My apologies, Don Miguel, for imposing on your hospitality." He turned to Star and saw the faint lines of weariness and anxiety in her face. He was sure that it was she who had nursed him these last three days. "I'm sorry to have worried you, *mi madre*," he said gently.

"Worried us!" Don Miguel exploded. "Did you think about worrying us when you stupidly enlisted in the

Union Army? Were you concerned for your mother when you wrote her only four letters in four years, and this last year none at all? And did you think about your family when you brought disgrace to our name by . . .''

"Michael!" Star shot her husband a quick warning glance, then tucked the coverlet closer around Patrick, her voice firm. "How can you speak of hospitality? This is your home."

So they knew about the court-martial, Patrick thought, surprised that he should feel a flicker of anger, his pride stung at the barely hidden contempt in Don Miguel's voice. He thought he had learned to control such point-less emotions. After all, as the top level aide from General Sheridan's headquarters had explained to Patrick at Fort Union, the court-martial would offer the captain at least a little protection. The French might not be so suspicious of a supposedly disgruntled and dishonorably discharged officer from the American Army coming into Mexico.

"You understand, of course," the colonel had said hastily, "there's no question of the American government stepping in to help you if you are arrested by the French. You will be operating as a civilian under unofficial orders from General Grant." The colonel frowned, disgusted. "Unfortunately, President Johnson, although he sides with President Juárez, has as yet taken no official stand on delivering guns and ammunition to the Juaristas. And it requires the patience of Job to abide the slow and poky methods of our State Department."

Patrick had not been too surprised when after the staged court-martial former friends hadn't bothered to hide their disdain, turning away when they saw him coming. There might have been more overt signs of disapproval, but Captain O'Malley's temper, his skill with a pistol, were too well known. Why, Patrick wondered now, had he expected it to be any different with Don Miguel?

Star said quickly, to change the subject, "I'm only sorry Carlos isn't here to see you."

Patrick saw the sadness shadowing Star's face when she spoke of her young son. Carlos had been only four when Patrick had left, a toddling, mischievous *muchacho* who had adored his older brother. "Carlos is all right, isn't he?" he asked apprehensively.

"Oh, yes." Star smiled. "He's staying with his grandfather in St. Louis while conditions in Mexico are so . . . unsettled."

Patrick grinned. "Be careful, Don Miguel, or you might end up having another Yankee in the family."

A smile tugged at the corners of Michael Kelly's mouth as his glance met his wife's. As if no one else in the world existed but the two of them, Patrick thought, remembering when he was young how jealous he had been of the love that ran so deeply and openly between Star and Don Miguel. And as he grew older, envious, wondering if any woman would look at him the way Star looked at her husband, her heart in her eyes for all to see.

"Oh, I've no objection to living with a Yankee," Michael drawled. Then, his voice tightening, "But after the United States invaded our country and stole almost half of Mexico, I can't imagine any Mexican worthy of the name foolish enough to fight a war for them."

"The Mexican War has been over for twenty years," Patrick protested. But the truth was, he thought wryly, he wasn't sure himself what had made him leave college and join the Union Army when the United States had plunged into its Civil War. Perhaps it was the pretty young abolitionist with her skin smelling of apple blossoms when he had tumbled her in her father's hayloft who had convinced him of the rightness of the Union cause. Or perhaps it was all his college friends rushing to join up, or perhaps, he grinned to himself, for no better reason than he knew how furious Don Miguel would be when he learned of his enlistment. Whatever the reason, the Union Army and its cause had become his and once giving his loyalty, Patrick was not the man to turn back.

The teasing smile returned to his young handsome face, sparks of amusement flashing in his dark blue eyes behind thick black lashes, so that for a moment there was nothing of the Indian about him, only pure Irish devilment as he baited Don Miguel. "Aren't you forgetting, your own father was American?"

I'm not likely to forget, Michael thought, wincing mentally. He had grown up split between two cultures and in some ways accepted by neither—his mother a Cordoba, the daughter of a proud, old *criollo* family, and his father a man he seldom saw, one of the first successful American traders on the Santa Fe trail, bringing goods from the United States to Mexico. He could even remember that when the Mexican War had started in '46, he had tried to keep from becoming entangled, straddling the fence, until he had seen Mexico being beaten to its knees by the swaggering Yankee invaders. He glared at his son. In the end, he, at least, had thrown in his lot with the Mexican Army, fighting for his country.

Star saw the anger gathering in her husband's face, and rose hastily to her feet. "We've tired Patrick enough. He needs to rest." She smiled impishly at her husband. "You two can argue later. . . . It'll be just like old times!"

Giving Patrick one last kiss, she whispered, "Sleep well, my darling boy."

But once away from Patrick's room, following the gallery that ran alongside the tiled patio, the smile faded from her face and she leaned wearily against her husband's arm.

"It's you who needs to rest," he scolded her, worried by the icy coldness of her hand in his. "You haven't slept for two nights, ever since Patricio showed up on our doorstep."

They had come to their large bedroom on the far side of the patio, and quickly now he started a small pinon fire in the fireplace. When he turned back to Star, she was seated on the bed, her hands clasped in her lap, as if she were too exhausted to move.

His hand caressed her hair, flaming red as the Aztec lily. "The boy will be all right, *querida,*" he said gently.

She lifted her face to him. "While I was with Patrick, I was remembering that time after the battle at Rio Churubusco,* when you were wounded and how frightened I was that you might die."

Silently Michael cursed Patrick for bringing back memories of those terrible last days of the Mexican War, putting that look of remembered horror in his wife's dove gray eyes. And bringing back to him, too, his own less than happy memories of his behavior toward Star, during that troubled time.

He smiled sheepishly. "Have you ever forgiven me, *querida,* for being such a proud, stubborn fool? When I think of how I hurt you . . ."

She put a finger across his lips, silencing him, but couldn't help smiling to herself. How alike they were, her husband and Patrick, even if the same blood didn't flow in their veins. Both proud, stubborn men, quick to anger but with a gentleness and strength beneath, like a bedrock that was always there when she needed it.

"What do you suppose Patrick is doing in Mexico?"

He shrugged. "*Quien sabe?*" He wondered if the man who had brought Patrick to the hacienda wasn't a deserter. There was something about the *mestizo,* a military bearing that hadn't completely disappeared. "It couldn't have been pleasant for Patricio after the court-martial," he said thoughtfully. "Perhaps he decided to leave the United States and return to Mexico."

"Patrick didn't steal those company funds," Star objected. "He's not a thief!"

Michael lifted an amused eyebrow. "But that's exactly what he was, my love, a thief and a *lepero,* when you discovered him picking your pocket in Mexico and decided to drag him back here to the rancho."

"But he was only a starving, homeless child then, living on the streets of Mexico by his wits," Star protested. She smiled innocently at her husband. "And if you weren't as fond of Patrick as I am, you would have forbidden me to keep him here at the hacienda."

Forbid her? Michael thought ruefully, gazing down

_____

*See Marcella Thum, *Blazing Star* (New York: Fawcett Crest, 1983).

into his wife's demure eyes but not overlooking the
determined set of her chin. When had he been able to
forbid his beautiful Yankee wife anything once she set
her mind to having her way? Not that she wasn't right
about his feelings for Patricio. After a difficult first year,
when the half-wild boy had constantly tested his foster
father's mettle, he and Patricio had managed to fight
their way to a mutual wary affection and respect for
each other.

Then he noticed Star trying to hide a yawn, and said,
pushing her gently back against the pillows on the bed,
"You should rest. I'll send for your maid to help you
undress."

When he started to turn away, she caught his hands,
her voice softly teasing. "Have you forgotten then, *mi
alma,* how to undress me?"

He gazed down into her silver gray eyes, saw the
warmth shimmering there, and felt a swift answering
passion so that he had to force himself to ask, "Are you
sure you're not too tired, *querida mia*?"

She laughed softly. "Never *that* tired, my love."

Swiftly then he removed the black woven cotton Mexican skirt, the white cotton camisa and few pieces of
undergarments beneath, the simple clothes that a peasant woman might wear, until the pale gleaming body
was finally revealed to him. Then he loosened the pins so
that her glorious hair fell over her shoulders, giving the
flesh where it touched a pale pink glow.

Smiling faintly, her lips half parted, she watched him
undress, finally pulling him impatiently into her waiting
arms. And that hadn't changed either, Michael mar-
veled, the pleasure they found in each other, not the
same as the first time they had held each other, but
better, as wine grows headier, lustier, more robust with
age.

Star sighed dreamily, contentedly, her eyes closed,
when at last he pulled away, but still holding her nestled
in his arms. He lay very still, thinking she had fallen
asleep, when all at once her eyelids opened, her gaze
searching his face anxiously as she asked, "How do you
think Patricio came to be wounded?"

"I don't know," Michael said, his brow darkening. "The first thing tomorrow, though, I intend to find out."

But the next morning when Star went to Patrick's room to bring his breakfast, she found the bed empty, the room deserted. Michael immediately questioned the servants, guessing what had happened even before the stable boy told him. Don Patricio had come to the stable before daybreak, saddled his sorrel horse, and tossing the boy a handful of pesos, ridden away.

Chapter 4

IT was late the next day after the bandit attack that Margarite and Frau Hundt arrived in Mexico City. The brigands had left the mules, but without horses and guns Lieutenant Schiller decided it was wiser not to press on to Mexico City in the dark but stop at the next village, report the robbery, and spend the night at whatever posada was available.

The villagers and the posada owner were eager to be of assistance to the tired and frightened passengers. A meal was hastily thrown together for the travelers, and several men set off at once to the nearest French garrison to raise the alarm.

Even Frau Hundt was mollified by the hospitality of the humble villagers. John Marsh, however, cast a jaundiced eye at the friendly reception they received. "Tomorrow, if that guerrilla band rides into this village, they'd be equally happy to see them," he commented wryly.

"Guerrillas!" Frau Hundt sniffed. "A band of robbers, that's all they were."

Mr. Marsh shook his head. "They were too well disci-

plined for ordinary bandits.'' He turned to Margarite
with a slight smile. ''And your common brigand would
not have allowed the countess Von Melk's heroic, if
foolhardy, behavior to go unpunished.''

Her behavior had been foolhardy, Margarite admitted
to herself. It had all happened too quickly for her to feel
terror at the moment the gun had exploded in her hand,
but now that it was over, she felt fear knotting inside of
her. Especially when she remembered the way the man
on the sorrel horse had looked at her, the glittering
arrogance in the eyes calmly assessing her, and her own
helpless feeling as if all strength were being drained
from her body by that flat, merciless gaze.

Had she killed the man, she wondered, shivering.
Frau Hundt mistook the shiver for a chill, and insisted
that Margarite must drink more of the hot chocolate the
innkeeper had prepared. Margarite obediently sipped at
the chocolate, although it tasted suspiciously and dis-
agreeably like goat's milk.

''*Mein Gott,* what a fright you gave me,'' her chaperone scolded her for the tenth time as they prepared for
bed in a tiny, ill-furnished room, which was, at least,
clean. ''What could you have been thinking of to behave
so recklessly? My heart was in my throat!''

Frau Hundt wasn't the only one unhappy with her,
Margarite thought. By their carefully stiff manner toward
her, she could tell that Lieutenants Schiller and Chazal
were equally annoyed with her, although she suspected
their annoyance was due to wounded pride that a mere
girl rather than a professional soldier had fired the only
shot at the bandits. Well, what else could I do, Margarite decided irritably. What sense would it have made
for Lieutenant Chazal or Franz to get themselves killed
just to prove their bravery. How foolish men could be,
she thought, surprised and a little guilty at such a heretic
thought, pushing it hastily from her mind as she fell
asleep.

By the time the *diligencia* had reached the heights
overlooking Mexico City the next day, Franz had thawed
enough so that, crowded into the carriage next to Margarite, he could smile at her enthusiasm when she caught

her first glimpse of the capital city. Surrounded by a
framework of magnificent mountains, including the snowy
peak of Popocatepetl and the distant volcano, Ixtaccihuatl,
the city lay like a jewel nestled in a fertile green valley.

"I never dreamed it would be so beautiful," Margarite
exclaimed, leaning out of the coach window so that she
could see better. Clouds enveloped the distant volcanoes through which snowy summits towered like marble
domes. The air was crystalline. Colors and shapes, church
spires and verdant fields had a quivering, translucent
quality.

As the carriage descended, however, the day became
more overcast and by the time the carriage passed over
the causeway into the city, rain was pouring down in
thick gray sheets. Peering only occasionally out of the
window now, Margarite could barely glimpse flat-roofed
adobe houses, crumbling churches, and flooded cobble-
stone streets. Men and women with straw capes pulled
over their heads like thatched huts huddled in doorways,
otherwise the streets were deserted.

After the *diligencia* reached the coach stop and the
passengers and their luggage were unloaded with much
confusion in the rain, it was still necessary to find a
hired cab to take Margarite and Frau Hundt to the Ortiz
home in the Calle de los Plateros. Lieutenant Schiller
and his small command had already said their hasty
good-byes, the lieutenant's hand lingering for a moment
longer than necessary in Margarite's.

John Marsh offered to accompany the ladies to their
final destination. "Many of the fashionable families leave
the city during the rainy season," he said. "Are you
sure your uncle and aunt are expecting you, Countess?"

"Oh, yes," she said confidently, pushing down a worrying sense of uneasiness again now that she was so
close to meeting her Mexican relatives. Would she remember them at all? she wondered. Other than her young,
beautiful mother, she had only a vague memory of se-
vere dark faces, of a house that had seemed enormous
and rather gloomy to a small child, except for the flower-
filled courtyard.

Frau Hundt, who had been keeping a sharp eye on the

baggage handlers to make sure that none of their luggage disappeared, asked, "Is the Ortiz house far from here?"

"El Calle de los Plateros?" Mr. Marsh said. "No, it's on the other side of the Plaza Mayor. The cab driver should know the way." He turned to Margarite. "I'll be staying for a few days at the Iturbide Hotel. Please call upon me if you or Frau Hundt should run into any difficulty."

Frau Hundt bristled a little. Did the Englishman think she wasn't capable of looking after her charge? "I'm sure we'll manage very well, Mr. Marsh," she said firmly, ushering Margarite ahead of her into the hired carriage, so that the girl had time for only a quick farewell of John Marsh.

When the cab, bumping over the uneven roads, finally pulled to a stop before a two-story dark pink stone house, the rain had let up somewhat. Stepping out of the carriage, Margarite gazed curiously at the ornate front of the house, completely covered with baroque-looking sculptures and guarded by a heavy oak iron-barred door that refused to open no matter how hard the coach driver pounded on it.

"Let me," Frau Hundt said impatiently, beating vigorously with her parasol at the door, so that when the door suddenly opened, she almost fell into the hallway. The servant in black and gold livery stared, startled, at the two drenched women. The feather on Margarite's jaunty bonnet was collapsed limply across her forehead, her skirt clung wetly to her hips, while her companion's shawl and parasol dripped water over the tiled floor.

When the man, speaking frantically in Spanish, tried to bar the way into the house, Frau Hundt simply pushed him aside, brandishing her parasol at him like a weapon as she demanded, "Don't stand there like an idiot. Go fetch your mistress."

Several more liveried servants came hurrying down the large stone staircase to assist the man guarding the door against the apparently mad interlopers trying to force their way into the house.

Behind Frau Hundt, Margarite tried to make herself heard, edging her way around her indignant companion.

"Por favor, Señor," she pleaded. *"Esta Señor Manuel Rojas y Ortiz en casa?"*

Relieved, the servant turned quickly to her, speaking swiftly in Spanish so that Margarite had a hard time following his words. Then a voice spoke sharply from the staircase. *"Que pasa, Raymond?"*

The staircase was dimly lit by flickering candles in wall sconces. Margarite could barely distinguish the stiletto-slim figure of a middle-aged man clothed completely in black, until he descended the stairs and crossed the hall toward her. The face was as gaunt as the body, with hollows gouged beneath the deepset eyes that drooped at the corners. The man's skin had an unhealthy bluish pallor, but the gaze looking down the long aquiline nose into Margarite's face was alert, and the voice, cold with disdain, as he asked in Spanish, "How may I help you, *Señora?*"

"Señor Ortiz?" she asked uncertainly.

He nodded stiffly.

"I'm Margarite Juliana Von Melk," she said slowly. "Juliana's daughter, your niece." Rebuffed by that frigid stare, she stammered, "You wrote . . . you asked that I should visit you. . . ."

A flicker of surprise touched those sunken eyes and Margarite knew at once that Elissa had lied. Her uncle and aunt were not expecting their niece to be visiting them.

Then, as quickly as it had appeared, the surprise was gone. Her uncle stepped forward, embraced her briefly, and immediately released her. His voice, if not warm, was at least cordial. "My apologies, Doña Margarite. I should have recognized you at once. You have Juliana's features, even the eyes." He gestured formally around him. "Everything in my house is yours."

His glance strayed toward Frau Hundt, and Margarite made hasty introductions. "May I present Señora Luise Hundt, my traveling companion."

"You are welcome to our home, *Señora,*" Margarite's uncle said gravely. "We are most grateful that you have brought our niece safely to us."

"My Aunt Josefa?" Margarite asked. "She's well, I hope?"

Her uncle nodded. "My sister is in the chapel at this hour or I would bring her the happy news of your arrival at once. She will be as overjoyed as I am," Don Manuel assured her. Bitterness etched deeper the gaunt lines in the narrow face. "There has been little cause for rejoicing in our house for too long a time."

"I—I only recently heard of my cousin's death. I'm very sorry," Margarite said.

"There seemed no need to write Don Johann of our loss," her uncle said, the bitterness slipping into the cold voice. "He takes little interest in his wife's family."

Margarite felt a rush of color to her face at the implied criticism of her father. Although her father had never spoken a word to her against her mother's family, she had long suspected that it was the Ortiz family, angered at Juliana's marriage to a man they obviously considered beneath her, who had turned their back on Juliana and her husband.

Forcing back her anger, she said quietly, "My father is dead."

Her uncle inclined his head. "I did not know. Then we share a common sorrow."

Frau Hundt, who did not understand what was being spoken in Spanish, nevertheless sensed the tension in the air, and said quickly, "It's been a tiring trip, Don Manuel. Perhaps we could be shown to our rooms?"

She spoke in German, but her gesturing toward the wet clothes of her companion and herself, made her meaning abundantly clear.

"Of course." Don Manuel merely lifted his hand and suddenly servants seemed to converge upon the hall from all directions. Immediately, the luggage was brought in from the cab and reached the bedrooms to which Margarite and Frau Luise were shown almost as soon as they did. Margarite's room was at the front of the hacienda. Like the rest of the house, the room was filled with French-style furniture, the chairs and bed covered with a pale blue brocade, a beautifully decorated ivory and gold Oriental screen in one corner, and a delicately carved commode and dressing table with tasseled blue velvet stool before it.

For all the beauty of the furnishings, though, there was no feeling of warmth in the large high-ceilinged room. Margarite was glad when one of the maids started a fragrant fire in the blue and white tiled fireplace and another maid brought up kettles of hot water for a bath. When she had finished a long, luxurious bath in the tulip-shaped iron tub behind the screen, using scented soap and drying herself with blissfully thick towels, she discovered that the maids had begun unpacking her traveling cases. There were at least a half-dozen chambermaids, all twittering like a flock of birds as they held up each gown for eager perusal and long sighs of pleasure.

Unlike the men servants, the women wore no uniform, all seeming to favor a loose-fitting chemise, a skirt over several colored petticoats, and white satin shoes. Their hair was worn long and loose, and Margarite couldn't help noticing that the white satin shoes were more often than not soiled, and the hair often matted and uncombed. Yet each one of the women was good-tempered and excessively obliging.

Margarite had washed her own hair, and one of the maids insisted upon brushing her hair dry before the fireplace, while another maid brought a silver tray loaded down with a silver pot of steaming chocolate, cold meats, fresh fruit, and several rich desserts. Then the women gathered in a circle around Margarite, watching her as she ate, giggling and talking rapidly, too rapidly for Margarite to follow.

I'll have to work at my Spanish, Margarite thought, casting a longing look toward the bed. She had had precious little sleep the night before and she wanted nothing so much as to put her head down on that great fluffy pillow, the first comfortable bed she had seen since leaving Vienna. In her halting Spanish she tried to convey that fact to the maids, but when they showed no inclination to leave, she finally got to her feet, marched across the room, and slipped into the bed, pulling the coverlet determinedly over her face.

When she awoke again, she was alone in the room and

darkness had gathered outside the window. For a moment she was disoriented, wondering where she was, until a soft knock came at the door leading to the next room. Without waiting for an answer, Frau Hundt bustled into the room and proceeded to light the lamps. "Good, you're awake," she said brusquely. "Your uncle sent word asking if we felt rested enough to dine with him and your aunt."

Margarite felt a quick twinge of dread at the thought of trying to carry on a conversation across the dinner table with her cadaverous-faced uncle.

As if sensing what the girl was thinking, Frau Luise shrugged and said, "He is your uncle. You cannot avoid him forever." She smiled hopefully. "And perhaps your aunt will not be so . . . formidable!"

However, when Margarite entered the large dining room an hour later, she discovered that her aunt Josefa was equally formidable, in her own way. She was her brother's twin in appearance, her body lean beneath the black velvet gown she wore, her face haggard, with the same long aquiline nose. But while her brother's eyes were coldly disdainful, Josefa's dark eyes beneath hooded lids burned with an inner all-consuming passion. For what? Margarite wondered, until she noticed how her aunt's tapered white fingers fondled the heavy jewel-encrusted gold cross around her neck, the only ornament she wore with her stark mourning clothes.

When she embraced Margarite, the girl could feel how skeletal the body was beneath the velvet, but the smile Doña Josefa gave her niece was warm. "How good to have you with us, child," she murmured. "The blessed virgin has answered my prayers." There was the same warmth in her voice, although a bit more guarded, when she greeted her niece's *dueña*.

The dining room, like Margarite's bedroom, was lavishly furnished with gilded furniture, gold framed mirrors, and a glittering crystal chandelier. As in the bedroom, there was a definite damp chill in the air that apparently permeated the whole house throughout the rainy season.

Margarite was amazed at the number of liveried servants who waited the table, one servant at each place

simply to keep the crystal goblets filled with the rich red
Spanish wine, and a half-dozen others to serve the numerous courses on gold decorated plates.

Although the food was abundant, Margarite could tell
by the expression on Frau Hundt's face that her companion was not impressed by the cook's culinary ability.
Considering the style in which her uncle and aunt lived,
she was surprised herself that the food was not better
prepared. At least, she thought, relieved, she didn't
have to carry on her end of the dinner conversation in her
struggling Spanish. In deference to Frau Hundt, her aunt
and uncle spoke French, which both Margarite and her
companion spoke almost as well as they did German.

At first the conversation was stilted, her uncle's formal manner matching the chilliness of the room, until
Frau Luise told of the guerrilla attack on the *diligencia*
on the road from Vera Cruz. Then Don Manuel's face
came to life, flushing angrily. "The guerrillas have grown
more and more bold these last months. Not even the
royal highway is safe from their outrageous attacks, and
Marshal Bazaine, who was sent to Mexico by the French
to destroy the Juaristas, does nothing but dote upon his
bride-to-be."

The deepset eyes filled with bitterness. "As for Emperor Maximilian, thrust upon us by Napoleon, he has
proven a disaster. Don Maximilian spends half his days
away from the National Palace, idling away his time at
Chapultepec while his French administrators wring the
last peso from the Mexican treasury for their own
pockets."

"Aren't you forgetting that it was the Mexican people
themselves who invited Maximilian to be their emperor?"
Margarite asked indignantly. "And that Maximilian gave
up his right to the Austrian throne to dedicate his life to
Mexico."

The thin face stiffened, gazing at his niece, as if Don
Manuel weren't accustomed to being contradicted at his
own dinner table. Then he replied coldly, "It was the
landowners and the church, yes, who in the beginning
thought Maximilian would be the strong leader that Mexico needed. Instead, Maximilian has alienated himself

from his own Hapsburg family by quarreling with his brother over a family pact that he now claims he was forced to sign. Worse, he has completely alienated himself from the Papal Nuncio by refusing to restore the ecclesiastical rights Juárez took away from the church. Not to mention the reform laws he has passed, championing the Indian workmen against the landowners."

Frau Hundt cast a quick warning glance at Margarite. Would the child never learn not to argue with men, she thought, sighing to herself. Then, before Margarite could speak again, she asked hastily, "And the empress Carlota? Is she popular with the people?"

"Oh, Doña Carlota is well enough liked," her host said grudgingly. "And clever for a woman. There are some who say she has a better head on her shoulders than her husband."

"The empress is barren," his sister said in a soft, horrified voice, as if no greater ill could befall a woman. "And we hear the parties and balls she gives at the palace and Chapultepec are little more than orgies."

"Then you don't attend the court?" Margarite asked, disappointed, for she knew if her relatives stayed away from the imperial court, then she would have little chance of meeting the emperor Maximilian again.

"We have only recently come out of mourning," her aunt reminded her reproachfully.

Don Manuel smiled thinly. "At first many of our friends were happy to accept the lavish court hospitality along with the orders and awards Maximilian and Carlota handed out so liberally. There were even those families who pretended descent from Spanish nobility so they could be given positions at court or their wives could become ladies-in-waiting to the empress."

By the disdainful curl of her uncle's mouth, Margarite was sure that the Ortiz family was not among those families. She studied the cold, remote faces of her uncle and aunt, the skin pulled as taut as yellowed parchment over the sharp bones. Would she ever feel at ease with her relatives, she thought in despair. She now realized wistfully how much she had hoped to find something of her beautiful lost mother here at the Ortiz home, some faint spark of Juliana in her mother's sister and brother.

As the weeks passed, however, Margarite discovered there was not even a picture or any memento of her mother anywhere in the *casa*, and whenever she deliberately brought up the subject of Juliana, her aunt and uncle politely but quickly changed the subject.

Not that she saw that much of her relatives except at mealtime. Her uncle was occupied with his many and varied business interests, while her aunt seemed to spend most of her time kneeling at her prie-dieu in the family chapel, attending services at the nearby cathedral in the great plaza, or devoting herself to sewing fine embroideries for the altar. Doña Josefa's absences from the house and her indifference to the day-by-day running of the large, sprawling house and numerous servants was a source of much annoyance to Frau Hundt.

When she complained to the major-domo, a slick-haired, disagreeable gentleman, he shrugged and said, "It is the tradition. Old maids dress the saints."

"It's no wonder the food is so execrable," Frau Hundt complained privately to Margarite. "I have never seen such slovenly servants. And it takes two people to do the work that one well-trained servant could do, that is, if any of them had any interest in being properly trained in their duties."

Margarite smiled faintly. "Still, they are very amiable," she pointed out.

Amiability was evidently not a quality Frau Luise considered essential in a house servant, as she irritably continued her tirade. "I spent two weeks instructing that young chambermaid, Rosita, how to clean a room properly, and then she quit. I found her begging food from the kitchen yesterday. I asked her, if she needed money so badly, why she had quit a perfectly good job, and do you know what she said? '*Señora*, if you only knew the pleasure of doing nothing!' "

Frau Hundt threw up her hands in despair. "It is no wonder nothing runs or works properly in this country."

Margarite did not mind the servants' lack of energy and efficiency as much as she minded her own lack of activity. In Vienna she had been accustomed to daily horseback rides and walks in the Prater, afternoons spent on lessons with her tutor, or shopping along the Kärntnerstrasse. In Mexico she quickly discovered that a woman from a wealthy home never rose from her bed before mid-morning, or put her small, satin-shod foot outside of the house except in a carriage. Horseback riding was considered a masculine sport, while education for a Mexican woman, if there was any, stopped at age twelve.

The Ortiz home had few visitors, and those who came were the age of her aunt and uncle. Only once had a young woman arrived at the house with her parents for dinner. To Margarite's surprise, the young woman had turned out to be her uncle's fiancée, Doña Guadalupe, a shy, pretty girl with a buxom figure and no conversation.

"She's at least a year younger than I am!" a shocked Margarite had protested the next afternoon to Frau Hundt while they took their daily carriage ride along the Paseo. "And Uncle Manuel has to be in his fifties."

Her companion shrugged. "So? Marshal Bazaine is past sixty and he was married in June to a girl of twenty. Anyway," she added practically, "with his wife and son both dead, your uncle must start another family as soon as possible. It is obvious your aunt will never marry, and there must be heirs to carry on the Ortiz family name." She gave Margarite an amused glance. "The servants tell me that if your uncle hadn't already been affianced, he would no doubt have married you."

At the girl's shocked glance, she laughed. "Apparently, it is a custom in Mexico, uncles marrying nieces. It keeps the wealth within the family, I suppose."

"My uncle has another son," Margarite reminded Frau Hundt, although she realized that all the time she had been in the Ortiz home, neither her uncle nor her aunt had ever mentioned Salvador's name. Remembering the cold clammy feel of her uncle's hands, the icy remoteness in his face, the thought of marrying him made her almost physically ill.

To push the distasteful thought from her mind, she returned her attention to the Paseo, to the handsome carriages driving slowly down the long, broad avenue.

Fashionably dressed women within the carriages flirted from behind their fans with the lavishly dressed *caballeros* on fiery horses, or nodded to friends as one carriage passed another. The scene reminded Margarite of the Hauptallee in Vienna, which on Sunday afternoons was crammed from one end to the other with pedestrians, horseback riders, and carriages, all intent on seeing or being seen.

Only, of course, in Vienna, she thought, there were no filthy *leperos* on the street plying their trade, exposing real and fake sores and mutilations, public letter writers, tortilla women and pulque vendors, hawkers selling everything from rosaries to love potions, and barefooted Indians in dirty white cotton trousers with earthen basins of sweetmeats and bread balanced on their heads, or Indian women moving with an unconscious grace while carrying babies cradled on their back. And although one often heard church bells in Vienna, it was not the neverending fountain of sound that constantly filled the air in Mexico.

The carriage had reached the Plaza Mayor, the heart of the city that sat like a colorful stage setting against a backdrop of snow-covered volcanoes in the distance. The National Palace, an enormous barracks of a building, dominated the east side of the great square, with the majestic cathedral on the north.

Around the gardens in the center of the square promenaded ladies in crinolines, accompanied by gentlemen in white sombreroes, short jackets, and tight silver-laced trousers. If it were not for the Austrian band playing noisily in the center of the square, and the soldiers of a dozen different nationalities, Mexican lancers to Chasseurs of Africa, walking their horses on the tanbark paths, Margarite could almost have forgotten that the war existed at all.

How handsome the Austrian soldiers were, she thought proudly as the carriage slowed down so that several Hussars, blond-haired with glittering medals across their chests, could cross the thoroughfare.

Then she took a closer look at one of the officers, and called to the coachman, "Stop! Stop!" Even before the carriage had completely halted, she had tugged the carriage door open. Gathering her skirt around her, she made an unladylike leap from the carriage into the street before Frau Hundt could reach out a hand to stop her.

Chapter 5

"F RANZ!"

The Austrian officer whirled, and smiling eagerly, left his fellow officers to join Margarite by the carriage.

"Countess, what a great pleasure. I was about to give up hope that I'd ever see you again."

"Oh?" Margarite smiled teasingly. "When you never bothered to call upon me I thought you'd forgotten all about me."

"But I did call," the young man blurted out. "Three times, and each time was told you weren't at home. I never stopped looking for you at the soirées at the palace and at the empress Carlota's balls on Monday nights at Chapultapec. . . ."

"My uncle and aunt have only recently come out of mourning," Margarite said, hoping the bewilderment she felt at the lieutenant's words didn't show in her face. No one had told her that the lieutenant had called. "I . . . we haven't attended any court functions." Then, quickly to change the subject, she asked lightly, "Your military duties haven't been too onerous then, if you can spend so much time at court?"

"I'm attached to the palace guard at Chapultapec," Franz said, unhappiness for a moment dimming the eager light in the young man's eyes as they clung to Margarite's face. "But I've asked for a transfer to the field. Not that there's been much fighting, except for a few guerrilla skirmishes, since Juárez has been chased to Paso del Norte. By now he's probably across the border."

"You paint a much more cheerful picture of the military situation than the newspapers do, Lieutenant," Frau Hundt said, joining Margarite outside the landau. "They say the guerrillas have recaptured many villages in the north, and that supplies from the United States for the Juaristas are pouring across the border."

"You shouldn't believe the lies that are printed in the newspapers," Franz said, nodding stiffly to the woman. "They print only what the ignorant masses want to believe." He turned to Margarite, his voice pleading. "Perhaps, Countess, we could stroll a short way together?"

Frau Hundt took Margarite's arm firmly. "I'm afraid that's out of the question, Lieutenant Schiller." Then, at the imploring look on the girl's face, sighed to herself, her resolution crumbling, remembering a long ago summer's day when there had been a handsome young officer whose arm the young Luise had clung to on a promenade much like this one.

"Fifteen minutes then, no longer," she warned, opening her parasol, and trailing a discreet distance behind the young couple as they joined the promenaders. No doubt Señor Ortiz would hear of his niece's meeting with the Austrian officer from the coachman, she thought dourly, but the poor child had had little enough pleasure since her arrival in Mexico.

Holding her own parasol of lilac lace over her head to divert some of the sun's rays, Margarite tilted her head to look up at Franz. He had stopped to buy her a nosegay of margarites at a flower stall. "Although I believe the Mexicans call them margaritas," he said, handing her the small bouquet of white-petaled flowers, then took her arm, his face fairly beaming with pride.

"What are the parties like at Chapultepec?" she asked curiously. "My aunt says they are orgies."

"Hardly that," Franz protested, then grinned sheepishly. "Actually, they're rather dull. There's a great deal of rich food, after which the older guests often nod off. The dancing is lively enough, though, after the emperor retires, which he does invariably at eight o'clock. Not many people know that the emperor retires early so that he can arise at dawn to work on affairs of state."

Margarite remembered her uncle's contempt for Maximilian and said slowly, "I've heard that the emperor idles away his days."

"Lies!" Franz exploded angrily. "Vicious lies spread by the rich landowners and the priests, who thought they could control Maximilian like a puppet. Both Emperor Maximilian and the empress Carlota work very hard at their duties and are dedicated to the welfare of the Mexican people. Why, one night when the emperor heard that Indian workers were being held as prisoners in a local bakery, he went himself to investigate. And he has such a kind heart, he is constantly pardoning military prisoners who have been court-martialed and sentenced to the firing squads. As for the empress, she has donated a fortune from her private funds to schools and hospitals and the poor."

It was Lieutenant Schiller's personal opinion that the emperor was entirely too kind-hearted, too blind to the venality and corruption around him, too willing to listen to any charlatan who happened to get his ear and told him what he wanted to hear. Like that American priest, Father Fischer, Franz thought gloomily, that the emperor put such store by. Any child could see that the man was nothing more than an unsavory trickster.

Margarite happily hugged the lieutenant's words to her heart, delighted to hear that Maximilian was as fine and noble a man as she had always known he was.

Looking down at his companion, Franz mistakenly thought the misty look of adoration in the emerald eyes, the glow that lighted the lovely face beneath the parasol, was for him. He caught one small hand in his, whispering, "Oh, Margarite, how I've missed you. I can't bear to be apart from you. There must be some way we can meet again."

Half startled, half embarrassed by the naked hunger she saw in the lieutenant's eyes, Margarite murmured, "I don't know how we can. Unless . . ." She kept her eyelids demurely cast down. "Unless there were some way the emperor could be persuaded to invite my uncle

and aunt to Chapultapec.'' Even her uncle, she thought
shrewdly, could hardly turn down a personal invitation
from the emperor. She smiled wistfully up at Lieutenant
Schiller. ''But then, I don't suppose you have that sort
of influence at court.''

The lieutenant laughed proudly, squeezing her hand.
''You'd be surprised,'' he said. At Hofburg, he knew, a
mere lieutenant wouldn't even be admitted to the imperial circle, but Maximilian was not like his brother, Franz
Josef. Although he might spend months writing a book
on court etiquette, and had imported the Hapsburg imperial trappings to his own court, Maximilian often sought
out the masculine company of the young officers in his
palace guard. He especially enjoyed entertaining the Austrian officers, with whom he could chat about home and
Vienna over cards, cigars, and wine. And Maximilian
was not averse, or so his courtiers gossiped in the royal
halls, to a little romantic intrigue himself.

When Margarite returned to the Ortiz carriage, Frau
Hundt was already regretting her leniency in allowing
her charge to walk, even for a few minutes, with Lieutenant Schiller.

''Don Manuel will be *fuchsteufelswild* when he hears
of your little escapade,'' she warned darkly.

''I don't care,'' Margarite said, shrugging with feigned
indifference. For she suspected that Frau Luise was
right. Her uncle would be hopping mad.

It was an indifference she had a hard time maintaining
when she was summoned to her uncle's spartanly furnished study that evening. If possible, her uncle's face
was more cadaverous, more haughty than ever as he
looked down his long nose at his niece and berated her
icily for her unseemly behavior in the Plaza Mayor that
afternoon.

''You will never see or speak to that *caballero* again.
Is that understood? If he comes to the house, he will be
turned away as he was before.''

From somewhere Margarite drew upon a courage she
hadn't known she possessed, as she faced her uncle's
wrath. ''You have no right to decide who I can or can't
see!'' she protested indignantly.

"No right?" Her uncle arched a furious brow. "This is my house, I am the head of this family, and you are my niece. I will not make the same mistake I made with your mother, foolishly inviting a foreigner like Don Johann into my home so that he could fill my poor sister's head with his romantic nonsense."

"My father loved my mother dearly!"

"Love?" Don Manuel's thin lips twisted, as if with a bad taste in his mouth. "Now you speak like a childish *Norteamericana*. I would have thought you would have learned more sense from your Austrian stepmother. Europeans are seldom so naive. A girl your age has no knowledge of love or marriage or what is best for her. With your father's death, it is my responsibility to act as your guardian and arrange a proper marriage for you."

As if the matter were closed, he got to his feet. "In the meantime, I have chosen another *dueña* for you to make certain no more unfortunate incidents like today occur."

"What of Frau Luise?" Margarite asked, shocked.

"There is a French ship leaving from Vera Cruz next week. Señora Hundt has passage aboard her."

"You can't! You can't send my friend away."

Once again the eyebrow lifted dauntingly as Don Manuel stared haughtily at his niece. "I am not accustomed to asking guests to leave my home. It is Doña Luise's own decision to return to Austria, not mine."

Margarite turned and ran from the study, finding Frau Luise in her bedroom, preparing for her journey. She flung her arms around the woman, begging tearfully, "You mustn't leave! Please say you'll stay."

"I'm sorry, child," Frau Hundt said gently, cradling the girl against her ample bosom. "I should have told you myself. But I was hired only to bring you to Mexico, you know, not to stay on here. It's better if I leave. Soon your uncle will find you a husband. You won't be needing a companion any longer."

Margarite's lower lip jutted ominously. "I'll find my own husband."

"Nonsense!" Frau Luise contradicted her briskly. "Only scullery maids pick their own husbands. Marriages for young women from good families are arranged in Austria just as they're arranged here in Mexico. Do you think you would have been permitted to marry whomever you chose even if you had stayed in Vienna?''

''What will I do without you?'' Margarite felt tears brimming in her eyes. ''Why can't you stay here in Mexico? I'll be so lonely without you.''

Frau Luise pulled a handkerchief from her sleeve and dabbed at her own eyes. ''I'll miss you, too, child.''

But Frau Hundt was under no illusion that she would miss Mexico. Oh, the country had a certain raw beauty, she had to admit as she returned to her packing, but the Mexican people themselves were a frustrating mixture of violence and indolence, impossible to understand, much less rule. As for Emperor Maximilian and the Empress Carlota, Frau Luise was much too shrewd not to have observed that that charming young couple sat on a throne supported only by French bayonets. And wasn't it Napoleon himself who had said that one can do anything with bayonets except sit upon them!

After Frau Hundt left, Margarite moped around the house or sat in the flower-filled patio, perfecting her Spanish, on those afternoons when the rain stopped for a few hours. Not that there was any point to improving her Spanish, she thought unhappily. She had no one to talk to except the servants and her aunt, who seldom spoke of anything except religious matters. She knew her aunt would have been happy if she had shown a religious vocation, but after one visit to a convent with Aunt Josefa, it had been painfully clear, even to her aunt, that Margarite had no interest in the religious life. She was sitting on the patio one warm August afternoon, a Spanish book in her lap and a glass of chilled orangeade in her hands, when her aunt came looking for her.

''Your hat, Margarite,'' she scolded.

Margarite did not have her aunt's Latin distaste for the sun. She liked the feel of the sunlight warm against her skin, but obediently she reached for the great soft straw hat tossed carelessly to one side of the chair and tied it beneath her chin.

Doña Josefa gazed, frowning a little, at her niece. The

girl was wearing a multi-colored Mexican skirt, an embroidered blouse, and a fringed shawl falling away from her softly curved shoulders. Although totally without fashion sense herself, the woman suspected that it was the sort of costume an ordinary Mexican woman might wear rather than the proper attire for a fashionable young lady.

"Your gown, Margarite?" she asked uncertainly.

Margarite yawned, stretching her arms so that the small breasts were pulled high, pushing against the soft cotton material of her camisa. "It's too hot for crinolines," she protested. Then, getting to her feet, she began to pace restlessly, her face unhappy, "Anyway, who's to see what I wear?"

Watching the girl's graceful walk, her regal carriage despite the simple gown she wore, her aunt thought proudly, that's the Ortiz blood in her. Juliana was the same. She remembered, without bitterness, that no man had ever looked twice at her when her beautiful sister was in the room.

But Juliana had always been such a happy girl, and Josefa was not so insensitive that she wasn't aware of the discontent shadowing her niece's young face. "Well, I'm sure someone will be looking at what you wear," she said, smiling faintly, "at the reception we've been invited to at Chapultapec next week."

"Uncle Manuel has accepted an invitation to court?" Margarite asked, startled.

"Your uncle may not agree with all of Emperor Maximilian's policies, but he is a loyal subject of the crown," her aunt said carefully. And in any case, she thought, frowning uneasily, not even her brother would be so impolitic as to turn down a direct invitation from Emperor Maximilian himself, not when Marshal Bazaine's French Imperial Guard was ready to imprison anyone of low or high estate showing signs of open disrespect to the emperor. "If you haven't any suitable frock," she said tactfully, "I've been told there are several good French modistes in the city."

But Margarite had already decided upon her gown, the flounced, white muslin crinoline, her carnival ball gown

that she had never had a chance to wear. If only the
bandits had not taken her only good piece of jewelry,
the pearl necklace, she thought as she dressed the night
of the reception. Thinking of the bandits, though, always
brought back memories of the man on the sorrel horse,
along with an odd, quivering sensation in the pit of her
stomach. Had she killed the man? Quickly she thrust the
question away. She didn't want anything to spoil this
evening.

When she was finally dressed and ready—the maids
who assisted her as much in a flurry of excitement as
she was—she presented herself to her uncle and aunt,
who were already dressed and waiting for her in her
uncle's study. Her uncle wore European clothes, expensively London-tailored, while her aunt was in her usual
black velvet gown and black lace mantilla. In honor of
the occasion, though, her aunt had put aside the gold
crucifix and wore a parure of diamonds around her neck,
on her ears, and in her smoothly coiffed black hair.

Margarite's own dark sable hair was pulled back in
the popular netted waterfall with a coronet above her
brow. A pink of excitement touched the creamy cheekbones, so there was no need for rouge, and her eyes
sparkled, emerald bright, behind dark lashes as she dipped
in a deep curtsy before her uncle. "Do I meet with
your approval, Uncle?" she asked demurely.

Don Manuel frowned at the bare expanse of bosom
and the simple camellia wreath that circled his niece's
hair. The long aristocrat nose twitched, and abruptly he
walked behind his desk. Opening a top drawer, he took
out a key. Then he swung open a wooden panel in the
wall behind the desk and used the key to unlock a
strongbox set into the wall.

He took out a black velvet box, removed an emerald
necklace, tiara, and earrings, and handed them to Margarite. "I prefer the old-fashioned style of women wearing diamonds, but colored stones would seem to suit
you," he said stiffly.

Margarite gave a pleased gasp when she took the
jewelry from his hands, each piece exquisitely mounted
in a running pattern of silver leaves. The fact that she

was sure her uncle wanted her to wear the emeralds only because it would not do for a member of the Ortiz family to appear without priceless jewels at a court reception didn't dim her happiness as the Ortiz carriage left the city and made its way over the Veronica causeway.

When they reached Chapultepec hill, it was still light enough so that Margarite could see the great, dark cypress woods hung with Spanish moss, like a primeval forest, already old when the Aztec chief Montezuma made his summer home here.

As the carriage ascended the hillside, Margarite clenched her hands in her lap, a fiery warmth then an icy cold sweeping over her at the thought of seeing the emperor Maximilian again. She had only to close her eyes and it was as if it had happened yesterday, that first meeting, the handsome golden-haired man, like a god smiling down at her. Would he remember her? she wondered. No, of course not. Why should he remember one frightened, awestruck eleven-year-old girl?

Engrossed in her own thoughts, she hardly heard her uncle explaining that Chapultepec had been the home of the Spanish viceroys for three hundred years. After the Spanish were ousted from Mexico, the palace had been turned into a military school, forever remembered in Mexican history because of the brave *niños* who had leapt to their death from the parapet rather than surrender to the American forces attacking the fortress.

As Margarite waited with her uncle and aunt in the great reception hall of the palace, she could see no reminders of a besieged military school. Hundreds of artists, masons, and carpenters had transformed the fortress into a palace fit for an emperor. Gold monograms had gone up over the windows and doorways, imported crystal chandeliers hung in the halls, and ornate wallpaper covered the walls. On the enormous terraces outside the castle, marble and silver statues stood amid the grottos and follies of eighteenth-century viceroys.

Within the long reception hall, the colorful crinolines of the women swayed like flowers beneath the glittering chandeliers, their lavish jewelry rivaling even the spectacular emeralds that Margarite wore. Most of the men present were foreign diplomats, military officers in the imperial army, or wealthy *hacendados*. There were even a few men looking very distinguished in salt-and-pepper cutaways, who Margarite recognized from their accents as Americans.

Following her gaze, her uncle shrugged. "Those gentlemen were officers in the Army of the Confederate States of America. Those and others like them have come to Mexico to start a colony of American expatriates near Cordoba. Matthew Maury, the well-known American scientist and officer in the Confederate Navy, is their leader and enjoys the close friendship of the emperor and empress." His mouth narrowed. "Although I doubt if the friendship will last very long. Don Maximiliano is much too fearful of further antagonizing the United States by encouraging Confederates to move to Mexico."

Margarite's attention had wandered from the American gentlemen to a new couple who had entered the reception hall. Although the woman's amethyst jewelry and her simple gray moiré gown seemed subdued next to the flashing jewels and colorful gowns of the Mexican women present, her flaming auburn hair, the blazing loveliness of the woman's beauty, would have made her stand out in any crowd. And the man with her, tall and strikingly handsome, with a streak of silver in his black hair, was in his own way equally eye-catching.

"Who are they?" Margarite asked curiously as the couple made their way through the gathering, coming toward where the Ortiz family stood.

Her uncle was already making introductions, nodding toward Margarite as he said, "Don Miguel, Doña Star, may I present my niece and ward, Countess Margarite Ortiz Von Melk, who is only recently arrived in Mexico."

Margarite curtsied. Doña Star was even more beautiful close-up, she thought, especially when she smiled. The woman's dove gray eyes were warm and friendly as she studied Margarite's gown. "Is that the latest fashion from Paris, Countess? How becoming. I'm afraid our gowns are months behind the time here in Mexico. You must visit our rancho soon so that you can tell me what the women in Vienna and Paris are wearing these days."

There was just the trace of an accent behind the almost perfect Spanish the woman spoke, and after the couple had exchanged a few more pleasantries and moved on, Margarite remarked, "What a beautiful woman, but surely the *señora* isn't Mexican?"

"Señor Kelly y Cordoba's wife is a *Norteamericana*," her uncle replied. "There was an unfortunate liaison and *yanqui* blood also flows in Don Miguel's veins, although the Cordobas themselves are an illustrious *criollo* family. They have a country estate in Cuernavaca near ours, where they spend a great deal of their time." Gazing after the couple, he said thoughtfully, "It's a surprise to see Don Miguel here. He has avoided the court of Maximilian from the very beginning."

Star Kelly was saying much the same thing about Don Manuel. "I never expected to see Señor Ortiz here this evening," she said to her husband. "Not after the way they say he stormed out of a council meeting when Maximilian refused to revoke the Indian labor laws."

"He's probably here for the same reason we are," Michael said grimly. "Because he doesn't want to be accused of treasonable behavior by refusing an invitation from Maximilian."

"Surely the emperor wouldn't do that?"

"Not Maximilian, Marshal Bazaine," Michael said. "I gather the general is growing notoriously intolerant of French detachments being lured into ambushes, of liberal Mexicans cooperating with the Juaristas, and of Maximilian pardoning those found guilty of treason by French courts-martial."

Star's gray eyes searched her husband's face. "It's Patrick you're worried about, isn't it, *mi alma*?" she asked quietly. "Is Patrick in some sort of trouble with the authorities?"

Michael saw the fear spring into those smoky gray eyes and felt a helpless rage that he could not protect this woman that he cherished more than life itself, from the slightest worry or unhappiness. He forced his voice to cheerfulness. "Patricio? The only trouble that one will have is from some irate husband."

But he knew Star wasn't deceived by his banter. They loved each other too well, knew each other as intimately as they knew themselves. He saw the questions gathering in her eyes, and was relieved when a rustling swept through the gathering that announced, even before the grand chamberlain made the formal pronouncement, that the emperor Maximilian and the empress Carlota had finally arrived to meet their guests.

Chapter 6

INSTEAD of canopied thrones in the reception room, there were two chairs, the arms carved in the shape of a plumed serpent, the symbol of the ancient Aztec god, Quetzalcoatl, which Maximilian had taken as his symbol too. And instead of a receiving line, and a marshaling of those to be presented to the emperor and empress by a gold-sticked grand chamberlain, the monarchs separated and moved informally in a circle around the room, greeting each guest by name.

When the empress Carlota reached Star and Michael Kelly, the American woman dipped in a deep, graceful curtsy that would have done credit to the royal circle at Hofburg.

The empress was wearing a sea blue gown and a splendid fire opal necklace, with matching opals at her ears and around her slender wrists. Star remembered hearing that the empress was particularly fond of the opal jewelry that had been mined at Querétaro and had been given to her as a gift from the Mexican people. Her dark lashes veiling her eyes, Star covertly studied the slim, erect figure standing before her. Carlota's classic features had strength and intelligence and would have been beautiful, she decided, if it had not been for a certain severity in the lines of the face, and a shadow of sadness that dulled the dark green-flecked eyes.

She greeted the Kellys in Spanish, without a trace of an accent. "It's a great pleasure, Señor Kelly, to meet you and your lovely wife at last." If the last words held a hint of reproach, it lasted only a moment, then her glance moved to Star, and a smile curved the small, passionate mouth. "It would seem stories we've heard at court of your wife's beauty were not exaggerated." She studied Star's hair. "The empress Eugénie, our dear friend, has hair much the same color as yours."

Star allowed her gaze, for a moment, to glance around the reception hall. "My husband and I have been admiring the changes Your Majesties have made here at Chapultapec."

A flush of pride softened the grave face as Carlota replied immediately, "It was the emperor who designed the renovations. His Majesty has great artistic talent. He supervised every detail of the construction of Miramar, our beautiful castle in Trieste." Briefly her glance left Star to look across the room at her husband.

Star, following the gaze, saw that the emperor was engaged in conversation with the Countess Von Melk. Watching the couple, the animation in the girl's lovely face, the attentive air of Maximilian, she felt an instant, vague alarm. Other guests in the room, Star noticed, were also watching the tableau, their faces amused or appalled or filled with a greedy eagerness to spread the word of Maximilian's latest conquest.

Star noticed that the empress was squinting a little and hoped Carlota was too nearsighted to see her husband's face clearly or the young woman with him. Or was Carlota already well aware of her husband's roving eye? Star wondered, remembering the gossip that the imperial couple never shared the same bed. Would that explain the sadness in Carlota's eyes? Star felt a wrench of pity for the empress for all that she wore the imperial crown of Mexico.

Margarite was oblivious of being the center of so much attention or the knowing glances being sent her way. At the moment, no one else existed for her except Maximilian. He looked exactly as she remembered him, if anything, even more handsome in the wasp-waisted dark green military tunic and white trousers with the wide tricolored ribbon of the Order of the Mexican Eagle across his breast. Perhaps his handsome face, the clear blue eyes, were a little tired, but when he smiled down at her as she dipped forward and down in a low obeisance before him, she felt an instant shock of recognition. And when he lifted her by one white-gloved hand, the faint pressure of his touch sent a giddy warmth surging through her.

After making sure that his equerry was successfully engaged in keeping the young lady's uncle and aunt occupied with conversation, Maximilian leaned forward and said in an amused, conspiratorial whisper that only Margarite could hear, "I have a message for you, Countess, from a lovesick Austrian officer by the name of Lieutenant Schiller. He is desolate he is unable to be with you today, but he and several of his brave fellow officers have been sent north to reinforce a French garrison." Gazing down at the young woman with eyes the color of jade, only brighter, more luminous, and with a familiar, adoring look in them, Maximilian's smile deepened. "Having met you, *Señora,* I can understand Lieutenant Schiller's malady. It is our court's great loss that your beauty hasn't graced our presence before this."

So it was Franz's doing, Margarite thought, the personal invitation to court from Maximilian, but memory of the young lieutenant flitted only briefly through her mind. How blue Maximilian's eyes are, she thought. That intense blue, admiring gaze on her face made her feel as if she were still a dumbstruck child of eleven.

Maximilian continued thoughtfully studying the young woman. "Perhaps, Countess, we can tempt you into accepting a position as a lady-in-waiting to the empress Carlota. Having someone like yourself at court, so recently arrived from Vienna, would be like a breath of air from home for her."

Overhearing the last part of the conversation, Don Manuel turned to Maximilian, his face punctiliously polite but his voice frigid. "You do the Ortiz family a great honor, sire. However, Her Majesty's ladies-in-waiting are all married, are they not? And my niece has not yet taken a husband."

The prominent Hapsburg lower lip jutted ominously for a moment as Maximilian recognized the rebuff behind the carefully phrased words. Then a lifetime of diplomatic training came to the fore, and the emperor conceded defeat graciously, smiling with winning charm at his guest. "With Doña Margarite's beauty, I'm sure her unmarried state is a temporary condition." Then with a last glance toward Margarite, he added firmly, "The empress Carlota and I look forward to seeing you and your family at court again soon, Señor Ortiz."

The rest of the evening passed in a delightful blur for Margarite. She scarcely remembered meeting the empress Carlota. With the careless cruelty of youth, she noticed that the empress looked older than her twenty-six years, and had a haughty, reserved manner, much different from her husband's charming affability.

A musical program followed after Their Majesties had completed their tour of the room. An Italian soprano sang several operatic arias, then gave her rendition of "La Paloma," a new popular love song that was heard everywhere in the capital and was a favorite of the empress Carlota's. Margarite couldn't help noticing that Carlota's white hand rested on Maximilian's arm during the performance, and as she gazed at her husband during the singing of "La Paloma," there was such a look of longing on her face that Margarite had looked quickly, guiltily, away.

After the performance, silent-footed Indian servants in livery moved among the guests with silver trays of small cakes, fruits, and bonbons. As was his custom, the emperor had retired by the time the ballroom dancing began, and although many young *caballeros* cast hopeful glances toward Margarite, there were none brave enough to dare approach the barrier of Don Manuel and ask the *señora* to dance.

The Ortiz family left Chapultapec before a late supper
was served to the guests. Margarite was aware of a chill
in the atmosphere around her as the carriage passed the
two guard posts within the castle grounds and traveled
over the poplar-lined causeway to the city gates. Maximilian was having a new road constructed connecting
the city with his castle at Chapultapec, but the present
road was in bad enough condition so that Margarite was
too busy trying to keep her balance in the coach, and
her crinoline skirt from being crushed, to worry about
her uncle's ominous silence or her aunt's nervous, unconscious clutching at the gold crucifix that was not
around her throat.

Once they reached the Ortiz *casa*, Don Manuel disappeared without a word into his study. Margarite turned
to her aunt, annoyed. "You'd think Uncle Manuel would
be proud that the emperor wanted me to be a lady-in-
waiting to the empress."

Doña Josefa's eyelids dipped over startled eyes, her
sallow face flushing in embarrassment. But then, of
course, she thought, the girl was too young and naturally too innocent to realize that there might be another
reason for Maximilian's wanting her near him at court.
Josefa, a virginal spinster herself, could not imagine
discussing the subject of a man's unholy, lascivious de-
sires with her niece. The girl would find out soon enough
once she was married.

Silently blessing the dear Savior for having saved her
from the indignities of the marriage bed, Josefa murmured an excuse of weariness to prevent further conversation.

Once in her own room, Margarite was sure she was
too excited to sleep. After she undressed and slipped
into bed, she went over and over again in her mind
every second of her meeting with Maximilian. It was a
disappointment, her uncle not allowing her to become a
lady-in-waiting to the empress, but he could hardly forbid her attending court functions in the future, not after
Maximilian had practically commanded the presence of
the Ortiz family at court. When she finally fell asleep, it
was to dream the by now familiar dream of a tall, golden-

bearded man with deep blue eyes, smiling and beckoning to her but as always, tantalizingly, just out of reach.

"Please, Doña Margarite, you must hurry." Rosita's face leaning over the bed, was puffy with sleep, her hair hanging in untidy wisps. "Don Manuel said the carriage will leave in an hour and you are to be packed and ready."

Rubbing the sleep from her eyes, Margarite saw that several of the other maids were already hastily pulling gowns from the armoire and packing shoes and undergarments in her leather trunk.

"Leave? Where are we going?" she asked, bewildered, gazing at the darkness outside her shuttered bedroom window. Why, it wasn't daybreak yet!

"I was not told," the maid said. "Only that you were to be packed and ready." Her voice dropped to a self-important whisper. "But the coachman told the cook and the cook told Maria and Maria told me that his grace, Doña Josefa, and yourself are all going on a visit to Real del Monte."

"Real del Monte," Margarite echoed as she allowed the maid to remove her night garments. "Where is Real del Monte?"

"Oh, in the mountains north of the city," the maid said vaguely. "Once or twice a year his grace pays a visit to the Ortiz silver mine at Real."

Margarite remembered the Englishman from the ship mentioning that her uncle owned a silver mine in a place called Real del Monte. But why should Don Manuel decide now, practically in the middle of the night, to pay a visit to the mine? She frowned at her reflection in her dressing table mirror as the maid fussed with her hair. Was it possible her uncle had arranged the trip to get her out of the city and away from Maximilian?

The maid helped her dress in a beige linen traveling gown with a matching bonnet and heavy veil. "It will be hot and dusty on the road to Real, and there will be times when you will have to walk or ride next to the carriage," Rosita cautioned. "Keep your face covered or you will be red as an Indio."

Her aunt was already seated in the carriage when

Margarite arrived in the front courtyard. The carriage
was not the black landau with the Ortiz coat of arms on
the door in gold, but a more sturdy, undecorated coach,
pulled by a team of horses, obviously chosen for their
strength, not looks. Her uncle was in a charro outfit on
horseback, along with eight well-armed outriders.

"Hurry, Margarite," her aunt urged, almost pulling
her into the carriage. "Your uncle wants to make Santi-
ago by evening."

Margarite had no sooner settled in the coach, when
her uncle gave the command to start. The carriage trun-
dled swiftly through the city, passing the great cathedral
and leaving by the gate of Guadalupe.

Once outside the city, the horses went at full gallop,
and it was all Margarite could do to cling to the leather
strap on the side of the carriage, much less try to engage
her aunt in conversation. It was still too dark to see
anything—even her aunt's face was in shadow—and at
last she fell into an uncomfortable half sleep. When she
was jolted fully awake again, it was daylight. They were
driving by great plains of gray-green maguey, villages
with roofless adobe houses, crumbling walls and arches,
and for miles, scarcely a tree to be seen. The view from
the lowered leather sides of the coach was so dreary and
desolate that Margarite soon closed her eyes again.

At the village of Santa Clara the carriage stopped so
the horses could rest a short time and be given water,
then raced off again. "What is the hurry?" Margarite
protested to her aunt, whose sallow face looked as exhausted as Margarite felt.

Her aunt nervously touched the crucifix that was once
more securely around her neck and said, "There are
many *ladrónes* on the road these days."

Margarite turned her gaze again to the road, then gave
a gasp of amazement. "What are those?" She pointed to
two huge stone pyramids coming into view, rising abruptly
from the flat plain surrounding them.

Her aunt crossed herself quickly, clutching at her
crucifix. Her deepset eyes burned with a zealot's fury.
"Heathen Aztecs worshiped at those temples, stained
with the blood of human sacrifices to their pagan gods.

The priests cut open the breasts and devoured the hearts of their victims. It was the mercy of our Lord that sent Cortés to Mexico to hunt down and destroy the heathen Indios, their golden idols, and bloodthirsty rituals.''

Margarite shivered as she gazed at the pyramids and the hundreds of smaller pyramids around them. Then she found herself remembering stories she had read of the Spanish Inquisition, priests torturing and burning at the stake, men, women, and children they considered infidels. And how Cortés and his men had murdered and plundered almost an entire race of people who had greeted the conquerors in peace. Were those any less blood-thirsty rituals?

The carriage was racing on again at a grand gallop, the outriders yelling encouragement to their horses with wild shrieks, the horses and carriage wheels raising so much dust that Margarite hastily drew her head back inside the coach. By afternoon they reached the pretty little village of San Juan and stopped for a quick meal of goat's milk, cheese, and biscuits. Margarite and her aunt would have liked to rest awhile at the posada, but Don Manuel didn't like the appearance of several rough-looking men hanging around the inn, and after changing their horses, decided they should continue their journey at once.

Several hours later, as the carriage sped through a wild-looking, rocky country of uncultivated plains and hills, the carriage wheels started to smoke. The outriders dismounted and began to extinguish the fire with the drinking water Don Manuel brought from the carriage, while the women stretched their legs. It was Don Manuel, grumbling at the delay, who first saw the riders appear suddenly from the hills as if springing from the ground itself.

Margarite and her aunt did not need his cry of alarm to hurry them back into the carriage. The outriders sprang upon their horses, Don Manuel already firing at the riders coming fast across the fields toward the coach, so fast that Margarite could see the leather jackets and trousers the attackers wore, the sunlight glinting against their carbines, the flashes of light when the carbines fired. The deafening sound of the exploding carbines mingled with the thundering hooves of the horses. The carriage started with a lurch that sent Margarite sprawling, but not before she saw her uncle sway and fall from his saddle, being dragged by his heel caught in the stirrup across the rocky ground, leaving a bright red trail behind him.

Terrified, the girl crouched low, making herself as small a target as possible as bullets slammed through the leather sides of the carriage. Then she saw, appalled, that her aunt was still seated calmly upright, her eyes closed, her hands fastened around the jewel-encrusted crucifix at her breast as her lips moved in silent prayer.

"Aunt Josefa! Get down!" Margarite tugged frantically at her aunt's arm.

The eyelids opened. For a moment, incredibly, Margarite thought her aunt smiled faintly, her voice very calm. "Do not despair, child. We are in the hands of God. He will . . ."

The dark head jerked forward beneath the mantilla. Without a sound her aunt slid slowly sideways and down, falling across Margarite's lap. Margarite stared down at the blood staining her gown, at her aunt's face with no expression there at all, only a horrible blankness to the waxlike pallor. Margarite felt herself flung forward across her aunt. The carriage was out of control now, swaying back and forth with a wild, uncontrolled motion as the horses, without drivers, raced forward in a panic.

Over the sound of the gunshots, the pounding hooves, and her own heart thudding in her chest, Margarite heard the screams of the bandits. *"Mueran los Franceses! Mueran Maximiliano! Viva la Mexico!"*

The runaway carriage hit a rock jutting in the road, shuddered, and tipped crazily, hanging suspended a moment before crashing over on its side. Margarite felt something hard hit her head, and there was an explosion of pain. She could not breathe. It was as if the world had turned over and fallen upon her, crushing her with its weight.

When she came to again, the pain was throbbing through her whole body. Whimpering softly, she cautiously opened her eyes. She was no longer in the coach. She was lying on the ground on a blanket that smelled bad.

There was noise and confusion at a large campfire not far from where she lay; terrible ululating screams mingling with loud roisterous laughter. Half conscious, she staggered to her feet and turned toward the sounds. And looked into hell. Her uncle's naked body, riddled with bullets and knife wounds, hung upside down from a tree. Near him, several of the outriders who had not been killed outright in the attack were also hung upside down from trees, their naked bodies slashed with knives, their right hands missing. The shadowy figures of the men surrounding the hanging men were half hidden in darkness, only the glint of a blade glittered in the firelight as a knife flashed downward, found the flesh of its victim, and extracted its toll of pain.

The scarcely human screams stabbed through Margarite. The bonfire flames dancing before her eyes, burned the scene into her mind before she mercifully collapsed again into unconsciousness.

Chapter 7

"HOSEA has returned, Captain. El Cuchillo's camp is just ahead in that abandoned hacienda. You can see their fires from here."

And so could any roving French patrol who happened to be in the area, Patrick thought, frowning, as he studied the crumbling walls of the deserted house, the rosy glow from campfires he could see reflected against the night sky. And as close as they were to the camp, why hadn't any sentries challenged them?

"Do we ride in, Captain?" Sergeant Valdez asked

quietly. Behind him, more than a half-dozen men on
wiry mustangs waited, along with twenty heavily loaded
pack mules. The men, like Patrick and Gabriel, were
dressed in the rough, much worn clothing of *arrieros*.

"What do we know of Cuchillo?"

Valdez shrugged. What did they know about any of
the Juaristas to whom they delivered the Springfield
rifles, received unofficially from the American military
in Brownsville, then smuggled across the border into
Mexico. Only their names and approximate rendezvous
points where the rifles were to be delivered.

"I've heard he's good with a knife. That's how he got
his name. And Hosea says there's about two dozen men
in the camp, as far as he could tell." The sergeant gave
Patrick a questioning glance. "A trap, you think?"

Patrick felt a prickling at the nape of his neck, a
warning signal that he had learned to respect over the
last years, when the wrong decision on his part could
mean life or death for himself and his men.

He drew his revolver and sheltered it beneath the dark
Saltillo serape he wore. Holding his reins in his left
hand, he turned to Gabriel. "We'll ride into the camp
together. Have Pablo stay behind with the mules, and
position the rest of the men on the right and left flank of
the camp, hidden, but close enough to hear my signal."

The sergeant gave the order and in a few moments
Patrick and Gabriel were alone, riding openly toward the
firelight. As soon as they were within hailing distance of
the campfires, Patrick saw the mutilated men hanging
from the thorn trees in the courtyard of the house.
Across the forehead of each man was slashed the letters
TAM for traitor to Mexico. *Triador a México.*

Beside him, Patrick heard Gabriel whisper, *"Madre
de Dios!"*

It was not the first time Patrick had come across dead
man with the marks of Juarista justice on their bodies, but
the sight never failed to sicken him. Still, it wasn't only
Juaristas who used torture, he reminded himself. He
remembered the villagers he had seen, men and women,
even children, murderously flogged to death by the French
for allowing the Juaristas into their villages, even though

there was no possible way the defenseless villagers could stop the armed guerrilla bands.

Patrick turned his gaze away from the dead men, studying the men sprawled, half drunk from pulque and blood lust, around the campfires. His eyes narrowed to angry slits. He knew that most of the Juaristas were not trained professional soldiers, but what sort of *stupido* was this El Cuchillo to allow such lax discipline, leaving his camp completely unprotected.

Several mangy-looking dogs had started barking when the two strangers approached the camp. Two of the men by the fire stumbled to their feet, yelling and brandishing their ancient carbines at the intruders. Others of the band came tumbling out of the roofless house, carrying knives, lances, swords, a few flourishing revolvers which they fired haphazardly over the heads of the two strangers.

Patrick and Gabriel sat perfectly still, Patrick's impassive gaze moving across the faces of the half dressed, wild-looking men, finally centering upon one fiercely mustached man who seemed more alert than the rest. "Are you the one who calls himself El Cuchillo? I have a message—from Brownsville."

"I'm El Cuchillo." The man who stepped forward, shoving the mustached man to one side, was a *mestizo*. Unlike Sergeant Valdez, there was more Spanish than Indian in his sharp features, sallow skin, and oily black hair that hung almost to his shoulders. Although he was several inches shorter than many of the men he led, there was a power in the brutally arrogant features, a hardness to the muscular, compact body, that made him somehow appear to tower over the men around him.

The small dark eyes fastened upon Patrick. A look of surprise, then vicious amusement, flickered across El Cuchillo's face. It was a face that might have been handsome except for the smashed nose that had been badly broken and never reset properly. The broad smile that split his features did not touch the flat black eyes. "Patricio, *mi amigo*! How long has it been?" He turned jovially to his companions. "Put away your guns, *compadres*. This *hombre* is an old friend. We grew up as boys together on the Cordoba rancho." The smile thinned.

"Only my good friend lived with the *patrón* and I lived with the other peons in dirt huts."

Patrick dismounted quickly, his revolver back in its holster but his hand still resting on the hammered silver handle. His face remained expressionless, his voice mild. "You always did talk too much, Juan."

The man laughed uproariously, slapping his knee. "That is true, Patricio, but never as well as you. How I admired the way you, a dirty *lepero* from the streets of Mexico, talked your way into the good graces of the oh so *bellissima* Señora Kelly." He winked broadly. "But then, perhaps, it was more than talking, *sí*?"

At the icy fury that suddenly glittered in Patrick's narrowed eyes, the man baiting him took an uneasy step backward, beads of perspiration breaking out on his forehead. Juan Heras all at once remembered the time when a young Patricio in a blind rage had beaten him to the ground and smashed his face with his bare fists, would have killed him, if Don Miguel hadn't come along in time and pulled his foster son away.

El Cuchillo's laugh was still loud but not quite so jovial. "I make a joke, *sí*? Come. We'll have time later to talk about old times, *mi hermano*. First, you must have something to drink, you and your *compadres*." He gestured grandly around him. "As you can see, we are celebrating a great military victory."

"Military victory?" Patrick's glance strayed to the Mexican features of the mutilated dead men. "I don't see any dead French soldiers here."

El Cuchillo swaggered over to the body of one of the dead men hanging from the tree and jabbed, almost playfully, with his knife at the corpse. "Don Manuel Rojas y Ortiz was as great an enemy to Mexico as any French pig. It is a great pity," he said regretfully, "that he died so quickly."

Patrick took a closer look at the disfigured body. It was Don Manuel, he realized, and swore softly beneath his breath. When word of the death of a powerful *hidalgo* like Ortiz reached Mexico, these hills would be swarming with Bazaine's soldiers, ready to take vengeance on

any hapless villager who was even suspected of being a
Juarista sympathizer.

He turned his gaze back to Juan Heras, his voice
edged. "No doubt the money and jewels you took from
Don Manuel will go toward the Juarista cause."

El Cuchillo lifted an eyebrow in feigned shock. "But,
of course, Patricio. Can you doubt it? Just as the rifles
you bring us will kill many French soldiers for our
beloved Presidente Juárez." He smiled greedily as he
added, "And the ransom money for the *señora* . . ."

"What *señora*?" Patrick interrupted sharply.

Juan shrugged. "She was in the Ortiz carriage with
another, older woman, when the carriage overturned.
The woman was dead, unfortunately, and of no use to
us, but the young *señora* will live, I think, and bring a
fine ransom." The small black eyes suddenly took on an
unpleasant sheen. "*Ai-ye,* and so beautiful a *señora* you
would not believe. Come with me and you will see what
a prize I have captured."

The room inside the house where the girl lay on a
crude pallet on the floor had only half a roof and three
walls still standing. A tallow candle was pushed into a
wine bottle, its flickering light touching only fitfully the
small body huddled beneath a dirty serape. An Indian
woman, her black hair plaited down her back, was
crouched on the floor beside the pallet.

El Cuchillo had only to gesture with his hand and the
woman scurried from the room. Juan picked up the
candle and the flickering yellow light fell fully across the
girl's face. Grinning widely, he reach down and flung
back the serape. The girl was wearing a shift of some
fine embroidered material, Patrick saw, torn in several
places so that the bruises and cuts that marred the softly
gleaming flesh beneath could be easily seen. There had
been a crude attempt to bandage some of the worst cuts,
but the bandages were filthy, and blood had dried against
the once white shift in ugly brown splotches.

Juan Heras moved the candle very slowly from the
girl's unconscious face, the dark lashes fanning out against
skin as finely textured as the richest, creamiest silk,
lingering over the small, perfectly formed pale breasts,

the slight, boyish swell of hips, then down the slender, curved legs to the tiny ankles and small feet.

"Not much to look at now, but clean her up and *bellissima, sí*?" He turned, smiling smugly at Patrick. "A daughter of the Ortiz family, of a certainty."

Even with the face bruised and her dark hair in a tangled mass, Patrick recognized the girl at once. The young woman who had picked up the Belgian officer's gun and shot him. What the devil had she been doing, traveling in the Ortiz carriage? he wondered. But none of his bewilderment showed in his face or voice as he said, "The Ortiz family have no daughters. The girl's probably a maid, traveling with her mistress."

Juan frowned, disappointed, but then he shook his head, his hand shrewdly fingering the expensively woven material of the shift. "No maid wears such fine undergarments. And the rest of the clothes we removed from her are just as rich. If not a daughter, then a relative, surely, and the family will pay dearly for her return."

"Who will pay?" Patrick pointed out almost indifferently. "Don Manuel is dead and the older woman in the carriage must have been his sister. His one son he disowned and the other is dead. Who is left of the family to pay dearly for the girl's return? The truth is, she's of no value to you, alive or dead."

Juan ran his tongue over lips that shone moistly in the candlelight as he gazed down at the unconscious girl. Smiling loosely, he pushed aside the torn shift and found one pink-tipped breast, caressing its softness roughly. "Oh, this one has value, *mi amigo*," he said thickly. "She will bring me and my men much pleasure when she has been broken properly from her fine ways."

At the touch of the man's hand, the girl's eyelids opened, the green eyes blank, blurred with pain, a half-delirious moan escaping the bloodless lips.

A murderous rage slashed through Patrick at sight of that rough, filthy hand at the girl's breast. Almost of its own volition, his hand moved to his revolver. At the same moment Juan, looking up, saw death almost upon him. He reached with reptilian swiftness for the knife at his waist, a second too late.

The bullet went through his wrist, and he screamed with the pain. The knife fell to the dirt floor, his hand dropping uselessly to his side. He glared at Patrick, his face yellow and contorted with agony, as he cursed, "*Cabrone!* My men will hang you in the tree with the other carrion. *Hijo de puta!* You will die, slowly, I pro. . ."

He gurgled into silence as Patrick stepped swiftly behind him, and an arm like an iron band went around his throat, crushing his windpipe so that he couldn't breathe, much less speak. He felt the muzzle of a gun shoved into his back. "It's very simple, *mi amigo*," Patrick said, his voice cold. "If I die, you die. Now, *vamos!*"

El Cuchillo stumbled out the door into the courtyard, the arm around his neck never loosening its grip. The men around the fire, already alarmed by the shot, were on their feet, muskets and revolvers in hand. They started to rush forward, then stopped, uncertain, at the sight of their leader, held like a shield in front of the stranger who had ridden into camp earlier.

Patrick loosened his grip. "Tell your men to put down their guns," he ordered Juan, jabbing him in the back with his revolver.

His captive screamed. "*Matar! Matar!* Shoot the dog down! There's just the two of them!"

On the other side of the courtyard, Gabriel fired two quick shots into the air.

"Not just two," Patrick said, gesturing to the crumbling walls around the house. "Take another look."

A volley of rifle shots landed around the feet of the clustered men, sending up puffs of dust. They whirled, gazing, startled at the men who had appeared, it seemed, from nowhere, rifles pointed with deadly accuracy into the courtyard.

Patrick's arm once more savagely closed around Juan's throat as a second volley of shots swiftly followed the first, closer this time, grazing the ears of the bandits, tearing through shirtsleeves. Guns and knives quickly clattered to the ground.

Gabriel gathered them up, threw them over the court-yard wall, then turned to the captain. Patrick jerked his chin back toward the house. "There's a girl inside. Bring her out. We're taking her with us."

Within two minutes Gabriel returned, carrying the girl wrapped in the serape in his arms. Patrick shouted to one of his men at the wall, "Hosea, drive off their horses and pull the men out. You, too, Sergeant. I'll catch up with you."

Gabriel looked as if he were going to protest, then shrugged and propped the unconscious girl on his horse, mounting swiftly behind her, wheeling the horse around and riding out of the courtyard into the darkness.

Patrick waited a few moments, then suddenly releasing his captive, he sent El Cuchillo sprawling into the dust at his feet, his revolver pointed at the man's head.

Juan landed on his knees and didn't bother trying to get up. Instead, he sat back on his haunches and started laughing, until tears came to his eyes, as if it were all a great joke they had shared. "Just like old times, *mi hermano, sí?*" he finally gasped, wiping his eyes with a bandanna. "We have one damn good fight. But if you wanted the girl so bad, you should have told me. I would have given her to you gladly. A woman should not come between friends."

He took the bandanna and wrapped it around his wrist. "There is still the matter of the rifles, *mi amigo*," he said, smiling cheerfully.

Patrick's finger itched to pull the trigger, to wipe that obscene smile off Juan Heras's face forever, but he knew he had no choice. Benito Juárez needed all the well-armed men he could get, no matter if some of the Juaristas were little better than thieves and cutthroats, as eager to rob and plunder as they were to fight French troops.

"The rifles will be left a mile down the trail," he said, holding the revolver carefully on El Cuchillo as he mounted his horse. "But if anyone comes after us, there'll be no rifles. Understood?"

Juan nodded, still smiling. "Sí, Patricio." He got to his feet. "*Vaya con Dios.*" Just for a second as he smiled, something cold and deadly flashed in the flat black eyes as he stared at Patrick. "Until we meet again, *mi amigo*," he said softly.

Patrick rode with deliberate slowness from the camp, putting spurs to his horse only when he was outside the range of the light from the campfires. Sergeant Valdez and his men were waiting a mile down the trail. While the sergeant helped unload the rifles from the pack mules, Patrick took the girl onto his horse. Although he moved her as gently as possible, she moaned as he took her in his arms and held her on the saddle in front of him.

When the troop moved on again, Gabriel rode alongside Patrick, speaking softly so that the men could not hear. "This is a great foolishness, Captain, taking the girl with us. You should have left her back at the camp."

The two men had grown to know each other too well for Patrick to remind the sergeant that it was not his place to question a direct order. Anyway, he decided ruefully, Gabriel was right. It had been quixotic to take the girl with him. She was sure to delay them in making their deliveries, might even put the whole command into jeopardy. Except, he thought, his mouth tightening, there was no way he could have left the injured girl to the tender mercies of Juan Heras. Not after Juanita. Juanita had been an Indian girl working on the Cordoba rancho. Because she had preferred Patrick to Juan, Heras had beaten the girl half to death and then raped her. If Don Miguel hadn't intervened, Patrick would have killed Juan rather than just smashing the man's face.

"There's a convent near San Miguel," he said. "We'll leave the girl there."

"San Miguel's more than three days' travel from here," Gabriel replied. "We don't know how badly *la niña* is injured. The trip could kill her."

Patrick gazed down into the girl's face, silver-gilded by the moonlight that lit the path through the hills ahead of them. Her head rested against his chest, and he could smell the faint rose perfume from her hair in his nostrils. For a moment, not sure that she was breathing, his own breath caught sharply in his chest. Then, leaning his head down, he felt relieved, the soft faint warmth of her breath against his face.

"There's a cave I remember not far off the trail ahead. We'll bed down there for the night and see how the girl is in the morning."

Gabriel recognized the stubborn look on the captain's face and knew it was useless to protest anymore. At the cave, while the men unpacked the mules, Patrick built a small fire, then spread some pine boughs on the floor and placed several blankets over them. Before placing the girl on the pallet, he carefully removed the bloody shift and the filthy bandages, then bathed the girl gently with warm water he had heated over the fire. With the dirt and grime and dried blood removed, he was able to study her injuries. The cuts on her legs and arms did not look too bad. It was the bruises, particularly those beneath the breasts, and the long deep cut on her head beneath the blood-matted hair that worried him.

Taking his knife, he cut away the hair from around the wound. The long black coils were not heavy and coarse, but soft as a satin rope as they slid through his hands. After washing the wound, he tore up his last clean cotton shirt and wrapped a fresh wet dressing around the girl's head.

Finally, he turned his attention to the ugly bruises beneath the girl's breasts, probing lightly at the rib cage with his fingertips. His patient, although still unconscious, groaned with the pain. The ribs didn't appear broken, Patrick thought, frowning, but he couldn't be sure. And even less sure that the girl hadn't been hurt internally.

He ripped up the rest of his shirt to make a bandage that he tied firmly around the girl's ribs, then he lowered her gently back onto the pallet, wrapping the blankets closely around her. Gabriel had brought him some food, and he debated whether or not to try to feed the girl. Then he remembered the surgeon at Fort Union who had told him never to try to force food or drink on an unconscious man. Gazing at the girl, her face so frighteningly white that he could see the pale blue veins beneath the skin at the temple, he only wished uneasily that the surgeon had taught him a little more about tending the wounded.

He settled on his haunches beside the pallet, his gaze never leaving the girl as he ate the corn and frijoles that Gabriel brought him, washing the food down with swallows of pulque. For several hours he remained, wrapped in a blanket, beside the pallet, half asleep, half awake, a condition to which his body had become accustomed on long night marches. But when his patient began to murmur fretfully, he came immediately fully awake, leaning over the girl, trying to make out what she was saying.

"Papa, papa," she moaned. *"Ich bin kalt, sehr kalt."*

Patrick recognized the language as German. What was a Mexican girl doing speaking German, he wondered absently, even as he piled his own blanket upon the girl, and when she still didn't stop shivering, quickly removed his clothes and slid under the blankets, gathering her icy flesh against his warm body. Finally she stopped trembling, gave a soft sigh, and fell into a natural sleep in his arms.

Chapter 8

AT first, when Margarite awoke, all she was conscious of was the pain. There was a dull throbbing in her head, and each time she drew a breath, it was like a knife stabbing into her chest. Cautiously she opened her eyes. Her head hurt too much to think of moving it, but gradually curiosity drove her to shift her head carefully, to look around her.

Where was she? Some sort of cave obviously, but how had she come here? And why did she hurt so? The last thing she remembered . . . her fingernails dug painfully into her palms. . . . *What was the last thing she remembered?* It was as if a dark, opaque curtain were pulled across her mind. No matter how she forced herself, she could not peer behind that curtain. And the harder she tried, the more her head ached.

She could see sunshine outside the entrance of the cave, but there was an icy core at the center of her being that had nothing to do with body heat. Then, suddenly, as she watched, the sunshine disappeared. The dark shadow of a man filled the small opening of the cave, blotting out the sun. Terrified, without knowing why she was terrified, she shrank back against the blankets, her head pounding. There was something frightening about shadows, black shadows . . . if only she could remember.

The man came to stand beside her, hunching down beside the pallet, when he saw her eyes were open. In the dimly lit cave, she thought at first he was black, with his swarthy skin and crisp black hair curling back from a wide forehead. Then, as her eyes grew accustomed to the dimness, she saw that the skin pulled taut over the broad flat cheekbones was more the color of burnished coppery bronze, the thickly lashed eyes an indigo blue rather than black. The face itself, with a rough growth of beard, had a curiously still quality, as if it were not made of flesh and blood but chiseled from some hard, smooth substance. Yet the long mouth beneath a carefully tended, luxuriant mustache was surprisingly warm and sensuous-looking, the voice, when he spoke, had a deep, rich timbre. "How are you feeling, *Señora*?"

She answered in a halting Spanish. "Who . . . are you? Where am I?"

So she did speak Spanish, Patrick thought, relieved. "Perhaps first you would tell me your name," he answered.

Margarite stared at the man, her green eyes widening, dazed. "I—I can't," she stammered, frightened. "I don't know my name." Hysteria crept into her voice, pulled it shrill. "I—I can't remember anything."

The man frowned, the dark intensity of his gaze fastened upon her face, unnerving. She felt tears spring to her eyes. Did he think she was lying? She felt the hysteria tighten, twisting inside of her. Why should she lie? Surely, he must know who she was. Why didn't he tell her? Why did he torment her this way? She reached out and clutched frantically at the worn leather jacket he wore.

"You must tell me who I am! What's happened to me?"

He removed her hand, his voice calm. "I don't know who you are, *Señora*."

The effort of talking had made her head throb even more. She had to clench her lips against the pain and force herself to continue speaking. "How did I come here?"

For a moment she thought he wasn't going to answer her, then he shrugged. "We found you alongside the trail. We brought you here."

We, who was we? she wondered, and then, grasping at straws, she said, "There must have been something, something I was carrying or wearing . . ."

The corners of the long mouth jerked upward in a brief smile. "You were wearing very little, *Señora*, little more than you are wearing now."

A warmth swept over Margarite's body as she all at once realized that beneath the blankets she was wearing nothing at all. She glared at the man, her voice taking on an unconscious arrogance that she wasn't even aware of as she demanded haughtily, "I want my clothes immediately."

"There was only your shift and that had to be cut away from you so I could clean and bandage your wounds."

The rush of color once more swept over her, her skin burning as she thought of a strange man's hands moving familiarly over her body. Her embarrassment wasn't helped by a faint flicker of amusement that she glimpsed for a moment in the dark eyes. "You . . . you shouldn't have," she stammered.

The amusement disappeared. He stared impassively down at her. "Would you prefer to have been left to die?" Then, coldly, "That can still be arranged if the *señora* wishes."

He couldn't mean it, she thought, outraged. He couldn't just leave her to die alone in this cave. Or could he? she wondered, suddenly shivering. What did she know about the man, or the other ferocious-looking men she glimpsed through the cave opening? How did she know that he wasn't lying; that it wasn't he and his men who had beaten her and dragged her to this cave?

The man must have guessed what she was thinking, for a scowl suddenly darkened his face, the deep-timbered voice impatient. "We are not bandits, *Señora*. We are *arrieros*."

"*Arrieros?*" she repeated blankly.

"Mule drivers," he said. "Surely the *señora* has seen *arrieros* before."

In a vague sort of way, a picture flashed in Margarite's mind, a long line of heavily loaded mules seen everywhere along the roads in Mexico, and even where there were no roads, being driven along by rough, hard-bitten muleteers. She grasped at the picture, but it quickly slipped away. Somehow, though, the fact that she could remember anything made her feel a little better.

"How long have I been here?"

"Two days," the man replied, and then, harshly, "We cannot delay any longer. Are you well enough to travel?"

"I don't know." She tried to sit up, and gasped at the pain that jabbed in her chest.

The man leaned forward, removed the bandage from around her head, and nodded, pleased. "The cut is healing well."

Before she could stop him, he had thrust aside the blanket covering her and had begun removing the bandage wrapped around her chest.

"Don't!" she protested indignantly, trying to pull the blanket back over her. But his hands were already examining the flesh beneath her breasts, their touch surprisingly gentle as he probed the bruised area. "I think perhaps the rib is cracked, not broken," he said thoughtfully as he rebound the cloth around her rib cage. "If the bandage is tight enough, you should be able to travel."

She snatched the blanket back over her. "How can I travel without clothes?" she demanded.

Without a word he got to his feet and left the cave. He returned in a few minutes and tossed upon her pallet a pair of leather trousers, a much worn cotton shirt, and a pair of huaraches. "Hosea is the smallest. These will have to do."

The girl picked the clothes up gingerly and gave the man a shocked glance. "They smell!"

"No doubt," he agreed placidly.

When she did not move, her chin setting obstinately, he reached down and took hold of the blanket, the dancing gleam of amusement again in the indigo eyes as he slowly began to pull the blanket away. "If you need assistance in dressing, *Señora . . .*"

She yanked the blanket from his grasp. "I can manage by myself," she said icily.

She waited until he had left the cave, then pulled herself slowly to her feet. As the blanket fell away from her, she gazed, shocked, at the black and blue bruises on her hips and legs. When she leaned over to pull on the trousers, a wave of dizziness swept over her and she had to brace herself against the wall of the cave to keep from falling. It was even harder, slipping into the shirt, biting her lips against the pain that curled like a whip around her as she lifted her arms. Both the shirt and the trousers were too large, but the shirt, at least, she could tuck into the waist of the trousers and the sleeves could be rolled up. The rolled-up trouser legs, however, kept falling over her ankles and the too large thonged leather huaraches slid off her feet.

Finally, triumphantly, she was dressed, although her nose wrinkled in protest at the smell from the much worn and obviously seldom washed clothes. She still ached all over, but at least the dizziness had passed. Even the throbbing in her head had eased somewhat. The man had not replaced the bandage on her head, and she touched the wound carefully, wincing a little. Then, in growing puzzlement, her hand examined the hair around the wound, and she cried out involuntarily.

Instantly the man was back inside the cave, his hand on the butt of the revolver at his waist, his eyes searching the cave swiftly before returning his gaze to Margarite.

"What's wrong?"

"My hair! What have you done to my hair?" she cried.

Patrick repressed a grin as he studied the girl. She did look peculiar, with half her hair hanging to her shoulders, the other half clipped short. Not to mention the oversized shirt, and the trousers trailing over her ankles.

He reached down, and taking a stiletto-thin wicked-looking knife from his boot, walked toward the girl. She retreated hastily, coming up hard against a wall of the cave. "What . . . what are you going to do?" she asked uneasily. Then as the knife flashed toward her head, panic-stricken, she tried to twist away.

"Hold still!" Patrick ordered irritably. His one hand clutched a handful of hair while the other hand wielded the knife. Soft coils of black hair drifted to the ground as the girl whimpered softly. When he had finished, the hair was at least evenly short, if not, perhaps, in the height of fashion. Then glancing downward, he decided he might as well finish the job, and swiftly slashed away several inches of trousers with his knife.

"Now, *Señora*," he growled, "we have wasted enough time. Come!"

Slowly, she followed him out of the cave, the huaraches flopping on her feet. After the darkness of the cave the sunshine made her blink, and it was several seconds before she could distinguish the faces of the other men, all unshaven, and looking as if they hadn't washed in weeks. And all looking, she thought, turning her gaze quickly from their rough cut faces, as if they would slit your throat without a second thought.

One of the men, older-looking than the rest, brought her some corn and tortillas. The dish was filthy, as were the man's hands as he handed her the food. Flinching, she shook her head, murmuring, "I'm not hungry."

"Eat, *Señora*." It was not a request but a command from the mustached man who was apparently the leader of the group. She started to protest, then saw the black, scowling look on his face and decided she was hungry after all. To her surprise she discovered she *was* hungry, and wondered how long it had been since she had eaten, as she quickly finished the last of the tortillas.

The older man then handed her a flask, and thinking it was water, she lifted it to her lips and swallowed quickly. It was like fire sliding down her throat, burning the lining of her stomach. She began to cough, her eyes tearing helplessly, while the men, watching her, laughed uproariously, punching one another in the shoulders, as if they had never seen anything so funny.

The man with the mustache did not laugh, but she saw one corner of his mouth twitch, and it was several seconds before he said curtly, "*Basta!*"

Something in the way the man said the word stirred a faint flame of memory . . . as if somewhere she had heard that same voice give that same command before, but the flame was feeble and died quickly, leaving her in the same frightening labyrinth of darkness. Tears, as much from frustration now as from the burning liquor she had swallowed, stung her eyes.

The men had turned away from her and were quickly finishing loading the mules. Each mule had what looked like a leather pillow stuffed with hay covering his back and halfway down his sides. As Margarite watched, appalled, a bandage was laced around the pad and the mule's body so cruelly tight that she was sure the poor animal, reduced to half its size, couldn't possibly breathe, much less move. The drivers seemed cheerfully oblivious to any agony they were causing the mules. They lifted great weights of cargo onto the backs of the animals, as easily as if they were tossing feather pillows around, all the while talking and laughing with one another like rough-housing schoolboys.

"You'll ride with me, Niña."

Margarite turned around, startled at the man's new, more familiar form of address. He shrugged. "That's what the men call you."

Patrick, amused by the girl in the outsized men's clothes, said, "Niño would perhaps be more fitting."

La niña . . . little girl, Margarite translated to herself. Well, she supposed she could be called worse. She stared coldly at the man. "And what do I call you?" she asked.

"Patricio," he said. He was holding the reins of a

sturdy, deep-chested bay mare. "Do you want to ride in front or pillion?"

Either way, Margarite realized, she would be forced to sit in uncomfortably close proximity to the man, her arms clasped around him, or his arms around her. She gave the man a wary glance, and gestured to the string of horses being tied behind the mules. "Why can't I ride one of them?"

She saw his eyes narrow and suspected that he wasn't used to having his commands questioned. At first she thought he was going to insist that she ride with him, then he shrugged and said indifferently, "As you wish."

The mule driver in charge of the horses quickly saddled one of the small, wiry mustangs. When Margarite saw the animal at close quarters, she swallowed nervously. The horse was ugly, with a shaggy coat and a nervous way of tossing his head. It wasn't until later that she learned that the small, wiry mustangs the *arrieros* rode were also the smartest, best-trained horses she would ever meet, obeying instantly their rider's commands, no matter how far-fetched or outrageous. But at the moment she could only wonder uneasily, Did she know how to ride?

She saw that Patricio was watching her, as if aware of her uncertainty. "If *la niña* is afraid . . ." he said.

She caught the faint note of derision as his voice trailed off, and her chin jerked up. "I'm not afraid."

"Well, then." The man picked her up and deposited her on the back of the small horse as easily as the other mule drivers had lifted their packs onto the backs of the mules. Almost as soon as she was astride the animal, Margarite realized from the way her body instinctively balanced itself in the saddle, and her feet found the stirrups, that horseback riding was not alien to her.

She smiled triumphantly down at the mustached mule driver, taking pleasure in the startled look that disturbed the impassive face for a moment.

She was certainly no stranger to riding, Patrick decided, watching the girl's hand wrap in a businesslike fashion around the rein, which was unusual in itself in a Mexican woman.

But then, he reminded himself, few Mexican women, largely uneducated no matter their wealth or family background, spoke anything but Spanish and perhaps a few words of French. They didn't speak German. He gazed thoughtfully at the girl. After all, how did he know she was Mexican, just because she spoke Spanish and had been traveling with the Ortiz family?

He remembered she had been with Austrian and Belgian troops when he had first met her. His shoulder still gave him an occasional twinge from that encounter! How did he know that she wasn't one of those foreigners like that Hapsburg upstart and his Belgian wife, who thought they had some sort of God-given right to rule the Mexican people.

Patrick's face darkened. With the lines of his face pulled cruelly flat, the blue eyes taking on an obsidian hardness, all trace of his Irish father disappeared and only his mother's Indian heritage was visible. It had taken the Mexican people three hundred years to throw out their Spanish conquerors, he thought grimly, but they would dispose of the French and Austrians in much less time.

The problem, though, was much more immediate, he realized. It was one thing to bring an injured Mexican girl into his camp; it was another to bring in a young woman who could be an imperialist sympathizer. What if she should regain her memory and discover she was traveling with a band of guerrillas smuggling guns into Mexico? The French were already well aware of the great amount of firearms being delivered secretly from U.S. Army depots along the border to Juárez's Republican Army in Mexico. French patrols were constantly scouring the countryside on the lookout for guerilla bands such as his.

Patrick shrugged. Well, it was too late now for regrets. A reckless glint touched the deep blue Irish eyes. He would have to play the hand as it was dealt him. He swiftly mounted his own horse, taking a last look at the woman. No, not woman, he thought, grinning to himself. On the back of the mustang, she looked like nothing so much as a scruffy boy. It was foolishness to think that even if she should discover the truth that he would have any trouble handling this slip of a girl.

Margarite grasped tightly at the rein when at Patricio's shouted cry of *"Adelante!"* her little mustang sprang forward, following the almost twenty mules and half-dozen mule drivers strung out ahead of him. At first her knees dug into her mount, until she realized that her mustang, no matter how narrow and rocky the trail winding through the hills, was as surefooted as any of the mules.

If the situation had been different, if an excruciating pain didn't stab through her chest each time she breathed, she might even have enjoyed the ride on the back of the well-trained mustang, who seemed to sense what she wanted him to do before she even gave the command. Had she spent a lot of time on horseback, then? She sighed. And if she had, what did it prove? It didn't help her remember who she was or how she had come here.

Impatiently, she tried again to peer beyond the darkness in her mind. Surely she could force herself to remember! And was startled by a vague, formless terror that suddenly swept over her as she mentally tugged at that black curtain in her mind, as if whatever lay behind that curtain was too terrible and frightening to be borne.

She shivered, feeling all at once cold, although the sun was high in the sky now, beating mercilessly down upon her uncovered head. It was easier, somehow safer, not to try to recapture her past but concentrate on the immediate present. She fastened her attention on the mule drivers walking along beside their mules, alternately cursing the animals when they proved obstinate, and lavishing them with praise when they behaved.

The curses, which were both obscene and graphic, made Margarite's ears burn even as she couldn't help being impressed by the picturesque language of the mule drivers, not to mention their expert skill at their jobs. Even when the packs worked loose and tumbled to the ground, which happened fairly frequently no matter how tightly the pack was bound to the mule, the *arriero* would adroitly lift the pack and tie it back onto the mule without stopping or breaking his stride.

As the morning wore on, though, and her body ached
as if not one inch of her wasn't bruised and battered, she
was less able to force her attention on the mule drivers
or withstand the pain and exhaustion that made the
crystal-clear air shimmer hazily before her eyes. Did
they never stop to rest? she wondered wearily, gazing at
the mules plodding ahead of her, following the bell mare.

Margarite had no idea how long they had been riding,
when one of the mule packers on horseback pulled his
mustang into step beside hers and handed her a canteen.
She started to lift it to her lips, then stopped warily,
remembering that morning.

The man beside her shook his head quickly. "*Agua*,
Niña," he assured her.

Her mouth and throat were coated with dust from the
trail. She drank quickly, the water warm but tasting
delicious as it slid down her parched throat. "*Gracias*,"
she said, handing the canteen back to the man.

"*De nada*," he answered gravely, pushing his sombrero back from his forehead. She recognized him then.
He was the *arriero* who had not joined in the laughter at
her expense that morning, she remembered, and he seldom engaged in the loud talking and horseplay of the
other men.

"When are we going to stop?" she asked.

"We cannot halt till we finish the day's run," he
explained. "The mules, if we stop, will lie down. It is
very difficult to make the stubborn beasts move again."

Margarite clenched her teeth against the pain. "How
. . . how much longer?"

The man squinted up at the sun. "The *jornada de
recua* is usually fifteen miles, so we have maybe two,
three hours to go." He studied the girl's white face, the
perspiration glinting on her forehead and above the small,
tightly set mouth. "Perhaps if you speak to Don Patricio,
he will stop early today."

"No!" she said sharply. She would not beg that . . .
that man. To try to take her mind off the pain and
weariness, she glanced around her, studying the countryside. They were coming down out of the hills now.
She could see a dry plain stretching before them and

then another low range of hills in the distance. Even farther away, jagged blue mountains blended into the horizon. "Where are we?" she asked. "Where are we going?"

The kindness she thought she had glimpsed in the man's face was all at once replaced by a blank wall. He shrugged. "*Quien sabe?*" he said, then spurred his horse ahead of hers down the trail.

Gabriel found Patricio riding with the *mulera* at the head of the train. "The girl's ready to drop," he said abruptly.

Patrick studied the horizon ahead of them, frowning. "We're already a day late for our next rendezvous." He glanced at the sergeant, his voice dry. "Why the sudden concern? You were the one who wanted to leave the girl behind in Cuchillo's camp. Don't tell me a pretty face is turning your head."

Gabriel said mildly, "The *señora* is indeed beautiful, and has much courage, I think. If you want to ride on, so be it, but you will have to tie the girl to her horse, or a few more miles and she will fall off."

Patrick's frown deepened into a scowl. Wheeling his horse, he rode to the end of the train, where the girl was bringing up the rear. One glance at her marble-white face glazed with exhaustion, her body swaying in the saddle, while her hand clenched the saddle horn as if for dear life, told him that the sergeant was right.

He shouted to his men, "*Hola!* We'll stop here for the night." Dismounting, he caught the mustang's reins in his hand. "You can step down, Niña."

When she stared down at him blankly, too exhausted to move, he lifted her from the saddle. He set her on her feet, and she swayed against him and would have fallen if he hadn't picked her up and carried her to a sheltered area, half-hidden amid the rocks.

As he left her propped against a rock, she saw that the men were already making camp. Working swiftly and efficiently, they unloaded the mules and placed the packs in rows upon the ground, covering them with a weatherproof sheet of sea grass, and finally digging a ditch around the packs to protect them if it should rain.

Although Margarite was too weary to move even a finger, the men worked as if they were no more tired than the moment they had started out that morning. Her own eyelids grew heavy; she dozed off.

When she awoke, it was dark. Someone had placed a blanket over her and a campfire had been started. The mule drivers were hunkered around the fire, talking and laughing boisterously as they ate. The firelight played across their dark-bearded faces, but somehow they did not appear as fierce or wild to Margarite as they had that morning; she even felt comforted by their presence.

When the same older man who had brought her food that morning came over to her with a stewlike mixture of meat and corn, she smiled her thanks. The dish was still filthy, the meat so highly spiced it burned her tongue, but this evening she did not hesitate, and swallowed the food greedily.

After she had finished eating, Patricio joined her. "Open your shirt, Niña," he said.

As she stiffened, her face freezing, his gaze wandered slowly, mockingly, over her. "You need have no concern," he drawled. "Your . . . charms are quite safe from me. I simply want to make sure that your bandage is still tight."

Embarrassed, she suddenly realized how unattractive she must look, her short, unkempt hair touseled around her no doubt dirt-stained face, the wrinkled and smelly shirt and trousers she wore. What was worse, she was sure the man was taking pleasure in humiliating her. She remembered a name one of the mule drivers had called a particularly recalcitrant mule. "*El hijo de puta!*" she muttered, beneath her breath.

"You said something, Niña?"

An eyebrow rose amused, but she saw a dangerous gleam in the indigo eyes and murmured hastily, "Nothing," as her fingers fumbled to unbutton her shirt.

His hands touching her flesh as he unbound and tightened the bandage were deft and impersonal, so that it shocked her, the unexpected, pleasurable sensation she felt when his one hand accidentally brushed against her breast.

When he had finished, he rose to his feet without speaking and started to turn away from her. "Wait!" she demanded, her fingers fumbling with the buttons on her shirt.

He turned back slowly.

"You haven't told me. Where are you taking me?"

For a moment she thought he wasn't going to answer her, then he said curtly, "The Convent of Santa Clara is several days ride from here. We'll leave you there."

A picture slipped into Margarite's mind, young, grave faces beneath dark folds of habits, bars and shadows and a depressing feeling of being imprisoned.

"Do you remember something, Niña?" Patricio asked, studying the girl's expressive face.

She shook her head, bewildered. "No, not really."

Patricio leaned back against the rocks, gazing thoughtfully down at her. "You're sure you remember nothing about yourself?"

She felt suddenly oddly guilty, as if somehow it were her fault that she couldn't or wouldn't remember. "I told you, I couldn't remember anything," she protested, half furious with him as well as at herself. "Why won't you believe me?"

She could barely make out his face in the flickering firelight that cast dark shadows against the rocks, but the feeling suddenly possessed her that he knew something he wasn't telling her. "You know who I am, don't you?" she demanded, her voice shaking with anger. "Why won't you tell me?"

"I don't know who you are, *Señora*," he answered, and there was no doubting that hard, cold voice.

At the despair he saw clouding the young face, Patrick's voice softened. "Your memory will return in time, Niña. I saw it happen during the war. A soldier who has seen one too many battles, or who has been struck on the head, loses his memory for a few days or weeks. Then, as suddenly as it left, the memory returns. You will see. It will be the same with you." Then, as he turned away, his voice hardened. "Sleep now. We'll leave early in the morning to make up for the time we lost today."

She did not have to be told to sleep. As soon as he left, she curled up in the blanket, her eyes already closing. It was just as she started to drift off that she suddenly remembered what the man had said. War? What war? she wondered, the last thing she remembered thinking before sleep overtook her.

Chapter 9

"THE convent isn't far now, Niña. Soon you will be safe with the good Sisters."

Hosea flashed his bright, eager smile at Margarite, his young face flushed with adoration. Although he claimed to be twenty and worked as hard as any of the other *arrieros*, Margarite was sure that the boy couldn't be more than sixteen.

Hosea's large dark eyes suddenly filled with unhappiness, his voice mournful. "It will be a great sadness, Niña, to have you leave us."

"I'll miss you too," Margarite said, smiling at the boy.

In the five days she had been with the *atajo*, she had quickly grown accustomed to the laughter and teasing and rough-housing of the *arrieros*, discovering an innate kindness and dignity beneath their rough exteriors. On the second day, Ramon, who had laughed the loudest when she choked over the pulque, sheepishly gave her a sombrero to protect "*la niña* from the sun." The man they called *la Madre*, who did the cooking and led the bell mare during the day's trek, had given her his own serape during a sudden rainstorm that had drenched the trail late one afternoon. When Lopez had noticed that the huaraches kept sliding off her feet, he had cleverly shaped from a piece of goatskin a pair of crude slippers that tied to her ankles and were as comfortable but afforded more protection than walking barefoot.

The other *arrieros* had been equally kind. They vied with one another to pay her outrageous compliments and particularly delighted, after the day's journey, to sit around the campfire and tell tall tales to *la niña* about their adventures on the trail and their prowess with the *señoras*. Some of the stories were so obviously exaggerated that Margarite had a hard time keeping a straight face as she pretended to believe every word.

Her ability in handling her mustang, she suspected, had helped gain her the admiration and respect of the mule drivers. The second morning on the trail, when her horse had reared unexpectedly at a snake that glided suddenly from the rocks, and she had managed to keep her seat and control the animal, the mule drivers had crowded around her, laughing and clapping and calling out proudly, "*Olé,* Niña. *Olé!*"

Even Gabriel, the *arriero* who had given her the water the first day, had grown more friendly, often pulling his mustang alongside of hers to talk for a few moments. Only the leader, Patricio, kept his distance, virtually ignoring her. And when he did occasionally bark orders at her, he often called her Niño, deliberately, Margarite was sure, because he knew it annoyed her.

Late in the afternoon of the fifth day, the caravan stopped not far from a small stream, where several Indian women were washing their hair and their clothes along its rocky banks. The *arrieros* were occupied with unpacking the mules, and Margarite, thinking longingly of a chance to bathe, managed to slip away without being noticed. When she reached the stream, though, she discovered, to her dismay, the *atajo* leader was there before her.

His clothes and revolver in a pile at the edge of the stream, the man was standing in the knee-deep water, his back to her as he scrubbed himself with a bar of soap. His black hair clung damp and curling to the nape of his neck. Water glistened on the broad back and shoulders, the muscles smooth and hard beneath the flesh. Soapy water ran in rivulets down over the narrow hips and flat buttocks.

Margarite stared at the man, shocked, and yet beneath the shock she was vaguely aware of another sensation, equally disturbing. She felt rooted to the ground, unable to tear her eyes away from that bronze, sculptured figure glistening in the sunlight. Then suddenly Patricio swung around, grinning broadly. He gestured toward the stream. "Come on in. There's plenty of room."

It was shock then and only shock she felt as she quickly averted her gaze from that embarrassing male appendage, her face growing warm as she stammered, "I—I've changed my mind."

"Don't be silly," he said casually. "Catch!"

Automatically she grabbed for the bar of soap he tossed her, missed, and the soap fell into the dirt at her feet. As she bent down to retrieve the soap, Patricio came splashing out of the stream toward her. Before she could flee, his one arm nonchalantly circled her waist, lifting her off her feet, her head and legs dangling. "You need a bath as much as I do, Niño," he said cheerfully.

The Indian women stopped their washing and gossiping for a moment to watch, giggling, as the man carried the young woman, kicking and squirming, out into the stream and dropped her unceremoniously into the water.

"Don't lose the soap," Patricio warned as Margarite came sputtering to the surface. "It's my last bar."

Without a backward glance he returned to the bank of the stream. Swiftly he toweled himself dry with a piece of blanket, and pulled on his shirt and trousers, returning the revolver to his belt.

As if she really were a boy, Margarite thought, furiously pushing the wet hair from her eyes as the man strode back toward the camp.

"Is something wrong, Niña?" Hosea asked anxiously, studying the señora's face, the green eyes flashing with a brilliance that took his breath away.

Margarite's anger faded as she returned to the present, to Hosea's adoring glance that made it perfectly clear that he, at least, did not consider her another boy!

"Nothing's wrong," she said, giving the young man a reassuring smile.

Later that afternoon her irritation returned when she listened to Patricio verbally rip a crestfallen Hosea up one side and down the other for taking too long to load his mules. Poor Hosea was not the only one to feel the lash of their leader's tongue, she had noticed. He was equally harsh and demanding with the rest of the men.

"Why do they allow him to treat them that way?" she demanded indignantly of Gabriel, who was riding alongside of her.

"Don Patricio is their *patrón*," Gabriel said. "He has much anger and much pride. The anger sharpens his senses and keeps us alive; the pride, I think, will one day destroy him."

At the calm, fatalistic note in the man's voice, Margarite threw him a startled glance. "Don Patricio mentioned a war. Were you in the war too?"

The man didn't answer, but she persisted stubbornly. "Where was this war?"

"There are always wars, Niña," he finally said slowly. "Do you remember nothing about the war we are having here in Mexico?"

She shook her head. "Who is fighting?" she asked, gazing around the beautiful, peaceful countryside, softly green now that the rainy season was finished. They were traveling across a high plateau that Gabriel called the Bajío, passing grand haciendas and lush fields filled with grain.

Gabriel shrugged. "Why do men always fight? For money, power, freedom. The French want money. They sent their soldiers and drained what is left of the treasury of Mexico. The Austrian and his wife who call themselves Emperor and Empress of Mexico want power. But they know nothing of Mexico and less of the Mexican people. And there is Benito Juárez," he said, pride creeping into his voice. "An Indian, elected President of Mexico, who tried to bring freedom to his people."

Suddenly, inexplicably, a picture flashed into Margarite's mind, a handsome golden-bearded man with pure blue eyes. The face was so clear to her that she almost cried aloud, no longer listening to Gabriel. Her whole being concentrated on retaining the man's face, even as it drifted away like smoke through her fingers. Who was he? she wondered in despair. He was too young to be her father. A lover? Perhaps even a husband? The thought that she might be married was somehow unnerving. She wasn't wearing a wedding ring, but then, the thieves who had attacked her and left her to die probably had stolen any jewelry she might have had. She frowned, remembering those moments at the stream with Don Patricio. Would she have been so shocked at the sight of a man's naked body if she were married?

She took a deep, ragged breath, hastily forcing that memory of Don Patricio from her mind, and returning her thoughts to the man riding beside her. What had they been talking about? Oh, yes, the war about which she could remember nothing. Was the golden-haired man somehow involved in the war? She could have cried with frustration but had learned it was useless to try to force herself to remember. It only made her head ache and brought back that unsettling feeling of terror, as if it were better not to remember.

She glanced curiously at Gabriel. "And the *arrieros*? What side of the war are they on?"

"We're mule packers, not soldiers," Patricio said sharply, hearing the last of the conversation as he brought his horse next to Margarite's. He turned a scowling gaze upon Gabriel. "Have you nothing better to do than waste time gossiping?"

Gabriel moved quickly away and Margarite gave Patricio a furious glance. "We weren't gossiping. How will I ever learn anything if no one talks to me?"

"The Sisters at the convent will tell you all you need to know," he replied. "Until we get there, stop bothering the men when they have work to do. Do you understand?"

"Perfectly," the girl said, looking down her short, straight nose at him in that irritatingly haughty manner he found particularly aggravating. "As long as you understand that I won't be ordered about like one of your *arrieros*."

She jerked at the reins of her horse to turn away,

when Patrick's hand shot out and caught her arm. He brought his own mount so close to hers that she could feel the muscular hardness of his thigh against her leg, see the fine white lines that fanned out from the narrowed eyes.

"Don't try my patience, Niño," he said softly.

She flushed and tried to pull away. "Don't call me Niño!"

The chiseled mouth curved into a tight-lipped smile as he stared down at her. "I'll call you what I wish, and while you're traveling with me, you'll do exactly as I say. Is that understood, Niño? Or is it your desire to walk the rest of the way to the convent?"

From the corner of her eye, Margarite saw that the *arrieros* were watching the scene quietly, but despite their fondness for her, she sensed that the mule drivers would not challenge any decision of Don Patricio's.

The man's hand continued to grasp her arm, painfully tightening its grip, as he continued inexorably, "I'm waiting for your answer, Niño."

He watched the defiance drain from the wide green eyes as her gaze lifted to his face, the color ebbing beneath the transparent skin as she struggled to regain her composure. "Yes, I understand," she said slowly, her eyes never leaving his face. "I—I won't cause any trouble."

Abruptly Patrick's hand dropped away from her arm. He gazed broodingly after the girl as she rode away from him, at her stiffly held back that still managed to look regal despite the ridiculous sombrero that bobbed on her head. Damn that stiff-necked arrogance of hers, he thought, as furious at himself as he was at the girl for making him lose his temper. *Gracias Dios* they would soon be at the convent and he would be rid of her, before she turned every one of his mule drivers as soft as mush, unfit to work, much less fight.

When the caravan reached the Santa Clara Convent, though, the convent doors were bolted shut. The walls were pockmarked with bullet holes, and it was obvious that the convent had been hastily abandoned.

"What now, Captain?" Gabriel asked Patrick.

"We've no more time to waste. We'll continue onto our rendezvous."

"And the girl?" Gabriel glanced at *la niña*, sitting on her mustang carefully apart from the *arrieros*.

"We'll take her with us to the mine," Patrick said. "After we drop off our guns, I have to go into Querétaro. The Juarista agent there will give me the location of the rest of our rendezvous sites. The girl will go with me. I'll leave her at the Convent of the Cross. There's a French garrison in Querétaro, so the convent should be untouched."

He spurred his horse away before Gabriel could reply. When he reached Margarite, he gestured toward the closed convent doors. "As you can see, it is not possible, after all, to leave you here. We have a delivery we must make up in the hills. You will come with us."

At the peremptory tone in his voice, Margarite seethed with anger. As if she had no more say in the matter than the cargo packed on the mules, she thought, being dragged willy-nilly wherever this man commanded. Almost, she opened her mouth to protest, but remembering her last confrontation with Patricio . . . she could still feel the bruise his hand had left on her arm . . . she thought better of it and instead merely nodded indifferently.

The truth was, she thought guiltily as she once again urged her mustang along, following in the rear of the column of mules, she was almost relieved that the convent had been closed. There was something about the thought of staying at a convent that somehow depressed her. Not to mention the unhappiness she would feel at leaving the *arrieros*. The mule drivers had given her their friendship and accepted her without question. They were, in a way, the only family she had. At the convent there would be strangers. She would have to endure curious stares and questions that she couldn't answer.

Then, as the caravan left the plateau and moved upward into the hills, she forgot about her own problems and concentrated on the rocky path, not daring to look down into the sharp dropoffs and deep ravines at the edge of the narrow trail. As dusk settled over the hills, the path ahead became harder to follow. Certainly, Don

Patricio must give the order to stop soon, she thought. Even her surefooted mount was picking his way nervously. This trail was dangerous enough in the daylight; in the dark it would be impossible.

She could hear Patricio at the front of the column berating the men, urging them on, when the accident happened. There was a sudden shrill scream of terror, then a crashing sound as two mules tumbled over the edge of the trail, dragging the man who had been walking beside them down with them.

Margarite dismounted, but when she tried to rush forward, Hosea stopped her. "It is best you stay here, Niña," he said quietly.

"Who is it? What's happened?"

"Lopez. I think perhaps he is dead."

Remembering that scream, Margarite shivered. "There must be something we can do. We can't just . . . leave him."

"Don Patricio would not leave a man to die," Hosea said, his young voice shocked. "See, they are lowering him now."

Torches had been lit and Margarite could see that ropes had been removed from the packs, one end quickly tied around Patricio's waist, the other end in the hands of four *arrieros*. Then she could no longer see the man as he descended over the side. She watched the four men brace themselves on the rocky ground. The rope looked so thin. Suppose it should break, too, she thought, hardly daring to breathe as she waited, what seemed like hours, but was only a few minutes before she heard Gabriel shout, "*Ahora!*" Then, "*Arriba, arriba!*"

"He's alive, Niña!" Hosea cried happily. Margarite could hear them, too, the pain-filled stream of curses coming from Lopez as eager arms lifted him away from his rescuer and laid him gently on the ground. Then, to Margarite's surprise, the four men immediately began to lower Patricio over the side again.

"What are they doing?" she protested. "Why is he going down again?"

"The packs, of course, Niña," Hosea said. "Don Patricio would not leave them behind."

"What do you carry that's so valuable?" she asked, surprised.

Hosea's usually open, good-natured face was all at once closed to her, his voice evasive as he answered. "Whatever is needed." He edged away from Margarite. "I must go help with Lopez, Niña. We are over the worst of the trail. Soon we will stop for the night."

Margarite flinched as she heard two revolver shots from the ravine, and knew the mules, undoubtedly injured in the fall, were being put out of their misery. Then she watched as the two packs were hauled back up onto the trail. They were in remarkably good condition except for a corner of one pack, where the binding had been torn. She picked up a piece of yellow paper that had blown free of the pack and landed at her feet. The paper felt smooth, wax-covered beneath her fingers.

Curious now, she stepped nearer to examine the packs more closely. From within the ripped pack, she caught the glint of steel in the torchlight.

"Niña!"

She whirled. Patricio had been hauled up from the ravine and was on the trail behind her, scowling at her. "Get back on your horse," he ordered brusquely. Then he turned to the men. "The rest of you start the mules. Ramon, help me make a litter for Lopez. We've still a half mile to go before we make camp."

A half hour later the weary mules and even more exhausted mule drivers had left the narrow, dangerous trail and come onto a clearing in the hillside. In the moonlight, Margarite could make out decaying, roofless buildings, the remains of water wheels, and some sort of gutted furnace. Luxuriant vegetation covered everything, vines trailing over broken shafts, moss creeping over jagged masses of rock.

"What is this place?" she asked Ramon, who was preparing the evening meal, while Madre helped Don Patricio with Lopez. There was something eerie about the surroundings, or perhaps it was just the pale silvery moonlight giving the whole scene a chilling, unnatural air.

"It's an abandoned silver mine." He jerked his thumb downward. "Down below, Niña, more than one thousand feet below, there still are tunnels. Years ago Indian workers descended a narrow shaft by ladders, a candle in their caps to light the way. Twelve, sixteen hours a day they labored in darkness with their picks at the veins of silver. The Spanish owner became so wealthy that when his son was christened, the whole party walked from his house to the church upon ingots of silver. But the hard labor, the dampness, caused much sickness among the workers. Many died. Others were forced to take their place. Finally water filled the tunnels of the mine and the owners were forced to abandon it.''

Margarite shivered, goose flesh rising on her arms, not sure whether it was from the story Ramon had told her or the sound of Lopez's screams from a nearby roofless hut as Madre held the man down and Don Patricio set the mule driver's broken leg. She drew her serape more closely around her and sat nearer to the campfire.

"Shouldn't someone fetch a doctor?''she asked Ramon.

"For a broken leg?'' the man asked, surprised at her question. "Why, I rode once from Guanajuato to Morelia with a broken leg and a broken arm,'' he bragged. "Of course,'' he conceded thoughtfully, "it was a matter of luck that it was my left arm that was broken so I could still pack my mules.'' As he talked, he stirred the *pozole,* a sort of hominy soup made from the inevitable corn, and Margarite no longer even noticed that the hands that handled the food were grimy with dirt.

When she still looked concerned, he said, "Don't worry, Niña. The *patrón* will take good care of Lopez.''

The pride in his voice when he spoke of Patricio, the same pride she had heard in Hosea's voice, irritated Margarite and she almost blurted out indignantly, "He should! It was his fault Lopez broke his leg. We should have stopped sooner,'' then bit back the words as she saw Patricio come out of the hut and walk toward the campfire.

He jerked his thumb toward Margarite. "Take some food and water and sit with Lopez,'' he ordered. "I've poured enough pulque into him so that he probably won't stir for a while, but he might be hungry or thirsty later."

Margarite stiffened with anger. It wasn't that she minded nursing Lopez; it was the high-handed way the man ordered her about that made her hands ball into fists of helpless rage at her side.

When she did not move immediately, Patricio snapped irritably, lines of weariness etched in his face. "Well, what are you waiting for?"

With as much dignity as she could muster under the circumstances, she took two plates of food and a canteen of water from Ramon and walked away from the campfire.

But she was still fuming inside as she entered the hut and settled down beside the injured man. Someday, somehow, she vowed, she would make Don Patricio sorry for playing the petty tyrant with her. As it turned out, there was very little nursing for her to do. Lopez was deep in a drunken sleep, his right leg in an improvised splint. There were bruises on his face and cuts on the rest of his body, but he was lucky to be alive, Margarite decided.

She ate her own dinner and put the second plate close to the fire to keep the food warm, wishing that she had thought to bring a blanket with her to keep herself warm. Her serape and the fire helped, but the flames heated only one side of her at a time, she discovered as she tucked her legs beneath her, trying to keep the rest of herself warm.

She thought the cold would keep her awake, but the long trek that day had tired her more than she realized, and she found herself dozing off, snapping awake when Lopez muttered in his sleep. She tucked his blanket more tightly around the man and poked the fire to make it burn better, then settled back again.

Drowsily, her eyes half closed, she noticed through the crumbling wall of the hut that the mule drivers had gathered around the cook fire for their evening meal. Oddly, it seemed there were more *arrieros* than she remembered in that circle. But it must have been her imagination, because when she jerked awake the second time, she counted only seven men, still haunched around the fire, passing a bottle of pulque and talking quietly.

Lopez had become restless and she spoke to him soothingly, trying to quiet him, although she wasn't sure he even heard her in his drunken, pain-filled stupor. When she finally fell asleep again, this time nothing awakened her, not even Patrick, who came to see how his patient was doing.

After making sure that Lopez was resting as comfortably as possible, he put some additional wood on the fire and turned his attention to the girl. She was lying curled up in a ball near the fire, the serape wrapped like a cocoon around her.

He leaned over her and touched her shoulder lightly, "Niña, wake up. Where's your blanket?"

She murmured protestingly in her sleep but didn't stir. He brought his own blanket over to the fire, then picked the girl up in his arms. Deep in an exhausted sleep, she didn't stir. Asleep, her face looked childishly vulnerable, with a smudge of dirt across one cheek, the short, touseled hair needing brushing, the sweetly curved lips drooping at the corners. The small body felt almost weightless in his arms.

Disconcertingly, as he held her he felt an unexpected tightness in his loins, his senses remembering the cornsilk softness of that hair in his hands, the shape and scent of that small body fitting snugly against his when he had slept with her in his arms that first night in the cave. He even found himself imagining his mouth covering those sweetly curved lips that could curl with such arrogant disdain, until all haughtiness was swept away and their softness parted, inviting entry into the even more intoxicating softness within. The sweet cries of rapture that he would coax from those lips as that small body grew warm and yielding beneath his seeking, coaxing hands.

Cursing beneath his breath, Patrick abruptly lowered the girl onto the blanket he had placed beside the fire. He had been too long without a woman, he decided. Why else should he have these ridiculous schoolboyish yearnings for a no doubt inexperienced girl with boyish hips and breasts small enough to fit into a man's hand.

Patrick liked his women well fleshed, with pillowy breasts and wide curving hips, mature women who knew exactly what a man needed and wasted no time fulfilling that need.

He smiled suddenly. They should reach the Adalid hacienda by tomorrow. He hadn't planned to stop there, but Lopez's injury gave him no choice. Doña Soledad, he was sure, would not only be willing to shelter Lopez until his recovery but, from past experience, would also be more than willing to provide Patrick with her own special skills and warmth in her bed.

Patrick rose to his feet, an amused glint in the narrowed gaze as he studied the sleeping girl, remembering the blazing defiance in her eyes earlier, when he had ordered her to bring food to Lopez, the way she had boldly stood up to him when he had forbidden her to talk to the men. He grinned to himself. The good Sisters at the Convent of the Cross would have their hands full with this little one, he decided wryly.

Then he wrapped himself in a blanket and hunched down by the fire to watch Lopez for the rest of the night.

Chapter 10

ARLY the next morning the caravan moved quickly down through the hills and turned southwest across the high plateau. When Margarite asked Gabriel where they were going, he shrugged, murmuring, "*Quien sabe?*"

"You must know where we're going!" she snapped irritably. It was ridiculous how secretive the *arrieros* were. It must be their Indian blood, she decided, the way they would suddenly stare at her, their faces going oddly blank whenever she attempted to question them. Even Lopez, who must be suffering dreadfully, jolting along on a litter behind his horse, accepted his lot stolidly, without making a sound.

But then, how did she know that she didn't have Indian blood too? she thought suddenly. Once Julio, who was the vainest of all the mule drivers, had lent her his broken bit of mirror and she had stared curious and a little apprehensive, into the mirror. The stranger who stared back at her had short cropped black hair, pale skin with a faint apricot color beneath from the sun, and eyes a fresh sparkling green like leaves after a rain. Did Indians have green eyes? she wondered. Or Mexicans, for that matter? Yet, if she weren't Indian or Spanish, then what was she?

Lately, other faces than the golden-haired blue-eyed man had been flashing into her mind; a young, plump-cheeked, dark-haired girl; an older, distinguished man with a full brown mustache, long sideburns, and a gentle smile that warmed her heart. But the other memory was always there, too, she sensed, just behind the dark curtain in her mind. Whenever she tried to pursue it, a cold panic gripped her, as if whatever the memory was, it was too frightening to be dragged out and faced.

What sort of person was she, then? Where had she come from and what kind of life had she led before her injuries, that she should have such a dark, terrifying secret in her past?

Wrapped up in her own unhappy thoughts, she hadn't realized that the column of mules and drivers had stopped. A small hacienda sat back from the road, almost hidden by the trees and fields surrounding its square, walled courtyard. She glimpsed through an open gateway, pink and white roses tumbling over stone walls. As she watched, the door to the house swung open and a woman stepped outside. She was dressed all in black, and although her figure was just this side of pleasingly plump, she moved gracefully on tiny feet toward Patricio, who dismounted and embraced her swiftly.

When the woman finally stepped back, a smile illuminated her softly rounded face and large, meltingly dark

eyes. "Don Patricio! How good it is to see you again.
It's been much too long." She gestured around her,
somehow managing to include all the *arrieros* as well as
Margarite in her greeting. "My house, though poor, and
all that is in it, is yours."

"We would not intrude upon you, Doña Soledad,"
Patricio said, "but we have an injured man who needs
attention."

There was a tenderness in Don Patricio's voice when
he spoke to the woman that Margarite had not heard
before. She gave the man a startled glance, before her
gaze moved speculatively toward their hostess. The
woman was no longer young, but she was not all that
old, she realized, and couldn't help noticing that Doña
Soledad's hand lingered possessively on Don Patricio's
arm.

Before further introductions could be made, the drivers were taking the mules around to the back of the
hacienda while Patricio and Gabriel were helping Lopez
into the house. Margarite trailed along behind, feeling
out of place and very conscious of her stained and worn
trousers and shirt next to Doña Soledad's immaculate
gown, her carefully coiffed hair.

If her hostess was curious about a girl's wearing a
man's clothes, she was too polite to display her surprise, only giving Margarite a brief sharp inspection
before summoning servants to assist her with the injured
man. A young woman servant led Margarite to a small
bedroom off an inner red-tiled patio.

Unlike her mistress, the servant did not try to hide her
curiosity, shooting off questions rapidly while she helped
Margarite undress. Where had the young *señora* come
from? Why was she wearing the clothes of a man? How
long had she, a woman alone, been traveling with the
mule drivers? Was the *señora* Don Patricio's sweetheart? To the last, Margarite gave an indignant no, but
managed to avoid answering the rest of the questions,
while the servant brought in buckets of hot water which
she poured into an old and chipped hip bath.

Margarite basked in the warm soapy water as the
servant briskly washed her hair, still asking questions.

What had happened to the *señora*'s hair? How had it
come to be short like a man's? She was still peppering
the girl with questions as Margarite luxuriously toweled
her hair and herself dry, then wrapped the towel more
tightly around her, when her hostess knocked then entered the room.

With a few curt words Doña Soledad sent the servant
hurrying away before turning to Margarite with a stiffly
apologetic smile. "You must excuse Carla. We have few
strangers here."

As she spoke, the dark eyes, without appearing to,
were closely examining the boyishly slim figure beneath
the towel. "I'll see if I can't find you some fresh clothing." With a sidelong approving glance into the mirror at
her own pleasingly curved figure, she murmured, "None
of my gowns will fit you, I'm afraid, but the cook's
young daughter is almost your size. We will be dining
early, around eight, if you should care to join us."

Margarite looked longingly at the bed, and her hostess
added quickly, "You must rest first, of course, *Señora*. . . ." Her voice trailed off, a faint embarrassed
pink touching her face as she turned quickly to the door.
"I'll send Carla with the clothes."

So Doña Soledad had been told of her guest's inability
to remember even her name, Margarite thought ruefully
as she slipped into bed beneath the colorful woven coverlet and promptly fell asleep.

She awoke to the sound of Carla bustling cheerfully
around the room, lighting candles and singing softly to
herself.

"Is it morning already?" she asked drowsily.

"Oh, no. I've brought you a gown so you can join the
family for dinner if you wish."

Margarite stretched languidly, sure that she could easily sleep for another twenty-four hours, but she was also
aware of a certain hollowness in her stomach. "I'll probably fall asleep at the table," she said, yawning, as Carla
helped her slip into the white embroidered chemiselike
blouse, several brightly colored petticoats, and a red and
green embroidered skirt. The maid finished the ensem-

ble by placing a rebozo over the girl's shoulders and
tying it, crossed, over the girl's breasts.

After she tied a pair of white satin slippers on Margarite's feet, Carla stepped back, sighing as she studied the
girl's bosom. "How very tiny you are," she said regretfully. She reached impulsively for a white cotton handkerchief, her face brightening. "Perhaps slipped within
the blouse, *Señora*," she said eagerly, "a little padding.
Don Patricio would never know."

Margarite quickly shook her head. "No, thank you,
Carla. The dress is fine the way it is." Not that a
handkerchief would deceive Don Patricio, she thought
wryly. He was only too well acquainted with how she
looked without a stitch of clothing. She studied her
reflection in the mirror. The gown was certainly more
becoming than the dirty pants and shirt, she decided,
although there did seem to be more leg revealed beneath the full, shortened skirt than she suspected was
respectable.

For a moment, staring at her reflection in the mirror,
she found herself grasping at a nebulous picture in her
mind, a fashionably dressed young woman carrying a
lilac lace parasol. There was a man with the woman. In
another moment she would see his face too. . . .

"You look *muy bonita*," Carla assured her loyally.
"Don Patricio will think himself very fortunate when he
sees you." She rolled her dark eyes soulfully upward.
"*Ai-ye*," she sighed. "How blessed you are to have a
strong handsome *caballero* like Don Patricio in your
bed." She giggled reminiscently. "The last time he visited our hacienda, the maid said Doña Soledad's bed
was not quiet all night."

By the time Margarite had absorbed this fascinating
bit of information about Don Patricio and her hostess,
the picture of the woman in lilac had exasperatingly
slipped away and Carla was taking her to the patio. A
tiny fountain set in a corner of the patio trickled musi-
cally against jadelike stones. A scarlet bougainvillea vine
climbed up one adobe wall. Several people were already
seated at a round candlelit table in the patio, which
evidently also served in fine weather as a dining room:

Don Patricio and Doña Soledad and two small girls who looked like miniature versions of their mother.

The girls were all in white, and although Doña Soledad was still dressed in black, it was a beautifully cut gown made of some shimmering material that clung revealingly to the luxuriantly curved breasts. A diamond necklace was clasped around the plump, unlined neck, a diamond pendant glittering in the candlelight against velvet white skin.

"My daughters, Pilar and Clara," their mother said. "This is a special treat, being allowed to dine with us tonight, and they have promised to be very good."

Don Patricio had risen at Margarite's entrance. The rough beard had disappeared, displaying a surprisingly square cut chin but the mustache, trimmed neatly now, still curved above the long, sensuous mouth. In place of the well-worn trail clothes, the *atajo* leader wore a handsome fitted black jacket and trousers of fine deerskin accented with a row of silver buttons. The trousers fit tightly around the muscular thighs and flared slightly at the ankle.

A frilled shirt made a striking contrast against the man's dark bronze skin, as did the flashing white smile that suddenly split Don Patricio's face. Annoyed because she had been caught gaping foolishly at the man, Margarite quickly lowered her eyelids and took her seat at the table.

Fortunately, with the two young girls chatting happily, there was little need for her to make conversation. After the monotonous corn and tortillas served on the trail, she had no difficulty concentrating on the delicious dinner of chicken and rice lightly seasoned, eggs poached in a tomato sauce laced with chiles and peppers, freshly baked bread, and a dozen different candied fruits for dessert along with little chocolate cakes. A sweet white wine was served with the meal and coffee thick with cream afterward. It was only when Margarite was sure she couldn't eat another morsel more that she began to pay attention to the conversation going on around her.

It was clear that Don Patricio was well acquainted with the family of his hostess and that it was not only

Doña Soledad who enjoyed his company. The two young girls flirted with him outrageously and he pretended to be smitten with each in turn, paying them extravagant compliments, making sure not to pay more attention to one girl than to the other. Margarite couldn't help noticing that for a supposedly uneducated mule driver, Don Patricio had excellent table manners and seemed as at ease with glistening crystal goblets and silver cutlery as he was with the crude dining arrangements on the trail.

He also seemed perfectly at ease with their hostess. When Don Patricio wasn't concentrating his charm on the young girls, it was Doña Soledad who received the compliments and warm smiles, the narrowed eyes lingering appreciatively on the thrusting breasts threatening to spill out of the shining black bodice. It was equally obvious that her hostess was not immune to the man's attentions, fluttering and blushing like a young girl at his compliments, and almost devouring the man with her large, rather bulbous dark eyes.

At the end of the meal, when their mother indicated it was time for the girls to be excused, they teased to be allowed to stay longer, but finally got to their feet obediently, dropping a shy farewell curtsy in Margarite's direction. Had they been warned of her odd illness? She then hastily covered her own mouth as she found herself unexpectedly yawning.

"Perhaps you would like to be excused also, Niña?" Don Patricio asked. It was more of a command than a question though, Margarite realized, bristling. No doubt he wanted to be rid of her, sending her off to bed like a child, so that he could be alone with Doña Soledad, who was undoubtedly his amorous target for the evening. Remembering the man's boorish behavior toward her on the trail, a spark of mischief leaped into Margarite's eyes. It would serve him right if she put a spike into his plans for a love tryst with his hostess.

She murmured demurely, "I'm not at all tired." Then, pouting prettily, and fluttering her lashes at the man across the table from her, she asked softly, "Would you send me off to bed alone, *amor mio*?"

She saw the quickly hidden look of shock on Doña

Soledad's face, but it was on Don Patricio's face that her gaze fastened, pleased at the annoyance that she saw flare up in those dark blue eyes. Before he could speak, she pushed her empty wineglass toward him. "May I have some more wine?" she asked sweetly.

When Patrick leaned forward to fill her glass from the crystal decanter, she allowed her hand to touch his caressingly. "Thank you, my sweet," she said softly, but not so softly that she was sure their hostess hadn't overheard the whispered endearment.

After a few sips of the wine, Margarite turned her wide, innocent gaze to her hostess. "You cannot imagine, Doña Soledad, how romantic it is to make love under the stars." Remembering Carla's words, she expertly mimicked the servant's soulful look, her voice rapturous as she smiled blissfully at Don Patricio. "How blessed I am to have a strong, handsome man like Don Patricio in my bed."

Patricio put down his own wineglass abruptly, his annoyance at the girl's obvious attempt to drive a wedge between Doña Soledad and himself giving way to a surprised, reluctant amusement. He studied the girl appraisingly. She was certainly playing the role well. Was it possible, he wondered, that the girl wasn't the virginal innocent he had thought her? He could swear the intimate smile she was giving him, her eyes sparkling like emeralds behind the thick cluster of lashes, was the smile of a practiced coquette.

He watched her drink the rest of her wine much too quickly, then hold out her goblet for a refill. Patrick lifted a questioning eyebrow. "You've already had several glasses, Niña."

"But it's so delicious," she protested. The wine was so much more pleasant-tasting than pulque, making her feel delightfully light-headed and relaxed, as if all at once it didn't matter that she had no memory or that she was deliberately flirting with Patricio to put Doña Soledad's nose out of joint. She could see a dark red stain of anger rising beneath the woman's white skin. Patricio wouldn't easily charm his way into his hostess's bed that evening, she thought smugly, delighted at the success of her maneuver.

Doña Soledad pushed back her chair. "If you'll excuse me," she said stiffly, "it's late and I must see that the girls are safely in bed."

After she had left the room, Patricio leaned comfortably back in his chair, but with a look in his eyes that made Margarite clutch nervously at the stem of her wineglass. Had she gone too far? Instead of ripping into her, though, for the lies she had told, Patricio's gaze rested on her face in a much too intimate manner. "Have I mentioned, Niña, how charming you look in that gown?" he asked, smiling.

She did look remarkably attractive, he thought, remembering the surprised pleasure he had felt when she had first walked out onto the patio. The dirty, scruffy boy had disappeared, and in his place was a young woman with an intriguing, gaminelike beauty. Short dark hair curled in petals around a lovely oval face, while the full short skirt emphasized a tiny waist and the delightful curves of legs and well-turned ankles.

The warmth of that smile upon her face made Margarite even more nervous, and she hastily took another sip of the wine, then studying Don Patricio over the edge of her wineglass and at a loss as to what to say, she murmured awkwardly, "Doña Soledad's husband is dead?"

"Killed in Puebla in 'sixty-two," Patrick replied, his face suddenly grim as he glanced down at his clothes. "These are his clothes Doña Soledad graciously lent me."

All at once Margarite no longer felt pleasantly light-headed but dismayingly giddy. She got quickly to her feet, holding on to the chair as the room whirled around her. "I—I . . . think . . . if you'll excuse me . . . I'll retire too," she stammered.

So quickly that she wasn't aware he had moved, Patricio was beside her, his arm slipping around her waist. "You must allow me to escort you to your room, Niña."

She tried to pull away. "That won't be necessary,"

she said hurriedly, but the arm only fastened tighter around her. Despite her reluctance, she found herself gratefully leaning on that strong arm for support against the dizziness that threatened to engulf her as they crossed the patio and walked down the candlelit corridor to her room. At the door of her room, when it was clear that her escort showed no inclination to leave, she managed to pull herself free, forcing her voice to a haughty dismissal. "Thank you, Don Patricio, but I have no further need of your services."

Before she could stop him, he was inside her room, closing the door behind him and leaning against it. His eyes were icily bright with amusement as he drawled, "Since you have chased one woman from my bed, *querida,* shall we say that I have need of . . . yours."

Watching him walk slowly toward her, she backed up hastily, coming up hard against the bed. If she were to scream, she thought desperately, would anyone hear her? The servants were undoubtedly asleep and the family's quarters, she knew, were on the far side of the patio from hers.

At the last moment she turned her head away, but a strong hand caught her chin and she was staring into Patricio's face, so close she could see the thin circle of gold around the indigo eyes, a tiny scar at the edge of a dark, finely arched brow. Then his face was blotted out as his mouth descended upon hers and took possession. With his hand still holding her chin in an iron grip, it was impossible for her to move. At first the warm mouth moved lazily over hers, brushing gently her tightly closed lips, teasing the corners of her mouth with a tongue that gently coerced but did not insist.

Beneath that gently teasing pressure that was sending delicious sensations of pleasure through her body, the light-headed sensation she had felt earlier returned. When the seeking tongue finally, triumphantly, found entry, she felt surprised, her own tongue touching his, at first timidly, then more boldly, seeming to know exactly what to do without any instructions from her bemused mind.

Even when his mouth left her lips and traced a path downward over her throat, she did not protest. Her eyes closed dreamily, she leaned back in his arms, the dizzying sensation growing stronger so that she clung to the man as if she would simply float away if he released her from the iron grip of his arms around her. She felt hands at the rebozo, loosening it deftly, so that it fell away from her breasts, those same warm hands slipping beneath the loose chemise to caress the soft flesh. And once again she felt an unexpected stab of pleasure as she had before, when that same hand, tightening her bandage, had brushed her breast. But this time the hand did not immediately move away, but found a soft nipple, and the pleasure intensified, almost too intense to be borne.

Then she heard Patricio murmur something, but there was a whirring sound in her ears and she could not determine what he was saying. Arms were lifting her, carrying her to the bed. She felt as if she were sinking into the downy softness of black feathers.

Patrick had turned quickly away from the bed and begun undressing. To be truthful, he hadn't expected to go this far. He had only meant to throw a scare into the girl for thwarting his plans with Doña Soledad. But the girl's eager response, her body growing soft and pliable in his arms, had changed those plans. And after all, he thought, throwing his shirt onto a chair, why not? The girl was obviously willing. What did it matter which woman shared his bed tonight?

Tossing aside his vest, he was loosening his trousers when he took a quick look back to the bed. It was like being dashed in the face with very, very cold water.

He stepped closer to the bed, but there was no doubting what he saw. Sprawled on the coverlet, her face blissfully, peacefully, asleep, *la niña* had passed out.

Chapter 11

CARLA awoke Margarite early the next morning. "You must make yourself ready, *Señora*," she announced, placing a tray of hot coffee, cheese, and rolls on a table beside the bed.

Margarite lay very still, not at all sure that she was able to move. There was a hammer pounding in her head, and the sunlight pouring into the room made her eyelids ache. When she forced herself to sit up, the coverlet fell away from her, and she discovered that she was wearing only her shift. Strange, she didn't remember removing her clothes last night. Had Carla undressed her?

As memory of the night before painfully pushed its way through the pounding in her head, a groan broke from her lips. It was embarrassing enough, the shocking way she had behaved at the dinner table, and then, later, here in this room . . . a warmth spread through her body, remembering. She could still feel the pressure of Don Patricio's mouth on her lips and breast, his hands pushing aside her rebozo and chemise, then arms lifting her, carrying her to the bed. And afterward? Margarite's heated body suddenly turned ice cold. *What had happened afterward?*

Carla came to the bed and handed her a glass of reddish liquid. "Doña Soledad is in a black mood this morning too," she giggled.

Ignoring the maid's knowing smile, Margarite stared at the glass being offered her and asked, "What is that?"

"Don Patricio said you were to drink this."

Cautiously, Margarite swallowed some of the liquid. It

120

tasted of tomatoes and hot spices and something else she could not identify. At first swallow she was sure she was going to be ill, but after a few more swallows, her stomach settled down. Although her head still pounded, she was able to swing her legs over the side of the bed. "Will the *arrieros* be leaving too?"

Carla shook her head. "I think not, just you and Don Patricio. You are to wear the clothes Doña Soledad gave you yesterday."

"How can I ride a horse in a skirt?" Margarite protested.

Carla shrugged. "That I do not know, only that Don Patricio ordered you should be ready to leave in half an hour."

So Doña Soledad's charming dinner companion of the night before had not changed after all, Margarite thought, annoyed. He was still giving orders. Well, she was in no great hurry to face the man again, not after what had happened in this room last night. If only, she thought desperately, she could remember exactly what *had* happened! Deliberately she took her time eating, washing, and dressing so that it was an hour before she strolled out into the front courtyard, where Don Patricio was waiting impatiently by his horse.

The only other person in the courtyard was Gabriel, and despite the mule driver's placid expression, Margarite sensed that the man was not pleased about something. She could not hear what the men were saying as Gabriel glanced toward her, then turned to Patricio and asked quietly, "Is this wise, Captain? Querétaro is a French stronghold. You could be walking into a trap."

Patrick shrugged impatiently. "What else can I do? We need the rendezvous points to make our deliveries."

"Then leave the girl behind with Doña Soledad. She can look after her."

Patrick shook his head. "We've put the *señora* into enough danger, leaving Lopez with her. And I can use the girl. The French will never suspect a *hacendado* visiting Querétaro for a few days shopping with his wife. After I've gotten the information we need from Jim Stout, I'll drop the girl off at the convent. And good riddance," he added, scowling as he glanced toward Margarite.

Gabriel had heard the amused whispers and gossip in the kitchen that morning among the servants about what had happened at the dinner table the evening before, Doña Soledad stalking off to bed alone, and Don Patricio's leaving Niña's bedroom later, his face like a black storm cloud. Gabriel cast an oblique glance at his companion's face, wondering if the captain didn't have something more in mind for the girl than just leaving her at the convent. But he also knew the captain too well to ask any further questions. The Indian shrugged philosophically. He was fond of Niña but, after all, it was none of his concern.

Margarite was deliberately dawdling, breathing in the cinnamon scent of the pinks that filled a flower bed along the wall.

Patrick called out sharply. "*Vamos*, Niña! *Vamos!*"

With a deliberate slowness, Margarite crossed the courtyard, keeping her eyes not on the man but on the horse.

"Where is my mount?" she asked.

"You'll be riding with me."

The girl's gaze swung back to the man, but before she could open her mouth to protest, Patrick growled a warning, "I'm in no mood for an argument, Niña."

She drew herself up haughtily. "Am I permitted to ask where you're taking me?"

"The Convent of the Cross in Querétaro."

"Oh," she said, surprised at the hurtful rejection she felt at the indifference in his voice. Then, afraid that her reaction might show in her face, she turned away, speaking quickly, "I want to say good-bye to the *arrieros* before I go."

Patricio caught her arm, swinging her back to face him. "That won't be necessary," he said curtly. "And there's no time."

"But Doña Soledad," she protested. "I must thank her for her hospitality." And apologize for her childish behavior at the dinner table last night, she thought, embarrassed, remembering how she had allowed the woman to believe that she had shared Don Patricio's blanket on the trail. She saw a flicker of amusement in the dark eyes watching her and knew Don Patricio was remembering last night, too, and enjoying her discomfiture.

Involuntarily her hands flew up to pull the rebozo tighter around her, as if her flesh could still feel the touch of those lips at her throat and breast. She remembered the stories the mule drivers had told around the campfire of their prowess with women, becoming more ribald after they thought she was asleep. Their tales had made it graphically and unmistakably clear what happened between a man and a woman in bed. Margarite's face burned. Surely she would remember if anything as shocking as the act the *arrieros* had described had happened to her last night! Or would she? Her memory lately had hardly been reliable. How did she know what had happened after Don Patricio carried her to bed?

She studied her companion's face, trying to read what he was thinking, but it was impossible, as if the face were carved from granite, only the eyes were no longer amused, but hard and cold. Her hands clutched at her rebozo, her voice stammering unhappily, "I . . . I'm afraid I behaved very badly last night. I don't suppose I'm used to wine."

Was it possible she didn't remember what had, or, rather, hadn't happened between them last night, Patrick wondered, studying the girl's embarrassed face. What a changeable little creature she was, either that or a consummate actress, last night all coquettish wiles and soft, yielding body, this morning flushed and stammering like a schoolgirl.

His gaze drifted slowly, deliberately, from the petaled hair to the enticing expanse of leg and ankle beneath the short, flirtatious skirt. "There's no need for apology, *querida*," he murmured softly, lifting her hand to his lips. "You were charming last night, everything a man could desire." And watched, amused, as the green eyes widened with alarm before he lifted her onto the saddle, mounting immediately behind her. Reaching around her, he picked up the reins.

As the horse started forward, Margarite winced, each jolt of the hooves against the rutted, rocky road making her head throb. "How far is it to Querétaro?" she asked, grasping at the saddle horn to keep from having to lean back against the man behind her.

"Not long, two or three hours," he said cheerfully. "Of course, the road isn't this good all the way."

Three hours with her head pounding as if it were being split in two! And with Don Patricio sitting so close to her, she could feel the buttons of his jacket press into her back, no matter how she tried to sit stiffly erect, away from him. "How very kind of you to go out of your way to take me into Querétaro," she said, gritting her teeth against the pain.

"It's not out of my way," he assured her. "I had business in Querétaro anyway." The horse stumbled and caught itself. The man's arm slipped around her waist to keep her from falling, his voice, warm and caressing. "You must not be unhappy, *poquita*," he whispered against her ear. "I promise you we will have one last night together before we must part."

Margarite might have heard the barely concealed laughter beneath the words if she had not been livid with anger. The conceit of the man! As if she were longing for his caresses, and didn't cringe at the thought of ever having allowed him to touch her in that way.

She jerked free of his encircling arm, her voice frigid. "I can assure you, Don Patricio, that what"—her voice choked on the words—"what happened last night will never happen again."

His laugh was softly triumphant. 'Oh, but it will, *querida,* never fear. And you need no longer play the teasing coquette with me now that I know how much you desire me."

Margarite bit back the angry retort that sprang to her lips. It was obvious he wouldn't believe whatever protestations she made. Her best defense was to ignore him. She held herself as far away from the man as possible within the confines of the saddle, and didn't speak another word, concentrating on the scenery which was monotonous enough, stretches of planted fields, an occasional hacienda, an Indian plodding by followed by an Indian woman carrying a pack. The combination of warm sunshine and her early arising made her drowsy, despite the jolting ride. Her head drooped, finally resting against the broad shoulder of the man behind her as she slept.

When she awoke, the dream still remained with her, so real that for a moment she stared around her, bewildered. The golden-haired man with the smiling blue eyes who had shared her dream was still clear in her mind's eye, so vivid that his name was almost there, on the tip of her tongue . . . in one moment she would remember. . . .

"Are you feeling better, Niña?"

Patricio's voice shattered both the dream and the name into nothingness. She could have wept with vexation. Then, all at once she became aware that her companion's arm rested in a much too familiar fashion around her waist, and that her body was nestling comfortably against the man, her head against his shoulder.

She jerked erect, fumbling at her rebozo which had fallen away from her shoulders, and glanced, flustered, around her. They had left the plateau and were descending through low hills into a valley. "Is it much farther to Querétaro?"

"We're almost there." Patricio gestured with his whip below them to a cluster of red-tiled roofs, church towers, and domes, completely surrounded by a wall of hills.

He was still acutely conscious of how the girl had felt in his arms as she slept, could still feel the weight of her head against his shoulder, the soft swell of her abdomen beneath his hand as he held her close. With her rebozo fallen open, and her chemise slipping from one shoulder, he had caught a tempting glimpse of one small, perfectly formed breast, and the desire to discover if he could, indeed, cradle its gleaming softness in one hand had been almost unsurmountable. He had almost forgotten his frustration over the fiasco of the night before, sending him to bed alone and in a foul humor.

She had smiled sweetly in her sleep, he remembered,

and murmured a name that he could not catch. A previous lover? he wondered, feeling a surprising twinge of jealousy. Then he frowned, annoyed at his own naiveté. After all, the girl meant nothing to him except for the pleasure she owed him, to make up for the disastrous evening. Naturally, she would have had other lovers. Her behavior at the table and in her bedroom had made it clear that she was no innocent as far as men were concerned, despite her girlish blushes this morning. Well, all the better as far as he was concerned, Patrick thought. He had never considered innocence in a woman a great prize.

He smiled, thinking of the evening ahead. Of course, there was the business with Stout to finish up first, but there would still be time before he left the girl at the convent in the morning and rejoined the *atajo*.

Looking over her shoulder, Margarite watched the smile wipe the brooding anger from the indigo eyes, softening and warming the harsh angles of the man's face, and felt vaguely uneasy. She wasn't sure but what she preferred the hostile, arrogant mule driver to this much too handsome, charming stranger who was pointing out the sights of Querétaro to her as they rode through the town.

"The Mexican war for independence against Spain began here in Querétaro in 1810," he explained. "A priest, Father Hidalgo, led that war, but it was a woman of Querétaro, called La Corregidora, who saved the revolution in the very beginning. When she learned that the plot to overthrow the Spanish government had been discovered, she risked her own life to warn the conspirators." He slanted a quizzical look down at Margarite. "You remember nothing of this, Niña, nothing of Mexican history?"

She shook her head, and he saw that her gaze fastened on soldiers passing them, some on horseback, some on foot. The uniforms varied in color and style, but whether French, Mexican, Austrian, or Belgian, the boots were brightly polished, the tunics crisply tailored. Patrick thought wryly of the ragtag uniforms, if they had any at all, of the Republican troops, the Juarista guerrillas.

Then he noticed the girl was staring at an Austrian Hussar in a scarlet tunic, making his way through the crowded thoroughfare, a tall, well-built young man with blond hair and a large flowing mustache.

Patrick frowned, his voice sharpening, as he asked, "Do you know the officer, Niña?"

She gave a little start, then shook her head again. Yet, for a moment, the man had seemed familiar, or was it only the bright scarlet uniform that had struck a chord of memory? Lately, it was as if gaping holes were being torn in that black curtain in her mind, allowing more and more flashes of memory to dart through.

"You're very sure?" Patrick remembered that it was in the company of Austrian and Belgian officers that he had first seen the girl.

Margarite heard the suspicion in Patricio's voice. "I thought . . . for a moment . . ." She gave her companion a puzzled glance. "Why are there so many soldiers in the town?"

"Querétaro is an imperialist garrison," he replied shortly. They were riding by a large plaza, passing colorfully decorated stalls, where Indians were selling fresh fruit, vegetables, pulque, and sweet cakes. Handsomely dressed couples strolled through the plaza, while others sat on benches, enjoying the sunshine and the passing scene. Patricio finally turned the horse off onto a wooded side street, stopping in front of a large building, its façade more ornate than the tile-roofed stores on either side.

From within the building Margarite could hear the sound of laughter and music. "Is this the convent?" she asked, startled.

"The convent's on the eastern edge of town." He lifted her down from the horse, then joined her, throwing the reins to a stable boy, waiting before the hotel. "This is the Español Hotel. I'll be only a moment."

Margarite followed him into the *sala* of the hotel, glancing curiously around her at the casinolike atmosphere. There were men crowded around tables gambling or playing billiards. Three musicians played their instruments in a rather bored fashion in one corner of the room. Several men cast admiring glances in her direction as she stood alone, and she was once again uncomfortably aware that her gown did not modestly cover her ankles. Still, her gown was modest enough compared to the shockingly low-cut chemises of the few Mexican women who inhabited the gambling casino. When they leaned familiarly over the men at the gaming tables, it was very obvious they wore nothing at all beneath their chemises.

Margarite looked quickly away and into the eyes of a French legionnaire who stood before her, kepi tucked under his arm, his heavy, muscular body filling the dark blue cutaway and red trousers. A pistol was stuck into a pale blue cotton sash, its butt as polished and gleaming as the eyes staring happily down at Margarite.

"Are you alone, Ma'm'selle? May I be of assistance?"

"My wife is not alone, Captain," Patricio said smoothly, returning to Margarite's side, resting his arm in a lightly possessive manner around her waist. "But thank you for your concern."

The edge of disdain in Patricio's voice brought an angry flush to the captain's face, but he nodded stiffly and moved away.

Outside the hotel Margarite pulled herself free of the arm still resting around her waist. "Wife?" she demanded indignantly.

Patrick shrugged. "It seemed simpler, to avoid trouble. Not even a French officer would interfere between a man and his wife, not in public anyway." Margarite was once again aware of that quick flash of suspicion in the narrowed eyes watching her. "Or perhaps you prefer the company of the Frenchman, Niña?" he asked softly.

"Of course not," Margarite replied, wishing irritably that the mule driver would not be so changeable, like spring weather, one minute warm and sunny, the next, stormy. Then she realized they were strolling west, not east, and asked, "This isn't the way to the convent, is it?"

The disarming smile returned to her escort's face. "I thought perhaps we'd have a bite to eat first. I can assure you that the food at the inn where we're going is much better than the plain fare the good Sisters serve at the convent."

Margarite's stomach reminded her it had been a long time since breakfast, not that she'd eaten much breakfast anyway, she remembered. It couldn't matter, she decided hungrily, postponing for an hour or so presenting herself at the convent.

The food was delicious at the small posada. She and Don Patricio sat at a table in a corner of the courtyard, away from the other diners. There were flowers on the table and the linen was spotless. Margarite had second helpings of everything, from the soup to the sugared sweet cakes and fresh melon. Only the dark red Spanish wine she refused.

She was reaching for a third sweet cake when she saw that her companion had stopped eating and was leaning back in his chair, an amused look on his face as he watched her eat.

Embarrassed, she started to put the cake back on the plate. Patricio grinned broadly. "Don't stop on my account, Niña. I like a woman with a hearty appetite."

All at once words flashed into Margarite's head, a woman's voice scolding her. *A young lady should eat like a bird, Margarite!*

"Margarite!" Her voice trembled with excitement. "My name's Margarite!"

He leaned forward intently. "Do you remember anything else?"

But the black curtain was back. Disappointed, she shook her head. "No, nothing, just a voice calling me by my name."

"Margarite . . . it sounds French. *Parlez-vous français, Mademoiselle?*"

The question was thrown out abruptly and, almost without thinking, Margarite answered, "*Un petit peu.*"

"So you speak French as well as German," he said thoughtfully. "It's not usual, a Mexican woman speaking so many languages."

The narrowed gaze searching her face made Margarite uncomfortable, as if once again he thought she was deliberately withholding some truth about herself from him.

"Not any more unusual than a mule driver speaking French," she replied, exasperated.

For a moment she thought the storm warnings would return, then that dazzling white smile flashed across the bronze face. *"Touché, Ma'm'selle."* He rose to his feet. "Shall we call it a draw?"

As they crossed the patio, Margarite noticed the gaze of the women patrons at the tables following Patricio, the flutter of their fans like the fluttering of hens at the presence of a cocky, handsome rooster in their midst. She gave her companion a mutinous glance. She was sure that Don Patricio was well aware of his disturbing effect upon women. Well, he needn't think that he had only to smile at her and she would fall at his feet just because she'd had too much wine last night and . . . hastily, she turned her mind away from last night.

Once outside the posada, Don Patricio suggested showing her some of the sights of Querétaro. "Unless, of course," he said with the utmost politeness, "you wish to be taken directly to the convent."

Margarite hesitated. There was no way the man could seduce her in broad daylight on a street filled with people. And it was a beautiful day. Golden sunlight drenched the tops of the hills surrounding the town and washed down the tiled rooftops.

Taking her silence for consent, her companion began the walking tour, which, several hours later, had taken them through most of Querétaro. At least it seemed that way to an exhausted Margarite. They had even climbed partway up on one of the hills that encircled the town. *Cerro de las Campanas*, the Hill of the Bells, Patricio had told her was its name.

Margarite sat and rested for a moment on a low adobe wall, enjoying the lovely, tranquil vista from the hillside, the green treelined avenues of the city below her, white birds wheeling through a blue sky, the sound of church bells drifting up from the town.

"*Ay, bonita,*" she breathed.

But when she turned, she saw that Patricio's eyes were not on the beauty of the town below them, but upon her. And there was an intensity in that narrowed gaze fastened upon her that made her realize uneasily that here upon the hillside she was not surrounded by crowds of people. They were completely alone.

"I—I think we should be going," she said nervously.

To her surprise, he agreed immediately, and his hands, almost completely spanning her small waist as he lifted her down from the wall, dropped away from her the minute her feet touched the ground.

And they were off touring again, walking through the alameda, past the Square of Independence, admiring the fountains and the flowers blooming everywhere. Once or twice Margarite thought she caught her companion gazing intently into the crowds around them, as if he were looking for someone, and sometimes, when they stopped, he seemed to delay deliberately. But he had told her he knew no one in Querétaro, so she decided it must be her imagination.

He did linger at a flower stall, where he bought her a nosegay of margaritas, which he handed to her with a flourish. His smile faded when he saw the sudden anguished look on her face.

"What is it?" he asked sharply.

She could see it so clearly, another day, another time, a blond man in a military uniform handing a young woman a nosegay of flowers. She did not recognize the man, but the woman she was sure was herself, in an elegant gown carrying a lilac lace parasol. But it was like looking at a picture of two strangers who meant nothing to her, one-dimensional figures caught in a terrifying limbo without a past and without a future. This time when the picture faded, tears of frustration stung her eyes.

"Another memory?" Don Patricio asked, his voice softening as he saw the tears trembling on the tangled eyelashes, spilling down her cheeks.

She nodded, unable to speak.

He smiled down at her as his thumbs gently traced the

delicate arch of her cheekbones, removing the tears. "Don't cry, *poquita*," he said tenderly. "It's a good sign. Each day you remember more."

"I'm afraid," she whispered. "I'm afraid of what I'll remember."

He stared at her, puzzled. "Why should you be afraid?"

She shook her head, smiling shakily. "I don't know."

"That's not fear," he said cheerfully. "That's hunger pangs you're feeling. It's been all of five hours since we ate. A *muchacha* with your appetite must be starved. The Hotel Español serves the best seafood in Querétaro. Come along. . . ."

The restaurant at the Hotel Español was much grander than the small inn where they'd had lunch. Meals were served on a second floor gallery that looked down upon a candlelit courtyard where gardenias floated in a pool, and a mariachi band played loudly. The women diners wore brightly colored crinoline gowns, jewels glittering in their hair and around their throats, but they were outshone by their male companions in military uniforms of scarlet, green, and bright blue, gold stripes running down their trouser legs, and gold braid tumbling over their tunics.

In her peasant-style dress and with her short, clipped hair, Margarite felt ill at ease amid such splendor. She soon forgot her own lack of a proper gown and jewels, however, when the waiter brought lobster and shrimp and iced caviar to the table.

Patrick had taken one quick look around the gallery when they had first entered, not that it was likely that Stout would take the chance of showing up with all the French and Austrian officers around. He turned his attention to the food, pushing down an uneasy feeling of concern. He had given the Juarista agent every chance today to pass along to him unobserved the information he needed. Still, there might be a good reason why the man hadn't appeared. And there was always tomorrow.

He glanced across the table at his companion, watching the girl happily devour the meat from a lobster claw. He grinned to himself. Margarite. What a fancy name for such an appealing little baggage. And wondered if his first guess about the girl hadn't been right after all, that she had been a maid, first traveling with that elderly German woman in the carriage, then employed by the Ortiz family. She could have picked up her haughty airs as well as bits of German and French from her former mistresses. And maids of wealthy women were often given their mistress's cast-off clothes, which would account for the expensive gown the girl had been wearing when Juan Heras had attacked the Ortiz coach.

Glancing across the table, Margarite saw the warmth of the man's eyes, a golden, dancing reflection of the candle flame reflected in their dark blue depths, and realized that for the last several hours she hadn't once seen the other Don Patricio, the *atajo* leader who had driven her and the *arrieros* so mercilessly on the trail. She had even found herself relaxing and enjoying the man's company, his teasing banter and infectious laughter, which made it impossible not to laugh with him.

Patrick was holding a glass of wine, his hand curled casually around the fragile stem. And all at once she was reminded of the touch of that hand at her breast, sending jolts of excitement through her body, making her feel oddly breathless and light-headed. But that had been due to the wine she had drunk last night, she told herself firmly, turning her silly and giddy and an easy prey for a man as undoubtedly experienced as Don Patricio was with women. She had no intention this evening of drinking even a drop of the pale golden champagne the waiter had poured into the goblet beside her plate.

Deliberately, she pulled her gaze away from Don Patricio and looked down at the strolling musicians in the courtyard below. "What a lovely song they're playing," she said. "Do you know what it is?"

" 'La Paloma.' It's a favorite of Mama Carlota's."

At the derisive note in his voice, Margarite swung her gaze back to him. "Mama Carlota?"

"That's what they're calling the empress of Mexico these days." His mouth twisted in a sardonic smile. "Maximilian is being called some even less flattering names."

Still, it was a beautiful melody, Margarite thought,

and gave her companion a quizzical glance. "I thought you said the *arrieros* weren't interested in the war."

Don Patricio shrugged indifferently. "One can't help hearing things, traveling through the countryside." And then the warmth was back in his face as he held Margarite's hand in his, stroking the soft pink palm with his finger. "It's much too beautiful a night to talk of war, Niña," he said softly, his glance caressing her face.

It was night, Margarite realized. Stars were strung across the dark velvety sky more dazzling than the jewels on the women around her. She pulled her hand free and rose hastily to her feet. "The convent," she said unhappily. "We should be leaving."

Patricio rose to his feet, too, smiling. "You surely wouldn't expect to arouse the good Sisters at this hour?"

"But . . . but we must." Margarite looked around her, panic-stricken, and then back at the man's amused, confident smile. How could she have been so stupid? It had all been planned, of course, the sight-seeing, the dinner. Don Patricio had never intended to take her to the convent. Hadn't he even boasted that they would spend one last night together?

Her companion gestured to the door behind them on the gallery. Margarite now saw that there were several such doors along the gallery. "Fortunately, I had the forethought to arrange a room for myself here at the hotel this evening. You are, of course, welcome to use it."

Margarite glared at him, her chin lifting haughtily. "No, thank you. I prefer to sleep alone."

Patrick sighed impatiently to himself. He had hoped he wouldn't have to go through the usual ridiculous charade. The indignant female's protestations of virtue that were meant only to encourage her lover to further heated pleadings and vows of undying love before finally permitting him to her bed as was her intention from the beginning. Somehow, he had hoped for more honesty from *la niña*.

He thrust a key into her hand, bowing gravely. "The room is yours. No one shall disturb you, unless it is your wish."

Margarite gazed at the key suspiciously. "Is this the only key to the room?"

He lifted his eyebrow in mock shock. "I assure you it is."

Despite her uneasiness, she found that she believed him. "Where will you sleep?" she asked.

"There are other rooms available in the hotel," he assured her. "And the first thing in the morning I will take you to the convent."

She clutched the key uncertainly. Still, she had no choice, she realized. She couldn't walk the street all night in a city filled with soldiers. She inclined her head graciously. "Thank you. I'll see you in the morning, then."

After she had disappeared into the hotel room, Patrick settled back at the table to finish his glass of champagne, his annoyance fading as he remembered with a pleasant glow of anticipation how vibrantly warm and alive the girl had been in his arms the night before. He imagined her now in the hotel room, undressing and bathing, making herself ready for him, then climbing into the bed, her young, eager body still warm and scented from her bath, waiting for him.

He poured himself a second glass of champagne. He would give her fifteen minutes, he decided magnanimously, then the charade would be over.

Chapter 12

MARGARITE was just about to extinguish the lamp beside the bed when she heard the sound of a door opening. Her glance flew to the gallery door, but it was still bolted shut on the inside. It was the door that

led to the inner hall of the hotel, and which she had
locked securely, that was now opening.

Don Patricio stepped inside, closed the door behind
him, then casually shrugging off his jacket, advanced
confidently toward the bed, his voice filled with tender
concern. "Are you comfortable, *poquita*?"

Margarite snatched the coverlet around her and hissed,
"Get out of my room!"

Don Patricio loosened the collar and began unbutton-
ing his shirt as he continued toward the bed. "It's my
room, Niña, and my bed," he said, grinning broadly.
"You surely didn't believe with all the military crowding
the town that I could find myself another hotel room?
And having spent a small fortune for this one, I can
assure you that I have no intention of sleeping in the
stable with my horse."

"You said I had the only key!"

He sat down on the edge of the bed and began to pull
off his boots. "I'm afraid I had a misspent youth," he
said regretfully. 'I learned to pick locks at a very early
age."

The boots fell with a thud to the floor and he was
reaching for the waistband of his trousers, when Margarite gave a small furious cry and started to scramble
from the bed. Swiftly an arm reached out and pulled her,
struggling wildly, into Patrick's lap. The coverlet fell
away from her as he deftly removed her shift, pulling it
over her head. Gently but firmly then he held her crushed
against his chest, his voice filled with mocking laughter
as he murmured, "To think that just last night, Niña,
you told Doña Soledad how blessed you were to have a
strong, handsome man like myself in your bed."

She felt his lips caress the bare flesh at her shoulders,
burning a path from the fragile collarbone to the hollow
in her throat, and she struggled even more frantically,
but it was like beating at an unyielding adobe wall.

He released her just long enough to gaze admiringly
down into her furious face. "What a little spitfire you
are, *poquita*," he said. "If you have this much fire when
we make love, I'll be sorry that I didn't finish what I

started last night. What the hell!'' he exploded as she ducked her head and sank her teeth into his wrist.

She tumbled from his lap, snatched the coverlet around her, and was heading for the door, when she realized what he had said. ''What do you mean, you didn't finish what you had started?'' she demanded, whirling to face him. ''You let me believe. . . .'' Her voice sputtered off, too incoherent with rage to continue.

He shrugged, grinning. ''There's no pleasure unless both parties are conscious. I'm sure you know that, Niña.''

He was walking slowly toward her as he spoke. Too late, she flung herself at the door, but the coverlet still wrapped around her legs tripped her. She would have fallen if his arms hadn't caught her and once more pulled her hard against him. This time the embrace was not gentle as she fought against him, beating at his chest with her fists, kicking at his shins with her feet, bruising herself more than the hard flesh she attacked. The arm never relaxed its hold, tightening inexorably around her waist, squeezing the breath from her body so that she could not whisper, much less scream.

''Enough!'' he growled at last, impatiently. ''You've put on a sufficient show of maidenly virtue. You'll wear yourself out if you keep this up.'' As he felt her struggles weaken, he swung her up in his arms, the coverlet falling away from her as he dropped her upon the bed.

He quickly removed his shirt and trousers, but when he turned back to the bed, he saw, dismayed, that the girl's eyes were closed. Had he held her too tightly? he wondered. Had she passed out on him again? Then he saw that her breasts were rising and falling rapidly, and when he touched her shoulder, her eyelids flew open and her green eyes blazed up at him.

He smiled down at her, relieved, his gaze lingering on the small, gleaming breasts, uplifted temptingly to him. His hand reached down to encircle one, discovering, pleased, that the soft cone shape did fit delightfully within his grasp, and wondered idly why he had ever thought great pillowy mounds of breasts attractive. His gaze wandered, delighted, over the rest of the small, exquisitely formed body, the tiny waist that his hands could span, the sweetly curved hips and shapely thighs. Even her feet were small and delicately formed.

"How beautiful you are, *poquita*," he murmured huskily, and as his thumb gently teased a velvety pink nipple, he grinned lazily down at her. "A pocket-sized Venus."

But the moment his hand possessed the silken flesh, he was startled to see that it was not passion blazing in those luminous green eyes, but something disturbingly close to fear as she whispered, "Please! Don't. . . ."

She twisted away from him and he stared down at her, half bewildered, half irritated. *Maldito!* What sort of game was she playing now? Last night she had clung to him as if she never wanted to let him go, and tonight her slender body was rigid, her legs pressed tightly together, denying him access.

He could feel his desire for her mounting, frustration biting in his loins, as he snapped, "Enough! You are trying my patience, Niña. Is it money you want? You shall have it." He found the cleverly concealed pocket in his right boot, pulled out several gold coins, and threw them contemptuously on the bed. The gold glittered brightly in the candlelight, but no brighter than the flash of anger he saw deep in the green eyes as she surged toward him, hands clawed to scratch at his face.

He caught those hands just in time, laughing triumphantly, knowing that anger was only the other side of the coin from passion. He held her small wrists imprisoned easily by one strong hand above her head as he lowered his lips to her breast, whispering, "That's better, *amada mia*. It's your fire I want, not ice."

She writhed within his grasp, sobbing and cursing him with all the swear words she could remember from the *arrieros,* but his mouth continued its assault relentlessly, his tongue teasing, flicking, at the soft peak of her breast, finally his lips covering, pulling gently, insistently, at the nipple until he felt its softness grow taut in his mouth. His one hand had been resting lightly, fingers spread, on the slight swell of her abdomen, and when he heard her give a soft, startled cry of pleasure, his hand moved downward to add its gentle persuasion, stroking lightly the satin soft thighs, tightly pressed together, until they parted instinctively beneath the seeking, questing hand.

At first Margarite thought the warmth racing through her body, her skin burning as if it were on fire, was due to rage. Except anger had never uncurled tendrils of pleasure in her stomach, or made her flesh quiver the way hers did wherever this man's hands or mouth touched. When he released his iron grip on her wrists, and she did not immediately begin to struggle against him again, she wondered almost absently: Was this something, then, her body was accustomed to, a man's mouth and hands exploring it intimately? Was that why it was no longer resisting but responding eagerly, as if with a will and secret knowledge of its own, her hips arching upward toward the hand that was bringing her such almost unendurable pleasure. Her own hands lifted seemingly of their own volition, pressing the dark head closer to her breast.

When he finally lifted his head, she could see that the chiseled lineaments of his face were suffused with a passionate tenderness as he gazed down at her. The hard length of his mouth softened in a smile as he lowered his head again and this time caressed her lips slowly with feathery kisses, while his hand continued its leisurely exploration of the curves and hollows of her body, seeming to know just where to touch to bring her the greatest pleasure, as if he knew her body better than she knew it herself.

Then his mouth on hers was no longer lightly teasing but covering her lips completely so that their breath mingled and her lips parted instinctively as if at an unspoken command. She felt a painful excitement mounting inside of her as his tongue plunged again and again into the softness of her mouth. When he took his lips away, she felt dizzy, weak with desire.

The narrowed indigo eyes searched her face, his voice gently questioning. *"Querida?"* But he was sure that she was as ready as he was. Behind the fringe of lashes her eyes glowed a deep misty green with desire.

She reached up and touched his face, tracing that long, sensuous mouth with her fingertip. As if from a great

distance she could hear the mariachi band still playing in
the hotel courtyard, music floating over the night air, the
sound of a woman's laughter, but it was all on the
periphery of her consciousness. Nothing really existed
for her but the closeness between herself and this man
that she never wanted to end, the tenderness in that face
gazing down into hers, engulfing her, making her feel
safe and warm and beloved.

When he swung his body above hers, and the gently
caressing hand was gone and what was in its place was
hard and demanding, she felt no sense of alarm. So the
sudden, sharp pain as he thrust deep into her brought a
startled scream to her lips.

She saw the look of shock flooding his face, felt him
withdrawing, and tightened her arms and legs around
him, holding him fast. For the pain was quickly gone
and what was in its place as he moved inside her, at first
slowly, carefully, then more swiftly, deeply, made the
earlier pleasure seem as nothing. This was a sensation
so intense, a series of swiftly mounting crescendos of
pleasure, reaching a sudden, exploding climax so shat-
tering that she cried aloud with rapture and a childish
sense of disappointment that it had ended so soon.

Her eyes closed in drowsy contentment, she sank
back on the bed, her body still throbbing faintly with
remembered pleasure, only vaguely aware of the weight
of his body leaving her and the bed.

"Margarite."

The sound of her name on his lips, a name he had not
used before, surprised her. She opened her eyes and
turned toward him, smiling. He was standing beside the
bed. To her surprise he was dressed, except for his
shirt. She could see the mat of black curling hair glistening against his chest, and she remembered the crisp feel
of that hair against her breasts when he had held her
close, the hardness of those muscular shoulders like
cords beneath her hands. Then she lifted her eyes to his
face and saw that all trace of tenderness was gone. The
eyes staring at her accusingly were a familiar stormy
black with anger.

"Why didn't you tell me you were a virgin?" he demanded.

"How was I to know?" she replied defensively, her smile fading. Then, childishly wanting to hurt him as he was hurting her by his behavior, added, "What does it matter? I'm not anymore, am I?"

She saw a muscle beside his mouth jerk, but his voice was flat. "Get dressed. I'm taking you to the convent."

"Now? In the middle of the night?" she protested. "You said the nuns would be asleep at this hour."

"Then we'll wake them," he snapped. He studied the girl in the bed. Her young, lovely face was still softened by the aftermath of passion, her eyes glowing a deep jade green, and her breasts with a faint shimmer of perspiration coating them had a nacreous, pearllike glow. He remembered only too vividly the scent and shape and texture of those breasts, each enticing curve of that small body.

He cursed himself silently, not only for unwittingly having deprived the girl of her innocence, but for another more disturbing memory. When he'd held her in his arms, a feeling had gut-wrenched him that he had never experienced before with any other woman, an emotion that he sensed was perilously close to love. And love was a luxury he dare not allow himself to feel. Affection, yes, even friendship, but there was no room in the precarious life he led for any deeper emotional attachment. What sort of life could he possibly offer any woman in the dangerous cat and mouse game he played each day here in Mexico? The fact that he was still alive was more a tribute to luck, Patrick thought grimly, than anything else.

He picked up her clothes and tossed them onto the bed. "Hurry up," he ordered brusquely.

He was reaching down to pick up his own shirt, when the muffled knock came at the hall door, and a voice, hardly recognizable, whispering, "Patrick . . . . open the door!"

In two strides he had crossed the room and pulled open the door. The man who fell into the room almost carried Patrick to the floor with him. Quickly Patrick

closed and locked the hall door, then knelt down beside
Jim Stout. The man's face was so badly battered and cut
that at first glance he wouldn't have recognized him.

Margarite had quickly left the bed and joined him,
staring, her eyes wide with shock, at the man crumpled
on the floor. "Who is he? What's happened to him?"
she whispered without knowing why she felt it necessary
to whisper.

"Get some water and towels," Patrick ordered, not
taking his eyes from the man's face. "Quick!"

The man's eyes opened. They were gray, Margarite
noticed, and a smile twitched the man's pain-filled face
as they fastened upon her, before, embarrassed, she
hastily turned away, remembering that there hadn't been
time for her to dress.

She heard the man speak, so softly that she had to
strain her ears to hear as she soaked towels in the water
pitcher. "You always were a lucky devil, O'Malley."

With a start of surprise, Margarite realized the man
was speaking English, and that Don Patricio was reply-
ing, also in English. "When did they get hold of you?"
he asked.

"Yesterday morning. I think they let me escape so
that I'd lead them to you. They know about the guns,
but not where the deliveries are to be made."

Margarite returned with the wet towels. "He shouldn't
be talking," she said in Spanish to Patricio, marveling
that the man had made it this far in his condition.

She tried to wash the blood away from a cheekbone
that was obviously broken, but the man pushed her
fretfully away. "No time," he muttered. He gave Patrick
a questioning glance.

Patrick glanced at Margarite, then nodded. "It's all
right. You can talk. She won't understand."

Quickly then, speaking through teeth that were broken and lips that were painfully swollen, the man gave
Patrick a short list of places, the names of two towns,
one hacienda, and a *pulquería*.

When he had finished, he sighed and closed his eyes.
Patrick took the towel from Margarite and gently held it

against the bloody face. "Jim?" he asked softly. "Can you hear me? How far behind you are they?"

As if in answer, another knock came at the door, a pounding that shook the frame of the door and brought Margarite to her feet. A man's voice demanded loudly. "Open the door, *Señor*. We are on official business from the French garrison."

Patrick already had his pistol held in a businesslike fashion in his hand. He handed Margarite her clothes and shoved her roughly toward the gallery door. "Get out of here! Don't come back."

She shook her head, her thoughts racing. "You can't hold them off with one gun. And how far would I get? They can't know for sure the man's here. Put him at the foot of the bed and throw the coverlet over him. You get into the bed too . . . pretend to be asleep. . . ."

She had dropped her clothes and was slipping into his shirt, her fingers icy cold with fear as she gathered it around her. The shirt came only as far as her thighs and hung loosely open at her breasts.

"What the hell are you doing?" Patrick demanded angrily.

She whirled on him, but she was more afraid of the men at the door than of Patricio. "Don't be stupid," she hissed. "Do as I say. The both of you, get into bed."

She waited until Patricio carried the stranger to the bed, flung the coverlet over him, then slipped into bed himself, only his naked shoulders and dark head showing above the coverlet.

"Close your eyes. Snore!"

An affronted look crossed Patrick's face. "I don't snore," he objected.

There was no more time; the pounding at the door was threatening to break it open by brute force. Margarite took a deep breath and pulled open the door. She recognized the French captain standing in the hallway, with two enlisted men behind him. He was the same officer she had met earlier that day in the hotel lobby.

He recognized her, too, Margarite saw by the sudden interest that sprang into his eyes even as he bowed formally and said, "Forgive this intrusion, *Señora*, but we must search your room."

She yawned and smiled sweetly. "Of course, but whatever for? There's just my husband and myself here." She held the door open so the captain could look into the room and see the man sleeping in the bed. "I believe you've already met my husband." The slightest look of contempt touched her face as she glanced, resigned, at the sleeping man. "As usual, poor Pablo drank too much wine and fell asleep the minute his head hit the pillow."

She sighed deeply, allowing her hands holding the shirt to fall away. The shirt parted still farther and the officer could not help catching a glimpse of a pert breast, or being aware that the young woman was not wearing anything at all beneath the shirt. "It is so difficult, is it not, Captain," she murmured, "to lie in bed, unsatisfied, unable to sleep." She stepped closer to the man, her voice a soft, unspoken invitation. "A Frenchman, I'm sure, would never treat a woman so cruelly."

The captain cleared his throat, uncomfortably aware of the two enlisted men behind him, whose eyes, like his, were fastened on the partially clad young woman in the doorway.

Behind her in the bed, the husband began to snore noisily, and the captain's face twisted with Gallic outrage. A man who'd drunkenly fall asleep without making love to his beautiful young wife, in the captain's considered opinion, deserved to be shot.

Margarite opened the door a little wider, her face wistful. "If you'd care to search the room, Captain, Pablo sleeps like the dead. Nothing will disturb him."

Remembering at the last minute his duty and the two men with him, the captain regretfully shook his head. "That won't be necessary," he said hastily. He bent low, kissing the small hand as he whispered, "Perhaps later, *Señora*, I can return?"

"Please do," she whispered back, giving the man's hand a fervent squeeze.

As soon as the door closed behind the soldiers, Patrick exploded from the bed. "Another minute and you'd have had Red Legs in bed with us," he snarled as he pulled the coverlet away from the injured man. Not injured, Margarite realized, staring, dismayed, at the too still body, the oddly blank face. Dead.

She felt a scream of hysteria rising in her throat, but before she could utter a sound, Patricio had his hand clamped over her mouth, until he felt her body grow quiet in his arms.

He withdrew his hand cautiously. "Are you all right? One scream and we'd have the whole hotel in here."

She nodded, unable to speak.

"Get dressed. We've got to get out of here." He grinned wickedly at her. "With the fetching picture you made in my shirt, I doubt if that French captain will wait very long before returning."

Margarite pulled the chemise over her head, flung on her petticoats and skirt, and was fumbling nervously with the ties and buttons, when Patrick impatiently pulled her to the gallery door.

"My shoes!" There was no time to put them on and she carried the slippers in her hand as she took a last look at the man sprawled on the bed. "What about him?" she asked in a shocked whisper.

For a moment a blackness settled over Patrick's face as he looked at the man, then he shrugged impassively. "There's nothing we can do for him now."

Then they were out on the gallery, making their way through the diners who were still enjoying their evening meal. They followed the gallery toward the far side of the hotel, where there were no more tables. The courtyard was dark below, and the sounds of music and laughter could be heard only faintly.

Margarite watched as Patricio climbed over the low iron railing that ran along the gallery, then glanced unhappily around her. "Isn't there a back staircase?"

"And no doubt posted with a guard," he replied impatiently. "It's not that long a drop to the courtyard. I'll go first."

She saw him hang for a moment over the edge of the gallery, then disappear from sight. She hurried to look over the railing. Patricio had landed with his knees bent to break the force of the fall.

He looked up at her and said quietly, "Hold on to the railing. When I tell you to, let go. I'll catch you."

She gazed down doubtfully. The drop didn't look that short to her. Supose he should miss. Patricio saw her hesitate and said grimly, "Or would you rather take your chances with Red Legs?"

Margarite remembered the way the captain's eyes had fondled her and she climbed quickly over the railing. Her hands clutching the railing, she let her body drop. For a moment she swung, suspended, her heart pounding in her throat.

"Now!" Patricio ordered.

There was no denying that sharp command. Margarite's hands loosened their death grip on the rail. She felt herself falling, then caught safely in arms that lowered her quickly to the ground. For a moment she clung to Patrick, her knees turned to water.

"The stable's this way." He was yanking her by the hand and she was stumbling after him in the darkness of a dank-smelling passageway that led from the courtyard to the stable.

The stable boy at first refused to give Patricio his horse, announcing importantly that he had orders from the French captain that no animals were allowed to leave the stable that evening. The boy quickly changed his mind, though, when he saw the way the man's hand rested lightly but professionally on the revolver at his waistband, the silver engraving on the handle of the gun as glittering as the man's cold, hard eyes.

As soon as the horse was saddled, Patricio tossed the boy several pesos, then pulled Margarite up behind him, ordering tersely, "Hang on."

Despite the late hour, the streets of Querétaro were still alive with people, music and laughter spilling out of the cantinas, soldiers weaving drunkenly from one *pulquería* to another. Candles flickered fitfully while half-naked *leperos* slouched asleep on the steps of the entrance to churches. Patricio took the unlit, narrow back streets that turned and twisted so that Margarite had no idea in which direction they were going.

Patricio hadn't spoken since they had left the stable

and, finally, she asked hesitantly, "Is this the way to the convent?"

"We're not going to the convent," he answered, biting off each word. "Or do you think that French captain will have any trouble remembering you?"

Margarite could hear the repressed anger in the man's voice, feel the tautness of the body her arms were clasped around, as if, she thought, bewildered, he were furious with her for some reason. Indignation replaced her bewilderment. It wasn't bad enough his breaking into her hotel room and raping her . . . well, seducing her, at least, she amended, but after she had gone to the trouble to save his life, he hadn't even bothered to thank her!

"I insist upon your taking me to the convent," she said haughtily. "I'll be perfectly safe there."

Patrick did not bother to answer, his mouth setting in a tight line. He would like nothing better than to do just that if he thought she would be safe there. But not even convent walls would protect the girl once they found the body of an escaped Juarista spy in her bedroom, and her supposed husband vanished.

They left the streets of the city, the horse climbing into the hills, following an almost nonexistent trail. Clouds had drifted across the moon and almost hidden the stars which barely pierced the cover. The darkness was so thick around them that Margarite felt she could reach out and touch it; the trail was so steep that she had to tighten her grasp around Patricio's middle to keep from sliding out of the saddle. Several times, when the horse stumbled on loose rock, she held her breath, sure they were going to crash off the trail into a ravine.

It was only after they made their way through the hills and Patricio stopped to rest the horse for a few moments that Margarite asked, "Was he a good friend of yours, that man back at the hotel?"

"It's better not to talk of such things," he answered brusquely. They had dismounted and were standing close together, the darkness wrapped around them. He couldn't see her face clearly, but he was very aware of her scent. The cameo loveliness of her small body was imprisoned in his mind with the same power to unsettle him as the feel of her breasts pressed against his back when she rode behind him. Despite the fact that her presence, which before had been a temporary inconvenience, had now become an almost insurmountable problem, he felt a sudden aching need to feel her beneath him again, her young ardent body opened, ready and eager to receive him.

Angered more at himself than at her—when had there ever been a time he had not been able to put a woman out of his mind? he thought derisively—he remounted and pulled her up behind him again. "Try and sleep," he ordered. "We've still several hours ride ahead of us."

"I can't sleep," she pointed out irritably. "I'll fall off the horse."

"Wrap your rebozo around you and give me the two ends," he said. When she had done so, he took the ends and tied them tightly around his waist. She must look like one of the Indian babies, their heads flopping, tied in a shawl to the backs of their mothers, Margarite thought, stifling a giggle at the image.

Of course, after everything that had happened, she wouldn't be able to sleep, she told herself. But the bay had an easy, restful gait. The rhythmic sound of its hooves, the creaking saddle, and jingling bridle, lulled her. Her head drooped, resting against Patricio's broad back. And she promptly fell asleep.

Chapter 13

A hand was shaking her shoulder gently, a familiar voice urging, "Wake up, Niña."

"Hosea?" She rubbed sleep from her eyes. It was not yet dawn, the earth stained an unearthly shade of pink in the half light between dark and daylight. Hosea was haunched down beside her. Her gaze fastened sleepily on the young mule driver, and then beyond him, to the other *arrieros* already busily fastening packs on their mules.

"Don Patricio said you are to wear these," the boy said, handing her the trousers and shirt she had worn when she rode with the pack train before. "They're clean," he said, flushing proudly. "The maid, Carla, at Doña Soledad's washed them herself, just for me." He nodded to a small stand of trees not far from the camp. "You can change there. No one will see," he assured her. "And Madre has saved some tortillas for you, but you must hurry. Don Patricio wants to be at San Angel by sunrise."

San Angel. The name sounded familiar. Then she remembered the man in the hotel room. San Angel was one of the words he had whispered to Don Patricio. And the man had spoken English, she remembered as she quickly removed her clothes behind the screen of protective trees. And even more surprising, she realized, Patricio had understood the man and so had she. Where would she have learned to speak English? And the man who died, who was he?

Remembering that horribly blank look on the dead man's bruised face, she shivered. Last night she had been too shocked and weary to question Don Patricio, but this morning, she decided firmly, she would demand some answers.

When she sought out Don Patricio, though, after swallowing several cold tortillas, she almost lost her courage. He was once again wearing the worn leather trousers and chamois shirt of a mule driver. The burnished bronze face beneath the dark sombrero, the hard indigo eyes, were the same, too, even the angry impatience in his voice as he snapped, "Get mounted, Niña." He glanced at the clothes she still held in her hand. "You can throw those away. You won't be needing them."

She tood a deep, steadying breath, and said, "We have to talk."

"There is nothing to talk about." For a moment, that

hard gaze flicked over the small, defiant figure standing before him, then he shrugged, as if amused. "If you're concerned about last night, I can promise you it won't happen again."

Suddenly, involuntarily, she found herself remembering those same eyes filled with tenderness and passion, that long mouth caressing her breast, sending waves of pleasure through her body. She flushed and said hastily, "I don't want to talk about that! I want to know about the man who died in the hotel room last night."

His eyes narrowed to slits, the muscles next to his mouth tightening with anger. She almost stepped back but forced herself to remain still, gazing calmly at the man, waiting.

At last he said indifferently, "He was a stranger who unfortunately stumbled into the wrong hotel room."

"That's a lie!" she blurted out. "He called you by name. And I heard him give you a list of places to deliver guns." She glanced at the mules, already packed and waiting and all at once understood. "There are guns in those packs, aren't there, guns that you're delivering to Juaristas."

She saw the look of surprise on his face, mingled with annoyance. "So you understand English too?"

"I suppose I must," she said slowly. "And if I'm to continue traveling with the *atajo,* I have the right to—"

"You have no rights, Niña," he interrupted, his voice softly menacing, sending a shiver of fear through her. "I lead this pack train. You will do exactly as I say, without question. And while you are traveling with us, you will be of some use. You'll take over the cooking from Madre."

"You can't make me stay," she said defiantly. "I can always turn myself over to the French and tell them the truth, that I wasn't involved with that man."

"Do you know how the French treat Mexican women suspected of being Juaristas?" he asked almost casually. "If you're lucky, they'll spread-eagle you and take turns raping you. If you're not lucky, they'll turn you over to Márquez's butchers. They have a special way of handling women who are even suspected of being Juarista sympathizers. They tie them to trees by their breasts and flog them before they leave them to die.''

''I—I don't believe you,'' Margarite whispered.

He shrugged. ''Ask Gabriel. That's what Márquez did to his wife, and only because she was married to a Juarista.''

Patrick saw the girl flinch, and schooled himself against the horror flooding her eyes. He had to shock her so that she would forget this insane idea of running off to the French. And become frightened enough of him so that like it or not, she would obey without questions his orders when her life might depend upon her instant obedience. As it was, there was precious little protection he could offer her. The French knew what he looked like now and the patrols would be out in force, looking for him and the guns.

He took the pistol from his belt and handed it to her. ''Keep this in your pack. It's loaded, so be careful.'' An eyebrow slanted sardonically. ''I wouldn't want you shooting the wrong people.''

He glanced around him, at the low-lying hills just beginning to take shape in the gray dawn. The first thing he had to do was to get away from these hills. The Indians around Querétaro were fiercely loyal to Mejia, one of Maximilian's most capable and loyal generals.

Hosea brought up Margarite's mustang, who seemed to recognize her, nuzzling her gently with his teeth as she patted his rough mane before gingerly sticking the pistol into her pack and swinging into the saddle.

The *atajo* reached the village of San Angel just after daylight. The village was so small that Margarite had seen it all in half an hour from the tiny church, with a decapitated statue of the Virgin Mary and Child, to a dirty open market smelling to high heaven from spoiled meat and decaying vegetables. The villagers living in little more than mud huts, the children with open sores on their naked bodies as they played in the dirt, did not seem discontented with their lot. The women smiled shyly at her as she passed, the men watching her with grave, placid faces.

Margarite could not help noticing that there were only

women, children, and old men in the village. "Where are all the men?" she asked Hosea. The young muleteer had stuck to her side like a shadow, she suspected on strict orders from Don Patricio, making sure that she did not roam too closely to an adobe hut at the edge of the village, where she assumed the business of delivering the guns was being conducted.

The young man shrugged. "The army came through with lariats, six, seven months ago, carrying off any boy or man able to carry a gun, to fight for Don Maximiliano. The men that tried to run off were shot. Two years ago they came to my village, too, and took my brothers and myself. They nailed shut the doors of houses where they kept us at night, but I managed to run away."

At Margarite's shocked look, he asked, surprised, "How else can an army be raised? General Porfirio Diaz does the same, raiding villages, gathering men for the army of President Juárez."

Margarite shook her head, half-smiling. "I'm sorry, Hosea, but your President Juárez and Emperor Maximilian sound much the same to me, one as much a scoundrel as the other."

"Ah, but Niña," the boy said eagerly, "you do not understand. President Juárez is Mexican; Don Maximiliano is a foreigner!"

Margarite glanced back at the hut. The sun was hot and she was getting hungry. "Will they be much longer, do you think?"

"Not long, Niña." The boy gave Margarite an unhappy sideways glance, then said slowly, "Ramon says that you are Don Patricio's woman now. Is this the truth?"

"No!" Margarite felt her face grow hot. "Why should Ramon say that?"

"Ramon says he can tell by the way Don Patricio looks at you."

"Ramon is mistaken," Margarite said firmly.

Hosea nodded, relieved. "I told Ramon so, that if you and Don Patricio were lovers, you would share your blanket with him, and Don Patricio sleeps alone."

Eager to change the subject, Margarite asked, "Are Ramon and the rest of the *arrieros* Juaristas too?"

Hosea looked away, his voice evasive. "We follow Don Patricio, Niña."

"Doesn't he have another name, your Don Patricio?" Margarite asked, suddenly curious.

"Don Patricio says it is safer if we do not know too much about each other," Hosea replied. Then added in a self-important whisper, "But once I overheard Gabriel call Don Patricio 'Captain O'Malley.' "

O'Malley, Margarite thought, puzzled. That was the name the man in the hotel room had called Don Patricio. It didn't sound like a Mexican name, but despite the deep blue eyes, Patricio's Indian heritage was stamped clearly on his face.

Before she could ask any more questions, the young mule driver gave her a pleading look. "Please, Niña, you won't tell Don Patricio that I spoke of this. He would be very angry with me that I spread tales like a woman."

"I won't say anything," Margarite promised. Not that she was likely to be spending any time talking to Don Patricio, she thought as the pack train left the village and, to the best of Margarite's reckoning, headed southwest.

The *atajo* leader seemed to go out of his way to avoid her company, and when he did glance her way, his gaze slid over her with that blank Indian stare she was beginning to hate.

As if, she thought, a sudden desolation sweeping over her, he had completely forgotten what had passed between them in the Querétaro hotel room. She only wished she could forget as easily the shameful eagerness with which she had encouraged and responded to the man's caresses. Was it possible she had only imagined the tenderness she had seen in his face, the pride and anger stripped away, leaving him as vulnerable as she was? As if for a moment in the intimacy they had shared a door had swung open between them and she had been allowed to see a Patrick kept carefully hidden from everyone else. And in that moment she had no longer been alone with that dark curtain in her mind and the terror always lurking behind that curtain. She had felt as if she would never be alone again.

Then, afterward, when he had turned upon her coldly, the door had swung shut. And the desolation she had felt then now suddenly returned like a stomach cramp, so that she cried aloud softly with the pain. Her hand tightened involuntarily on the reins and her horse stopped short, turning his head to give her a surprised look from wide brown eyes. She leaned forward in the saddle, blinking her eyes against the treacherous tears. The heat beating down through her sombrero made the horizon shift and blur and she could feel the perspiration trickling down between her breasts.

She was not even aware that the mules and *arrieros* had pulled well ahead of her, when Patricio suddenly appeared alongside her. There was a growth of beard on his dust-coated face, and his eyes were red-rimmed with weariness. He pushed his horse next to hers and yanked savagely at the reins. "If you aren't a good enough rider to keep up, you'll be left behind," he warned.

"I can ride as well as any of the *arrieros*," she protested indignantly. And she had been doing more than her share, what with taking over the cooking chores and packing and unpacking her own mustang each morning and evening. Even the mule packers had praised her, telling her she was fast turning into an *arriero*.

Anyway, why was Don Patricio pushing so hard? They hadn't seen anyone in days, except a few Indians trudging along the trail. Yet the train leader insisted upon their being on the trail before daylight, not stopping until both the mules and men were almost dropping with exhaustion. "Why are you in such a hurry?" she complained.

He jerked his thumb over his shoulder, his voice clipped. "Trying to stay ahead of them."

She saw the dust cloud in the distance bearing down upon them. Her heart leaped in her breast. Soldiers? The *arrieros* had already seen the approaching horses, and they and their mules were drifting swiftly off into the folds of the hills, disappearing from sight in draws and washes.

Margarite started to urge her horse after them, but Don Patricio still held her reins. "There's no time." His narrowed gaze was scouting the terrain around them, fastening on a wooden, slatted bridge over a culvert where a stream had once flowed but, with the rainy season passed, was now bone dry. He pulled Margarite's mustang after him, down the rocky side of the culvert and under the bridge.

Margarite slid off her horse, holding the reins loosely. Patrick did the same. A moment before, Margarite had been flushed with the heat. Now all at once she felt ice cold as she heard the hoofbeats of the troop of soldiers riding close, heard the jingle of bridles. The bridge was narrow, the slats far apart. Surely the soldiers would see them. She bit her lower lip, terrified, trying to stop her chin from trembling.

Unexpectedly, she felt Patricio's arm slide around her waist, pulling her against him, her sombrero falling off as he pressed her against his chest. She could hear the steady beat of his heart as she buried her face in his shirtfront, trying to blot out the sound of those horses, the voices and curses in French from the soldiers passing overhead, complaining of the heat, of the search for the gun smugglers that had been futile so far.

When finally the last hoofbeat had clattered over the bridge and faded away in the distance, the arm around her did not loosen. It seemed to her that the heartbeat beneath the chamois shirt was no longer quite so steady. She stirred cautiously in his arms. Could it be that he was not as indifferent to her as he pretended, she wondered hopefully.

She felt her shirt being pulled loose from her waistband, his hands slipping beneath, sliding over the soft moist warmth of her back. She raised on tiptoe to more easily reach his mouth, her tongue mischievously teasing at his mouth before slipping between the sun-dry lips. He gave a strangled groan. His arms lifted her off her feet, fitting her small body snugly against his growing hardness. Her lips were comfortably on a level with his now. She did not have to bend her neck as his mouth captured hers in a deep, searching kiss. The blazing sunlight seemed to have entered inside of her, was racing through her body. She felt as if she were melting with desire and even the worn shirt she wore was a hindrance. She wanted nothing to be between them, to have his hands reach and touch every part of her.

He was well aware of the urgency of her response, and when he finally set her gently down again, he grinned wryly down at her, then at the hard ground, the rocky soil beneath their feet. "Not here, *poquita*. I won't tumble you in the dirt."

"I don't care!" she whispered fiercely, burrowing against him. Then with a half sob of relief, "I thought you didn't want me. . . ."

His arms tightened around her convulsively so that for a moment she felt a jab of pain where her ribs had been injured when the carriage had turned over. He felt her wince and instantly released her. "I'm sorry, *querida*. Did I hurt you?"

She shook her head. "No." Then, indignantly, "Don't treat me as if I would break!" She suddenly smiled up at him, her hands caressing the crisp hair at the nape of his neck as she whispered, "If not now, where? And when?"

He laughed, half startled, half pleased at her boldness. Who would have thought so much passion could be contained in so small a package? But it wasn't only her passion that pleased him. There was something about the girl that reminded him of Doña Star. Oh, not in appearance. His American foster mother with her blazing hair and cool gray eyes had an entirely different type of beauty. It was Margarite's courage and intelligence, even her spirited, stubborn independence that reminded him of Star. Was it possible? he wondered. Could Margarite be American? Except what would an American girl be doing traveling with the Ortiz family?

Well, who she was wasn't important at the moment, he reminded himself. What was important was that somehow he get her to a place of safety. Even if the French didn't run them down, the bad food, sleeping on the hard ground, the constant physical exhaustion of the trail, were sure to take their toll of the girl.

By tomorrow or the next day they should be at Morelia. A *diligencia* ran from there to Mexico and on to Cuernavaca. He was sure his foster parents would take the girl in and look after her until she recovered her memory. Or until if and when he was still alive and able to join her at the ranch.

Margarite tilted back her head, studying his face uneasily. "What are you thinking about?"

He reached down to pick up her sombrero. "That we'd better be on our way before Gabriel sends someone back to make sure we're all right."

She made a face at him, her voice cajoling. "Can't we stay a few more minutes?" Without his arms lifting her off her feet, she stood only as high as his heart. If they stayed even a few more minutes, he thought ruefully, they wouldn't leave at all.

Swiftly he scooped her up and lifted her up on her horse. She looked as if she were about to object further, but then she saw his face. She knew him well enough now to recognize that hard, closed look, closed even to her.

Well, there was still tonight, she thought. The *arrieros* always slept like the dead. And once they were asleep— she smiled to herself, aware for the first time of a pleasurable sense of pride in the power a woman held over a man, even this man riding beside her, who always appeared so self-suffcent and controlled. Don Patricio wouldn't put her away from him this evening, she promised herself smugly.

It was almost dusk when the caravan reached the outskirts of a village that was only a little larger than San Angel. Several thorn trees, twisted with age, grew in a clump just outside the town on the far side of a stream. Patrick, who was in advance of the caravan, noticed uneasily how quiet the town was. There were no signs of inhabitants as his horse splashed across the shallow stream. Then he saw what was hanging, roped to the trees. He shouted back to Margarite, who was riding a short distance behind him, "Don't come any closer!"

But she had already seen what hung in the trees, the mutilated bodies of three men, one a boy, not even yet a man. The bodies were hung upside down, still bleeding from the knife wounds, one man's hand had been cut away. The blood gathered beneath them, soaking into the dry earth.

Cursing helplessly, Patrick spurred his horse, trying to put his mount between the girl and the obscene dangling bodies in the trees. He heard her scream, her eyes, behind the black lashes, glazed with horror as she stared at the men.

But it wasn't those particular bodies, Margarite was seeing. The opaque black curtain in her mind had been abruptly and brutally torn aside and she saw the horror behind that curtain clearly. It was another three men, screaming, writhing in the firelight as knives were plunged again and again into their quivering, still-breathing bodies. And one of the men was her uncle Manuel.

Frightened at the bone-whiteness of her face, Patrick reached for her reins, "Don't look, *querida*."

It wasn't the men she was staring at with horror now; it was Don Patricio. She was remembering awakening in the bandit's camp, those shadowy figures around the hanging men, their faces hidden in darkness, only their knives glinting in the firelight. She hadn't been found alongside the road, she thought, sickened with the knowledge. It was Don Patricio and his Juaristas who had attacked the carriage and killed her aunt and uncle.

"Keep away from me," she whispered. When he didn't remove his hand, she lifted her whip and brought it savagely across his face. Jerking her reins free, she whirled her horse around and raced away into the gathering darkness.

Although her little mustang was fast, it was no match for Patrick's powerful bay. Within a quarter of a mile he caught up with her, grabbed her reins, and yanked her horse to an abrupt halt. The mustang stumbled and almost fell before stopping, her flanks heaving and welted where Margarite had put the whip to her.

She scrambled from the saddle, but Patrick had already dismounted. She ran only a few steps, when his arms encircled her and pulled her roughly against him. She was sobbing and gasping for breath as his arms tightened around her. When he felt the resistance leave her, he lowered her gently to the ground.

She was still sobbing, but softer now, burying her face in her hands as if she could not bear to look at him. He moved a few steps away from her and waited, his face expressionless as he watched her.

When she finally dropped her hands and got to her feet, lifting her tear-stained face to his, he thought he had prepared himself for what he might see in her eyes. But it was like an unexpectedly violent blow to his mid-section when he saw the loathing in their green depths as she whispered, "You butchered him, my uncle and those other men. I saw you . . . you and the others at your camp."

His eyes narrowed, his voice cold. "I assume your memory has returned, then."

"I remember," she said tonelessly. "Oh, God, I wish I didn't." Because she was remembering other things now, lying in this man's arms, begging him not to let her go. A revulsion shook her, a humiliation so complete that her voice trembled. "Why didn't you kill me too? I wish you had. I wish I were dead."

She turned blindly to the mustang, her groping hand finding in the saddlebag the pistol Patrick had given her, not sure when she held the gun in her hand whether she meant the bullet for him or for herself.

Patrick did not wait for her to make the decision. His left hand whipped out and knocked the gun from her hand while his right hand, curled into a fist, struck her chin. This time when he lowered her to the ground, she didn't make a sound.

Chapter 14

WHEN she recovered consciousness, she was lying on a blanket on the ground near the stream and it was night. There was a fire with men gathered around it, their dark bearded faces leaping in and out of the shadows the firelight cast. It was so much like the time she had awakened after the attack on the coach that she shuddered, terrified. But at least this time there were no agonized screams ripping through the night, no tortured men hanging from trees. While she was unconscious, the relatives of the men had crept out from the village and removed the bodies of their dead.

She became aware that Hosea was crouched beside her with a plate of food. "Don Patricio said I could untie your wrists and you should eat."

She hadn't realized that her wrists were tied. Now she turned her gaze away, unable to bear looking at Hosea. To think that she had been fond of the boy, she thought, and he was one of *them*.

"Please, *Señora*," he said, his voice beseeching. "It wasn't the *arrieros* who killed your family. It was El Cuchillo."

Patrick joined them. He made a quick gesture with his hand. The boy took one last forlorn look at the young woman, then slipped away.

Patrick haunched down beside Margarite. "*Señora*," he said.

Although the voice was mild, the authority beneath could not be dismissed the way she had dismissed Hosea. Reluctantly she turned to face the man, feeling a savage pleasure when she saw the cut still livid across his cheek where her whip had caught him.

"What is your name, *Señora?*"

"Von Melk," she said, that unconsciously haughty note creeping back into her voice. "Countess Margarite Juliana Von Melk. My father is . . . was Count Johann Von Melk, attached to the diplomatic service of Emperor Franz Josef."

So that explained her ability to speak so many languages, Patrick thought. The daughter of a member of the imperial diplomatic corps, she had probably lived in many countries. And her title explained her arrogant airs, he thought, staring hopelessly into the gaping abyss that had widened further between them.

"What were you doing in the Ortiz coach?"

"My uncle is . . . was Don Manuel Rojas y Ortiz." She gave him a sharp glance. "How did you know it was the Ortiz coach?" Her eyes flashed contempt. "But, of course, you must have known it was the Oritz coach when you and your men attacked it."

The flattened Indian look to his face did not alter in the slightest, but for a second something flickered deep in the indigo eyes, then was still.

She glanced down with disgust at the shirt and trousers she wore. How could she have ever allowed herself to wear such garments? And the rest, she remembered, cringing mentally, living with thieves and murderers as if she were one of them. Even without a memory, how could she have sunk to their level so quickly, as if the generations of careful breeding had been, after all, only a thin veneer, easily broken. The thought was somehow even more frightening than this man hunched quietly beside her.

She held out her hands to him, her voice imperious. "Why am I tied this way? I demand you release me at once."

He rose slowly to his feet. "The ropes are necessary to make sure you don't try to run away again."

She drew in her breath incredulously. "But now that I know . . . now that you know who I am, surely you can't hold me."

"Unfortunately, you also know who we are," he pointed out. "And since you also understand English, you know the location of the rendezvous points where the rest of the guns are to be delivered." He inclined his head toward her gravely, his voice holding a formal, mocking politeness. "You understand, Countess, my men and I have no great desire to be stood up against a wall and shot." He turned away from her abruptly. "Sleep now. We'll be leaving before daybreak."

When Margarite first awoke the next morning, in the foggy world between sleep and full wakefulness, for a moment she thought she was still Niña and stretched blissfully. Until she remembered. Then she jerked to her feet, a jumble of confused memories filling her mind, the girl in the white crinoline with her uncle's emeralds gleaming at her throat being presented at Chapultapec to the emperor Maximilian, and the girl in dirty pants and shirt riding a wiry mustang, following a dusty mule train. For a moment, bewildered, it was impossible to believe the two women were actually one, as if she had been split in two and the other, the grubby girl in the too large sombrero, still existed somehow inside of her.

When Gabriel saddled and brought her her mustang, no sign of confusion showed in her face, however, as she murmured a cold *"Gracias"* to the man and mounted the horse, disdaining the unappetizing breakfast the man had also brought her.

During the next hours she spoke to no one as the *atajo* headed south toward Morelia, and she carefully kept her gaze averted from the *arrieros*. She discovered that even with her hands tied, she could still manage easily the clever little mustang that followed the mule train obediently. She did observe the countryside, which was wilder now, with fewer and fewer haciendas to be seen. And those they did pass were mostly in ruins. Destroyed by the war, she wondered, or had the *hacendados* who owned the homes taken their families and fled to Cuba, to escape the chaos of war.

Midafternoon, Gabriel brought her a canteen of water. She would have preferred to refuse the gesture, but despite the fact the countryside was much greener, with woods and numerous streams, she was still thirsty, and her thirst spoke louder than her pride. She drank greedily before handing the canteen back to the man. When he started to turn away without speaking, she blurted out, "Gabriel."

He turned back. "Yes, *Señora*?"

She spoke softly, urgently. "If you were to help me escape, I'm sure you'd receive a handsome reward. My uncle was very wealthy." Her voice fell away under that impassive Indian gaze that suddenly, it occurred to her, held more dignity than some members of nobility she had met.

Exasperated, she looked around her at the scruffy group of dirty, bearded mule packers, cursing their mules almost monotonously as they urged them forward. With one part of her mind she felt vaguely shocked that the profanity didn't bring even a blush to her cheeks. "It makes no sense," she protested. "How can untrained guerrilla bands expect to stand up against thousands of well-trained professional soldiers?"

Gabriel shrugged, the brim of his sombrero casting a deep shadow across his face. "If it was your land stolen from you, *Señora,* would you fight?" he asked quietly.

Margarite flushed, annoyed. "The Mexican people asked Emperor Maximilian to take the crown of Mexico," she objected. "They sent signed petitions."

A faint smile touched the impassive face. "The French soldiers came to our villages and fired their cannon into our walls. The people were forced to sign, many not even knowing what they were signing. Most put their marks, unable to write their names. Others—landowners, churchmen—signed because President Juárez had taken away their privileges, giving the church and the land back to the people, to Indians like himself."

Was it possible? Margarite wondered uneasily. Had the petitions been only a hoax? Well, even if it were true, she was sure that Maximilian had not known of the deceit practiced upon him by Napoleon when he accepted the throne of Mexico.

"Your President Juárez has fled Mexico," she said scornfully. "He's not even fighting beside you."

"Juárez sent his family to the United States," Gabriel said calmly. "Juárez would not leave. And when the French bayonets are gone, it is your Austrian emperor who will die."

A chill, like ice water, ran down Margarite's spine, even as she told herself firmly that it was not possible. Even if by some miracle Juárez should win, the mighty Hapsburg empire, the emperor Franz Josef himself would not allow any harm to come to a Hapsburg, to the emperor's own brother.

The mule train did not stop again until almost dark. Then they took shelter within the crumbling walls of an abandoned hacienda. Margarite did not join the *arrieros* after they had unloaded their mules and gathered for the evening meal. A cold meal, Hosea apologized when he brought her a plate of food. Don Patricio had ordered there would be no campfire that night.

Margarite had found a room in the small hacienda that for all its dirt floor actually had a bed of sorts. After making sure there were no scorpions lurking in the rope springs, she gratefully threw her blanket down upon it. A full moon cast a harsh silvery light through the window of the room and what she could see of the cold tortillas that Hosea had placed upon a dusty table did little for her appetite. She pushed the food away.

"You must eat," Hosea said, worried. "Nothing this morning and no food this evening. . ."

"Go and have your own meal, Hosea," Patrick said from the doorway. "I'll take care of the *señora*."

After the boy left, Patricio came into the room, jerking his chin toward the food. "Eat, Señora," he said flatly.

"I'm not hungry."

"I didn't ask you if you were hungry," he replied.

Anger turned her eyes a pure crystal green in the moonlight, her voice childishly defiant. "You can't make me eat," she cried.

"Oh, but I can," he said, his voice still quiet, only the indigo eyes holding a warning spark beneath the slashing black brows. "And you know that I can." He sighed softly. "Be sensible, Margarite. What good will it do to starve yourself to death?"

"Why should you care if I live or die?" she demanded. Then, tauntingly, "Or is it that dead, you'll receive no money for my return? That's what you're doing, isn't it, kidnapping me and holding me for ransom?"

He leaned back against the wall of the room, his arms crossed, considering her thoughtfully. "Who would pay for your ransom? Your uncle and aunt are dead. Do you have relatives in Austria? Would they pay for your return?"

No, Margarite thought, wincing, thinking of her stepmother. She remembered Elissa had been only too happy to ship her off to Mexico to her unsuspecting relatives.

At the girl's silence, Patrick continued. "How much value do you place on your life, Countess?" His glance swept over her appraisingly. "No doubt you wear clothes well and can speak several languages, but what other value do you have? Can you cook for a man, bear his children, warm his bed? Who would pay a ransom for you, Margarite?"

Margarite felt her cheeks flame, not sure whether she was angrier at his deriding her worth or at his implying that she had been lacking somehow when they had made love.

"The emperor Maximilian would pay for my return," she retorted impulsively, not sure whether it was true or not, but remembering the disturbing warmth in those pure blue eyes when they had looked at her that evening at Chapultapec.

Patrick smiled tightly. "Yes, I've heard Maximilian has a fondness for young, pretty girls. I've even heard that he has a special door into his sleeping quarters at Chapultapec where they are brought to him at night, from Carlota's ladies-in-waiting to young Indian girls. Did you go through that door, Niña?"

Margarite sprang to her feet, her small, slim body rigid with rage. "That's not true! Maximilian wouldn't . . . he couldn't—" She broke off bitterly. "But then, how could you possibly understand a man of Maximilian's kindness and nobility?''

''Is that the same kind and noble Maximilian who issued the Black Decree?'' Patrick asked jeeringly. ''Anyone found with arms or even suspected of being a Juarista, according to your emperor's law, will be automatically executed within twenty-four hours without the benefit of a trial.''

''Is the law so much worse than what Juarista bands like yours do to their victims?'' she demanded hotly. ''Were those three poor souls hanging in the trees last night given a trial?''

Patrick shook his head. ''The French troops that passed us yesterday stopped at the village. The mayor and his family gave them food and grain. After the French left, the guerrillas rode in and killed the mayor, his brother, and son, as punishment for helping the French.''

Not, he thought wearily, that that excused the senseless brutality on both sides. But what had bothered him even more than the guerrillas band's vicious cruelty was his discovery of the name of the leader of the band. It was El Cuchillo and his cutthroats who had ridden into the village and butchered the mayor and his family. That was why Patrick had ordered no campfires and put on extra guards this night.

Margarite was standing within a few inches of him, her body tensed, her head thrown back as she glared up at him, the moonlight limning the lovely features of her face. He suddenly remembered how they had stood together in the culvert, with the French troops riding by on the bridge overhead, how her body had fit firmly and sweetly against his, their heartbeats intermingled as if she were a part of him. Had that exquisitely curved little body fit as sweetly into Maximilian's arms, he wondered, the thought like a searing knife plunged into him. ''You haven't answered my question, *Señora*,'' he rasped. ''Did you use that little door into Maximilian's quarters?''

She gave a muffled gasp of fury. ''You know you were the first, God forgive me. For I'll never be able to forgive myself. Do you think I won't regret the rest of my life how you forced yourself upon me. I only wish I could forget. . . ."

"Do you?" he asked, his voice suddenly so menacing that, all at once frightened, she started to step away, but not quickly enough. His arm was around her, pulling her inexorably against him, his hand on her chin, forcing her head back so that she had a glimpse of his harsh dark face before his mouth descended swiftly on hers. She knew better now than to offer resistance. She forced herself to remain perfectly, coldly still, to allow his mouth to plunder hers ruthlessly. But there was nothing ruthless about his hand that had left her chin and was stroking her throat gently, then suddenly dipping down to circle and enclose one small breast.

Even through her shirt she could feel the burning warmth of that hand and suddenly, shockingly, it wasn't the man who was her enemy but her own treacherous body responding to that touch, as if it had a mind and will of its own. Recognizing the danger now, she tried to twist away from that seeking, caressing hand that was bringing her body to vibrant, throbbing life, a sharp urgent need building deep within her. The more she struggled, the tighter his arm encircled her, and neither the lips nor the hand ceased their knowing seduction. She felt her lips forced apart beneath the brutal pressure of that mouth, his tongue, hard and insistent, probing her mouth again and again, while the hand swiftly and skillfully undid the shirtfront.

"Don't!" she whispered against that bruising mouth, but if he heard her, he paid no attention. The hand slipped inside the shirt and boldly captured, then lazily pulled at the taut peak. It was only when the aching need throbbing within her, the overwhelming desire to hold him as tightly as he was holding her, was in complete possession of her, everything else mindlessly forgotten as her arms rose to encircle him, pull him closer, a soft moan of rapture starting deep in her throat . . . that he suddenly thrust her away from him. She stumbled and sat down on the edge of the makeshift bed.

"Lie to yourself if you want," he growled, his eyes glittering icily beneath the narrowed lids. "But don't ever lie to me, *poquita*. You gave yourself willingly. There was no force between us.''

Then he turned and strode from the room, Margarite staring after him blankly, her hands clutching the side of the bed to stop their trembling.

Chapter 15

I T was not the first pale ray of the sun creeping through the window that awakened Margarite the next morning. It was the sound of gunfire. The unmistakable thud of a rifle bullet ploughed into the crumbling adobe wall of the hacienda. Sharp explosions ripping through the cool gray morning brought her flying from the bed.

She was halfway through the bedroom door when Hosea appeared and thrust her back into the room. ''Stay inside, Niña, away from the window.''

''What is it? What's happening?'' Through the opened window that had only one shutter left she could see men on horseback, circling the house, brandishing rifles over their heads, bandarillas crossed over their breasts. They were shouting uproariously as they rode, occasionally sending a rifle shot in the direction of the hacienda almost as an afterthought.

''They're not soldiers,'' she said, bewildered.

Hosea shook his head. ''No, *Señora*. It's El Cuchillo. He and his men claim to be *Chinacos* but they don't fight for Juarez, only for themselves.''

''Why are they attacking us? What do they want?''

''The rifles.'' His young face looked suddenly old, his voice trembling with anger. ''They killed the night guards, Ramon and Tomas. They shot the bell mare and drove off the mules.''

Margarite remembered with a painful wrench that it was Ramon who had given her his sombrero to protect her from the sun. She clutched at the boy's arm. "Don Patricio?"

"He is alive, Niña." He pulled himself free, his voice once more steady. "I must go. Stay in the room. You'll be safe here."

But it wasn't only the rifles El Cuchillo wanted, Margarite discovered later that morning, when, unable to stay cowering in her room a moment longer, not knowing what was happening, she edged her way carefully through the door. The firing that had continued spasmodically all morning in ragged volleys had stopped almost completely.

She found Patricio and Gabriel in the small *sala* of the hacienda, crouched beneath the open windows, their rifles beside them.

When Patrick saw Margarite, he crossed to her side and yanked her down to the dusty, tiled floor. "Damn it, do you want to get yourself killed!"

She saw the blood on his shirtsleeve. "You're hurt!"

He frowned impatiently. "I thought Hosea told you to stay in your room."

"He did." Then, unable to keep the fear from her voice, she demanded, "Why don't you give them the rifles? They're not worth our lives."

Patrick smiled grimly. "They have the rifles. That's how I got this. . . ." He gestured toward the wound. "Trying to stop them from reaching the packs."

"Why? Why are they still here?"

As if in answer, she heard a man's voice call from outside the house. "Patricio, *compadre*, let us talk." Before Patrick could stop her, she had crawled to the window and lifted her head carefully to peer out. The man on horseback carrying a dirty white cloth on a lance was wearing a white sombrero with enormous amounts of gold braid wound around it. The sombrero was pushed back on the man's head and she could see his face. She would never forget the brutality in its features, or the almost obscene cheerfulness in the man's voice as he called out. "Give me the *niña*, Patricio. It is only fair. I

had her first. Surely by now you have tired of her
charms. And you and I, we will have a drink together and
talk over old times, *sí, compadre*?"

There was a sharp burst of gunfire from within the
house, so close to Margarite that she jumped and clutched
at Patrick, who had jerked her away from the window.
The smell of gunpowder burned, acrid in her nostrils.
The man on horseback swayed, then cursing wildly, he
fired off his gun at the house before, slumped forward in
his saddle, he raced away from the house.

Gabriel gazed sadly at his rifle, then at Patricio. "I
apologize, Patricio. I forgot, this rifle pulls to the right."

Margarite twisted free of Patrick's arm. "What did he
mean?" she demanded. "He had me first?"

When Patrick didn't answer, Gabriel said quietly,
"We found you in El Cuchillo's camp after he and his
carrion had killed your uncle and his vaqueros."

"But then, why . . . why did he leave me alongside
the road?"

"He didn't," Patrick said, his mouth quirking in a half
smile. "You might say Juan gave you up, under protest."

"You know him? He called you by name."

Patrick shrugged. "Juan Heras and I knew each other
years ago."

As if in angry response to their leader being shot, the
bandits suddenly burst out of the trees a short distance
from the hacienda and, screaming wildly, once again
began to ride around the house. Their sombrero brims
flapped in the wind, the manes and tails of their horses
flying, the earth seeming to shake under the pounding
hooves. They fired off their rifles almost haphazardly
toward the house, so that although a few bullets thudded
into the walls, others whined harmlessly overhead.

Nevertheless, Patrick thrust Margarite down to the
floor, sheltering her body with his own as he crouched
by the window, taking careful aim at the circling riders
before firing. Finally, when the more accurate rifle fire
of the *arrieros* from within the hacienda began to take its
toll, the guerrillas withdrew again to the trees, leaving
their comrades who had been shot off their horses to
scream in pain and rage, writhing on the ground. A few

managed to crawl off into the trees; the others finally grew still.

Patrick turned to Margarite. There was blood on her shirt, he saw, alarmed, then realized that it was his own blood from his arm when he had shoved her down onto the floor.

"Are you all right?"

She nodded, unable to speak. The muscles in her throat were so tight with fear that it hurt when she whispered, "It's me, isn't it? It's me they want."

Patrick scowled. "Not just you. Juan has an old grudge against me. He'll kill us all anyway."

"How much longer . . . before they . . . before we. . . ?" She could not force herself to put it into words.

"Before we run out of ammunition?" Patrick finished the sentence for her. "One, two days if we're careful. At least they didn't get our water and food." He suddenly smiled, a devil-may-care smile that set the indigo eyes to sparkling. "Don't worry, Countess. We've been in worse spots."

He acted almost as if he were enjoying himself, Margarite thought, exasperated. She was frozen with terror. At any moment she had expected one of those whining bullets to find its mark in her body. And what happened when they ran out of bullets and water?

Her gaze flew, panic-stricken, around the empty room. She could feel the hysteria rising in her throat like a silent scream. She didn't feel Patrick's hand gripping her arm, but his voice somehow penetrated the icy fog of her fear. "Hosea has been shot," he said. "He's in the back room with Madre and Julio. Would you stay with him?"

"Yes. Yes, of course." She forced the words past her trembling lips, her own fear forgotten for the moment in her concern for Hosea. Julio and Madre were at the back windows, talking calmly, passing a cigarillo back and forth between them, when she entered the room. Hosea lay in a corner, a blanket thrown over him. His eyes were closed and for one heartbreaking moment, she thought he was dead. A makeshift bandage had been bound around his chest and it was already stained red, but he smiled weakly at Margarite when she knelt down beside him. "Are you still angry with me, Niña?"

She shook her head, forcing herself to smile back at the boy. Hosea's lips were drained white, his face drawn with pain. "Don't talk." She saw the canteen beside him, and lifted it to his mouth, but his eyelids had already closed. She held the canteen to his lips and stroked his throat gently until he swallowed. She had no cloth to replace the bloody bandage. She cast Madre a despairing glance. "Isn't there anything we can do for him?"

The man shrugged. "We are all in the hands of God."

The *arriero* sounded almost indifferent to the boy's plight, but Margarite had already learned that the Indians accepted death with the same good-humored fatalism they accepted their hard poverty-stricken lives. And, after all, she thought bitterly, why not? Life was cheap in Mexico. What did one boy's life matter? There was nothing she could do except sit beside Hosea and hold his cold hands in hers, rubbing them between her own hands to warm them. Every now and then she wet her kerchief in the canteen of water and wiped the cold, clammy perspiration from the boy's face. The skin was childishly smooth. Had he even begun to shave yet? she wondered absently.

Finally, she realized by the boy's shallow breathing that he was unconscious. Perhaps it was for the best, she thought wearily, getting to her feet and stretching the stiffness from her cramped muscles. Unconscious, at least, Hosea wouldn't feel the pain.

She joined Madre at the window. It was almost sunset, the western horizon filled with lilac and gold clouds floating against the bright, clear blue of the sky, the sun sinking in a blaze of gold and crimson. "*Muy bonita, sí?*" Madre said proudly.

"Yes," Margarite answered, thinking that she had never seen such glorious sunsets anywhere else in the world as she had in Mexico. What a beautiful, yet savage land, she thought, shivering. It was impossible to believe that anyone could tame this country or its people.

She looked toward the trees. She couldn't see the

bandits, but she was sure they were there. As if guessing what she was thinking, Madre said, "They won't attack anymore tonight, Niña." He knew El Cuchillo's reputation. The man would deliberately prolong the siege until the defenders were forced to surrender. El Cuchillo didn't want dead men that would provide no enjoyment for him and his men and their knives.

Madre pulled some hard cheese from a sack, and taking his knife, sliced off a piece for Margarite. "Eat, Niña," he said, grinning. "There is courage in a full stomach."

Margarite forced herself to swallow the cheese and the two swallows of water that each *arriero* was allowed. Without Hosea to occupy her attention, she could feel the terror returning, her heart thudding in her chest. She suspected that that was why Patricio had sent her to sit beside the boy, to take her mind off the bandits waiting in the trees. Ashamed that the fear was clear in her eyes so that everyone could see what a coward she was, she slipped back to her room to huddle in the bed, the blanket wrapped around her. At last she drifted off into an exhausted sleep, only to jerk awake when the wind rose and rattled the dangling shutter at the window.

To her surprise, over the rattling sound she heard music, guitar music, faint but clear from the guerrilla camp. She sat up in bed, the blanket clutched around her, not to protect her from the chill night air but from a different sort of coldness, an iciness in the very marrow of her bones, making her shake convulsively.

"Margarite." Even before Patricio spoke, she was aware he had come quietly into the room, was standing beside the bed, watching her, although his face and body was shrouded in darkness. He was holding something out to her, a canteen. "There is some pulque left. It will help you sleep."

She lifted the canteen to her lips. Although she disliked the taste of the liquor made from the maguey plant, this night she welcomed the pulque's burning sensation down her throat, spreading its warmth through her body.

She gestured toward the window, the music still drifting into the room, a lovely poignant melody. "What is that song they're playing?"

Patrick hesitated a moment, then said, "I don't know." But of course, he did know. It was the "Diana," the tune Mexicans played at their military victories . . . and at executions. "Try to sleep," he said harshly, starting to turn away.

She reached out and touched his arm. He could feel the coldness of that hand through his shirtsleeve. "Don't go," she whispered. When he turned back, she had leaned forward so that her face was caught in the path of moonlight that fell across the bed. Her eyes were wide and shimmering with fear, her lips trembling. "They'll be back tomorrow, won't they?"

"Yes." He had lived too long with death as a young boy on the streets of Mexico, then during his years as a soldier in the Civil War in America, and this last year smuggling guns into Mexico. Death to him was no more than an old acquaintance whose face he knew well. But he could not bear to see Margarite's terror, and even harder to endure, the knowledge ripping him apart, that he was partly to blame for her being here, trapped in this hacienda with those jackals outside moving in for the kill.

She shivered suddenly and gave a plaintive sigh. "I'm so cold."

With a low, furious curse, Patrick pulled her, blanket and all, into his arms. She clung to him, then frantically pushed aside the blanket so she could feel the comforting warmth and hardness of his body pressed against hers as she burrowed like a frightened little animal into the dark safety of his arms. "I'm such a coward," she whispered. "I can't seem to stop shaking."

He smoothed the soft hair that swirled like a cap around her head, then cupped her face, the skin cool in his hands as he lifted her mouth to his. "*Callate, amor mio*," he ordered gently before his mouth descended upon hers. "Be quiet, my love."

She rested almost passively in his arms while his mouth stroked her lips with a languorous, feather-soft brushing movement, and his hands moved down the graceful line of her spine, molding her body closer against him. Then his mouth moved more insistently against hers and her lips parted with a sigh, her body no longer still, her hips moving sensuously beneath those caressing hands. She made no resistance as his hands swiftly removed her shirt and trousers and lowered her upon the bed, his own clothes quickly following hers to the floor.

When he laid down beside her and gathered her in his arms, her body no longer felt cold to his touch. In the moonlight her pale skin was gilded with silver, but her flesh was warm and vibrantly alive, turning a rosy pink wherever his stroking hands touched. Her mouth sought his blindly, urgently, as she turned in his arms to fit her body more easily against his hardness. But it was not like the last time at the hotel in Querétaro when he had taken her quickly, the rapture she had felt hardly begun when it had ended all too soon. This time all his movements, his caresses, his tongue teasing her breast to hardness, his lips trailing over the length of her body, were slow, deliberate, as if they had all the time in the world, as if he could continue to prolong the pleasure he was bringing her indefinitely.

She could not begin to know his own agony at postponing his own almost overwhelming desire for fulfillment. He groaned softly to himself at the hot, throbbing pain, the relief denied him, but knew that the deeper, the more prolonged her desire, the longer he could banish that look of terror from her eyes, keep her from remembering the horror that the morning would bring.

Then his hand slipped down to find that she was as ready for him as he was for her. She whispered, "Please . . . please . . . ," her body arching beneath him, her hands sliding down his chest over the flat hard stomach to find at last what she was seeking. At the touch of those hands shyly then more boldly caressing, he knew he could no more wait any longer than she could. He slid her beneath him, her body open and eager for him as he took possession in one swift, deep thrust, his mouth covering hers quickly to smother the low cry that leaped to her lips.

Then he lifted his head and looked down into her face, the green eyes blurred with desire, the soft, delicate lines of her face stiffened with passion, but with no trace of fear left, no trace at all.

"*Querida,*" he said thickly. "My love, my soul."

She smiled, a smile like a benediction as she tightened her muscles against the hardness inside of her. Her body arched, her hips moving beneath him as slowly, rhythmically, he began to deepen the hard, driving strokes until Margarite felt as if she could not endure the twisting, aching desire building within her a moment longer, nor endure for it to end. Her world had narrowed down to this room, to this bed, to this man who was becoming part of her. Only this fragile moment existed, all else forgotten. She felt the shuddering explosion within her at the same moment that Patrick thrust one last time deeply within her and found his own release.

For several moments he remained quietly within her, as if neither could bear to part, his lips lazily kissing away the salty tears from her thick, tangled lashes, his hands smoothing the damp curls back from her forehead.

Gradually she became aware that the music had stopped playing as night sounds crept into the room, a bird calling sleepily, cicadas chirping in the leaves. She could see Patrick's face above hers clearly in the moonlight, the dark beginnings of a beard along the strong chin, the tenderness and adoration in the indigo eyes, even the faded but still angry red mark on his face from her whip. She touched the scar with her fingertip, as if trying to erase it, her voice filled with self-reproach, "I am so sorry, *amado mio.*"

He grinned suddenly, and rolled away from her, but still cradling her in his arms. "That's not the first time you marked me," he teased, taking her hand and drawing it down to his shoulder, where she could feel the slight indentation of a scar.

At first she didn't understand, then all at once remembered the bandits' attack on the *diligencia* when she had first arrived in Mexico. "You were the man on the sorrel horse!"

"And you were the little spitfire who grabbed the

lieutenant's gun and shot me. I'm fortunate that you're a rotten marksman, *poquita*."

"I didn't mean to shoot," she protested. "I was trying to stop the lieutenant from shooting. Your men would have killed him, wouldn't they?"

"Yes." At her instinctive recoil, his arms tightened, pulling her back into his embrace, his voice sober. "There's nothing pretty or heroic about war, *querida*. You kill or be killed. It's that simple." He smiled grimly. "I should have killed Juan back at his camp that day I found you there." But it was his Irish softness that had ruled him that day, remembering that Juan and he had been friends as children on the Cordoba rancho, so that he had shot the man in the wrist instead of through the heart.

"Do you know El Cuchillo well?" she asked curiously.

He hesitated a moment, then said slowly, "We grew up together on a ranch."

"You own a ranch?" she asked, startled.

He laughed. "No, my sweet. I'm not one of your rich *hacendados*. All I own in the world are the clothes on my back and a small ranch in Texas that I won in a poker game."

"I don't understand," Margarite said, puzzled. "You're Mexican and yet you fought in the American Civil War? You risk your life smuggling guns for the Juaristas, yet your real name is O'Malley?"

"How did you know that?" Patrick asked, slanting a dark eyebrow at her, his hand for a moment stopping its slow, drifting caressing of the small body cuddled in his arms.

"In the hotel room," she said. "The man who was killed called you that, remember? How did you come by an Irish name like O'Malley?"

For a moment she thought he wasn't going to answer her, then he said, "My father was an Irishman, a fortune hunter who came to Mexico to look for a gold mine. Instead, he married my mother, an Indian from Michoacan, and lost everything in a gold mine that had no gold." He smiled wryly. "But Patrick O'Malley never stopped looking and never gave up hope. He was always

convinced that next month or next year he'd find his
fortune, dragging my mother and me from one mining
camp to another."

Despite the cynical twist to his mouth when he spoke
of his father, Margarite could sense the deep affection
the half-Indian son must have had for his eternally opti-
mistic, foolhardy father.

"What happened to your parents?"

Patrick's voice hardened. "My father was killed in
the Mexican War in forty-six. Mother died a year later.
By then I'd become a *lepero* on the streets of Mexico,
stealing the food to keep us both alive."

Now it was Margarite who wanted to wipe the unhappy memories from those dark, indigo-shaded eyes.
She lifted her head to kiss the narrowed lips, the muscle
clenched along the jaw, her hands running lightly over
the dark curly mass of hair on the muscular chest. Then
she took his hand and placed it on her breast, removing
her lips an inch from his as she murmured, smiling
teasingly, "I'm growing cold again."

A sudden volley of gunshots from the bandit camp
split the night, and Margarite stiffened in Patrick's arms
even as she lowered her eyelids swiftly so that he couldn't
see the fear there.

His hand stroked her hair soothingly. "Don't be afraid,
querida. They won't attack tonight." The gunshots, he
knew, were just El Cuchillo's way of making sure the
defenders in the hacienda slept badly.

"I'm not afraid," she protested, then knowing she
could not lie to him, smiled faintly. "Yes, I am, but not
of dying." It was the thought of being at the mercy of
that man with the cruel, smashed face that froze her
blood with horror.

As if guessing at once what she was thinking, Patrick's
arms pulled her closer, as he said quietly, "I'll never let
him hurt you, *querida*. You know that, don't you?"

She knew what he meant, that a bullet from Patrick's
gun would find her before Juan Heras could touch her.
She sighed, relieved, and felt his hands once more move
lightly over her body, finding the dark, silken hair beneath the slight, soft curve of her stomach, the fingers

stroking the inner softness of her thighs, moving upward to the even more tempting softness between. As thrusts of pleasure shot through her stomach, and desire leaped again inside of her, she forgot El Cuchillo and tomorrow and everything else but her need and love for this man.

Perhaps because they both knew this might be the only night they would have, their lovemaking took on a bittersweet intensity, passion flaring like a wildfire between them, consuming them, so that at the last moment, looking up into that hard, driven face above hers, feeling Patrick moving inside of her, Margarite felt herself lifted to a height of ecstasy, a happiness so complete, that it was like a small death, and no other deaths could possibly matter. Afterward, exhausted, she fell contentedly asleep in his arms.

Gunshots awoke her again the next morning. Instantly she reached out for Patrick, but the bed was empty. She got to her feet, and taking what water was left in her canteen, she cleaned herself as best she could before she carefully pulled on the shirt and trousers. As if she were preparing to meet a lover, she thought, running her fingers through her hair, trying to put it into some semblance of order.

There was, as usual in any Mexican bedroom, a small niche in the wall where a statue of the Virgin Mary had once stood, but was now deserted. Margarite paused a moment before the niche, then kneeling, crossed herself, her lips moving in silent prayer.

The gunshots were louder, closer now. Margarite lifted her head and rose, puzzled, to her feet. The gunshots sounded different. The bandits had been using American Springfield rifles; the gunfire she was hearing now was not so sharp, more of a muffled explosion.

She went to the window, and watched, amazed, the *banditos* riding away in a panic back into the trees, as troopers in kepis, dark blue tunics, and red trousers, firing carbines, chased after them.

She turned to see Patrick standing in the doorway, his smile wry. "It seems we've been saved by the French." Which, he thought grimly, was a little like jumping from the frying pan into the fire, avoiding death from El Cuchillo's bullets only to stand before a French firing squad. At least, though, Margarite would be safe. For one brief second he allowed his gaze to fasten upon the small, lovely face lifted to his, as if impressing it forever, feature by feature, in his mind, then he said abruptly, turning his back upon her, "Well, shall we go meet our deliverers?"

Startled, Margarite stared after him. She had almost run into his arms, but the coldness of his voice, the Indian blankness that had suddenly masked his face, had stopped her.

When the French sergeant strode into the small *sala* of the hacienda fifteen minutes later, his gaze swiftly took in the small weary group of men gathered there. If he were startled to see a young woman dressed in men's clothes in the gathering, his face carefully displayed no surprise, as he introduced himself crisply, "Sergeant Louis Carpentier, Third Company, First Regiment, the Foreign Legion, regularly stationed at Chihuahua."

Patrick gazed at the man thoughtfully. "You're a long way from your post, Sergeant."

A flush turned the sergeant's face, already deeply tanned by his previous military duty in Algeria, even ruddier. The sergeant, like the other men in his regiment, had been delighted with the news that they had been ordered by Marshal Bazaine to withdraw from Chihuahua and move south, hopefully to return to France. Nevertheless, it galled him, a proud French legionnaire, who would die before admitting defeat, to retreat before an enemy.

Not, he thought, annoyed, that the Juaristas ever stood and fought. You could search for them for days and then when you least expected it, a band of guerrillas, wildly yelling, would suddenly appear out of the barrancas or hills, decimate a troop, then just as swiftly vanish before the legionnaires could even put up a battle. The same way the regiment occupied a village, enforced the people's loyalty to the emperor, always knowing that the minute they withdrew, the Juaristas would once again take over the town.

Well, it was none of this Mexican's concern, the regiment's withdrawal, he decided, giving Patrick a stern glance as he gestured around him. "I want to know what's happened here and your name and business."

"We are *arrieros*," Patrick said placidly. "The men who attacked us stole our mules and packs. *Gracias Dios*, you chanced by."

The other men in the *sala* might be mule packers, the sergeant thought shrewdly, but there was something about their leader that didn't ring true for all his docile air. "What is your name, *Señor*?" he asked suspiciously.

Before Patrick could answer, Margarite, who had been kneeling beside Hosea, relieved to discover he was still breathing, even if his chest hardly moved, rose quickly to her feet. "May I introduce myself, Sergeant? I am the countess Margarite Juliana Von Melk." She smiled graciously at the sergeant. "And I want to add my thanks for your saving us from those bandits."

The name registered at once. Even miles away from the capital, the sergeant had heard of the murder of the Ortiz family, the disappearance of the niece, the Countess Von Melk. The emperor himself had ordered an exhaustive hunt be made for the young woman, but after several weeks had passed and there had been no word on the whereabouts of the countess, not even the expected ransom note, the woman had been given up for dead.

Where had the countess been all this time? the sergeant wondered, giving the *arriero* a speculative glance, then turning his gaze back to the young woman so outlandishly dressed in a man's shirt and trousers. Surely not traveling, dressed like that, with a troop of rough mule packers?

"The *señora* escaped before the bandits reached her carriage," Patrick interposed smoothly. "An Indian family found her and took her to the Convent of the Cross in Querétaro. Unfortunately, the shock had robbed the *señora* of her memory until only a few days ago. Then the good Sisters at the convent paid us to deliver the countess to her home in Mexico." He shrugged practically. "The money they paid us was very little and the city is not on our regular trade route. Perhaps the sergeant would be willing to take the *señora* off our hands and escort her the rest of the way to her home?''

The sergeant saw the shocked look that flooded the girl's face, as if the *arriero* had suddenly reached out and struck her. The sergeant grinned to himself. Well, the Mexican was a handsome greaser, for all that he was an Indian, and he supposed even a countess could stumble. He had no doubt the story of her spending all the time safely in a convent was a lie, but he was equally sure that the good Sisters would be paid well to back up the tale, to protect Countess Von Melk's reputation.

He bowed gravely to the woman, thinking happily what a coup it would be when he showed up in the capital with the countess. There might even be a reward in it for him and his men from a grateful family. ''It will be our pleasure to return you to your home, Countess.''

Margarite tried to catch Patrick's eye. How could he send her away like this with no more words between them, as if they were two strangers? Not after last night.

When the French sergeant stepped outside to see to a horse being saddled for her, she caught Patrick's sleeve, her voice, pleading, ''Patrick, I want to stay with you.''

''Do you fancy yourself as a *soldadera,* Countess?'' he drawled, amused. ''Do you know what a woman who follows the soldiers does? She sleeps with any man who will have her, has her baby in the dirt, then carries it on her back, with the chickens and the pigs on strings behind her. She washes clothes on rocks, cooks the food, then eats what's left after the men have finished. Is that what you want, Countess?''

Why was he doing this, Margarite wondered, bewildered. What had happened since last night? ''I don't care,'' she insisted stubbornly. ''I want to be with you.''

He shrugged impatiently. ''I don't want you with me,'' he said coldly.

''Last night . . .'' she said desperately. ''Last night you said . . .''

He laughed softly, almost sheepishly. ''A man will say and do many things, Countess, when he thinks it is his last night on earth.'' He glanced through the window at the sergeant returning and shrugged, his voice growing hard. "You can always tell Red Legs the truth about us if it will make you feel better."

Margarite felt her face grow hot then cold, an impotent fury whipping through her body, shaking her as if she stood in a high wind. Damn him! she thought helplessly. She would gladly turn him over to the sergeant as a Juarista, but that would mean the deaths of Hosea and the rest of the *arrieros*. And she was sure that Patrick knew that she couldn't bring herself to that betrayal.

The sergeant came in the door. "We're ready, Countess," he said, slapping the dust from his uniform with his hand. He turned to Patrick, frowning regretfully. "My men chased down some of those bandits, but I'm afraid that most of them and their leader got away."

Margarite knelt for a moment beside Hosea, placing a kiss on the closed eyelids. "*Vaya con Dios, niño,*" she whispered softly. Tears stung behind her eyes, but there was no sign of them on her face as she bid good-bye to the rest of the mule packers, carefully not looking at Patrick as she left the hacienda.

It was only after she mounted the horse the sergeant held for her that the searing grief swept over her, worse even than when her father had died. Her hands tightened on the rein. It took every ounce of strength she possessed to stop herself from jumping off the horse and running back into the hacienda, back into Patrick's arms.

Then, remembering her father, she could hear his gently chiding voice, "*Kopf hoch, liebchen.* A Von Melk always holds his head high."

Margarite straightened her shoulders, her back ramrod straight, and without a backward glance, she rode away from the hacienda.

Chapter 16

"**L**OOK, Countess! There, below you, is Cuernavaca."

The childlike pleasure in Doña Isobel's voice jogged Margarite from her half-sleeping state. They had left Mexico when the snow-capped peak of the volcano Popocatepetl had turned scarlet then gold in the first splintering rays of the sunrise. As the Ortiz carriage had made its long, slow ascent into the pine-forested mountains between Mexico and the valley of Cuernavaca, she had tried to stay awake, but gradually her eyelids had grown heavy and she had lapsed into the listlessness that never seemed to leave her these days.

At least, she thought, twisting her body to find a more comfortable position against the cushions of the carriage, she didn't feel as wretched as when the French legionnaires had deposited her at the Ortiz home in Mexico two months before. That morning, as hands had helped her dismount from her horse, her face had been flushed and feverish and she had to be carried into the house. The servants still living in her uncle's *casa* had crowded incredulously around her, murmuring of miracles and crossing themselves as if she had, in fact, risen from the dead. Every bone in her body aching, all she could remember was thinking, surprised, that it was true after all. One could sicken and die from a broken heart.

Except she hadn't died. She had been racked with painful chills and fever, drifting in and out of consciousness for two weeks. When she had finally fully awakened, drenched in perspiration, Doña Isobel had been sitting beside her bed.

"*Gracias Dios*," the woman had smiled down at her, relieved. "The fever has broken. You will be better soon now, Countess." She brought Margarite a glass of chilled orangeade, which her patient drank greedily.

"I've been ill?" Margarite asked, glancing around her, recognizing the French furniture and the bedroom as the one that had been hers when she had lived at the Ortiz house before.

"And no wonder," her companion murmured, her round, olive-skinned face sympathetic, "after the terrible ordeal you've been through. First, those bloodthirsty *banditos* murdering Don Manuel and Doña Josefa, then losing your memory and traveling with rough *arrieros*, then being attacked by more *banditos*. The doctors say it's God's mercy that you survived at all."

So it *had* happened, Margarite thought wearily; it hadn't just been a product of a feverish mind. Not only the attack on her uncle's carriage and living with the mule packers, but lying in Patrick's arms, the tenderness in his face as he had made love to her. And the most bitter memory of all, the cold indifference in that same face as he had sent her away with the French legionnaires. Scalding waves of humiliation washed over her, remembering those last moments with him, the pain in the wounded green eyes so intense that Doña Isobel leaned over her patient anxiously. "Try and sleep now, child. Rest is what you need. Don Francisco is waiting to see you, but he can come back another day."

Margarite closed her eyes and gratefully felt sleep pulling at her, banishing memories. How unfortunate that you didn't die from heartbreak, after all, she thought, and, who was Don Francisco? before sleep relentlessly pulled her under.

Don Francisco, it turned out three days later when Margarite, propped up with pillows, was able to receive visitors, was the administrator of her uncle's vast estate . . . her estate now, Margarite learned to her surprise.

"Surely, there are other, closer relatives," she protested, more alarmed than pleased at the prospect of her uncle's wealth and the responsibilities for that wealth being dropped in her lap. "Don't I have a cousin, Salvador?"

Don Francisco seemed surprised that she knew about her cousin. "I wouldn't have thought your uncle ever mentioned his name. Unlike his older brother, Salvador was always at odds with his father. Don Manuel sent him to Spain to school and he returned with all sorts of new liberal ideas that are so popular among the young in Europe today, then he ran off and joined the Republican Army of General Salazar."

"His father's estate should still belong to Salvador," Margarite said.

Don Francisco, white-haired with a strong aquiline nose, frowned at the girl's protests. "Don Manuel disowned his son and anyway, there is a question whether or not Salvador is still alive. I've heard that he was one of the officers captured with General Salazar and executed along with the general under the Black Decree." He shrugged. "In any case, a known Juarista has no standing in Mexican courts."

Don Francisco's face softened as he gazed at the girl, looking so small and forlorn in the large bed. Despite the peculiar short hair and the illness that made the remarkable green eyes seem enormous in the too thin face, there was still something about Doña Margarite that could stir the senses of even an old man like himself. Don Francisco took himself firmly in hand. The very first thing, he decided, he must find a suitable husband for the young woman, a man of mature years competent to look after the vast Ortiz estate and a young wife.

He glanced across the room at Doña Isobel, who, of course, very properly had not left the countess alone in the room with a man, but sat in a chair by the window, working at her embroidery, pretending not to hear the conversation by the bed. Silently Don Francisco commended himself for having found such a satisfactory *dueña* as Doña Isobel for his young charge. Señora Isobel Lopita Costello was a woman of impeccable character and family, even if the Costello family had fallen on hard times. Señora Costello's very presence in the Ortiz household would be enough to dispel any scandalous rumors that might cling to the young countess and her mysterious whereabouts these last weeks.

He turned his attention back to Margarite, discovering that the heavy black lashes had lowered, veiling her eyes, her thoughts obviously elsewhere, although she listened politely as Don Francisco quickly itemized the most valuable of the properties she would inherit, from the silver mine at Real del Monte to a sugar and coffee plantation near Cuernavaca. Finally, realizing that a young woman would be bored and confused by such matters, he smiled indulgently. "Well, now that's enough business for today. You mustn't worry about anything. All the necessary legal questions are being handled. All you need do is rest and recover your health, isn't that so, Doña Isobel?"

The *dueña* came quickly to the bedside, smiling in agreement, but the bright black eyes were troubled as they gazed down at the girl in the bed. It was normal, Doña Isobel told herself, that the girl should grieve for the deaths of her uncle and aunt, but as the weeks passed, despite the return of her health, Margarite continued to be sunk in a curious apathy, and Doña Isobel became uneasy. After all, the girl could not have known her uncle and aunt all that well, and, although Doña Isobel wouldn't have spoken such a disloyal thought aloud, neither Don Manuel nor his sister, Josefa, struck Isobel as the types to inspire deep affection in their niece or unending remorse at their deaths.

It was the *dueña* who, finally, at her wit's end at what to do to arouse the young woman from her withdrawn sadness, suggested that she and the countess move to the Ortiz villa outside of Cuernavaca for a few months. "The weather is much more agreeable in the warm country," she said temptingly. "And since Don Maximiliano has refurbished the Borda *quinta* at Cuernavaca, many fashionable people have moved there and a quite gay social season has developed."

"How far is Cuernavaca?" Margarite asked, not really caring but not wanting to hurt Isobel's feelings by cutting off the conversation.

"Only seventy-five kilometers, a day's journey." Then,

quickly, thinking the girl might be afraid after her terrible experience, "And one doesn't have to worry about bandit attacks. With the emperor and empress staying so often at La Borda, the road between Mexico and Cuernavaca is constantly patrolled by Colonel Lamadrid's municipal guard."

Margarite had finally agreed to the move to the Ortiz country villa because it was easier than disagreeing, just as now she obediently looked out the carriage window. The carriage was rounding a curve in the road, and through a break in the dark green pines she could see far below, as if caught in a golden bowl, a sun-splashed green valley and, in its midst, the rooftops and church spires of Cuernavaca.

When the carriage began its descent into the valley, she began to feel a difference in the air, a soft, moist warmth after the clear, crisp air of Mexico City's high plateau. A fragrance from orange and banana and lemon trees, along with rich semi-tropical growth drifted through the open windows of the carriage as they left the dark pines behind. When the carriage stopped at the post house of Las Tres Marias to rest the horses, Margarite removed her shawl before she stepped down from the carriage. Lifting her face like a sunflower to the sunlight, the odd, tight feeling in her chest began to loosen slowly.

There was a meadow and groves of fruit trees near the post house. Feeling a need to stretch her legs, Margarite walked across the road toward the meadow, the hem of her black skirt trailing over trimmed meadow grass. The mourning gown she wore all at once felt too heavy, as if it were making it difficult for her to breathe. It was the Mexican custom, she knew, to wear white as mourning during the hot months. She would switch to white, she decided, when they reached the Ortiz villa. It was the first decision she had made on her own in weeks, and she turned, feeling suddenly vaguely triumphant, back toward the road.

The carriages rumbling down the road toward the post house announced their approach, and Margarite stepped back safely away from the road and the clouds of dust the carriages stirred up as they passed. She caught a swift glimpse of a bodyguard of Austrian Hussars, twelve plumed and blue-velvet-harnessed white mules, their bells jingling, pulling an obviously new carriage with the motto EQUITY AND JUSTICE painted below the imperial blazon on the door. She glimpsed a golden-bearded man in the carriage, and a young boy's face at the window, before the carriage and the long procession of other escort vehicles rapidly passed.

Doña Isobel quickly crossed the road to Margarite's side. "Are you all right?" she asked anxiously.

Margarite shook the dust from her black skirt. "Yes, of course."

Doña Isobel cast an annoyed glance after the procession of rapidly disappearing vehicles, then said, her voice lightly malicious, "Don Maximiliano must be in a hurry to visit his Indian mistress at La Borda."

And was startled when Margarite whirled upon her furiously. "I won't listen to backstairs gossip about the emperor!"

Doña Isobel flushed. "But, Countess . . ."

"And don't call me Countess!" Then, ashamed of her outburst, because she had grown fond of her good-natured companion these last weeks, she smiled coaxingly. "Surely, we know each other well enough by now for you to call me Margarite."

"As you wish, Count—Margarite," the woman said stiffly.

Margarite gazed after the carriages, now only a cloud of dust disappearing down the hill, her voice puzzled. "I could have sworn I saw a child in the emperor's carriage."

Doña Isobel had too sunny a disposition to carry a grudge for more than a minute. "That would be Prince Agustin de Iturbide, the emperor's heir," she said, and then, her eyes sparkling happily at the chance to gossip, "At least, that's what he's being called. Actually the boy's a grandson of the last emperor of Mexico, Agustin de Iturbide, who reigned for less than a year over forty years ago. The boy's mother is a commoner, an American woman, that Maximilian bought off, along with the rest of the Iturbide family, so that he could bring the child into his household and train him as his successor."

"What of the empress Carlota?" Margarite asked, shocked. "Surely she can't be happy, accepting another woman's child."

Their carriage was ready and the conversation was discontinued while the two women climbed back inside and adjusted their voluminous skirts to the close quarters, before Doña Isobel shrugged and said practically, "I don't suppose Carlota was pleased with having the boy foisted upon her, but what could she do about it? The emperor must have a successor and everyone knows the empress is barren. And even if she weren't, she and Don Maximiliano never share the same bed."

At the warning look in Margarite's face, she added hastily, "And that's not gossip, it's the truth. One of the ladies-in-waiting at the court is a dear friend of mine. She told me that not only do the emperor and empress never share the same apartment at Chapultepec or La Borda, but when they travel together, the emperor always carries along his own cot." Her voice dropped to a hushed whisper. "It's said that Carlota discovered her husband in some infidelity years ago. The empress is very proud and never forgave her husband or permitted him back into her bed again."

Doña Isobel sighed. "Poor Doña Carlota. How painful it must be for her. Sometimes I think it is a mistake for a woman to have too much pride."

Margarite winced. And a worse mistake, she thought bitterly, remembering how she had begged Patrick to take her with him, for a woman to have no pride! And then realized, startled, that it was almost a half hour since she had thought of Patrick, who had tormented her every waking thought these last months.

With an almost physical effort she tore her thoughts away from that crumbling hacienda where she had last seen Patrick, and concentrated her attention on the passing scene outside the carriage, the neat white haciendas behind groves of flowering trees, the chimney of a sugar mill, rich pasturelands, and everywhere she looked, flowers and sunshine. She would forget Patrick O'Malley, she told herself fiercely. Somehow she would make herself forget him. Then realized, her spirits lifting a little, that for the first time she was, at least, accepting the possibility that she *could* forget him.

When the carriage reached the Ortiz villa a few miles southwest of Cuernavaca, her spirits lifted even higher. Although the walled villa was smaller than the Ortiz home in Mexico, it had a charm all its own. The graceful arched gateway into the cobblestoned courtyard, the open, spacious rooms, were filled with sunlight and sparkling clean, unlike the dark, often dust-coated rooms of the hacienda in Mexico City. The bedroom to which Margarite was shown had a tiled floor, freshly cut flowers, and the furniture, obviously of local origin, was simple but comfortable.

From one window of the room she could view the blue-tinged Tres Marias mountains in the distance, and from the other, a patio, the flower beds filled with star lilies, tuberoses, pinks, and climbing roses. A pool in the center of the patio reflected the pink clouds overhead, and the soft murmur of a fountain was almost drowned out by the song of a golden warbler and a raucous purple and gold parrot. A snow-white flamingo walked in stately dignity beside the reflecting pool.

Margarite stood by the window, lifting her face to the sun as she had done earlier at the post house, as if its rays were reaching inside her, melting an icy core at the very center of her being. A young servant girl, with a shy smile and a neat, clean dress, helped her change from her travel-stained gown to a white muslin dress trimmed with black ribbon at the throat and waist. Then Margarite went down into the main *sala* to meet the villa's overseer, Don Pedro, a short, stocky man with a grave, courteous manner, and his wife, Doña Delores, the villa's housekeeper. Only a few minutes' conversation with the housekeeper, and Margarite knew by the woman's brisk, competent air that it was Doña Delores who took pride in keeping the villa in perfect order.

Talking with the overseer, she discovered that the villa was only part of the Ortiz holdings here at Cuernavaca. There were coffee and sugar fields, a refinery, ranch land, and a complete village, where over three hundred Indian plantation workers and their families lived; even a store from which the workers bought food and clothing, all belonging to the Ortiz family. All belonging to her now, Margarite thought suddenly, incredulously.

To her own surprise, she heard herself asking Don Pedro if he would show her around the estate the next day. He nodded graciously, "Of course, if the *señora* wishes. But it will be hot and dusty," he warned, "and will take all day."

Doña Isobel gave Margarite an anxious look. "Are you sure you shouldn't wait a few days, Margarite, until you're stronger?"

"Tomorrow," Margarite said firmly.

When she awoke early the next morning, the familiar dark depression was there sitting on her chest. Even before she opened her eyes she was aware of a sense of loss like a keening inside of her so that for a moment all she wanted to do was curl up in an anguished ball, hugging her pain to her. But this morning she did not allow the pain to rule her; she forced herself out of bed and without bothering to ring for her maid dressed in her voluminous riding skirt and jacket of dark green merino, with a bit of white muslin shirtwaist showing at the collar, and adjusted the veil of her small, dark green hat over her face.

The horse that Don Pedro had waiting for her had obviously been chosen for his gentle nature. He stood patiently as Margarite swung herself onto the lady's saddle, her riding skirt falling gracefully around her as she hooked her knee over the saddle horn, pushing aside the sudden sharp memory of her little mustang that she had ridden astride in a boy's trousers.

If only everything didn't remind her, she thought. As she forced herself to smile at Don Pedro and follow him, as he led the way from the small corral, she could feel the misery inside her. The ride was a mistake, she thought unhappily. She should have stayed at the hacienda. And then she felt an unexpected jolt of anger.

No! She was tired of feeling hurt and ashamed and

miserable, tired of hiding in her bed like a child pulling
the blanket over her head, as if by refusing to face the
truth of Patrick's callous treatment of her she could
somehow make it not real.

Anyway, it was too late to turn back to the hacienda
now, and gradually, in spite of herself, she found herself
listening, even asking questions as Don Pedro and she
rode by the sugar fields. The cane had been cut in
November, he explained. The next planting wouldn't be
till May. He showed her the sugar refinery, the tall,
white stone chimney spearing at the blue sky, the sweet
smell of molasses still hanging over the now empty tanks.
They rode through groves of banana and orange trees,
inspected the coffee mill where the heady fragrance of
newly milled and bagged coffee beans mingled with the
scent of trailing geraniums covering one wall of the mill.

Midday Don Pedro stopped at the plantation *tienda*
and bought the *señora* a straw sombrero in place of the
tiny bit of riding hat and veil she wore. She thanked him
gratefully. She had already removed the jacket of her
riding habit, but the sun was still uncomfortably warm
through the sheer muslin blouse and she could sympa-
thize with the workers who, when the noonday bell had
rung, had tilted their sombreros over their faces and
were sensibly taking siestas in the shade of whatever
trees were handy.

As they left the plantation store and rode past small
adobe huts where the Indian workers lived, children
playing in the dusty street as their mothers sat in front of
the huts, grinding the corn for the evening meal, Margarite asked curiously, "Do all the workers live here in the
village?"

"Of course," the overseer replied, surprised. "They
belong to the plantation. Where else would they live?"
He shrugged. "Besides, it is forbidden for them to leave.
They are all in debt to the *patrón,* debts their fathers and
grandfathers contracted before them, buying food and
clothing from the *tienda.* If they should try to run away,
the law would only bring them back."

"I thought Emperor Maximilian had abolished peonage."

"It was the empress Carlota's idea," Don Pedro corrected her. "And a foolish law it is, too, impossible to enforce. Oh, there were some landowners who allowed their workers to leave, but in a few weeks they were back, starving, unable to find jobs elsewhere, blaming the empress for their misery." He sighed philosophically. "Ah, well, Doña Carlota is a foreigner like her husband. They do not understand the Indians, who want nothing more from life than to work as little as possible, have some food for their families, and enough pulque to drink. What would they do with freedom?"

Margarite remembered, as a child living in Washington with her diplomat father, that much the same thing had been said about the black slaves in America. She glanced at the open, friendly faces of the Indian women, their dark eyes following her curiously as she rode beside the overseer. At least, she thought, the village was much cleaner and more prosperous-looking than the Indian villages she had seen when she had ridden with the mule train. Thinking of the mule train, though, reminded her of the Indian *arrieros,* their fierce independence, pride, and courage. They would never be content with a peon's lot, enslaved for life on a plantation, she thought. Nor did it sit well with her, the knowledge that with her uncle's death the Indian laborers on the plantation were enslaved now to *her.*

"Would it be possible for me to cancel the debts of the workers?" she asked Don Pedro.

The overseer gave her a shocked glance. "But why should you, Doña Margarite? The workers are happy enough. We've never had any trouble here on the Ortiz plantation."

"But is it possible?" Margarite asked stubbornly.

"It would cost a great deal of money," he said uneasily. "And with the war hurting the sale of our sugar, our profits are little enough these last years. In any case," he said firmly, "it is not a decision I can make. You must speak to Don Francisco." Eager to change from an uncomfortable subject, he said hastily, "We should be returning to the hacienda. Your *dueña* said particularly you were not to become overtired."

Margarite discovered she was tired by the time they

reached the hacienda, and a scolding Doña Isobel insisted that she go straight to bed. Still, it was a good tiredness, she thought, stretching, a physical aching in muscles too long unused to any activity. And that night she slept the whole night through without waking suddenly to stare dry-eyed into the darkness, reliving over and over again those last moments with Patrick, the icy indifference in his face, the almost amused contempt in his words as he had dismissed her.

After that first morning she went riding every day, quickly discarding the too heavy riding habit for Mexican riding attire—a woven cotton skirt, a comfortable white camisa tucked into its waist, and a straw sombrero. Since the overseer was too busy with his own duties to accompany her, he assigned two stalwart vaqueros to ride along with her whenever she took a horse from the stable.

Margarite studied the two grinning young men, evidently delighted with their assignment of protecting the young, beautiful *señora*, great pistols stuck in their belts. "Is it necessary?" she asked the overseer, preferring to ride alone. "After all, with the emperor so often in residence at Cuernavaca, surely this area is well protected from bandits."

Not wanting to alarm the girl, Don Pedro decided not to tell her that even here in Cuernavaca, an imperialist stronghold, each time the emperor or empress left La Borda, French soldiers were always sent ahead to sweep the roads and make sure the way was safe for Their Majesties. "You might be thrown from your horse," he said instead, and added firmly, "And, of course, it is not proper for a young woman to ride alone."

There was no question of her *dueña* riding with her, Margarite knew. Doña Isobel was terrified of horses and grew faint at even the thought of riding one.

So each day when she took her ride around the estate, the two vaqueros trailed at a respectful distance behind her but close enough to make sure that no harm fell upon the young *señora*. After the third day's ride, Margarite refused the patient mount Don Pedro had chosen for her. She selected instead from the stable a more spirited black mare with a white blaze and mouth, named Pico Blanco, who, she quickly discovered, loved to gallop and had to be kept firmly in hand as she and her escort cantered over the fields and meadows of the estate.

At first, the vaqueros were nervous, watching the small woman on the back of the powerful mare, but they soon relaxed when they realized that she was easily able to control the horse. Sometimes, mischievously, Margarite would allow Pico Blanco her head. She enjoyed the feel of the mare lengthening her step, stretching out happily into a gallop while the wind blew into her face and, behind her, she could hear the hoofbeats of the horses of the vaqueros, their whoops and loud cries, as they tried in vain to catch up with her.

It was when she was galloping Pico Blanco one morning over a dirt road that ran along one edge of the Cordoba rancho, the horses of her escort pounding behind her, that she became aware of another riding party on the road. The dust thrown up by the hooves of the horses hid the riders from view, but as Margarite checked her horse to a halt, she could make out a small detachment of Austrian Hussars advancing toward her. Two of the Hussars had drawn their swords as they cantered toward her. The leader drew up alongside Margarite, and with a quick glance at the two glowering vaqueros behind her, said in French, "I am sorry, *Señora*, but we must ask you to identify yourself."

Margarite answered in German, "I am the Countess Von Melk." She gestured toward the two vaqueros, whose hands were resting, she noticed, close to their pistols. "And these are vaqueros from the Ortiz Ranch, where I live."

"Countess!" A man in a gray charro costume, a white and silver sombrero covering his golden hair, rode forward. The Hussars parted quickly before the white Arab charger.

Almost at sound of that familiar voice, Margarite slid off her horse and dipped in a deep curtsy. "Your Majesty," she said, startled.

Maximilian had dismounted almost as quickly as she had and now reached out a long aristocratic hand to pull her to her feet. He was smiling, his dazzling blue eyes sparkling with pleasure as he studied the young woman standing before him. "It's a great pleasure to see you again, Countess, and looking so well. The empress and I were desolate when we heard of your misfortune. The deaths of your uncle and aunt must have been a terrible loss to you, as they were to all of us. We were much relieved to hear that with God's providence, you, at least, had been spared." The warm blue gaze flicked swiftly over Margarite's small trim figure, then back to her face. "We heard you were in seclusion or we would, of course, have offered our condolences in person."

"Thank you, Your Majesty," she said, aware of the magnetic charm of the man reaching out to her, even as she thought: How tired he looks. There were lines around the bright blue eyes that had not been there the last time she had seen him at Chapultapec, and she noticed he had developed a nervous habit of twisting at one of the points of his beard.

With his innate tact, Maximilian quickly changed the subject. "I must apologize for my Hussars interrupting your ride, Countess. They take their responsibilities of guarding me too seriously, I'm afraid." His appreciative gaze ran knowledgeably over Pico Blanco. "What a splendid mount. And you ride her beautifully."

He turned and smiled down at Margarite. "I believe you feel as I do about riding, Countess, to walk one's horse is death, to trot is life, but to gallop is bliss." Then, almost as if they were sharing a secret between them, he leaned toward her and said softly, "It is not given to some of us to ride slowly, is it, Doña Margarite?" Then, before she could answer, he stepped back briskly. "But we mustn't keep you from your ride any longer. The empress and I will be looking forward to seeing you at La Borda, now that you have recovered from your terrible ordeal."

He had remounted his horse before his aides could assist him. Margarite saw that the two men who had held their horses to one side as she and the emperor spoke now fell into place, cantering a short distance behind as the Hussars once more closed rank around

Maximilian. There had been a cynical smile, she had
noticed on the blond mustached and sideburned face of
one of the officers that made her feel an instant aversion
to the man.

Her dislike would have been even stronger if she had
heard the baron von Muller turn to his fellow officer and
say with an amused smirk, "Another conquest for Maximilian, wouldn't you say? How long do you think it will
take before the countess goes through the little door?"

As it was, Margarite felt only a rather pleasant excitement as she mounted her own horse and spurred Pico
Blanco away from the road and across the pastureland.
Pico Blanco, who never liked standing, instantly responded to the pressure of her legs, shifting from a
canter to a gallop, her legs stretching out beneath her.
Was the emperor still watching her? Margarite wondered, and then knew that, of course, he wasn't. The
royal party was well out of sight by now. And it was
foolish racing Pico this way over rough ground, she told
herself, at the same moment she felt the horse stumble.

Although Pico quickly recovered her stride, Margarite
could tell she was favoring her right leg. Quickly she
halted the horse and was speaking soothingly to the
trembling mare, when the vaqueros joined her.

"She's not badly hurt, is she?" If only she had not
tried to show off before Maximilian, urging Pico into the
gallop, she thought, guilt-stricken, as the vaqueros examined the mare's leg.

Antonio, the older of the two vaqueros, shook his
head. "She cannot be ridden, though, not for several
days. Take my horse, *Señora*. I'll walk Pico back to the
stable."

Margarite glanced around her. They had ridden farther than usual that day and they must be miles from the
hacienda. "Isn't there someplace closer where Pico can
be taken?" she asked. "She shouldn't be walking on that
leg at all."

"The Cordoba hacienda isn't far. We're already on
their land. They have an excellent stable and I'm sure
would tend Pico until her leg has healed. Tomas can stay

with you, and I'll ride ahead to ask permission to use the stable."

"No," Margarite said. "It's my fault Pico hurt her leg. I'll ask permission of the Cordobas. You can show me the way."

There was something familiar about the Cordoba name, she thought as she mounted Tomas's horse and followed Antonio, while Tomas slowly led the injured Pico. She couldn't place where she'd heard the name before, though, until they reached the Cordoba hacienda. The soft-voiced Indian woman who answered the door went to fetch her mistress, while Antonio and Tomas went off to the stable.

Margarite immediately recognized the red-haired woman who walked briskly into the *sala* a few minutes later. It was the American woman she had met at the emperor's reception at Chapultapec.

Star held out both her hands to Margarite, a smile of greeting on her face. "How wonderful to see you again, Countess."

"I apologize for the intrusion, Señora Kelly," Margarite said ruefully. "My mare pulled up lame. If you could give Pico Blanco stable room for a few days rest and perhaps loan me a mount—"

"Of course," Star interrupted quickly. "Your horse is already being taken care of but, please, you mustn't rush off. I heard you were staying at the Ortiz plantation and had planned to visit you, but I wasn't sure that you had completely recovered from your"— there was only a moment's hesitation before she finished—"accident." She gestured toward the Indian servant who had returned to the room with a silver tray upon which sat a pitcher of fruit juice and several silver glasses, along with a plate of crisp sugary cakes. "You must, at least, rest and refresh yourself before leaving."

"I shouldn't stay," Margarite said, gazing regretfully at the frosty pitcher. "My *dueña* will be worried if I'm not back by noon."

"Well, then that's no problem at all," her hostess said cheerfully. "If you'll excuse me for a minute, I'll send one of the stable boys with a note to your *dueña*, explaining that you'll be visiting with me for a few hours. It'll give us a chance to get better acquainted.''

Without waiting for her guest to offer polite objections, Star strode gracefully from the *sala*. Taking off the straw sombrero and tossing it onto one of the comfortable chairs in the room, Margarite gazed curiously around her. The house was built in much the same style as the Ortiz hacienda, and the large room with the plump, colorful pillows, books and newspapers scattered in pleasing disorder, made her feel immediately at home.

As at the Ortiz hacienda, there were bowls of flowers everywhere. One particularly eye-catching arrangement of full-blown crimson roses sat on a table near Margarite, and as she bent closer to catch their spicy scent, she noticed several daguerrotypes in matching silver frames on the table.

One picture was of a young boy of ten or twelve in a charro costume; the other was a man who wore the uniform of an American officer in the Union Army. Despite the stiffly posed daguerrotype, the man had a relaxed air, his hand resting lightly on his sword hilt, a carefree smile on his handsome face. It was a smile that Margarite knew well. For it was Patrick's face staring up at her from the silver frame.

Chapter 17

"COUNTESS." A hand gently touched Margarite's arm, the voice with an undertone of concern. "Countess, is anything wrong?"

Margarite tore her gaze away from the daguerrotype. How long, she wondered, embarrassed, had she been standing there, staring like a ninny at Patrick's picture?

She took a deep breath, trying to calm the trembling inside of her before she turned to her hostess. "Nothing's wrong," she said, smiling with lips that felt strangely wooden. "And please call me Margarite."

"Only if you call me Star," her hostess agreed. Margarite could see the concern still caught in the gray eyes, as Señora Kelly poured a glass of fruit juice for her guest, then insisted she must sit down. "The weather in Cuernavaca is delightful, but it can take a bit of getting used to after the cool, rarefied air of Mexico City."

"Have you lived here long?" Margarite asked, to make conversation while she gathered her scattered wits. What was Patrick's picture doing here in the Cordoba hacienda? And what was he doing wearing an American Army officer's uniform?

"Almost twenty years," Star said, seating herself across from Margarite and sipping from her own glass of fruit juice. "Ever since my marriage to Don Miguel."

"But you're an American, aren't you? It must have been difficult giving up your own land, moving so far from home."

"Not difficult at all," Star said, smiling, a faint pink running along her cheekbones, the gray eyes softly glowing so that for a moment she looked Margarite's age. "Wherever my husband is is my home."

Yes, Margarite thought, remembering. That was how it had felt when she had been wrapped in Patrick's arms, as if she had, at last, come home. Then she winced at the pain that was never far away, as other humiliating memories intruded.

Star put down her glass and leaned forward, studying anxiously her young guest's unhappy face. "Are you sure you're all right, Margarite? I've heard what a terrifying experience you've been through. How fortunate for you that you were able to reach the safety of the convent at Querétaro."

"I was never at the convent," Margarite said impulsively, suddenly not wanting to lie to this woman. She had never felt able to talk openly of her experiences to Doña Isobel, who was so easily shocked, yet she felt a desperate need to talk to another woman, especially one

who seemed as open and caring as Doña Star. "A group
of mule packers rescued me from the camp where the
bandits had taken me. I—I had lost my memory. I didn't
even know my name. I traveled with the mule train for
several weeks." Her hands tightened together in her lap
as she spoke in a rush. "They . . . the *arrieros* were
very kind to me."

She would not, could not, talk of Don Patricio, even to
this woman who was listening sympathetically, her serene gray eyes undismayed as Margarite told how she
had dressed as a boy and lived and rode with the *arrieros*
as if she were one herself. Nor did the serenity of that
gaze falter, even when Margarite told how, after her
memory returned, she had discovered that the mule
packers were in fact gun smugglers, working with the
Juaristas.

When she had finished her story, Star said quietly,
"I'm honored that you've taken me into your confidence, child. I never keep any secrets from my husband,
but you can be sure that what you've told me will never
leave this hacienda."

Margarite gazed down at her clenched hands. "I
couldn't!" she blurted out. "I couldn't tell the French
soldiers that the *arrieros* were Juaristas, even after what
the Juaristas had done to my aunt and uncle."

"Of course you couldn't," Star said firmly. Sadness
shadowed the lovely gray eyes. "Poor Mexico. When I
first came to this country, it was the Americans they
were trying to drive out. Now it's the French. And when
the Mexicans aren't fighting off foreign invasions, they
fight just as bitterly among themselves, one revolution
following another."

"I met the emperor this morning, while riding," Margarite said. And then, puzzled, "I didn't recognize the
uniforms of some of the guard that rode with him."

"Black trousers, gray felt hats with black plumes?
Those would be members of the Cocks Club, a group of
youngbloods who form a guard for Maximilian whenever
he leaves La Borda." Star smiled. "And who also, I
gather, furnish the emperor with male talk and compan-
ionship when he wants to relax with wine and cards,

away from La Borda." Unspoken was the rest of the sentence. . . . *And away from Carlota.*

Margarite remembered how tired Maximilian had looked. "I'm sure the emperor needs his few moments of relaxation," she said stiffly. "He works very hard for the Mexican people."

Star gazed thoughtfully at her young guest. "So does Carlota, and there are those who believe she has the wiser head of the two. But somehow, despite their best intentions, between the two of them they've succeeded in turning not only the landowners and the church against them, but with the Black Decree, the very people they've tried to help. The truth is, I feel sorry for both of them. I'm afraid neither one really understands the Mexican people."

She shrugged ruefully. "But then, Patrick always said you have to be a Mexican to understand Mexico."

"Patrick?" Margarite asked, putting down her glass of fruit juice so abruptly it clattered on the table.

Star gestured toward the daguerrotypes. "My sons," she said proudly, "Carlos and Patrick. Carlos is visiting his grandfather in St. Louis. And Patrick . . ." She hesitated a moment. "Patrick is away too."

"They're both very handsome," Margarite said as she gazed, bewildered, from the picture of Patrick to her youthful hostess.

Star laughed. "Oh, Patrick's not my natural son, although he's just as dear to me as if he were. We brought him into our home when he was just a child."

"That uniform he's wearing, it's American, isn't it?" Margarite couldn't resist asking.

Star nodded, sighing. "I'm afraid that's my fault. I insisted that Patrick be sent to the United States to college and he joined the Union Army when the Civil War broke out. My husband was furious, but Patrick always did go his own way. In many ways, Patrick is very like my husband," she said, smiling. "Both hotheaded, stubborn, and proud. I remember the first time I met Michael . . ."

At first, as she listened to her hostess, Margarite's gaze kept wandering to Patrick's picture, but gradually

she found herself becoming fascinated by the story that
Star told of her adventurous trek down the Santa Fe trail
from St. Louis with Don Miguel, of a marriage that had
first not been a marriage at all because of the horror that
had stayed with Star from her first marriage, and finally
being caught up in the war that had split Star's loyalties
between her own countrymen and Mexicans like her
husband.

It was Star who finally broke off apologetically. "I
didn't mean to bore you with my life's story, Margarite.
Please forgive my rambling on. . . ."

"Oh, no. I'd love to hear more," Margarite said eagerly. Almost involuntarily her gaze slipped back to the
daguerrotype of Patrick, to that long narrow mouth curved
in a devil-may-care smile, remembering the way those
lips had felt against her own, the way her flesh had
burned and her heart pounded wildly against her rib
cage as that mouth had moved slowly, tantalizingly,
over her body.

She heard Star ask, puzzled, "Have you perhaps met
my son, Doña Margarite?"

Margarite flushed, turning her face quickly away from
the picture and from her hostess's too searching gaze.
"No . . . no," she stammered. "He . . . he reminds me
of someone I once knew."

"But she was lying. I'm sure she was," Star told her
husband that evening. "You should have seen her face
when she saw Patrick's picture. As if she were looking
at a ghost."

Michael was enjoying his after-dinner brandy as he
stretched out comfortably on the sofa in the *sala*, and he
smiled with amused affection at his wife. "And just
where do you suppose our Patrick would have met an
Austrian countess? Especially since Patrick has probably been back in the States for months now."

"We don't know he crossed back over the border,"
Star said. "For all we know he could still be here in
Mexico." She gazed suspiciously into her husband's
suddenly too bland face. "Patrick is here in Mexico,
isn't he?" she demanded accusingly. "And you didn't
tell me."

Michael sighed. He should have known it was futile to try to hide the truth from his wife. He said cautiously, "One of the vaqueros was up in the hills the other day, checking out the arroyo that carries the water supply to the sugar refinery. He almost ran into a small band of Juaristas. He turned tail and ran before they saw him, but he insists that one of the Juaristas looked like Patrick. Of course, he was probably mistaken," Michael added hastily as he saw the fear spring into Star's face.

"You think Patrick has joined the Juaristas?"

"Who knows? It would be like the young fool," her husband growled. "First, fighting with the Americans in a war that was none of his business and then joining a Juarista guerrilla band."

Star smiled at her husband. "If you were twenty years younger, you know you'd be fighting with the Juaristas, too."

"Well, thank God I'm older and wiser," her husband said, shifting uncomfortably, as if his wife's words struck too close to home. "All wars are stupid, and this war, worse than most. I have no great love for Benito Juárez, who seems determined to destroy *hacendados* like myself, but Napoleon was insane to think a charming dilettante like Maximilian could pull his chestnuts from the fire for him here in Mexico. And you can be sure if the war continues to go badly for the French, Napoleon will cut his losses and run."

"Has the situation grown that serious, then?"

Her husband nodded, his face grim. "The rumors are growing stronger each day that Marshal Bazaine has begun unofficially to pull his French forces back, and the Juaristas are taking over the villages in the north the minute the French leave. The Juaristas have even grown strong enough to begin attacking the customhouses up and down the coast. And the customhouses were Maximilian's sole financial support."

Michael put down his brandy glass and got to his feet, striding restlessly around the room. "Of course, Maximilian never had any money except what Napoleon gave him, and much of that he recklessly squandered on rebuilding his palaces at Chapultepec and here at La

Borda. Instead of relying on the French, he should have been building himself an army of his own to fight the Juaristas." He turned, worried, to his wife. "But if the vaqueros are right and there are guerrilla bands so close to the ranch, I want you to stay near the hacienda. No more rides alone into the hills."

Star was sitting with her feet tucked beneath her, watching her husband prowl around the room, noticing that he still walked with the lithe panther stride he had learned when he had lived with the Comanches as a young boy. The years had been good to her husband, she thought fondly. His body was still as hard and muscular as a young man's.

Then, realization of what he was saying jerked her erect in protest. "Cuernavaca has always been loyal to the emperor. And surely the Juaristas won't try anything this close to La Borda."

It was true enough, Michael thought. The imperial family was well protected at their summer palace. He had been surprised himself to hear of Juaristas in the area. If it had been Patrick in the hills, what was the young fool thinking of? He must know of the danger of his position with a strong French garrison at the Cortés Barracks in Cuernavaca.

In one graceful gesture Star swung her legs to the floor and rose to her feet. "In any case, I don't see why I should give up my rides. We've always treated our people fairly. The Juaristas have no reason to bother us."

Michael stopped his prowling to stand before his wife, lifting a cynical eyebrow. "Remember, I warned you years ago not to put too much trust in the honor of soldiers?" His voice roughened. "I want your word, *querida,* that you won't go riding without an armed escort."

For a moment he thought she was going to protest further, catching a familiar, stubborn glint in the wide gray eyes. He decided ruefully it would be easier to play the stern husband if his wife had not been wearing the green sprigged-cotton gown which was a particular favorite of his. The sheer stuff of the gown revealed the

lissome curves of her still firm, upthrust breasts, while
the lace-filled fichu provocatively concealed their loveliness from his gaze.

He drew her gently into his arms. "I lost you once to
bandits, remember, my love?" he said quietly. "I'll not
take the chance of it happening again. Promise me. . . ."

Star felt her resistance slipping away as she saw the
concern in her husband's dark green eyes, eyes so striking in the sun-darkened Mexican face. As much as she
hated the thought of giving up her daily rides alone, she
knew, of course, that she could not refuse. But then, she
thought, smiling to herself, it had been a long time since
she had been able to refuse her husband anything.

"As you wish, *mi amor*," she said meekly enough.
But couldn't help thinking: She had promised only not
to go riding alone; she hadn't promised not to go into the
hills, looking for Patrick!

Perhaps her voice was too mild, for Michael's eyes
narrowed in sudden suspicion. Before those eyes could
probe too deeply, Star said hastily, "We should send a
message warning the Ortiz hacienda. Margarite's *dueña*
will be in an uproar if she discovers the countess has
been out riding, with Juaristas in the area."

The Ortiz household and Doña Isobel, however, were
already in an uproar when Margarite returned. As soon as
she entered the cool, arched hallway, Doña Isobel moving with unusual swiftness on her tiny, silk-slippered
feet, came rushing toward her. "*Gracias Dios,* you've
returned," she said, alarmed.

"I sent word where I was," Margarite said. "There
was no need for you to be upset."

Doña Isobel shook her head, her voice flustered. "No,
no. I received the message that you were at the Cordoba
ranch. It was another message that arrived just an hour
ago, delivered by an aide to Emperor Maximilian. His
Majesty requests your presence at a luncheon tomorrow
at the Borda Palace." She spread her hands helplessly.
"What could I say? You were not here and I couldn't
refuse an invitation from his imperial highness, now,
could I?"

"Of course you couldn't," Margarite said soothingly,

thinking, surprised and flattered, that the emperor certainly hadn't wasted any time in offering her the hospitality of La Borda!

"But it isn't proper," Doña Isobel wailed, trailing after Margarite as she headed for her bedroom to remove her hot, dusty riding clothes. "A young unmarried woman cannot possibly attend a social engagement alone. What will people say?" More particularly, the *dueña* thought unhappily, what would Don Francisco say?

Margarite gratefully allowed a servant to remove her soft leather riding boots. "Naturally, you'll come with me to La Borda, Doña Isobel," she said firmly. "I'm sure the emperor meant to include you in the invitation."

She went to stand at her bedroom window, the tile floor deliciously cool against her bare feet. She shook her head to loosen her hair that had been pressed down by the sombrero. One nice thing about having short hair, she thought absently, it was much cooler. Although her hair had grown long enough so that it covered her ears now, she supposed her unconventional short hair style would cause conversation at the royal luncheon.

As her thoughts turned back to the invitation, she was surprised to discover that she felt none of the excitement and elation she had felt when she had last attended a reception at which Maximilian was present. It was even difficult to imagine that other young girl, delirious with happiness at the thought of being presented to the emperor.

Margarite gazed without seeing down into the courtyard. Was it always going to be this way? she wondered, misery suddenly knotting in her stomach. Was Patrick's dark, handsome face, that derisive smile, always going to stand between her and any other man?

She would not let him, she thought determinedly, turning away from the window. These last weeks, hours had gone by and she had not thought of Patrick. It was only seeing his picture in the Cordoba hacienda that had brought back all the unhappy memories. In time, she was sure those memories, like the daguerrotype, would fade. In time, she would be the same girl she once had been.

Margarite's mouth twisted into a bitter smile as she slipped out of the white cotton camisa, the dark blue skirt, and into the tulip-shaped tin tub of cool water scented with rose lotion that the maid had prepared for her. No, not the same girl, she thought, gazing down into the water at the pale creamy flesh where the sun had not touched its golden fingers. She could never be that same innocent, naive young woman again, no matter how she might try.

What was it the Mexicans called a despoiled young woman . . . a soiled dove? She flinched at the description. Perhaps Doña Isobel was right, she thought uneasily. Perhaps she shouldn't accept the emperor's invitation. Was it possible that men could sense, just by looking into her face, what she had become?

She scrubbed herself furiously until her skin burned, then, wrapping a towel around her, got out of the tub and studied herself carefully in her dressing table mirror. Except that her face was thinner, the cheekbones more pronounced, she was relieved to see that she looked exactly the same. And as her maid helped her dress for the luncheon the next morning, in a demure white dimity crinoline gown, black mourning ribbons at her sleeve and neck, and a sweeping brimmed straw hat, she even began to feel a little of the nervous excitement she had felt when she had dressed for the imperial reception at Chapultapec.

La Borda, however, was not Chapultapec, she discovered an hour later as her carriage drove through the wooden gate into a cobblestoned courtyard. La Borda was not even a palace but a simple country mansion, surrounded by terraced, still semi-wild gardens, fountains, and pools. Mango trees had been planted around the *quinta,* probably at the time Señor La Borda had built the mansion and gardens many years before with the profit from his silver mines. Margarite and Doña Isobel held up the hems of their skirts, picking their way carefully around the pulpy, overripe fruit that had fallen onto the garden paths.

As she and Doña Isobel followed the servant past dark, stagnant pools and under trellises laden with tea roses, she could hear a murmur of voices in the distance over the soft, oppressive trickling sound of water that could be heard everywhere in the Borda gardens. Then they came to the lower pool, almost the size of a small lake, where ducks paddled lazily between water lilies, and a bathing villa had been built at one end.

"They say the empress swims in the lake every day," Doña Isobel said in a low, shocked voice. As if swimming were associated with some lewd, shocking behavior, Margarite thought amused, but then, most well-bred Mexican women considered any sort of physical exercise for a woman declassé.

Margarite was surprised when she saw the large number of luncheon guests gathered by the lake. Carlota's ladies-in-waiting were still in mourning white for the death of the empress's father, King Leopold I of Belgium, who had died several months before. The other dozen or so women present wore pastel gowns with hoop skirts that swayed gently around them as they moved. The men present were in military uniform or white frock coats and carried Panama hats. Somehow Margarite hadn't expected such a sizable garden party, then shrugged, amused. Had she really expected that she had been invited to an intimate tête-à-tête with the imperial family? A tall, slender figure separated himself from a group of men and walked toward Margarite, several small white spaniels frolicking around his legs.

The emperor was not wearing a charro outfit today, but the white frock coat of a country gentleman. Although Maximilian had looked handsome in the Mexican riding costume, Margarite decided that somehow he looked more natural dressed as an Austrian country squire.

Maximilian bent, smiling, over Margarite's hand. "How good to see you again, Countess." The blue eyes, twinkling, immediately noted the bouquet of margarites at her waist. "And how charming that you should be wearing your namesake flower."

Margarite felt a glow of pleasure that he should remember her given name, then reminded herself that royalty were always well informed before a social engagement about the guests that would be present.

His Majesty turned to Doña Isobel and bent with the same courtly grace over her hand. "We're delighted that you were able to attend our little luncheon today, *Señora*. Her Majesty's lady-in-waiting, Señora del Barrio, has told us of the devoted care you've taken of the Countess Von Melk."

Margarite was amused to see Doña Isobel flush a bright, pleased crimson, melting as she suspected most women did, under the effect of Maximilian's disarming smile, his easy charm.

Then Señora del Barrio came rushing over to Doña Isobel, and drew her friend away, while Maximilian said softly, for Margarite's ears alone, "Might we walk together for a few moments, Countess? I have a favor to ask of you."

"Of course, Your Highness." She fell into step beside him, her hand resting lightly on his proffered arm as they followed a garden path leading away from the lake.

When the emperor spoke again, the smile had left his eyes and his voice was sober. "Once before, at Chapultapec, I asked if you would serve the empress as a lady-in-waiting. Now, an unhappy situation has arisen, and I'm asking again, this time for you to serve, if only in a temporary capacity, as a lady-in-waiting to the empress while we reside at La Borda."

"Her majesty already has her ladies-in-waiting," Margarite said, her voice uncertain.

"Yes, and they all are devoted to my wife. These last months, however, have been very difficult for the empress, ever since her royal trip to the Yucatan. I blame myself for sending her in my place, but circumstances did not allow my leaving. She did a splendid job of representing the crown, but returned, exhausted and ill, only to be greeted with the sad news of the death of her father."

Maximilian tugged unhappily at a point of his golden beard. "The empress is not as strong as she appears and has pushed herself much too hard ever since we accepted the crown and came to Mexico. And since the countesses von Kollonitz and Zichy, who traveled with the empress to Mexico, have returned home, Carlo is too much alone. Unhappily, state matters keep me too occupied to spend as much time with her as I would wish, and her Mexican ladies-in-waiting have little knowledge or interest in the world outside of Mexico. I thought, perhaps, if someone young and energetic, with, shall we say, a wider viewpoint of the world, would spend some time with my wife, it might help her take her mind off her unhappiness at the loss of her father."

They stopped walking, and Maximilian swung around to face Margarite, gazing intently down into her face. "I can assure you, Countess, you would be performing a great service, not just for the empress, but for myself. Of course, though, it must be your decision."

Looking into those sunny blue eyes, Margarite pushed aside the uneasy feeling that it would be difficult for anyone to refuse Maximilian, even as she replied cautiously, "I'm not sure I have the qualities or experience to be a lady-in-waiting, Your Majesty. If the empress wishes it, however, I will be glad to serve her temporarily, at least, in any way that I can."

Maximilian smiled, relieved. "It's settled then. Countess del Barrio can instruct you in your duties. I haven't spoken to Carlo yet, but I'm sure she'll be as pleased as I am by your decision." And then, almost casually, he added, "You can, naturally, return to the Ortiz rancho each evening, but, if you wish, a room can be prepared for you here at La Borda."

The uneasiness grew stronger within Margarite. It was not the emperor Maximilian smiling warmly down at her, but simply a man looking with desire at a woman, waiting for some subtle intimation that she returned his feeling. And if she would? Shocked, she hastily thrust the thought aside. She was being ridiculous. It had been only her imagination, of course. But she took a step backward as she said slowly, "I think, perhaps, Your Majesty, it would be best if I returned to my home at night."

Behind the golden beard, the full red lips tightened for a moment, then Maximilian shrugged gently, his smile affable. "As you wish." He turned and glanced over his shoulder. "And now I must return you to my guests. Count von Kevenhuller and Barons von Kulmer and von Malbough are already, I'm sure, annoyed with me for monopolizing the loveliest young *señora* to be present at La Borda today."

As soon as Margarite returned to join the other guests, Maximilian withdrew and Margarite was immediately surrounded by several young Hussars, all with golden mustaches and sideburns, two of whom she remembered seeing with the emperor on the road the day before. Their gallant compliments and easy banter soon made her forget her momentary uneasiness with the emperor. One of the officers, Count von Kevenhuller, she had already heard about. The eldest son of one of the oldest families of Hungarian nobility, the count had already gained a reputation in Mexico for his numerous love affairs and duels.

Now he insisted over his friends' vociferous objections that Margarite must sit next to him at the luncheon table. "How has it happened we haven't met before, Countess?" he asked while his gaze wandered, pleased, from the tiny waist, made even smaller by the voluminous crinoline skirt, to the startling vibrant green eyes. "You're like a breath from home. Surely we must have met in Vienna, riding in the Prater, or attending a ball at the Hofburg." He sighed nostalgically. "How I miss Vienna, don't you, Countess? Try as they may, their imperial highnesses have not managed to change their court here in Mexico into another Hofburg."

Listening, Margarite felt an unexpected pang of homesickness herself. Not just for Vienna, she thought, but for Paula. She had written her stepsister several times since her arrival in Mexico and had never had a reply. She would write her again that very evening, she decided, and send the letter out in the emperor's mail pouch.

Then she became aware that the laughing voices around her had fallen silent, the handsome young officers clustered around her drawing stiffly to attention. She glanced up curiously to see that the empress had arrived, at last, to greet her guests. Dressed completely in black, Carlota moved with a stiff dignity, her head held regally erect, nodding without speaking to the men and women she passed, her lips in a set smile.

When she came closer, Margarite saw, dismayed, that the emperor had been right. Carlota did not just look tired, but ill, her skin with a deep pallor, a drawn, unhappy expression around her eyes as she stopped before Margarite and the Hussars.

Margarite dropped into a deep curtsy, and when she arose, saw that Carlota's gaze ignored the others present and was fastened upon her. The empress spoke in Spanish to Margarite. "I understand you are to be my new lady-in-waiting, Countess Von Melk." The voice was cold, and, for a moment, something shone in the oddly flecked eyes, a furious brightness that made Count von Kevenhuller take an unconscious, protective step closer to Margarite.

Then the stilettolike brightness was gone and Carlota's face was carefully, blandly indifferent as she murmured before moving on. "We are pleased to have you serve us, *Señora*."

Margarite let her breath go with a sigh, not even realizing she had been holding it, only aware of one uncomfortable fact. Despite what Maximilian had said, the empress Carlota was not at all pleased with her new lady-in-waiting.

Chapter 18

JF Margarite had not already promised Maximilian, her meeting with Carlota would have made her change her mind about accepting the position as lady-in-waiting to the empress. As it was, she had enough second thoughts

so that the next day she began drafting a note of polite
refusal, when Don Francisco arrived unexpectedly at
the Ortiz hacienda. His horses were spent. Don Francisco, unlike his usual well-groomed, impeccable self,
was disheveled and out of sorts. He had evidently been
roused from a sound sleep, then driven all night, pro-
pelled by a frantic message to come at once to Cuernavaca, a message no doubt sent by Doña Isobel, Margarite
decided, annoyed.

In no uncertain terms, Don Francisco stiffly informed
Margarite that he could not possibly allow her to serve
as lady-in-waiting to the empress Carlota.

"The emperor himself requested that I accept the
position," Margarite said, forgetting in her irritation at
Don Francisco's high-handed manner that she had been
about to turn down the position herself. After all, she
was no longer a child to be ordered about, she thought.
She had turned eighteen only a few weeks before.

Don Francisco frowned. That was precisely the reason why Doña Margarite should not step foot in La Borda.
Don Francisco was only too aware of the emperor's
reputation with women, even as discreet as Maximilian
was with his affairs. With a cold, barren wife like the
empress, Don Francisco did not begrudge the man turning to other women, but certainly he would never allow
Don Manuel's niece to become one of those women.

He cleared his throat and forced a paternal smile to
his lips. "There are . . . reasons . . . beyond a young
woman's understanding, aside from the obvious fact
that you are too young and inexperienced to hold such a
responsible position, why I cannot permit you to attend
Her Majesty."

They were talking on the patio, where Margarite was
having a late breakfast after an early morning horseback
ride. A touch of irritation crept into Don Francisco's
voice as he studied Margarite, still wearing her riding
habit. "I must also insist that these rides of yours cease.
I can't imagine why Doña Isobel allowed them in the first
place. It's not seemly at all, a young woman riding
horseback all over the countryside, like a vaquero."

He was disconcerted at the look of icy haughtiness

that froze the young woman's face, the imperious air with which Margarite rose to her feet and confronted him. What had happened to that sweet, helpless child he had visited in the bedroom of the Ortiz home in Mexico? Don Francisco wondered, bewildered. There was no trace of that young girl in Margarite's cold, composed voice. "I appreciate your concern for me, Don Francisco, but I wasn't aware that you were my father or uncle . . . or legal guardian."

The last words brought the frown quickly back to Don Francisco's face. "Under Mexican law, and as a young unmarried woman, you are required to have a guardian and trustee appointed by the court—"

Margarite interrupted swiftly. "You forget that I'm not a Mexican citizen," she pointed out. "I'm a citizen of Austria. Of course, I could speak with General Count Franz Thun," she added thoughtfully. "I understand he's in charge of the Austrian forces here in Mexico, and I'm sure he could explain about my legal rights as an Austrian citizen."

At the look of consternation on Don Francisco's face, as if a friendly puppy had suddenly turned around and bit him, she smiled sweetly. "I am glad you've come to visit me, Don Francisco. I've been wanting to talk to you about canceling the debts of the peons on the estate. It hardly seems fair, does it, that a man should be saddled with his grandfather's debts? And I can't help feeling that the charges the workers pay for the food and clothing at the estate store are entirely too high. Don't you agree?"

It was a still sputtering Don Francisco who was finally ushered from the Ortiz hacienda an hour later, while Margarite returned to her hot chocolate and rolls. After a moment she tore in half the note of refusal she had been writing to the emperor. It wasn't only Don Francisco's stiff-necked, overbearing attitude, immediately arousing the rebel in Margarite, that had made her change her mind though. Nor was it her dislike of breaking her word to Maximilian. It was the look she had glimpsed briefly in Carlota's eyes and could not put out of her mind. Had it been hostility . . . or fear? Even the reserved coldness in the woman's face had been overshadowed by a haunting sadness. Was it possible Maximilian had been right, that Carlota did need a friend at court?

When Margarite arrived at La Borda Quinta the next morning to take up her duties, Señora Manuela del Barrio met Margarite at her arrival at the mansion. The *señora* escorted her into the garden, where dew-laden branches hung low, and a rich moist earth scent mingled with the fragrance of crushed mangos and roses.

The empress was seated on a balustrade beside the lake, watching the young heir apparent, Agustin Iturbide, sail a small boat amid the water lilies.

Margarite heard the young boy cry eagerly, his native English mingling with the new Spanish he was learning. "Look, Mama Carlota. *Mucho* fish!" A small hand reached out to tug at Carlota's skirt, to gain her attention. Carlota's gaze, which had seemed centered at some faraway point, returned to the young boy with the bright yellow curls who was now her son.

"Speak Spanish, Agustin," she said, but her voice, though stern, was not unkind as she gently removed the child's dirty hand from her skirt. Then she saw Doña Manuela approaching with Margarite and rose gracefully to her feet as Señora del Barrio presented her new lady-in-waiting to the empress.

There was no hint of a desire for friendship in Carlota's voice, nor anything but a cold, reserved politeness in her eyes as she nodded to Margarite after the girl arose from her curtsy. "Doña Manuela will acquaint you with your duties, Countess." The small, lovely mouth, marred by a fever blister, twisted in a faintly ironic smile as she gazed at Margarite and murmured, "We hope you won't find life here at La Borda too dull."

Then she turned abruptly and, taking Agustin by the hand, walked away. Doña Manuela made a small apologetic gesture toward Margarite. "You must excuse Her Majesty. She . . . she has not been well."

Margarite gazed after the retreating black figure. What odd eyes she has, she thought, the green rim around the darkness, the brown flecks around the pupils. And although Carlota's pale face was carefully, almost rigidly controlled, the eyes burned with a feverish brightness against the dull, fine-grained skin.

"What are my duties?" she asked her companion.

Apparently very little, Margarite learned. Her duties would consist mostly of sitting with Her Majesty and the other ladies-in-waiting while Carlota read and embroidered, going for an occasional carriage ride, and filling in at the table when guests were invited to La Borda. "Is that how she spends her days?" she asked Señora del Barrio, surprised. "I thought . . . that is, I heard Her Majesty often sits in on council meetings with the emperor and his advisors."

Doña Manuela shook her head. "Not anymore. Oh, she still has the many charities she runs, but she is no longer allowed to attend the council meetings." Her glance rested, worried, on the departing empress. "That is when it began, I think, her sadness and depression." She glanced around, then, as if deciding to trust Margarite, lowered her voice. "Don Maximiliano said it was because the Mexican people don't want their country to be run by a woman, but I think he is annoyed because he heard whispers that his wife was more respected in the council chamber than he was."

Doña Manuela shrugged. "Of course, here at La Borda, the emperor does very little work anyway. Official papers to be signed come each morning from Mexico, but the emperor hardly looks at them. He is much too busy playing with Agustín, or riding off to Acapantzingo with his cronies, or chasing butterflies with Señor Bilimek."

"Señor Bilimek? Have I met him?"

"You would remember him if you had," her companion said, smiling. "He is a most odd gentleman, but amusing to look at, with his beard and yellow umbrella and cork helmet and jacket with pockets everywhere. He and the emperor chase over the countryside, collecting butterflies, insects, and reptiles for a museum the emperor plans to open here in Mexico. Often the emperor talks the ladies-in-waiting into helping with the collecting." Doña Manuela gave a little sniff of distaste. "I myself have no interest in such activities. Nor does Doña Carlota."

She glanced at the diamond-encrusted watch on her bosom. "While the empress is engaged in her morning constitutional, this will be a good time for you to meet the other ladies-in-waiting and staff."

It was not, all things considered, a very large staff for a royal residence, Margarite decided after introductions were made. The emperor and empress were economizing, Doña Manuela explained, having belatedly discovered, much to Maximilian's surprise, that the personal royal funds they had brought to Mexico had almost disappeared, and the incomes they had been promised to receive from France had never arrived.

Carlota had limited herself to fourteen personal attendants, all from prominent Mexican families, only three of whom, Margarite gathered, received any honorarium for their work. Margarite was introduced to four of the ladies in attendance that morning, and their dark eyes studied the new lady-in-waiting, some amused, some openly questioning. One of the ladies, Countess del Valle, who assisted her husband in making the arrangements for all the royal functions, was dressed as elegantly as if she had just arrived from Paris, and had an irritating way of looking down her long nose at Margarite.

The chamberlain in charge of La Borda was Doña Manuela's husband, Felipe Neri, a thin, hawk-faced man with a frosty air. Then there was overworked Frau von Kuhacsevitch, who had come with the empress from Austria, and whose duties as lady of the bedchamber as well as dealing with the dozens of Mexican servants left her looking harassed and irritable so that her husband, Jacob, with the thankless job of imperial treasurer, looked almost jovial in comparison.

The only person with whom Margarite immediately felt at ease was a young man who came hurrying by with a stack of papers in his hands, and who was introduced as José Luis Blasio, secretary to both Their Majesties. He gave Margarite a shy, pleasant smile before hurrying away again.

Before Margarite could be introduced to the rest of the staff, it was time for the ladies-in-waiting to join Her Majesty on the terrace, overlooking the garden. Embroidery was promptly whipped out, while one of the women read aloud in Spanish from an extremely dull book of Mexican folklore. Margarite, who had never been fond of needlework, and was, as a matter of fact, very bad at it, jabbed her finger several times, drawing blood. The third time she muttered beneath her breath one of the profanities she had learned from the *arrieros*, and little Señora Maria Pacheco, who was sitting beside her, gave a startled giggle.

Carlota looked up from her embroidery hoop. "There is something amusing, Pacheco?" she asked coldly.

"No, Your Highness." The young woman, who was one of the paid attendants, nervously returned her gaze to her embroidery.

Margarite had to restrain a giggle herself. For suddenly the scene reminded her of those afternoons she and Paula had spent with their tutor, a very proper widow, pretending to study while really thinking of ways to bedevil the poor woman. She must add a postscript to the letter she had written Paula the night before, she decided, and describe the scene on the terrace. How Paula would laugh if she could see her sister in the role of a sedate and proper lady-in-waiting.

The next few days, however, Margarite had a hard time maintaining her sense of humor. It was soon obvious that as much as possible, the empress was ignoring her presence. It was always one of the other ladies, never Margarite, she asked to accompany her on carriage rides, to walk with her through the gardens, to bring messages from Carlota's living quarters, on one side of the mansion, to her husband's, on the other side.

The only time Margarite's presence was specifically requested was when the emperor and empress entertained, and she suspected that Carlota included her only because Margarite could speak French and German to the guests who could not speak Spanish. Carlota, Margarite noticed, was always very quiet at these gatherings, almost withdrawn, making stiffly polite conversation only when necessary, but Maximilian seemed to thrive on the small informal parties. With a cigar in one hand and the inevitable glass of champagne in the other, he would speak enthusiastically of the school for Indian painters, the new museum, the reforms in the Mexican education system he was planning.

As if, Margarite thought, bewildered, as she listened, the emperor were not aware of the gathering storm outside of Cuernavaca, the Juarista raids that were becoming more and more daring and closer to the capital, the Mexicans who were defecting each day from the French Army to the Juaristas.

When one of the guests ventured the thought that perhaps more fundamental reforms were first needed, Maximilian's full Hapsburg lower lip jutted out ominously. "Yes, I agree," he said at once. "It's as I've always said, the reforms must first begin with the judicial functionaries, the army officers, and the clergy. The judges are corrupt, the officers have no sense of honor, and the clergy lack Christian charity and morality." Then suddenly, unexpectedly, the bad humor was gone and he smiled winningly, in one of his quick changes of mood. "But all this does not make me lose hope for the future."

Margarite happened to be looking toward Carlota, when the emperor spoke, and saw the expression that flitted swiftly across the darkly brooding face as Carlota gazed at her husband. It was a look of pity mingled with such passionate adoration that Margarite, shaken, felt as if she were violating a privacy and looked quickly away. Somehow it had not occurred to her, after seeing for herself the separate apartments the emperor and empress occupied at La Borda, how very little time they spent in each other's company, that Carlota might still love her husband passionately. To be sure, in public, Maximilian was always circumspect in his behavior toward his wife, treating her with a charming deference. It was Carlota who appeared reserved, almost indifferent.

If she loves him, why doesn't she fight for him? Margarite thought angrily. I would. If I were Carlota, I'd scratch the eyes out of any woman who went through that garden door into Maximilian's quarters.

"And now that the mourning period for her father is past, why does she continue to wear those awful black gowns?" she protested to Señora Pacheco, who was standing beside her. "The empress would be beautiful if she would only smile more and wear brighter colors."

Despite the fact that Maria Pacheco was a widow and shy as a nun, a closeness had sprung up between her and Margarite, who were nearer the same age than the other attendants to Carlota. Now Maria's gaze rested with loving anxiety on the empress, who had grown so thin that her black gown hung shapelessly on her slender body. For all that it was still only February, the day was warm and perspiration glistened on Carlota's oval face. Doña Maria shook her head sadly. "I don't think it would matter," she said.

She glanced around to make sure no one could overhear—Margarite had already discovered that nothing spread faster than court gossip—then said softly, "The emperor's valet, Grill, told me in the strictest confidence, of course, that the chief gardener's wife is pregnant by the emperor."

A flush stained Maria's cheeks as she glanced over at the emperor, looking very dashing in the uniform of a general in the imperial army. "Don Maximiliano. . . ." Señora Pacheco shrugged with a Mexican woman's acceptance of masculine peccadillos. "Well, he's *mucho hombre,* is he not? And very attractive to women. Yet, in his own fashion, I believe he loves and respects Doña Carlota, and is concerned for her health and well-being, as we all are."

She frowned as she noticed the empress was tearing at a corner of her handkerchief with her small white teeth. "Her headache is worse, I can tell. She should have remained in her room, but she insisted upon making an appearance today."

"Can't the court physician help her?"

"The empress dislikes doctors. She is taking a medicine that was given her by a servant when she became ill in Yucatan, an Indian brew called *totoache,* made from mushrooms. Dr. Brasch doesn't trust its effects upon the empress, but she felt so much better after taking it, that her maid, Frau Doblinger, tells me Her Highness has been using the medicine ever since." Then, noticing that the empress was beckoning to her imperiously, Maria said anxiously, "I must go to her."

As she hurried away, Margarite was aware that a young Austrian officer with only one arm and a limp was approaching her. There was something about his face, the sharply waxed brown mustache and pointed chin, that seemed familiar, but she could not place where she had seen him before.

She started to smile a greeting, but something in the stiffness of the young man's manner made her nod her head graciously instead, when he asked, "May I speak to you for a moment, Countess Von Melk?" Then, abruptly, "You don't remember me, do you?"

When she shook her head, puzzled, he said, "I sailed on the *Louisiane* with you and Lieutenant Franz Schiller." His young voice was suddenly vicious. "You do remember Franz?"

"Of course," she said, startled. "How is the lieutenant?"

"He's dead. Lieutenant Schiller was killed a week ago outside of Matamoros."

Chapter 19

*T*HE captain's voice slashed cruelly through the bright afternoon sunlight so that the very air around Margarite seemed to shiver as he continued inexorably. "Lieutenant Schiller was with an imperial supply column when it was attacked by a Juarista force under General Escobedo. The Mexican imperial troops deserted to the Juaristas and left the Austrians to be slaughtered. I was one of the few who managed to escape. Franz wasn't so lucky."

Margarite had the odd sensation that she could actually feel the blood drain from her face. How was it possible? Franz had been so young and alive. How could it happen so quickly that his life was ended? And she hadn't even known. Suddenly she thought: Patrick could be dead, too, and I would never know. The pain that twisted through her then filled the vivid green eyes with such a look of agony that the captain was all at once ashamed of how brutally he had imparted his news. He leaned forward anxiously. "Are you all right, Countess? Shall I get you a glass of champagne?"

Margarite shook her head, fighting to regain her self-control as her gaze drifted aimlessly around the garden party, the gaily dressed women in their sheer summer gowns, servants moving among them with iced drinks in silver glasses, the emperor himself chatting and laughing with his guests, his golden beard as always immaculately combed into two points, the back hair carefully swept upward to hide a balding spot. It was impossible to imagine that outside of this charming, romantic setting was a world of sudden, violent death.

"Franz's last thoughts were of you, Countess," the captain said. "He was wild with grief when he heard that you had been killed with your uncle and aunt. When he heard you were safe, he tried to get leave to come and see you, but with the French pulling back, there aren't enough imperial troops to hold the garrisons. Every man is desperately needed. He wrote you at your home in Mexico. . . ."

"I never received any letters," Margarite said. Had the mail been lost as happened so often in Mexico, or, she wondered suspiciously, had any letters from what Don Francisco would no doubt consider an improper suitor simply been kept from her?

The captain looked down into the girl's stricken face and apologized awkwardly. "I'm sorry I blurted out the news of Franz's death that way." He gestured around the garden party with his good arm. "It's just, coming from the hell where I've been, to . . . to this. And then after all you had meant to Franz, when I heard that you were here at the palace, that Maximilian had picked you himself as a lady-in-waiting to his wife, I assumed . . . I thought . . ." His pink face flushed a bright, embarrassed red.

Six months ago, Margarite realized, she wouldn't have

had the faintest idea what her companion was talking about. Now she knew only too well what he was implying, what, she suspected, a great many others at court believed; that she was Maximilian's latest mistress. "You thought wrong," she said sharply. Then, feeling all at once sorry for the young man's embarrassment, added more gently, "The emperor asked me to take on the temporary position as lady-in-waiting because he thought I could be of some assistance to the empress. She hasn't been well lately. . . ."

That, at least, was true, she thought the next morning as she walked through the Borda gardens. Whether or not Maximilian originally had any other plans in mind for her, he had made no further overtures to her. He was always unfailingly charming, nothing more, when she saw him, which was not that often, since he kept to his own quarters of the palace most of the time. Perhaps the latest rumor that the chief gardener's wife was pregnant by the emperor might have discouraged him from any further romantic adventures, she decided wryly.

She turned up a garden path that led to a covered cul de sac with stone benches, the view looking out across the countryside at an old church on a hillside and an ancient Spanish viaduct running through the barranca below the hill. It was one of her favorite spots, with the fragrant beauty of the garden behind her and the sun-warmed countryside before her. As she stood gazing out over the countryside, at first she didn't realize she wasn't alone, until the black shadowy figure seated on one of the benches stirred. Margarite swiftly curtsied, then started to withdraw, murmuring apologies. "I'm sorry, Your Majesty, I didn't mean to intrude. . . ."

Carlota's face was quiet, almost as still as the garden with its occasional bird cries, the step of a sentry beneath the wall, the faint trickle of water. For the first time when she looked at her lady-in-waiting, there was no wariness in Carlota's glance, almost a friendly curiosity as she gestured to the bench next to hers. "Please stay, Countess."

So she knows there is nothing between her husband and myself, Margarite thought, relieved. She was begin-

ning to realize that there was little that went on at La
Borda that Carlota didn't know. Even the official reports that came down from Mexico each noon, and
which Maximilian usually tossed aside, Carlota read
through patiently each night, the lamps in her bedroom
burning long after the lights in Maximilian's quarters had
been extinguished, the young secretary, José Luis, had
confided to Margarite.

And what of Concepcion Sedano, the gardener's wife,
Margarite thought. Did Carlota know about that liaison,
too, that the Indian girl was bearing her husband's child.
No doubt she did, she decided with a sharp stab of pity.
For whatever had driven the empress from her husband's
bed, she was sure Carlota still loved Maximilian deeply.

Carlota turned her gaze back to the green hills, the
weathered stones of the church looking butter-colored in
the early morning sunlight. "It is a lovely vista, is it
not?" Her voice grew faintly wistful. "Not as lovely as
our Miramar in Trieste, of course. There we could see
the ocean from every room. Have you visited Trieste,
Countess?"

"No, Your Highness."

"How we hated to leave our beautiful Miramar, I
think the emperor even more than I. But we had our
duty and our dream of building a great empire here in
this new world." Carlota sighed softly. "We were so
sure we could reach the Indian masses, make them
understand how our new humane laws would change
their lives for the better after the oppression they had
suffered for so long." She shrugged helplessly. "Only
it's as if there is a 'nothingness' within the Indian people
that's made of granite that no one can reach or change.
Sometimes I think it would be less hard to erect the
pyramids of Egypt than to vanquish Mexican nothingness." She glanced up at Margarite. "Have you noticed
that too, Countess?"

Margarite thought of the Indian *arrieros* she had grown
to know so well in just a few weeks, their passion for
living, their humor and loyalty and courage in the face of
death. She hesitated a moment, then said slowly, "It

takes time, I would think, Your Highness, time and patience, to change people."

An irritation crept into the sad voice. "Why can't the people realize that the empire is Mexico's only chance for salvation? The emperor Maximilian has pledged his life, given up his own royal inheritance to save Mexico. We cannot fail." With an almost physical effort, her slender shoulders stiffened and she smiled fleetingly at Margarite. "Perhaps it is as the emperor says, I worry too much. The emperor is a true Viennese. With him, the condition is serious but never critical!"

Then, as if sensing that even that remark smacked of disloyalty, she turned her gaze away from Margarite, her voice once more imperious as she said, "You may withdraw, Countess, and send Matilde to me with my shawl. I feel a chill in the air."

If Maximilian didn't regard the conditions in Mexico as critical, he was abruptly forced to change his mind two days later, when an envoy from Paris came riding down the road from Mexico, bringing a letter from Napoleon. Maximilian had been lying in a hammock outside his quarters with Prince Agustin playing on his chest, but the letter brought him swiftly to his feet and to Carlota's private apartment, where she was sitting with her ladies-in-waiting, embroidering.

"Carlo, listen to this! After giving us his solemn word, Napoleon has betrayed us. He has ordered Marshal Bazaine to withdraw all the French troops."

In his anger, Maximilian was speaking in German as he flourished the letter, his face flushed, the full Hapsburg underlip trembling with rage. The ladies-in-waiting present, who, with the exception of Margarite, spoke only Spanish glanced uneasily at one another, sensing the emperor's anger but not understanding the reason.

Carlota's face grew pale. Swiftly she put aside her embroidery and rose to her feet. With the slightest motion of her head she indicated the ladies should leave the room. As Margarite followed the other women out the door, she heard Carlota speaking quietly, soothingly, in German to her husband. "We always knew, Maxl, that someday the French would leave. We will raise our own army, as we should have done from the beginning. . . .''

The next few days the ladies-in-waiting had even less duties to occupy them. Envoys rushed back and forth from the capital to La Borda. And for the first time since Margarite had come to La Borda, the empress and the emperor were inseparable. Margarite could watch them from a distance as they paced up and down the garden walks, talking earnestly, their heads bent together. Outwardly, when they were in public, neither Carlota nor Maximilian gave any indication that they were disturbed in the least by the news of the withdrawal of the French troops. Only when she was close enough to Maximilian did Margarite see that the bright blue eyes were now always clouded with worry, and a champagne glass was always in his hand. Carlota's lips had become even more set, her lacy handkerchief torn to shreds by her small white teeth.

She learned through the palace grapevine that Maximilian, in his written reply to Napoleon, and in a white hot rage, had insisted that the French troops should leave Mexico immediately. "For himself," he had announced proudly, "he would place his life and services at the disposal of his new subjects . . . "Every drop of my blood is Mexican!"

"How can the empire survive without an army?" Margarite asked José Luis one evening, when the young secretary, looking harassed and worried, stopped a moment to speak to her in the garden.

"There are still the Austrian and Belgian troops, and some of the French officers are leaving the Legion to join Maximilian's army. And the emperor's brother will be sending additional troops for the Austrian Legion soon. We've heard they're already recruited and sent to Trieste, awaiting shipment to Mexico."

"Then it's only rumors I've heard," Margarite asked, "that the emperor is planning to abdicate?"

José looked around to make sure they were alone. He had learned to trust the young Austrian lady-in-waiting, but one could never be too careful. "Maximilian will not abdicate," he said quietly. "The empress has said that abdication is cowardly, unworthy of a prince of the House of Hapsburg. And there is the new army Maximilian is building," the young man added loyally. "Many Mexicans, like myself, are still devoted to the emperor, and Mexicans, formerly Juaristas, are joining the imperial army every day. Soon they will be marching north to drive Juárez back across the border."

Margarite had been aware of the new Mexican faces that were appearing daily at court as old, less loyal faces faded away, many former imperialist supporters fleeing the country as Napoleon withdrew his support of his puppet government. And it was true that Maximilian was engrossed in plans for his new army, paying a great deal of attention to deciding on the uniforms for his troops, the braid, epaulettes, and color schemes.

As she left José Luis, crossing the garden toward the empress's private apartments, she wondered about her own future. The imperial family would be leaving for Chapultapec any day now. If the empress asked her, should she go with them? Even though she had lost her girlish illusions about Maximilian, that he was not, after all, a golden, all-powerful god, but a very mortal, fallible man, she had learned to respect the empress, to admire Carlota's intelligence and fierce loyalty to her husband. Nevertheless, the subservient role of lady-in-waiting was not one that Margarite relished.

Perhaps I should return to Europe, too, she thought. As much as she had grown to love Mexico, she couldn't imagine living the rest of her life here, where everything and everyone reminded her painfully of Patrick. And if she did stay, she was sure Don Francisco would become more and more insistent that she marry.

She tried to imagine such a marriage, a strange man taking her to his bed, his hands caressing her body intimately, the way Patrick had, and a sickening feeling swept over her, so that she felt suddenly faint and sat down on one of the stone benches beside the garden path. How could she endure it? she thought. She had been so sure these last weeks that she had managed to banish Patrick from her mind, that she was dismayed at how easily the memories rushed back, knocking down the careful barriers she had erected, filling her with such a storm tide of longing that she had to bite her lip against the cry that rose in her throat.

Engulfed in her misery, she didn't notice the Mexican officer approaching her until he spoke. "Countess Von Melk, is it not?"

She looked up, at first not recognizing the man's face, half hidden in the shadow of the mango trees, or the timbre of the voice, that had an unpleasant, grating roughness.

She smiled uncertainly. 'I'm sorry, I don't believe we've—'' She broke off abruptly as the man stepped closer, into a splintered ray of sunlight, and she saw his face, the harsh, brutal features, the small black eyes and battered nose of El Cuchillo.

At first, remembering what she and her family had suffered at this man's hands, all Margarite felt was an anger so intense that for a moment her throat closed and she couldn't speak.

Seeing the rage flooding the girl's face, Juan Heras smiled almost smugly. "I am flattered, *Señora*. I see that you remember me."

"Remember you! How dare you show yourself here?"

Juan spread his hands reproachfully. "But why should I not be invited to La Borda? I am a colonel in the emperor's imperial service, assigned to the Cortes barracks here in Cuernavaca."

"You're a Juarista," she spat out. "No, not even that, a common bandit and a murderer. Even the Juaristas wouldn't have carrion like you."

She turned to call the sentry, when the man's hand shot out and gripped her wrist, his grasp slowly, deliberately, tightening, even as he smiled innocently at Margarite. "I wouldn't disturb the sentries, Doña Margarite. After all, why should the emperor believe a hysterical young woman who never actually saw the faces of the men who held her? No, I think Maximilian would be more willing to believe me, the man who attacked a band of Juarista gun smugglers and brought his imperial army many needed guns."

He was standing so close to her that Margarite could

smell the sour odor of tequila and cheap cigarillos on his breath. "Take your hands off me," she said sharply, refusing to give him the satisfaction of crying out against the pain that shot agonizingly from her wrist to her shoulder.

Juan shrugged and dropped her wrist. "As long as we understand each other, *Señora*." The small black eyes filled with vicious pleasure as they surveyed the young woman before him, the small breasts rising and falling rapidly against the pink muslin bodice of her gown, the creamy skin that glowed in the shadow covered pathway.

"And I don't think Maximilian will be pleased to learn that he is sharing his bed with a woman who gave herself willingly to a known and dangerous Juarista." The black eyes turned coldly calculating. "And perhaps is still slipping away from Maximilian's bed to creep into her lover's arms?"

At Margarite's eyes widening in surprise, Juan shrugged impatiently. "There is no need to pretend the innocent with me. We both know Patricio is in the area. My men almost caught him a few days ago, when his band attacked a supply column on the road to Cuernavaca, but, like an eel, he slipped away. The next time you see him, tell Patricio he won't be so lucky again. And when I catch him, you can be sure he will die slowly, your lover, this I promise you." The smile grew greedy in anticipation, the black eyes suddenly oily-looking, as if he were savoring each word. "What pleasure it will give me to hear him scream and beg for death before my knife finishes with him."

The man's hatred was palpable in the air, like the foul stench of his breath. He's insane, Margarite thought, staring into the small, virulent eyes, the stream of saliva running from one corner of the loose, red lips. It was not as an imperialist officer the man was hunting down Patrick. It was a case of private vengeance. The man would never rest until he had killed Patrick.

She heard the sound of footsteps on the path behind them and turned, relieved, to see Colonel Van der Smissen marching briskly up the path toward her.

The colonel frowned at the retreating back of Colonel

Heras, and gave Margarite's flushed face a searching
glance. "Are you all right, Countess? That . . . officer
wasn't bothering you?" He spoke the word *officer* with
scarcely concealed contempt.

Margarite shook her head. El Cuchillo was right, she
thought helplessly. She hadn't seen the faces of the
bandits who had killed her aunt and uncle. It would
only be her word against a colonel in Maximilian's
army. Yet she couldn't resist protesting angrily. "Why
does the emperor accept such men into his army?"

Colonel Van der Smissen smiled dourly. "Unfortunately, the emperor has little choice. His imperial army
is composed of mostly jumped-up rascals, ex-Juaristas,
five or six thousand bandits, mule drivers, and bakers'
boys suddenly turned colonels. Soldiers are recruited by
force and brought to the barracks between rows of bayonets. As soon as they are led through a field of sugar
cane where they can hide, they desert."

It was the colonel's glum opinion that the day the
French Army sailed, the empire would collapse with a
bang. Still, Van der Smissen was a professional soldier,
devoted to his trade, and, some said, even more devoted
to the empress Carlota. He had come to Mexico with the
Belgian Legion to serve the cause of Carlota. He would
not desert her even when the emperor sent him on such
futile missions as he was now about to embark upon, to
attempt to reach Benito Juárez and negotiate some sort
of settlement with him. As hopeless, Van Smissen thought
grimly, as Maximilian's constantly trying to convince
the Americans they should withdraw their support from
Juárez.

He glanced down at Margarite. "Will you be returning
to Chapultepec with the empress?" he asked.

"No," Margarite answered, suddenly making up her
mind. "I—I have matters I must attend to here in
Cuernavaca."

Behind the fan of dark lashes, her eyes shone like
jewels, so that Van der Smissen found himself wondering, a little enviously, who the fortunate fellow was who
was holding the Countess Von Melk here in Cuernavaca.

Chapter 20

"**S**HALL we stop and have lunch here?" Star asked Margarite as the two women rested their horses in the shade of a group of cottonwood trees. Not far behind them, a half-dozen vaqueros, heavily armed, pushed their sombreros back on their heads and passed around a flask of tequila. Although the morning had been cool when the horses left the Cordoba rancho, the June sun now blazed overhead.

Margarite slipped easily from her horse to the ground before any of the vaqueros could move forward to help her dismount. She glanced around, pleased. It was a beautiful spot. She could hear a waterfall in the distance and the air was so clear that the snowy peak of Popocatepetl seemed almost within reach instead of miles away. Far below her she could glimpse the pink and gold rooftops and church spires of Cuernavaca, even the red-tiled Cortés barracks nestled in the shelter of the peaks of the Tres Marias.

Star had dismounted, too, and was already spreading a blanket on the turflike grass, untying a wicker basket of food from her saddle. Margarite hurried to help unpack the cheese, poppyseed rolls, and fruit from the basket while a vaquero took a bottle of wine up to the falls to cool. There were even flaky, sugary cinnamon cakes in the basket.

"I knew they were your special favorite," Star said, smiling at Margarite as the two women settled their skirts around them and spread the food on crisp white napkins. When the vaquero returned later with the chilled wine, the two women, with appetites sharpened by their early morning ride, had almost finished every morsel of the simple meal.

Star poured the wine into plain glass goblets, then lifted her glass to Margarite. "It's not exactly La Borda," she said teasingly.

"No," Margarite agreed, gazing happily around her. "It's much nicer."

"You're not sorry then that you didn't return with the court to Chapultapec?" Star asked curiously.

Margarite shook her head. When Maximilian and Carlota occasionally returned to La Borda, she still acted as one of Carlota's ladies-in-waiting, but each time became more difficult. Those few moments in the garden when Carlota had let down the barriers between them, and Margarite had glimpsed the unhappy, lonely woman behind the icy reserve had never happened again. If anything, Carlota had withdrawn more and more behind the imperial façade, snapping irritably at her ladies-in-waiting, or lapsing into dull, brooding silences. And Margarite couldn't help noticing that at the elegant parties that were still being given at La Borda, Maximilian drank more and more heavily his favorite champagne.

The war news had grown steadily worse as Benito Juárez and his Republican troops advanced south, reoccupying Chihuahua, and closing in on the important port of Matamoros. With the bad news, the guest list at the parties at La Borda had dwindled to the few loyal followers who remained in the royal entourage along with Mexican officers like Colonel Miguel Lopez and Colonel Juan Heras. They strutted through the gardens in their splendid new uniforms, jealously vying for favor with the emperor, and fighting among themselves to guard their new exalted positions in the imperial army.

It was a drunken Colonel Lopez who had caught Margarite alone in a corridor during such a party and attempted to kiss her. When she tried to push him away, he had smiled loosely at the girl struggling in his arms. "Don't you think I've seen the ardor in your eyes, *Señora*? There's no need to pretend with me." His hands pawed at her bodice as he mumbled, "Colonel

Heras has told me about you. You will see. I will treat you better than that *ladrone*."

Furious, Margarite had shoved at the man, pushing him off balance. "*Hijo de puta!*" she hissed. "I'd sooner lie down with a cockroach!"

In spite of her anger, she felt almost amused at the drunken shock on the man's face at such unladylike words coming from the countess Von Melk as she turned and stalked away.

Remembering that unpleasant episode, Margarite decided that it was time she left her duties as lady-in-waiting permanently. The emperor and empress were returning to La Borda the next day, according to a message she had received from Maria Pacheco. She would hand in her resignation then.

"It can't be too happy a time for the imperial family," Star said. "First the news of the withdrawal of the French forces, and then Franz Josef refusing to send the Austrian troops he had promised his brother. They say King Leopold has also refused to send any more Belgian soldiers to Mexico, despite his sister, Carlota's, urgent request."

"It was cruel of Napoleon to place Maximilian and Carlota on the Mexican throne, promise them support, and then withdraw it," Margarite said indignantly.

"No one forced them to take the throne," Star pointed out gently, then sighed. "Still I suppose it was difficult for Maximilian and Carlota to turn down an empire. If only Maximilian would abdicate. It would save so much bloodshed." Her gray eyes darkened unhappily. "I worry so about Patrick. . . ."

Margarite pretended to sip at her wine while she fought back the bitter taste of guilt. In the beginning she had sought out Star's company deliberately, to try to find out as much as she could about Patrick from his foster mother. But as she and Star almost immediately struck up a close friendship, she disliked more and more the deception between them.

She could not bear to look into her friend's face now as she murmured, "Your adopted son? I thought he was in the United States?"

She did not see the look of amused sympathy on Star's face as she gazed at Margarite. How transparent the girl is, Star thought. The minute I mention Patrick, her face lights up like a Christmas candle.

"My husband thinks Patrick is here in Mexico, fighting with the Juaristas," she replied, and then, afraid of worrying the girl unduly, added hastily, "Of course, he could be mistaken."

"You've never told me, how did you happen to adopt Patrick?" Margarite asked.

Star laughed in memory. "I was shopping in Mexico along the Calle de los Plateros, when my husband caught Patrick with his hand in my pocket. Patrick was an orphan, living on the streets of Mexico as a thief, like so many Mexican children after the war. In spite of his ragged clothes and dirty face, though, he was a handsome, engaging lad. I persuaded my husband that Patrick should return to the rancho with us."

"And you never learned any more about him?"

"Only that his mother had been an Indian, his father, an Irish-American adventurer who came to Mexico to look for gold and died in the Mexican War, fighting for Mexico. When we took Patrick to our rancho, he insisted on working with the vaqueros, paying his own way. We wanted to adopt him, but he always proudly refused to give up his own name. Still, I think, in time he accepted Michael and myself as the parents he had lost."

Star's face glowed with maternal pride. "Of course, I had accepted him as our son from the beginning. Even after we had a child of our own, Patrick was still very special to Michael and me. Though he could get into the most outrageous mischief," she said, laughing. "But when I'd be furious with him, he'd smile—he has the warmest, most captivating smile—and I never could stay angry with him for long."

Margarite remembered that smile only too well, how it could so easily disarm her. She felt bruised, remembering. It was torment to talk about Patrick, and even more torment not to, she discovered as she clung eagerly to Star's every word as the woman continued her reminiscences.

"Even when he got into the worse scrapes, though, he was never spiteful or cruel. And he had too much pride to behave dishonorably. That's why I could never believe—" Star broke off, then shrugged wryly. "Well, you might as well hear the story from me, although we heard it only secondhand ourselves. Friends of my husband's in Texas wrote that Patrick was dishonorably discharged from the Union Army for stealing from the mess funds." Star's voice grew taut with anger. "But I'll never believe it."

Margarite tried to hide the bewilderment she was feeling. If Patrick were dishonorably discharged, how was he able to get the United States Army guns he was smuggling into Mexico?

For a moment she was tempted to tell Star the truth; that her foster son was not the stranger to her that she pretended him to be. Far from it! But that would mean telling the whole story about Patrick and herself, including the humiliating ending. And that she could not force herself to do. Not yet.

At the girl's silence, Star smiled apologetically. "You must be tired of hearing me talk about Patrick. What I had really planned to tell you today is that I've decided to give a costume party for my husband's birthday next month and, of course, I want you to come. Michael absolutely refuses to wear a costume," she said cheerfully, "but I've assured him that as guest of honor, he won't have to."

For a while, the two women discussed various costumes they might wear to the party, then the wine and sunshine made them drowsy, and they stretched out on the blanket for a siesta. Margarite awoke first. Star was still asleep, as were the vaqueros, stretched out on the grass not far away, sombreros over their faces, their pistols beside them within hand's reach.

Margarite yawned and got lazily to her feet, deciding to investigate the waterfall she could hear in the distance, the murmur of the fall the only sound except for the occasional calling of a mockingbird as she climbed the hill behind her. The actual waterfall was still tantalizingly hidden from her when she finally reached the boulder-strewn hilltop and stopped to rest a moment on a flat rock.

She had forgotten to put on her sombrero when she started the climb and the sun beat unmercifully on her head, reminding her of those days she had spent with the *arrieros,* riding astride her mustang through the hill country. She braced her hands against the rock, against the memories that immediately rushed back over her in dizzying waves, her eyes shut as if to physically refuse them entry. If only there were some way she could burn the memories from her mind, she thought miserably as the sun burned like a firebrand against her skin.

"Don't move, *poquita,*" a voice said quietly behind her.

Her eyes flew open. She stared, petrified, at the arched-tailed scorpion on the rock beside her, within an inch of her outspread hand. She was too terrified to move. A boot descended on the venomous creature, crushing it. Arms circled Margarite's waist, yanked her to her feet, and she was staring disbelievingly into a pair of indigo blue eyes, a face as hard as if chiseled from granite beneath a dark sombrero.

"Haven't you enough sense to watch where you sit?" Patrick demanded, his voice rough with fear. "One sting from that one and you'd be dead in an hour."

When she couldn't find her voice, he snatched up her hand and examined it closely. "He didn't touch you?"

His nearness evoked suffocating sensations, the way as a child she had always felt before a violent storm, her skin prickling, her heart thudding in her chest. Somehow she managed to pull her hand free, her voice sounding rusty as she asked stiffly, "What are you doing here?"

He pushed his sombrero back from his forehead, and she saw that his face was tired, the lines around his eyes and mouth like tiny gashes, but the smile was the same mockingly lighthearted one she remembered. "I might ask the same of you. Picnicking in a countryside swarming with Juaristas—that doesn't seem a trifle foolhardy?"

"There are a half-dozen vaqueros with us," Margarite said defensively, clenching her hands at her sides as if to physically prevent them from doing something terribly foolish, like reaching up and touching that face, which held no hint of what, if anything, he was feeling. "We're perfectly safe."

"Your bodyguards are sound sleepers, and they haven't posted a guard," he pointed out. "If you were attacked, they'd be dead before they could fire their guns." His eyes narrowed as they roamed over Margarite, the smile fading, his eyes as hard and cold as his face. "Although any Juaristas would be happy to keep you alive. They'd take pleasure in holding for ransom Maximilian's latest mistress."

Almost, Margarite blurted out, "That's not true," but bit back the protest as she fought to hold on to her pride. After all, he had made it clear how little she meant to him, hadn't he? she reminded herself bitterly. She owed him no explanations if she took a dozen lovers. She forced an indifferent smile to her lips as she murmured, "I wouldn't have thought you bothered with court gossip."

"Gossip can prove useful," he said, moving away from her to lean back against a stunted cottonwood tree, but his eyes never leaving her. "You'd be surprised how much information can be learned from servants who talk too freely."

She remembered her conversation with Juan Heras in the garden at La Borda. "Information about the movement of military supplies?" she asked. "Is that how you knew when and where to attack the military supply train?"

"You seem to have your sources of information too," he said dryly.

"Heras will kill you," Margarite blurted out. "He told me to tell you."

He stiffened, his voice suddenly softly menacing. "So you're a confidante of El Cuchillo now, *poquita*? Or have you made another conquest? Perhaps I should have left you at his camp in the beginning."

Margarite's cheeks stung with anger, but one thing at least she had learned as Carlota's lady-in-waiting was to hold her tongue, no matter how provoked. Deliberately she turned her gaze away from Patrick, staring down into a barranca where Corono de Cristoes flowered.

The petals, like drops of blood caught amid the spiny thickets, brought back another painful memory, and her gaze returned to Patrick. "Hosea? Is he with you?"

For a brief moment she saw pain charge the narrowed eyes before Patrick said harshly. "The *niño* died."

Yes, Margarite thought dully, she should have known the boy couldn't have survived such a terrible wound.

"For what?" she demanded, her voice trembling with anger. "Is it worth it, a young boy dying so that an illiterate Indian can be placed in the National Palace in Mexico!"

The face beneath the sombrero did not move a muscle but something stirred in that indigo gaze and then was still. Patrick's voice, when he spoke, was deceptively mild. "Hosea was more man than boy, and President Juárez is an educated man, a lawyer."

Margarite was immediately ashamed of her outburst, knowing that she had wanted to hurt this man as he had hurt her. And she sensed that she had succeeded. But the taste of triumph was dust in her mouth. She turned away from that pitiless gaze. How many more would die, she wondered wearily, adding their blood to the already bloodstained Mexican earth. Patrick himself could be next.

What was he doing here anyway? she suddenly wondered. He must know that Heras's men were combing the hills around Cuernavaca for him. Her gaze wandered down to the road in the distance below her, the road that ran between Cuernavaca and the capital. Then she swung back, facing Patrick, all at once understanding the reason for the glasses slung over his shoulder.

She motioned toward the road. "That's why you're here, isn't it?" she demanded. "You're watching the road." No doubt, his men weren't far away, perhaps hidden from view on the other side of the barranca, waiting for Patrick to give the signal to attack the next unsuspecting military traffic to travel the road to Mexico. Or, she thought, all at once alarmed, travelers from Mexico to Cuernavaca? Such as Maximilian and Carlota coming over this road tomorrow on their way to La Borda. Although the plans for their travels were kept secret as much as possible, Patrick was right. There was always gossip at La Borda about the court's coming and going.

She stared at Patrick, horrified. "It's Maximilian you're waiting for, isn't it? You plan to attack the imperial coach!"

Patrick silently cursed his own stupidity. He had forgotten how intelligent the countess was. Not that he had forgotten much else about her, he thought grimly, annoyingly aware of the hunger even now twisting inside of him as he studied Margarite's slim figure. A vagrant breeze pulling at the simple woven riding shirt outlined the soft curve of her hips, and tugged loose a tendril of blue-black hair at her temple, hair that still curled, gamine-fashion, around her face. A healthy peach glow from the sunlight ran along her cheekbones, and he saw that she was not as boyishly slender as he remembered. Her forearms and throat were softly rounded, her breasts showing a more womanly curve as they pushed against the embroidered white camisa.

How many countless nights had he lain on his blanket, trying to sleep, and instead remembering every detail about the countess Von Melk: the small, exquisitely formed body, the childlike way she slept, curled up in a ball beside him, the haughty way her back stiffened, her chin lifted, when she was angry, even the slight stutter that crept into her voice when she was embarrassed.

Yet not once had he questioned the decision he had made when he had sent her away. Oh, he had no doubt that she would have gone with him, turned herself willingly into a *soladera* for him, but for how long? How long before she would start comparing her hard, comfortless life with him with the luxurious life she had known before she met him? And how long before she would start remembering that she had been born a countess, her mother a wealthy *criolla,* and begin regretting attaching herself to a man who was not only half Indian but without wealth, whose only title was captain in the United States Army. If it were agonizing to be without her now, how much more agonizing to have her look at him one day with reproach and disillusionment in her gaze.

Nothing of what he was thinking showed in Patrick's face. All Margarite could see was the cruel, hard cast to his features, and she shivered, not sure whether it was concern for Maximilian and Carlota or the knowledge that the imperial coach was heavily guarded on its trips between Chapultapec and La Borda. It would be suicide to attempt such an attack on the imperial family.

"I can't let you do it," she whispered. "I won't!"

Shocked at the blaze of anger that leapt into the indigo eyes, she stepped back, but not quickly enough. Patrick's hands were hard on her arms, hurting her as he pulled her toward him so abruptly that she stumbled and fell against him. The fury in his voice seemed to sear her face as he scowled down at her. "Does he mean so much to you then, your emperor Maximilian? Is he so special when he takes a woman? Tell me, does he perform differently in bed than other, ordinary men?"

His mouth descended on hers with a ferocity that forced her lips apart, his tongue searching, plundering, giving her no chance to answer. There was no way she could combat his anger, which she sensed vaguely with one part of her mind was directed as much at himself as at her. She forced herself to remain still, as if she were standing in the midst of a violent storm and knew the only way to remain safe was not to run but to remain perfectly motionless, to allow the storm to run its course.

Then suddenly she realized the hands on her arms were no longer hurting her, the mouth no longer cruelly bruising, but moving insistently, coaxingly, against her lips. His hands on her back pressed her softness against him, lifting her from the ground so that she felt the hardness of his legs, her body molded against his. His tongue was no longer ravaging but skillfully penetrating the softness of her mouth slowly, rhythmically. This was a different sort of storm racing through her blood, his caresses arousing a hunger she thought she had forgotten but her body, so long starved, remembered well.

When she lifted her arms to pull him closer, when her lips moved beneath his with an eagerness to match his own, he suddenly pulled away, his smile, triumphantly taunting as he looked down into her flushed face and murmured, "So you haven't forgotten me completely, *Niña*."

He set her abruptly on her feet, his voice contemptuous as his gaze raked her from soft leather boots to the dark, shining hair that swirled around her face. "Or is it that you're one of those women who are natural-born *putas*, who spread your legs for any man."

Margarite stared at him with loathing, even as one part of her mind thought bewildered: How was it possible to love and hate a man at the same time? "I hope El Cuchillo does find you," she said hotly. "I hope he finds you and kills you."

Patrick laughed softly. "Do you now?" His hand reached out almost casually to touch the small breast pushing against the loose, cotton camisolelike blouse she wore. Furious, she felt her nipple harden beneath the fingers pulling gently at it, saw the laughter in his eyes at her discomfiture.

"Are you so sure it's my death you want, *poquita*?" he asked, grinning down at her, but startled himself at the immediate reaction, like a knife thrusting within himself, when he felt the response of the small, upthrust breast beneath his hand. Then, he thought coldly, why not? Why should he deny himself the pleasure he would find in that soft, willing body? And he couldn't afford to let her go running off to Heras with word of his plans to attack the imperial carriage, now, could he? "Shall I keep you here with me, *poquita*?" he asked, his eyes narrowing, studying the girl. "Shall I make you forget that strutting popinjay at La Borda?"

His hand slipped inside the cotton blouse, pleased that she wore no stays beneath, not that her firm, slender body needed any, he thought, remembering the litheness of her body beneath the boy's clothes she had once worn. His hand found and captured the softness of her breast, which was not boylike at all, but fit snugly into his hand, while his thumb continued to brush teasingly at the proud nipple. He heard her catch her breath, saw her eyes widening, the iris growing a darker, lustrous green with desire. No, not just desire, he realized with an odd feeling of dismay. He had seen the quickening of desire in too many women's eyes, glittering, ephemeral, flaring up and dying away just as quickly, not to recognize the difference. The green eyes gazing into his were filled with a soft, wondrous glow, a shining warmth that had remained in her eyes, he remembered, even after they finished making love.

"I'll stay," she said quietly. "But I'll not be a party to murder." And she waited, bracing herself for his anger to once more explode around her.

Instead, she saw a look of almost grudging admiration in the indigo eyes, the hand growing quiet, then withdrawing from her breast, leaving her body strangely cold and aching.

Patrick's mouth twisted in a wry smile. He had forgotten the girl's courage, the way she had stood up to him, defying him from the beginning. Oh, she would keep her word, he knew. She would go with him, but would he ever know? Had she stayed with him because she loved him or because she wanted to keep Maximilian alive?

He frowned. "It won't make any difference, you know. Maximilian is finished. It's just a matter of time. And those who stand with him will go down with him. There'll be no place for foreigners like yourself in Mexico after Maximilian is gone."

"What of you?" she asked, clasping her hands before her so that he could not see their trembling. "Aren't you a foreigner too? Your father was an American, and don't you take your orders from the United States Army?" Her voice sharpened indignantly. "Although I can't believe that the United States government would order you to kill the emperor."

He shrugged indifferently. "There was no question of killing Maximilian. He would be held safely. Without him to rally around, his imperial army would soon collapse. Then he and his wife would be placed on a ship, waiting in Vera Cruz, and sent back to Europe, where they belong." Unexpectedly he smiled, that charming, reckless smile that made the indigo eyes sparkle, and wiped all trace of his Indian ancestry from his face.

"But you're right, Countess. Capturing your Maximilian was entirely my own idea."

"He is not my Maximilian!" she protested. She gazed, exasperated, at the man smiling so light-heartedly down at her, her words coming in a rush. "And if you weren't so blind, you'd know—" She broke off abruptly, feeling her face grow warm, and turned her gaze quickly away from those too searching eyes.

"Know what, *poquita*?" A hand was on her chin, gently forcing her to face him. And for one heart-twisting moment, she saw in that suddenly unguarded face what Star must have glimpsed in the eyes of that young thief prowling the Calle de la Plateros, a desperate pride and an equally desperate hunger warring within the boy and now the man.

Her gaze clung helplessly to his as she said softly, "You know I've never lain with any other man. I never could."

Then she waited, her head held high but her face pale, a trembling starting deep inside her as she watched his face with that stony look, shutting her out.

Embarrassment put a slight stutter into her voice as she laughed nervously and murmured. "You needn't be alarmed. I don't plan to throw myself at you again." But she couldn't stop the tears stinging her eyes, from sliding helplessly down her face.

"*Querida, mi alma.*" Her face was cupped in his hands, and he was kissing her eyes, as he stroked her hair and whispered, "Don't cry, *poquita*. It destroys me to see you cry." His arms hungrily closed around her.

She stood on tiptoe to reach his lips, laughing and crying at the same time, her voice joyfully, childishly, triumphant. "I won't let you send me away again. No one can stop us from being together now."

Star's voice spoke quietly but firmly behind her. "I'm sorry, Margarite, but you're wrong. I'll stop you."

Chapter 21

UNLIKE Margarite, Star had thought to put on her sombrero before she had climbed the hill. Now she pushed it back from her face so that the still bright auburn hair flamed in the sunlight, the silvery gray eyes warm with concern and affection as she turned to Patrick. "You're looking tired, *mi hijo*."

Patrick took the woman quickly in his arms, placed a kiss on one smooth cheek, then smiled down at her. "And you are as beautiful as ever. How is Don Miguel?"

"Fretting about you, as I do," she said briskly. Then glancing at Margarite, "What mischief are you up to now, Patrick?"

The smile did not waver, only the indigo eyes hardened a little. "This matter does not concern you."

"Of course it concerns me," Star said, giving her son an impatient glance. "I promised Margarite's *dueña* that I would look after her. And even if I hadn't, do you think I'd let the girl do something so foolishly reckless as to ride off with your band of cutthroats."

"Soldiers, not cutthroats," Patrick corrected her lightly. "And how do you propose to stop me? With that band of sleeping beauties riding with you?"

"They are no longer sleeping," Star said, gesturing behind her to the vaqueros, who, crouched low below the ridge of the hill, hidden in the brush, now rose in a half circle, their guns drawn.

Star sighed and shook her head. "Oh, I know your men must be somewhere near, but I can't believe you'd put Margarite's life at risk if my vaqueros or your men should start shooting." She smiled faintly. "Not to mention that I'm sure you know Don Miguel wouldn't be too happy if anything happened to me."

"You should have been a general, *Mamacíta*," Patrick said, smiling grimly. "But don't you think Margarite has the right to make her own decision?"

"I have decided," Margarite said quickly, moving to stand beside Patrick.

For a moment, looking into the girl's glowing face, as if reflecting the passion banked in the green eyes, one small hand resting proudly on Patrick's arm, Star felt a wrench of pity. How could she have forgotten, she thought, how it felt to be young and terribly in love, so that nothing else in the world mattered but the man who held you in his arms. And she remembered, as if it had been yesterday rather than years before, those weeks and months of anguish when she had been separated from Michael. But that had been different, she reminded herself firmly. She had been married, or thought she was, to Michael before she had been kidnapped away from him.

She forced her gaze away from Margarite and back to her son. "This is madness, Patrick," she said quietly. "Do you really expect the girl to lead your sort of life? How long do you think she'll last? And if something should happen to you, what will become of her then?" Her gaze swung accusingly back to Margarite. "And what of Patrick? How can he protect himself, or his men, if half the time he's worrying about you, your safety, your welfare?"

She motioned to the men behind her to lower their guns then walked a short distance away before turning back and saying to Margarite, "I'll wait for you by the horses."

At the picnic site Star kept herself busy, packing the remains of the lunch into the wicker basket, folding the blanket, trying to ignore her misgivings. Had she been wrong to interfere? Would Margarite, or Patrick, ever forgive her?

When, ten minutes later, Margarite came slowly down the hillside, she did not look at Star but went directly to her horse. Star could sense the despair in the young, stiffly held back, and she held out her hand, then let it drop helplessly. "I'm sorry," she said. "I wouldn't blame you for hating me."

Margarite turned, her face pale but her voice steady. "I don't hate you. I should have told you about Patrick and me in the beginning. And you were right, of course. I just would have been in his way." The composed young face suddenly shattered as she buried her face in the saddle, her voice muffled, heartbroken. "But it hurts so, losing him again."

The sound of that young, heartbroken voice still echoed in Star's ears that evening as she prepared for bed. She stopped brushing her hair to turn to her husband pleadingly. "I did do the right thing, didn't I? I feel so guilty."

Michael was already in bed, waiting, as usual, a little impatiently for his wife to join him. Now he tore his attention from Star's auburn hair spilling loosely over the shoulders of her lacy nightdress, the brush making a faint crackling sound as it rose and fell rhythmically, burnishing the already smoothly shining hair, a nightly ritual that never ceased to delight him.

For a moment, some of the fury he had felt earlier when he had learned of his wife's meeting with Patricio returned, a fury that had vented itself upon the shame-faced vaqueros who had been asleep when they should have been guarding Doña Star and the countess Von Melk. "Of course you did the right thing," he said brusquely. Seeing the unhappiness on his wife's face, his voice softened. "Patricio might be headstrong, but he's no fool. I'm sure he knows that taking the girl with him would have been the height of folly." He frowned as he reached for a long black cheroot from a mosaic-lidded box beside the bed. "I can't imagine how such an unlikely pair ever met in the first place."

"Margarite told me it was Patrick who rescued her from the camp of Juan Heras after Heras's men had killed her aunt and uncle. You remember Juan, don't you? He grew up here on the ranch. Margarite says he's now a colonel in the imperial army."

Michael's face darkened as he lit the cheroot. He

remembered Juan Heras only too well. He had often regretted that he had stopped Patrick from finishing with his fists the job he had started, in dealing with the cold-blooded bastard. "If the emperor is depending upon *cazadores* like Juan Heras to fight his battles for him, then he's in more trouble than I thought." He shrugged impatiently. "Anyway, the girl will no doubt get over her infatuation with Patrick."

"I don't think so," Star said, shaking her head. "I saw the way she looked at Patrick. And she's not a child, you know. She's the same age I was when I married you." Her gray eyes clouded in memory. "And I can't help remembering how I felt when you and I were separated. I never want to endure such pain again."

But Michael didn't want to think about that terrible time in their lives, how, in part, their separation had been due to his own pigheadedness and pride, and he said gruffly, "Well, the countess will have to get over whatever her feelings are for Patrick. When I was in Mexico last week, I heard that Margarite's guardian has arranged a marriage for her with a very suitable gentleman from an old *criollo* family."

Star's hand clenched her hairbrush as she gave her husband a furious glance. "How can you be so unfeeling? Arranged marriage! This isn't the Middle Ages, you know. Sometimes I forget how very Mexican you are, Michael."

Her husband got out of bed, and since he slept in the raw, his wife was very aware of the wide shoulders, the taut strength of the muscles, still firm and hard across the broad chest, as he walked slowly toward her with his lithe Indian stride. "And I sometimes forget how very much a Yankee you are, *mi amada*," he said, smiling down into her beautiful, angry face. "As for unfeeling. . ."

Her husband's mouth on hers caused Star the same shock of pleasure she had felt the first time they had kissed. She gave a murmur of protest quickly stilled as his mouth increased its pressure, parting her lips, and his hands moved gently, persuasively, over the curves and hollows of a body that was as familiar to him as his own, yet a familiarity of which he never tired. When he

felt the angry stiffness disappear from her body, her
thighs parting to receive his caress, her mouth opening
fully, eagerly, beneath his, his arms scooped her up and
carried her to the bed. His voice was husky, his eyes
warm with amusement as he quickly stripped the sheer
gown away and pulled her beneath him. "Let me show
you, my love, just how much I do feel," he said, laughing softly.

Later, blissfully content, curled snugly next to her
sleeping husband, her outflung hand resting on his chest,
Star was still not able to keep a nagging sense of fore-
boding from gnawing at a corner of her mind when she
thought of Patrick and Margarite. The uneasy feeling
remained with her even as she threw herself into preparing for the costume ball she was giving for Michael's
birthday.

Although she had sent Margarite and her *dueña* an
invitation to the party, she wasn't sure the girl would
attend and was pleasantly surprised the night of the ball
when she looked up from greeting late arriving guests to
see Margarite and Doña Isobel crossing the room toward
her. She might not have recognized Margarite, who was
wearing a mask and attired as a Poblana peasant girl
dressed for a fete day, but there was no mistaking the
buxom figure of Doña Isobel, who had apparently refused to wear a costume but did have a black lacy mask
over her face.

"How charming you look, my dear," Star said, giving
the girl a quick embrace, then stepping back to admire
Margarite's costume. The white muslin shift, trimmed
with lace and embroidery around the skirt, was sheer
enough so that the petticoat could be seen beneath, the
bottom half of the petticoat of scarlet, the upper part of
white satin. A red satin vest embroidered with silver, a
colored sash wrapped twice around Margarite's tiny waist,
silk stockings and white satin shoes trimmed with silver
completed the costume.

It was evident from the rather pained expression about
Doña Isobel's mouth that Margarite's costume did not
meet with her approval, but she said nothing, allowing
her hostess to lead her to the refreshment table which

was piled high with fresh fruit on beds of ice, sweet
cakes of all sizes and shapes, crisp tortillas filled with
sour cream, pitchers of fruit juice, and bowls of brandy
punch.

Leaving Doña Isobel happily sampling the delicacies
on the table, Star pulled Margarite to one side. "I was
afraid you might not come," she said, then hurriedly,
afraid that she was being tactless, "that your duties at
La Borda might keep you away."

"The emperor and empress returned to Chapultapec
yesterday. In any case, I'm no longer one of Carlota's
ladies-in-waiting," Margarite said. "I informed the empress of my decision to leave my post last week."

Something in her voice made Star ask curiously, "Was
Her Majesty upset with you for leaving?"

"No," Margarite said slowly, remembering she had
been worried herself when she had approached the empress with her decision, knowing Carlota's uncertain
temper these days. Instead, the empress had seemed
indifferent to the news. Her green-flecked eyes, with
their intense, feverish quality, had dark circles around
them as she gazed broodingly at a point just above
Margarite's shoulder, and accepted without a word her
lady-in-waiting's resignation.

It was Maria Pacheco who had burst into tears when
Margarite told her friend she was leaving. "How will I
manage without you here at La Borda?" she had protested. "It's bad enough at Chapultapec, where the whole
court lives as if under a state of siege. Frau Kuhacsevich
is in constant fear of being poisoned, and the emperor is
either up in the air or down in the depths of despair,
while the empress goes for days without speaking to
anyone except her maid, Matilde, and the emperor. Even
when she speaks with the emperor, you can tell how
worried she is about him, afraid that he will abdicate.
Frau Kuhacsevich tells me that Doña Carlota is determined to return to Europe by herself and plead the
emperor's case before Napoleon."

"If she goes, will you go with her?"

Maria nodded forlornly. "If she asks me, of course.
What else can I do? I can't desert her now, although I'm

sure I will not know how to behave before the French court."

"I'm glad you've resigned your post at court." Star's worried voice drew Margarite back to the present. "In the beginning, I think the people accepted Carlota, but now, even in Cuernavaca, you can hear them singing in the *pulquerías,* cruel songs about 'Mama Carlota.' "

Margarite had heard the songs, too, calling Carlota barren and a whore, that soon she would be snared and captured along with her husband. She was sure that Carlota knew about the songs too.

"Michael says that Maximilian can't last much longer, that both the British and French ministers have begged him to abdicate."

Margarite remembered that Patrick had said much the same thing, but it hurt too much to think about Patrick and she concentrated instead on the black, jewel-encrusted costume her hostess wore, the farthingale skirt and starched white lace ruff around Star's slender neck. The auburn hair was set in the elaborate coiffure of the seventeenth century, entwined with ropes of pearls. "Queen Elizabeth?" she hazarded a guess.

Star nodded, laughing. "I decided it might be fun to become a queen for a night, and I remember reading that Queen Elizabeth had red hair."

As Margarite strolled among the guests gathered in the torchlit courtyard and under the arched gallery that surrounded the patio, she noticed that some of the other women guests had indulged in their fancies to be queen for a night. She spotted, amused, two Queen Isabellas and one Mary Queen of Scots. Remembering the unhappy empress Carlota, she wondered if royal life wasn't vastly overrated. She decided she much preferred her peasant attire, which was drawing admiring glances, if not from the women guests, then from the men.

The musicians with their guitars, violins, and horns had gathered for the dancing in the grand *sala*, beginning the set with a gay mazurka. Star and Michael led the way onto the dance floor. Michael, like many of the men present, wore a mask but had refused to wear a costume, although there were some young gallants in silver-studded charro costumes and colorful military uniforms of a bygone day. Margarite watched Star and Michael, thinking wistfully how well they looked together, Michael's arms resting lightly, possessively, around his wife, Star gazing adoringly up into her husband's deeply tanned face.

She felt a touch on her shoulder. The guest had come up behind her so quietly that Margarite hadn't noticed him. He was dressed as a Carmelite monk, his body wrapped within a black cape. His face, covered by a black mask, was almost hidden within the hood of his costume. He nodded to her, then signaled to the dance floor, indicating a desire for her to dance with him. She was about to refuse. There was something a little offputting about the caped and hooded figure, and, in any case, she was in no mood for dancing. Then she saw Doña Isobel heading determinedly toward her. She was sure that her *dueña,* who had fussed unendingly about Margarite's attending the party at all, was determined to attach herself like a leech to her young charge for the rest of the evening.

Margarite slipped quickly into the monk's waiting arms and out onto the dance floor before Doña Isobel could reach her side. As the man's arms closed firmly around her, leading her effortlessly through the intricate steps of the mazurka, she smiled up at her partner. "For a man who has given up the sins of the flesh, you dance very well, *Señor.*"

Her partner didn't answer her, only holding her more tightly. Margarite saw that Doña Isobel was standing, watching the dancers, annoyed, while her hostess, whirling around in her husband's arms, had a slightly puzzled look on her face as she caught sight of Margarite and the monk.

Feeling all at once ill at ease, Margarite tried to make conversation several more times with her companion, only to meet with a black silence. Well, really, she thought, annoyed. Had he taken a vow of silence to match his monk's costume?

Then, to her surprise, she was being danced out into

the courtyard, where several other couples, romantically inclined, had found the torchlit patio, fairy lamps flickering like fireflies among the trees, more to their liking. It was even more difficult now to see the face of the monk in the flickering torchlight, but there was no doubt the arms around her were pressing her scandalously close so that she could feel the hardness of the body beneath the all-encompassing cloak. Not just the hardness of his body, she realized suddenly. She was sure the man was wearing a pistol in a holster beneath the cape. Not that it was unusual for men to carry guns, even to a social gathering, with so many brigands on the road, but while he was dancing? Margarite's irritation turned to anger.

"We should return to the *sala*," she said coldly. "I think it's going to rain."

It had rained that morning, forecasting an early beginning of the rainy season, and the warm night air, filled with the scent of flowers from the flower beds, had a softness to it, as if more rain would soon be forthcoming.

Before she realized what he was doing, the arms around her tightened in an iron grip and she was pulled into the shadows of the trees.

"What do you think you're doing?" she whispered, outraged, struggling to free herself. Was the man mad to handle her this way with help only a scream away?

A hand covered her mouth firmly, and then a voice whispered into her ear, "Not so loud, *poquita*." She felt the warm breath of his laughter. "Or I'll know Gabriel was right in calling me a fool for coming here tonight."

"Patrick!" She lowered her voice quickly, her hand reaching up to touch his face as if she still could not believe it.

He took her hand and held it to his lips, then pulled her gently toward the outer wall of the courtyard, where oleander bushes spread their sharp sweetness into the night. She did not even see the door he opened, so well hidden it was among the stones, only that they stepped from the courtyard into complete darkness. She sensed she was in some sort of small enclosure, open to the sky overhead. As her eyes became accustomed to the darkness, she could see tall walls of another, smaller courtyard surrounding her.

"Where are we?" she asked, startled.

From his cape, Patrick took out sulphur matches and a piece of candle. He lit the candle, shielding it with his hand, and Margarite could see overgrown flower beds and tangled, untended shrubbery, even a small, cracked fountain in the middle of a pool, empty now except for stagnant rainwater. At one side of the courtyard was a small octagonal structure, one side open toward the courtyard, reminding her of the gazebos she had seen in gardens in America.

"One of the Cordoba family, years ago, built this private courtyard, with its own hidden entrance and exit. The story is he was a scholar and built it so he could study his books without being disturbed, but Doña Star always claimed it was a secret rendezvous for his mistresses." Patrick grinned as he lit Margarite's way across the damp grass. "I'm inclined to agree with Doña Star."

"Does your mother know you're here?" Margarite asked.

Patrick shook his head. "I shouldn't be here at all, but I was sure you would be attending the party tonight, and I couldn't pass up the chance to see you one last time."

Margarite stopped abruptly on the steps of the small gazebo, her heart like a fist closing in her chest. "One last time?"

Patrick put the candle on a small table, its light hidden by the windowless walls. The wicker furniture in the room was old and shabby, but still comfortable. He turned toward Margarite, removing his mask. She could see his features in the flickering candlelight, the indigo eyes, black and opaque, against the burnished copper face. "I'm heading north tomorrow to join General Diaz."

"But you're not in the Mexican Republican Army," she protested. "You're an American Army officer."

Patrick shrugged. "Not anymore. I've sent in my resignation. I should have done it long ago." He leaned forward and undid the ties that held Margarite's mask. She could feel his gaze travel intently over her face, as if, she thought, suddenly terrified, he was memorizing each feature, as if he never expected to see her again.

She flung herself into his arms. "I won't let you go," she said furiously. "I won't let you go off and be killed."

He rocked her in his arms as if she were a child he was comforting. "Who said anything about being killed?" he said, his voice chiding. "Why should I do anything as foolish as that?" He kissed her lightly on her eyelids and temples, the kisses as soft as the rain she could hear beginning to fall on the tiled roof, until the trembling that shook her body with fear changed to a different type of shivering. Impatiently she lifted her own lips to claim his, unable to wait any longer to assuage the wild fever that burned within her. Then she sighed with contentment as his mouth moved across hers with a growing urgency.

He took off his cape and flung it over one of the couches whose pillows were still there although the covers were split and stained from rain that had blown into the small house. He smiled wryly down at the starched white muslin shift she wore. "That's a charming costume, but very easily wrinkled, I'm afraid."

Understanding, she flushed and started to turn away, her hands fumbling at the fastening at her neck, when he gently turned her around to face him. "Why do you turn away from me?" he asked quietly. "Are you ashamed that I should watch you undress? Do you think anything you could do, *querida,* would shame me or yourself?" And then, laughing teasingly, "Shall I help you?"

She shook her head, her hands steadying as they quickly undid the fastening at her neck, the sash at her waist, and lifted the shift over her head. Standing proudly erect, her eyes fastened on Patrick's face, she slipped off the tiny lace chemise that covered her breasts, and allowed the colorful, stiff petticoats and her lacy undergarments to fall with a soft, whispering sound at her feet. Slimly beautiful, the silken sheen of her flesh catching the candlelight, she gloried in the warmth of Patrick's gaze roaming over her, the look of burning desire she had put into his eyes only making her own desire burn that much more hotly.

When he threw off his own clothes, hanging the gun belt carefully over a chair, she stepped into his arms. The shock of his flesh, warm and hard, against hers, made her gasp, and when he pulled her down on the couch beside him, she knew she was as ready and eager as he was. But he did not immediately possess her. Instead, he kissed her slowly, murmuring words of love as he caressed her, his lips lingering wherever the veins beat close to the surface of her skin, deliberately prolonging, stretching her desire until she moaned softly, reaching blindly for him, guiding him to the warm, waiting softness. "Please . . . please . . ." she whispered.

Almost the moment he slipped inside of her, she felt both their bodies' exploding response, the emptiness she had felt for so long inside of her filled with a happiness so complete it was almost like pain. Even Patrick was shocked at the depth of the passion that had consumed them both. He braced himself above Margarite, slowly parting from her, but his hands continuing to fondle her, stroking the now soft, pink-tipped breasts, brushing the dark tendrils of hair back from her face. "What a little passion flower you are, *mi alma*," he whispered. "How could anyone guess how much fire there is behind that beautiful, haughty face?"

She smiled, running her hands lightly, teasingly, along his rib cage. "And do you believe me now, my love, that there has never been anyone else but you? There never will be."

To her surprise, she watched his face darken into a scowl as he abruptly moved away from her to sit on the side of the couch. "Don't say that, Margarite." Oh, he intended to survive, he thought grimly, but only an idiot expected any guarantees in the middle of a war. And he suspected Margarite had no understanding at all of her own deeply passionate nature. If anything should happen to him, did he want her to remain faithful to a dead man, all that sweet unspent passion curdling and shriveling inside of her?

"I'd want you to find someone else if I shouldn't come back to you," he said harshly.

"You will come back!" Margarite sat up abruptly. "Promise me that you will!"

She watched that impassive, fatalistic Indian look that she hated close over his face, and she burrowed into his chest, her voice muffled against his neck. "I'd die if anything happened to you."

Patrick laughed softly. "Oh, no, you wouldn't, my love. You have too much courage, too much spirit to ever turn your back on life." He lifted her chin and kissed the tip of her nose, resisting the almost overwhelming impulse to pull her body, that he knew would be already soft and yielding, into his arms, feel those small breasts grow firm and proud beneath his stroking fingers. With a smothered groan he pushed her away and got to his feet, his voice hoarse. "You can't stay away any longer, little one. Your *dueña* is probably already raising an alarm." It had been dangerous enough, his coming here tonight, he thought. He wouldn't put Margarite's reputation in jeopardy too.

She got slowly to her feet, understanding now why he had prolonged their lovemaking, knowing they would have so little time together. She felt tears like a hard knot in her throat, but she wouldn't let him see her cry, she thought furiously. She wouldn't have his last glimpse of her, perhaps for months, be with her eyes red and puffy. He helped her dress, dropping a kiss at the nape of her neck as he fastened the back of her shift, holding her for a moment in his arms after he had tied the sash around her tiny waist. Then he dressed himself quickly, restrapping the holstered pistol around his waist before drawing on the monk's cloak and hood. The candle had died out and he held her around the waist as they walked through the darkness back to the hidden door in the wall.

He opened the door, and as she stepped through, he pulled her back into his arms, not kissing her, simply holding her close in an embrace that was like an unspoken commitment, more binding somehow than the act of love.

In the darkness neither saw the men waiting beyond

the wall with pistols drawn, until they heard guns being cocked, and a man's voice sliced sharply through the blackness toward them. "Don't move, Don Patricio. You and the countess Von Melk are both under arrest."

Chapter 22

PATRICK stiffened, his hand moving instinctively to the butt on the gun beneath the cloak, then realized that Margarite would be in the line of fire and let his hand drop to his side. The men were wearing the uniform of Maximilian's newly formed *cazadores*, and Patrick was not surprised when he and Margarite were taken, not to the main *sala*, but to a smaller, informal room which was Don Miguel's study, to find Juan Heras waiting there for them. His foster parents were also in the room, and Star gave an involuntary gasp of despair when she saw Patrick. Her husband's face darkened, but he didn't make a sound.

Juan, who was apparently making himself at home, seated behind Don Miguel's broad desk, got to his feet and smiled jovially when three of his men escorted Patrick and Margarite into the room. "So I was right, *compadre*. I was sure if the countess was here tonight, you would not be far away." He winked broadly at Patrick. "You forget, *hermano,* I was brought up on this rancho too. Like you, I would bring my *novias* to the small, secret courtyard." He bowed gallantly toward Margarite. "What better place to enjoy the charms of the beautiful countess."

The muscles in Patrick's face pulled taut, his eyes seeming to flatten in his face. Michael looked at his son, then said quickly to the man behind the desk, "How

long do you plan to hold my family and my guests
captives?''

Heras made a shocked face. ''Your guests are not
captives, Don Miguel. Not at all. My men are protecting
them from any foolishness on the part of your vaqueros.
As for your wife and yourself, I have no proof that you
knew that Don Patricio would be here this evening.''
His voice thickened, all amusement leaving the mutilated face as he turned toward Patrick. ''But Don Patricio
and the countess are my prisoners and will return with
me to the Cortés Barracks.''

''And then?'' Contempt laced Michael's voice. ''That
is, assuming they live to reach Cuernavaca.''

Juan spread his hands in feigned helplessness. ''But,
patrón,'' he said with exaggerated mock servility. ''You
surely know Emperor Maximilian's decree of last Octo-
ber. All persons who are members of armed bands not
authorized by law shall be tried by a military court, and
executed within twenty-four hours.''

''And the countess?'' Michael asked coldly. ''Or are
you fool enough to think that anyone in his right mind
will believe a lady-in-waiting to the empress is a member
of an armed band?''

''That is not my decision to make,'' Heras said loftily.
''The military guard will decide.'' His small black eyes
were suddenly bright with malice as he added, ''But under
the decree, even *hacendados* as grand as yourself, Don Miguel, can be executed if they are found to be in complic-
ity with the Liberals.''

Michael gazed at the man a long moment, then asked,
his voice very quiet, ''Are you threatening me, Juan?''

Behind Heras, his second in command, Captain Ramon Ghivera, an Indian who had grown up on a ranch
much like this one and who was still in awe of the rich
hacendados, shuffled his feet uneasily.

Heras turned and scowled at the captain. ''Why are
you standing there, you fool? Escort the prisoners
outside.''

''I think not, *compadre*.''

Heras whirled and looked into the barrel of a pistol
held in Patrick's hand.

"You should train your men better, Colonel Heras," Patrick said, his smile taunting. "One of the first military rules—always search a prisoner for hidden weapons." Without looking at Margarite, who was still standing beside him, he said, "Move over beside Don Miguel, Margarite."

"Patrick, what . . . ?"

"Now! Move!"

She did as she was told, Don Miguel's arm reaching out to pull her beside his wife, his own body shielding theirs.

Juan's face, a mixture of anger and confusion, dissolved into a loose-lipped smile. "You are running a bluff, I think, *amigo*. You brought no men with you this time. Kill me, and my men will shoot you down."

Twisting to see around Don Miguel's broad shoulders, Margarite watched Patrick, his face completely blank and still except for the long mouth that curved into a death's-head smile. His voice was almost casual as he said, "Then we'll die together, *amigo*."

Juan's small black eyes scurried toward his three men, standing, as if in a frozen tableau, unsure what to do. His crushed face stained an ugly yellow, not with fear, Margarite saw, but fury, the loose smile exposing a great many blackened, decayed teeth. "Put down the gun, Patricio, and I'll forget about the woman. She is of no use to me. I swear on my mother's grave. . . ."

Even as he was speaking, Juan's hand was creeping downward to the gun at his waist. The impact from Patrick's bullet hitting his forehead spun him around, so that for a moment Margarite saw what was left of the bloody, lower part of his face. The smile still hung obscenely on the loose mouth as he pitched forward and crashed to the floor. Almost the same moment, jolted out of their paralysis, two of the soldiers fired their guns at Patrick.

The sound of the gunfire reverberated against the walls of the room, so that she could not hear her own screams above the explosion. Nor did she know later how she had managed to get out from behind Don Miguel's restraining arm. All she knew was that she was kneeling on the floor beside Patrick, cradling his head in her lap, moaning his name over and over again while her white muslin shift turned scarlet with the blood pouring from his wounds.

The soldiers had lifted their guns again for a final volley into the fallen man but with the *señora* there, shielding the body in her arms, they hesitated. Don Miguel stepped forward, placing himself between Margarite and the men with their drawn revolvers.

"*Bastante!*" he ordered sharply. "This is my home, not a *carniceria*. It's finished. I'll have no more killing here."

The air of authority, the bark of command in his voice, made two of the men turn uncertainly to Ramon, who was their leader now. With command so suddenly and unhappily thrust upon him, Ramon swallowed, licking suddenly dry lips as he stared into the *patrón*'s hard face. Weakly he tried to bluster. "I must make certain, you understand, that Don Patricio is dead."

"As you wish, but first I'm going to take my son into the next room, where my wife will see if there is anything she can do for him. And I want a priest brought. Father Alfredo is among the guests."

Ramon made a last-ditch attempt to establish his authority. "You do not give the orders here, Don Miguel!"

Michael studied the captain almost pityingly. "Do you plan to kill me too? Do you think my vaqueros will allow any of you to leave here alive if harm comes to me?" He shrugged. "You can post a guard outside the room if it will make you feel better."

Without waiting for the man's reply he turned, and with infinite gentleness lifted Patrick into his arms. Margarite started to follow him, but Star stopped her at the door. "It's best if you wait out here, child," she said. Turning to one of the soldiers, she said, "Fetch the *señora*'s *dueña*."

At a nod from the captain, the man left the room and returned in a few seconds with Doña Isobel, who took one look at Margarite's bloodstained dress and promptly collapsed into the man's arms. In the confusion, Star slipped into the bedroom, closing the door behind her.

The priest arrived within minutes and joined Star and Michael at Patrick's bedside. It was not ten minutes later that he reappeared in the doorway, his face somber as he turned to Ramon. "Your prisoner is dead, Captain. You may go in and make certain if you must." The compassionate eyes sought out Margarite, his voice gentle. "Be grateful he lived long enough to receive the holy sacrament, my child. May God have mercy on his soul."

"No!" Margarite pushed blindly past the priest into the room. It was, she remembered vaguely from a tour she had taken of the house with Star, a small, makeshift surgery, where the mistress of the hacienda doled out medicines and tended, as best she could, the hurts and ills of those who lived on the ranch. A candle had been lit at the foot of a narrow bed; otherwise the room was dark. Star and Don Miguel were kneeling beside the bed, their shadows falling across the face of the man lying on the bed.

Star stood up and moved to one side so that for a moment, in the flickering candlelight, Margarite saw Patrick's face, with its curious, terrible emptiness.

Then as Margarite swayed, Star moved quickly to the girl's side, her arm slipping around the small waist as she half-led, half-carried the girl from the room.

Chapter 23

"**D**RINK your chocolate, Margarite, before it cools," Doña Isobel urged. "And the cook has made those cinnamon cakes that you particularly like."

Because her *dueña*'s voice was so anxious, Margarite obediently picked up the cup of chocolate. She had

forgotten, she thought, welcoming the warmth of the
cup in her hand, how damp and chill the Ortiz home
was, especially during the rainy season. Even the mirrors in the *sala* where she and Doña Isobel were having
their afternoon chocolate had a faint haze over them
and the chill of the tile floor crept up through her silk
slippers. Although the curtains were drawn, she could
hear the rain tapping insistently against the windows.
And she was reminded suddenly, wrenchingly, of the
soft sound of the rain that last evening, when she and
Patrick had made love in the small, secret courtyard.

Oh, God, she gasped as pain ripped fiercely through
her.

Doña Isobel leaned forward, her pleasant face drawn
with worry. "Are you all right? You're not ill?"

Margarite shook her head, her hand gripping the side
of the chair until her knuckles turned white. If Doña
Isobel hadn't been sitting beside her, her round eyes
fastened anxiously upon her face, she would have
screamed aloud with the pain, but she knew that would
have scared her poor *dueña* to death, sent her scurrying
for the doctor and Don Francisco.

Doña Isobel gave a sigh of relief. "I was afraid you
might have caught a chill. And Don Francisco would be
upset if you weren't able to receive him tomorrow. He's
bringing the marriage contract for you to see."

Margarite took a cautious breath. She could feel the
pain withdrawing slowly, oh, not for good, she knew,
only to hide somewhere deep within her, behind the wall
of numbness, to claw out at her again when she least
expected it. But she had learned over the last two weeks
not to fight the waves of pain and to be grateful for the
numbness when it crept back.

She put down the cup of chocolate, her palms damp.
Her gaze drifted to the windows, listening to the sound
of the rain. "I don't want to see Don Francisco, and I
have no intention of marrying Don Roberto."

Her voice was apathetic but with a mulish quality to it
that made Doña Isobel sigh. Don Francisco would be
furious with her if Margarite refused to see him again.
He already blamed his ward's *dueña* for the terrible

happenings at the Cordoba hacienda, for the folly of permitting Margarite to attend the costume ball in the first place without a proper escort, and then allowing the girl out of her sight.

As if, Isobel thought as she nervously awaited Don Francisco's arrival the next day, she hadn't done everything she possibly could to avert any hint of scandal afterward. Hadn't she rushed Margarite, half unconscious, back to the Ortiz ranch, and without even bothering to pack had bundled herself and her charge into a carriage for the trip to Mexico City. It was important, she realized, that the girl be removed at once from Cuernavaca and placed under the powerful protection of Don Francisco, to avoid the alarming possibility of her arrest, and, of course, it was equally important to put as much distance as possible between Margarite and the scandalous rumors that were sure to spread through Cuernavaca about the countess and Don Patricio.

When Don Francisco arrived at the Ortiz home the next afternoon, he scowled when Doña Isobel unhappily informed him that the countess was indisposed, then impatiently brushed by her. When he knocked then entered Margarite's bedroom, she was resting in a chair and turned, startled, at the man's abrupt entrance. "I left word that I wasn't receiving visitors, Don Francisco," she said, for the first time in weeks an angry flush of color in her face.

Don Francisco was shocked himself at the young woman's appearance, her face ravaged, her eyes dull. It was just as well he hadn't brought Don Roberto along, he thought. It wouldn't do for a prospective bridegroom, even one as eager as Don Roberto, to see his intended bride looking so ill.

"Please forgive the intrusion, Doña Margarite," he said hastily. "I wouldn't be bothering you, but there are certain matters that must be settled. I've brought the marriage contract for you to see. Don Roberto has been very patient, but with the unfortunate incident at the Cordoba rancho, you can understand that the sooner the marriage is consummated the better."

"I will not sign any marriage contract," Margarite

said almost indifferently, the color fading from her face, leaving once again the gray lifelessness as she listlessly turned her gaze away from Don Francisco.

"You misunderstand, Doña Margarite, if you think your signature is necessary to the marriage contract," Don Francisco said coldly. "I simply brought the contract for you to see as a courtesy, in case there are any stipulations you wish changed. As your legal guardian, I have already given my permission for your marriage to Don Roberto."

When Margarite opened her mouth to protest, he held up his hand. "Please, Doña Margarite, I have spoken to the Ortiz solicitor. You are inheriting a large estate under Mexican law. As a young unwed woman, it is required by law that a legal male guardian be appointed, as I have been, to oversee the management of the property and yourself, for your own protection and well-being." He smiled grimly. "And it is pointless to think of running to General Thun with your rights as an Austrian citizen. With the emperor's army crumbling around him, General Thun is much too busy to become involved with a young girl's legal technicalities."

Por Dios, Don Francisco thought, annoyed. Couldn't the girl see that marriage was her only choice? It had taken every bit of his influence to prevent an official investigation into the countess Von Melk's relationship with the known Juarista traitor, Don Patricio O'Malley. And if it hadn't been for the wealth of the Ortiz estate, he had no doubt but that Don Roberto would have withdrawn his offer of marriage when the scandalous rumors about his intended and Don Patricio had reached Mexico from Cuernavaca.

A look of surprise touched Margarite's face, and she smiled faintly. "And how will you force me to marry Don Roberto? Will you have me dragged screaming to the altar?"

Then she felt a spurt of fear at the icy black anger she saw gathering in Don Francisco's dark eyes, reminding her all at once of her uncle. There was the same arrogance in the sharp, aquiline features of a man accustomed to having his own way.

"I hope there will be no need for such drastic measures," Don Francisco replied. "But you will marry Don Roberto. Be assured of that. You will remain in this house for as long as it takes for you to come to your senses."

"I'm to be a prisoner in my own home?" Margarite demanded, startled out of her lethargy.

Don Francisco shrugged. "If necessary." Feeling suddenly, vaguely guilty looking into the girl's wide, shocked eyes, he said more gently, "I have no wish to be your jailor, child. But I was your uncle's closest friend and I could not betray his memory by behaving dishonorably toward you. Your virtue and reputation are as dear to me as if you were my own daughter. If God had spared him, I'm sure this marriage with Don Roberto is what your uncle would have wanted for you. In time, you will see that I am right."

"Never! I will never marry!"

A look of amusement touched Don Francisco's wintry black eyes. "When you are young, *Señora*, never can be a very short time. If you had a regard, a feeling for the church, I could understand your desire to withdraw from the world and become cloistered." At the girl's look of dismay, he smiled dourly. "I thought not. Then, if it's not marriage to Christ, then it must be marriage to a man. A woman cannot be happy living alone. It is not in her nature."

He bowed gravely. "I will be away from the city for a few days, and when I return, I'm sure you will have reconsidered. In the meantime, I will give instructions to your servants that you are not to leave the hacienda without my permission."

The door closed quietly behind him. Margarite stared at the door disbelievingly. Did Don Francisco really believe he could keep her a prisoner? Even in Vienna, where arranged marriages, she knew, were often the rule, she could not imagine being treated in such a high-handed fashion. Although she had no great desire to leave the house, and hadn't, in fact, left the premises since her arrival two weeks before, she went to her armoire and took out a bonnet and shawl. Then she made her way to the great brass-decorated front door of the villa. A young man in the black and gold Ortiz livery, seated by the door, sprang to his feet at her approach.

"Please fetch my carriage," Margarite said.

The young man flushed unhappily. "I'm sorry, *Señora*, but Don Francisco has given strict orders. The *señora* is not to leave the hacienda."

"This is my house, not Don Francisco's!"

The man shook his head helplessly, giving Margarite an imploring look. "It is not permitted. For the *señora*, I would lay down my life gladly. Her beauty lights my days and nights. It grieves me to deny you anything. . . ."

In the midst of his impassioned declaration of loyalty, Margarite turned and stalked away. She was brooding in her room when Doña Isobel knocked and came in hesitantly.

"Señora Pacheco is here to see you," she said. "She is waiting in the *sala*."

"Am I allowed to see her?" Margarite asked bitterly. "Have you forgotten that you're my jailor now?"

And then immediately she regretted her words at the tears that sprang at once into Doña Isobel's stricken eyes. After all, her imprisonment wasn't her *dueña*'s fault. Doña Isobel was simply following her employer's instructions.

"I'm sure Don Francisco wouldn't object to a visit from a lady-in-waiting to the empress," Doña Isobel protested.

Probably not, Margarite decided. Don Francisco was too clever to antagonize the imperial family, although she suspected that like many other wealthy landowners who had first supported the emperor, Don Francisco had become disillusioned with Maximilian's liberal ideas.

When Maria came rustling into the room in her black widow's weeds, embracing Margarite quickly, Margarite was surprised at the pleasure she felt at seeing her friend. Taking pleasure in anything was something she had been sure she would never do again, and she felt a guilty pang, as if in feeling anything she was somehow betraying Patrick.

"I'll see about tea . . . or would you prefer chocolate, *Señora*?" Doña Isobel asked before bustling from the room.

Maria stepped back and studied Margarite's face, but she was too tactful to say anything about her friend's haggard appearance. Nor did she make any comment about what had occurred at the Cordoba ranch, although Margarite was sure everyone at court had by now heard the shocking story.

For a moment an awkward silence ensued which Margarite finally, determinedly, broke. "You must tell me all the news from the court," she said more to put Maria at ease rather than because of any great interest in the latest gossip that always swirled around Carlota and Maximilian. "Is it true that the empress is leaving for Europe to plead her husband's cause before Napoleon?"

Maria nodded sadly. "Yes, the announcement was in the *Diario del Imperio* yesterday. She'll be leaving the day after tomorrow, July ninth, for Vera Cruz."

"So soon?" Margarite asked, surprised. "Will you be going with her?"

Maria shook her head. "It is to be a very small party accompanying Her Majesty. The only women will be Señora del Barrio, Frau von Kuhacsevich, and, of course, her maid, Matilde." Maria plucked unhappily at her skirt, then said in a rush, "I worry so about the empress making such a difficult trip in the rainy season and with the yellow fever in Vera Cruz. She—she has not been well, you know."

But when Margarite tried to discover what was wrong with Carlota, Maria became evasive, almost distraught, as if she felt she had already said too much. Seeming eager to change the subject, she delved into her skirt pocket and brought out a letter.

"I almost forgot. This piece of mail for you came in the emperor's mail pouch from Austria yesterday. I thought as long as I was visiting you, I'd bring it along rather than having it sent on to you."

Margarite recognized the round childish scrawl on the envelope immediately. Paula. As she eagerly tore open the envelope, she realized that this was the first piece of

mail she'd had since she had returned to Mexico City.
Not that she knew that many people who would write to
her, but she had thought she might hear from Star. Or
was it possible, she wondered unhappily, that Star blamed
her for her son's death. Patrick would never have risked
his life and come to the costume ball that night if Margarite hadn't been there.

Hastily Margarite thrust such a wounding thought
from her mind. It was difficult enough accepting the fact
of Patrick's death. How could she bear it if she thought
she was partly to blame for his death?

She concentrated on the letter from Paula which was
brief for all that the scrawling handwriting covered a full
page.

> Dearest sister,
>
> This is the second time I have written, begging
> you for help without any answer. If I do not hear
> this time, then I will know all is lost and I have
> nowhere else to turn except to throw myself into
> the Danube. Mama says you are very grand and
> wealthy now and no longer think of us but I cannot
> believe this. You are still my dear sister and clos-
> est friend. Can you not return home, if only for a
> visit? Oh, please, please do! You are the only one
> who can save me from a life of misery.
>
> Your devoted and heartbroken sister. . . . Paula.

Maria, watching Margarite's face as she read the
letter, asked, "Is it bad news, then? Your family in
Austria is not well?"

"It's from my sister," Margarite said slowly. The
letter sounded typically melodramatic, like Paula herself, and yet she could sense an undertone of despera-
tion, as if her stepsister really were in some sort of
trouble and needed her help.

"You and your sister are very close?" Maria asked
sympathetically.

Margarite nodded, remembering how she had depended
upon Paula those lonely months after her father's death.

Paula, who could somehow always find a way to make her stepsister laugh when Margarite was feeling unhappy.

Doña Isobel returned with a servant and a tray of hot chocolate and tea. Margarite put the letter into her skirt pocket and whispered quickly to a surprised Maria, "Please don't say anything to Doña Isobel about the letter."

For the rest of the hour as the three women chatted, Margarite's thoughts were occupied elsewhere. Her hand closed over the letter in her pocket. Why not? she asked herself, a pulse of excitement beating in her throat. She had no wish to be forced into a marriage with Don Roberto, and with Patrick gone, there was nothing to hold her here in Mexico. And it was obvious, that for whatever reason, Paula needed her. Why not return to Austria?

When Maria finally rose to leave, Margarite accompanied her guest. At the door she suddenly pulled her friend to one side. "I have a great favor to ask of you, Maria," she whispered urgently. "Will you ask the empress if I may travel to Europe with Her Majesty's party?"

Maria blinked. "I—I don't understand. I heard you were to marry Señor Aguardiante."

"I will never marry Don Roberto," Margarite said fiercely. "That is why I must leave Mexico as soon as possible. And even Don Francisco can't stop me if I'm traveling under the protection of the empress Carlota."

Maria's hands fluttered, frightened, to her breast. "But I don't think . . . I'm not sure I should interfere."

"What harm can it do just to ask?" Margarite pleaded. "Please, Maria, it would mean so much to me."

Maria wavered. "Well, I suppose I could inquire, but there's so little time," she said anxiously. "How could you possibly be ready to leave so soon?"

That was not her only problem, Margarite thought. How was she going to leave the house without being stopped? The next day, when Maria returned, she discovered she had yet another problem.

"I spoke to the empress," Maria said, glancing around nervously for Margarite's *dueña*.

"Doña Isobel is shopping, but she'll be back in a minute, so tell me quickly, what did Carlota say? Did she give her permission?"

Maria nodded. "That is, you won't actually be a member of the imperial party, of course, but Doña Carlota did say you could travel with them as far as Paris. She is still very angry at Emperor Franz Josef and has no intention of visiting Vienna. Also"—Maria's face flushed, embarrassed—"Her Majesty said I was to make it very clear that you would have to pay all your own travel expenses."

Margarite had not thought of having to pay for her own passage on the ship. Always when she had traveled, someone else had taken care of such details. As for having any pocket money of her own, that had never been necessary since her arrival in Mexico. Her *dueñas* had always carried any money she might need.

At Margarite's look of dismay, Maria said apologetically, "That is why the empress is traveling with such a small party. There are no funds to pay for any more people to accompany her. I'll gladly give you what money I can. . . ."

"No, I'll manage somehow," Margarite said quickly. She knew that Maria received only a small stipend from the royal family. "I will need one more favor, though. Could you arrange for a hack carriage to wait for me at the plaza on the corner tomorrow evening, shortly after midnight? Will the royal party be leaving from the National Palace?"

"No, from Chapultepec." Maria gave a shiver of fright. "Surely you don't plan to travel all alone to Chapultepec at that hour of the night?"

"Don't worry. I'll be fine," Margarite said, then seeing Doña Isobel come into the room, said loudly, "Be sure to give Her Royal Highness my very best wishes for a safe journey."

Maria rose quickly to her feet, giving Doña Isobel a nervous glance, sure that the guilt she was feeling was written plainly in her face.

"I—I . . . must return at once to the palace," she

stammered. "There is so much to be done before the empress leaves."

At the front door she embraced Margarite, whispering unhappily, "Please change your mind, Margarite." Then seeing the obdurate look settle across her friend's face, sighed, "*Vaya con Dios.* I will pray for you."

When Margarite turned away from the door, she saw her *dueña* watching her from the stairs. Was it possible that Doña Isobel suspected something? she wondered uneasily. But if she did, her companion gave no indication. After the midday meal both women went to their rooms for a siesta. First, making sure that Isobel was indeed asleep and the halls deserted of servants who always promptly took their siestas, too, Margarite hurried down the stairs to her uncle's study.

The curtains were pulled. The room, shrouded in darkness, had a moldy, unused smell. Margarite lit a candle and went over to her uncle's desk. Then she shut her eyes, trying to recall exactly what her uncle had done the night he had given her her mother's emeralds to wear to the imperial reception at Chapultapec. He had gone to the desk, she remembered, and pulled out the top righthand drawer, reached in, and taken out a key that had opened the strongbox in the wall behind the desk. She placed the candle on the desktop and pulled open the drawer eagerly. All that her questing fingers found in the small drawer were a stack of old bills and receipts.

Frowning, she took the drawer all the way out, dumping its contents on the desk. What if Don Francisco had taken the key? But why should he? The contents of the strongbox belonged to her. He might not even know about the key or the strongbox. No, more than likely the key was hidden so that servants cleaning the desk wouldn't be tempted to steal from the strongbox. She remembered her father had had a desk with a secret drawer that had fascinated her as a child, but with her father's desk, the drawer itself had been secret. It had been necessary, she remembered, to slide a piece of veneer to one side to find the drawer.

Carefully, she moved her fingers over the inside of the drawer. Whatever the secret was, it must be easily within reach, she realized, remembering how quickly her uncle had retrieved the key. After pushing and probing for several minutes, a piece of the wooden bottom of the drawer suddenly gave way beneath her finger, exposing a tiny hiding space beneath. And there was the key.

The panel swung open easily with the slight whining sound she remembered from the last time. Opening the lock box itself was more difficult. The key was worn and she had to twist it within the lock several times before the door to the box opened.

She was startled at the amount of jewelry within the box, mostly diamonds and mostly old-fashioned pieces, but the stones looked valuable for all that the settings were out of date. It was the black velvet jewel case that had belonged to her mother, though, that her hands reached for and opened. Not knowing how much she would need to pay her boat passage, and her expenses once she reached Europe, she scooped as many necklaces, earrings, and rings as she could into the pockets of her skirt, leaving behind the more awkwardly shaped coronets and heavier diamond parures. Then to her delight, she discovered a leather bag filled with gold pieces pushed to the back of the case and dropped that into her pockets, too, pushing down a feeling of guilt as she did so.

After all, everything in the case belonged to her mother, and now to her, she reminded herself firmly. It wasn't stealing to take her own property, especially when she needed money so desperately. Quietly closing the box and the panel, she returned the key to its hidden place in the desk drawer, along with the papers, and extinguished the candle. Once in her own room again, she hid the jewels at the bottom of a canvas traveling bag, then retired, all at once exhausted, to her bed. She might as well get as much sleep as she could now, she decided. She would be getting very little that night.

It was shortly before midnight that she crept down the stairs again, carrying the traveling bag crammed with as many clothes and necessaries as she could push inside of it. She made her way to the back kitchen area. As she had expected, a porter was posted at the back gate from the courtyard off the kitchen, but also as she expected, he was sound asleep. In the flickering light from a lantern hung on the wall near the man, she could see his face, his mouth open as he snored heavily, a half-finished jug of pulque beside him.

She pushed open the gate cautiously, and froze in her tracks when it groaned so loudly that she whirled around toward the porter, her heart pounding in her throat. Then she went limp with relief when she saw the man had not stirred.

She did not dare push the gate open any farther. Taking a deep breath, she slid sideways through the half-opened gate, pulling the heavy bag after her, and with the bag bumping awkwardly against her leg, hurried off into the darkness.

Chapter 24

"*Gott in Himmel*, what next?" Frau Kuhacsevich muttered as Margarite and she, along with the empress Carlota and the rest of the imperial party arrived at the Gare Montparnasse in Paris, only to discover that there was not one French official at the railroad station to greet the empress of Mexico upon her arrival in the French capital. In fact, there was no royal welcome at all for the weary travelers.

"Perhaps Señor Almonte was right," Margarite said, sitting down wearily upon her carpet bag. The August heat within the station was stifling. "With Napoleon ill, perhaps the empress should have gone to her family in Belgium." The Mexican ambassador had been the only one to wait upon Carlota on her arrival at the port of St. Nazaire the day before. After informing the empress that Louis-Napoleon was ailing and unable to receive her at his summer palace at St. Cloud, he had urged her to visit her home at Miramar or her family in Belgium instead.

"Illness is no excuse for such an insult," Frau Kuhacsevich hissed angrily. "And you know, the empress insists upon seeing Napoleon personally. She will not rest until she fulfills her promise to her husband."

Margarite rubbed absently at a spot of soot on her blue linen traveling suit, already stained from six weeks of travel. The few other gowns she had in her traveling case were not in much better condition. She longed for a hot bath, fresh clothes, and a clean bed. Instead, it seemed with this latest calamity, there were no accommodations prepared for the royal party, much less carriages waiting to take them to a hotel.

Not that she should be surprised, Margarite thought. The whole journey had been a disaster from the beginning. Well, no, she corrected herself, the beginning had gone surprisingly well. The hack had been waiting for her at the plaza which at that late hour was lit only by the lights from the cantinas and the candles burning within striped red, green, and white glasses on the church steps, where Indian vendors sold jugs of pulque. The *leperos,* who usually begged on the street during the day, were sleeping in ragged heaps beneath the arcade on one side of the plaza.

Arriving at Chapultapec, Margarite was taken under the wing of Frau Kuhacsevich. The woman remembered the girl from La Borda, and although they had never been close friends, she had always regarded Margarite as a fellow Austrian, like herself and her husband, exiled into a world of mad foreigners. And the emperor had been kindness itself to Margarite.

Carlota had only nodded absently toward Margarite while they had waited in the courtyard for the long line of carriages, escorted by Austrian cavalry, to leave. Maximilian, however, had drawn her to one side and smiled warmly down at her. "I am glad you will be going with the party, Countess. The empress will need all her friends on this difficult trip." His eyes saddened.

"My Carlo's leaving is the heaviest sacrifice I have yet made to my new fatherland."

Maximilian pressed Margarite's hand lightly, studying the girl's face, still disturbingly beautiful despite the look of sadness, as if a light had gone out behind the once sparkling emerald eyes. "But then, I understand you know something of the pain of losing a loved one," he said gently before a conspiratorial, almost mischievous, smile touched his lips for a moment. "And I promise you we will keep your whereabouts a secret from Don Francisco as long as we can."

How very kind he was, Margarite thought, staring into the handsome face that had once haunted her schoolgirl's dreams. Why couldn't the Mexican people see how kind and gentle he was? But then, perhaps gentleness wasn't what made a great leader, she thought. Perhaps it was a ruthlessness, a strength of purpose that would not be swayed, qualities which Maximilian lacked. Or was it more simple than that? Would the proud Mexican people have ever accepted any foreigner to rule them?

But then Frau Kuhacsevich was hustling her into a carriage, the canvas bag, which Margarite insisted upon keeping with her at all times, serving as a footrest in the crowded carriage. Maximilian accompanied Carlota as far as Ayula, where he said good-bye privately to his wife in a small adobe hut in the mountain village. It seemed to Margarite it was after that leavetaking that the journey turned into a nightmare.

Torrential rain had washed out sections of the mountain roads, and it took fifteen hours to reach Puebla, where the weary party spent their first night at a hacienda that had been hastily opened to them. The whole party had retired early. Margarite had fallen at once into a sound sleep, awaking the next morning much refreshed, so that when she joined Frau Kuhacsevich in their coach, she was surprised to see the older woman looking as tired as if she hadn't slept at all.

It was only after the other coach riders fell asleep, despite the rough ride, that her companion whispered to

Margarite, "What a terrible night we had with the empress. Did you hear nothing?"

Margarite shook her head, mystified. "Was Her Highness ill?

"Her Majesty awoke at midnight, and after rousing her servants, insisted upon being taken to the house of the prefect of Puebla. It was storming, and not knowing what to do, Matilde fetched me and Señora del Barrio, but none of us could dissuade Carlota from going to the prefect's home. Even when we reached the hacienda and the servants informed us that the prefect was out of town, the empress demanded to be admitted. Finally, they let us inside and she roamed through the house like a woman possessed, remembering aloud how she and the emperor had been given a triumphant welcome to Mexico in this very house."

Frau Kuhacsevich gave a little shudder. "I would swear, listening to her, it was as if Her Highness thought it had all happened yesterday instead of two years ago. Sometimes I think the servants are right, that her Indian servants have been secretly poisoning the empress with a herb that produces the symptoms of madness."

At Margarite's appalled stare, Frau Kuhacsevich pulled herself together. "It's only servants' gossip, of course," she said quickly. "It's the terrible strain of the last months that have upset the empress. She'll be better once we're aboard the ship and away from this cursed country."

Then neither Margarite nor Frau Kuhacsevich had any more chance to talk as the carriage was suddenly mired down in a sea of mud and had to be physically lifted and carried by the Austrian soldiers, along with the other carriages which were also stuck. Time after time the rain-soaked passengers had to climb out into the mud and rain while the carriages were moved to drier ground.

Margarite's carriage was several removed from the carriage in which Carlota rode, but it was impossible not to hear Carlota complaining loudly to anyone who would listen, that the delays were all a plot so that the steamer waiting for them at Vera Cruz would sail without her.

When, near the railroad station at Paso del Macho, a small band of guerrillas suddenly appeared through the rain, cut off the road ahead, and drove away the mules and horses, Margarite was too exhausted to feel any alarm or even annoyance at the military escort for not firing a shot at the marauders.

It was a bedraggled company that finally reached the quays at Vera Cruz, only to have Carlota make another scene when she discovered the mail steamer that was to take them to France flew the French flag. How the empress was finally pacified and persuaded to board the launch that took her to the ship, Margarite never knew. She had her own troubles aboard the ship, convincing the captain to accept a pair of diamond earrings and a ruby-encrusted brooch as passage for her trip to France.

She had to share her tiny cabin on the crowded ship with one of the servants who had been hastily added to Carlota's entourage just before she left Chapultepec. The girl spent most of her trip being seasick, as did Carlota, Margarite learned from the few times Frau Kuhacsevich was able to spend any moments alone with her during the voyage.

"At least her mind is clear once more," the lady of the bedchamber said, relieved. "She refuses to leave her cabin, though, and spends all her time reading the papers she plans to present to Napoleon when she has her audience with him."

If the empress was ever given a chance to visit with Napoleon at all, Margarite thought now as she watched the royal entourage mill helplessly around the station, trying to decide what to do, with no one to greet them and no idea where they should stay in Paris.

She couldn't help wondering cynically if Napoleon's illness hadn't been carefully planned so he wouldn't have to receive Carlota, who could only be an embarrassing reminder of the failure of his once grandiose dreams for Mexico. The small circle around the empress parted for a moment and she caught a glimpse of Carlota, dressed completely in black, her face puffy, with dark shadows around the febrile eyes, making her look years older than her age. Despite the commotion around

her, Margarite could hear Carlota's voice, shrilly agitated, as she insisted upon being taken straight to the
palace at St. Cloud and an immediate audience with the
emperor of France.

Somehow wiser heads prevailed, and the whole company was finally taken in hired hacks to the Grand
Hotel. The hotel, despite its name, was not grand at all,
but on the seedy side, with worn-thin rugs in the lobby
and the unpleasant odor of stopped drains in the halls.
With a few of her gold coins Margarite was able to
secure a room alone, which she moved into gratefully.
She was delighted to be away from the disturbing presence
of Carlota and a royal entourage made irritable and
worried with the growing realization that the journey
which was to accomplish so much was fast turning into
an embarrassing fiasco.

The next few days Margarite was too busy to see any
of the imperial party. Hesitant to appear at her stepmother's door without some sort of advance notice, she
sent a letter to Vienna, letting her stepmother know she
was in Paris. Then she busied herself with buying a new
wardrobe to replace the few gowns, now travel-worn,
that she had been able to take with her from Mexico.
Not just travel-worn, she realized as she studied the
gowns of the fashionable Parisian women in the hotel
lobby, but outdated. The awkward crinolines had been
replaced by much slimmer skirts with draped backs, and
the hats were small and saucy instead of demure bon-
nets that covered the face.

As she tried on a small tocque decorated with velvet
violets and lavender ribbon at a millinery shop, wondering if the lavender was the same shade as a new walking
dress she had bought, she saw Señora del Barrio also
completing a purchase of a new hat.

When she saw Margarite, Carlota's lady-in-waiting hurried to her side, and displaying the white broad-brimmed
hat to the girl, asked, worried, "Do you think this will
look attractive on Her Majesty? After her meeting
with the empress Eugénie yesterday, Her Majesty was
upset that she and her ladies-in-waiting looked so
unfashionable."

Margarite had heard of the unexpected arrival of the empress of France at the Grand Hotel the day before. When Margarite had returned to the hotel from her shopping trip, the guests seated in the lobby were abuzz with descriptions of the beautiful auburn-haired Eugénie and the charming Mediterranean blue-green Worth gown she had worn for her visit with Carlota.

If Carlota hoped to compete with a fashion plate like Eugénie, Margarite thought unhappily, she was sure to lose. She said tactfully, "I always thought the empress Carlota looked lovely in a *mantilla*." Then she noticed the twine bag of food the *señora* had at her side, filled with a jug of fresh milk and pastries. "Don't you like the food at the Grand Hotel, *Señora*?" she asked, surprised.

Señora del Barrio looked flustered. "Oh, it's not for me. It's for Her Majesty. The food at the hotel doesn't . . . doesn't agree with her." Then in a rush, "I must be returning to the hotel. The empress will be leaving for St. Cloud this afternoon."

"Her Majesty has secured an audience with Napoleon then?" Margarite asked, relieved.

"Oh, yes. The empress Eugénie tried to discourage her, but Her Majesty would not be put off." The *señora* sighed. "I only wish she would allow her diplomatic advisors to conduct the interview with the emperor instead of insisting upon handling the affair herself." Then, as if afraid of having sounded disloyal, she said hastily, "Not that the empress Carlota won't manage very well, I'm sure. After all, she is a Bourbon as well as empress of Mexico. Even if he is ill, Louis-Napoleon must see the justice of her claim that Mexico not be abandoned."

However, when Margarite returned to the hotel later that afternoon, she arrived just in time to see Carlota being ushered hurriedly through the curious crowds in the Grand Hotel lobby by the faithful Señor Castillo and Count del Valle. Margarite caught only a glimpse of Carlota's face but knew at once that the audience with Napoleon had not gone well.

Margarite wondered what had happened at the meeting as several afternoons later she joined the promenade along the Bois de Boulogne. However, neither Frau

Kuhacsevich nor Señora del Barrio had appeared again in the lobby or the dining room of the hotel, evidently staying closeted with the empress, so there was no way Margarite could question them.

Margarite adjusted her lacy parasol to protect her face against the sun. Well, since she wasn't an offical member of the imperial party, it was probably best if she minded her own business, she decided. Determinedly, she put out of her mind the dazed look on Carlota's face, the way Señor Castillo's arm had had to support the empress, and concentrated instead on the bustling cosmopolitan street scene around her, so different from Mexico. Here there were no *leperos* to impede your progress by their insistent begging, no blank Indian faces or Indian women gliding by with babies strapped to their back, no colorful booths where tortillas were being baked and pulque sold. The only resemblance to Mexico were in the flower booths at almost every corner and the occasional sound of church bells.

But then, in Mexico, Margarite thought, waiting for a fiacre to pass before she attempted to cross the crowded thoroughfare, she wouldn't have dared walk down the street in broad daylight without a *dueña* to accompany her. Idly, her gaze rested on a man walking ahead of her. Something about the set of the shoulders, the way he walked, even the dark hair she could glimpse beneath the homburg sent a shock of recognition like a lightning bolt through her body. It was Patrick! Somehow miraculously he had survived the bullet wounds and was here in Paris. Not thinking, only feeling, she rushed after the man, pushing aside couples who stood in her way, to reach him, tugging at his coat sleeve, and whispering hoarsely, "Patrick . . . Patrick, *mi amor*."

The man, a total stranger, turned to stare at her, at first startled, then uneasy. "What do you want, Ma'm'selle?"

Other people passing by turned to stare curiously. Margarite felt her face drain of blood, disappointment so acute it was almost as agonizing as watching Patrick die all over again.

The man's gaze softened as he gazed into the lovely

face of the young woman who had accosted him, then he smiled knowingly. "I am late to an appointment, ma'm'selle, but if you care to come by my hotel later. . ."

He thought she was one of the young demimondaines who plied their trade openly on the streets of Paris, Margarite realized, not even caring as she murmured an apology and turned quickly away. She walked stiffly back toward the hotel, gazing blindly ahead of her, unaware of the tears that rolled down her face, or of the covert glances cast her way by the guests in the lobby as she made her way to her room and flung herself across the bed. Finally, when there were no more tears to be shed, spent and exhausted, she went to the washstand. As she splashed cold water on her face, all she could think of were the empty, desolate years stretching out ahead of her. How would she ever face them, all those years, alone?

When the soft knock came at her door an hour later, she thought it was the waiter. She had ordered her evening meal to be served in her room, but when she opened the door, Frau Kuhacsevich hurried in. The woman sighed with relief when she saw Margarite. "I was afraid you might be out. The empress wishes to see you immediately in her suite."

If she noticed that Margarite's face was tear-stained, she was too concerned with her own problems to ask any questions. Her own plump face was worn, as if she hadn't had a good night's sleep in days.

"Why should Doña Carlota want to see me?" Margarite asked.

"Please don't ask questions, just come with me," Frau Kuhacsevich urged. "We daren't upset Her Highness more than she is already."

"The audience with Napoleon then, it didn't go well?"

Frau Kuhacsevich frowned unhappily. "*Mein Gott,* it could not have gone any worse. The emperor flatly refused to provide any more money or troops to Mexico. He as much as told the empress that her husband should abdicate. When he refused her a second interview, the empress went out to the summer palace at St. Cloud with only poor Doña Manuela for company, and forced her way into Napoleon and the empress Eugénie's presence. She accused Napoleon of terrible things, of stealing large sums of money from the Mexican people, all the while screaming at him hysterically. When, to calm her down, a cold drink was brought, she flung the glass away from her and cried the emperor was trying to poison her. It's only through sleeping powders that Dr. Bouslaveck has been able to make the empress rest; otherwise she paces the floor all night long.''

"What can I do?" Margarite asked uncertainly.

Frau Kuhacsevich shrugged impatiently. "She asked to see you. That's all I know. I was sent to fetch you. You must come with me," she said sternly. "Would you turn your back on her too?"

Margarite reached for her shawl and reluctantly followed her companion down the hall. The suite of rooms into which she was escorted was a far cry from the grandeur of Chapultapec in which the empress had held court. But she was grateful to see, after she had risen from her curtsy upon her presentation to Carlota, that the woman's face, though almost a pale blue-white, was composed, even if her voice was frosty as she said, "So finally you tear yourself away from your own enjoyments to remember your duties as a lady of the court, Countess Von Melk.''

Almost, Margarite protested that she was no longer a lady-in-waiting to Her Royal Highness, but instead, remembering Maximilian's kindness to her in the courtyard of Chapultapec, said quietly, "I am sorry, Your Highness. I didn't want to intrude."

"No matter," Carlota said, her mood changing abruptly. She began to walk back and forth, her movements stiff, jerking, unlike her usual graceful carriage. "I've been told that you've been traveling the streets of the city daily. And you understand French. You must be informed on what the people in Paris are saying about me, about my visit here, and what they feel about that vile charlatan with no sense of honor who calls himself a Bonaparte." The last was spit out angrily, the fine eyes bright with evangelistic fury. "My husband always said if you want to know about a country, you must speak with its people, not its rulers. If I could bypass Napoleon and appeal directly to the French people, I'm sure they would listen."

"I'm afraid, at the moment, Your Highness, it is Prussia, not Mexico, that concerns the French people," Margarite said, choosing each word carefully. "With the Prussian victories over Austria, they worry that Bismarck will now turn his troops upon France. The newspapers say the Austrians suffered terrible casualties because of the new weapons the Prussians are using."

"Oh, there are always casualties in wars," Carlota said. Then, spitefully, "Still, I would like to have seen the emperor Franz Josef's face when the people jeered at him upon his return to Vienna, after being forced to sign that disastrous treaty with Bismarck. At least in Mexico we are stopping Juárez with much less of an army than Franz Josef had at the battle of Sadowa."

Margarite cast a startled glance toward Frau Kuhacsevich. Surely, the empress must have heard the latest news from Mexico received over the new transatlantic electric cable, news that could be read by anyone in the Paris newspapers. Monterrey and Saltillo had been evacuated, Tampico had fallen. Juárez himself was leading an army towards Durango.

"Napoleon thinks he has bested me," the empress continued, walking more quickly, her eyes darting, agitated, around the room. "But I will never give up. There is still the Pope. The Holy Father will give me money to raise an army."

Margarite lowered her eyes so the empress could not read her thoughts there. Did Carlota really believe the Pope would provide her with any support after Maximilian had turned his back on the clergy in Mexico?

"You will travel with us to Rome, Countess," Carlota said almost casually. "You may be of some use. Your father was in the diplomatic service, was he not?"

Margarite blurted out without thinking, "No, I'm not able to accompany you, Your Highness. I'm waiting word from my family in Vienna."

Carlota's glittering eyes narrowed. In the light from the overhanging gas lamps, her cheeks looked sunken in her face. Her voice rose shrilly. "How dare you? How dare you refuse a royal command?"

Frau von Kuhacsevich gave Margarite an annoyed glance, then moved forward quickly to Carlota's side, her voice soothing, as to a child. "I'm sure the countess meant no offense, Your Highness." She poured a glass of sweetened orange juice, Carlota's favorite drink, from a pitcher into a glass and handed it to the infuriated woman. "I've prepared this myself, Your Highness. It's perfectly safe."

Carlota stared at the glass a long moment, then her mouth tightened suspiciously as she glanced from the glass to Margarite. "How do I know *she* hasn't placed poison in it since she came into the room? How do I know she hasn't been sent by Napoleon to poison me?" A look of feral cunning crept into the narrowed eyes. "Or is it my husband that has sent you, *ma'm'selle*? To poison me and rid himself of a barren wife? Do you think I'm blind? Don't you think I know what went on between you two at La Borda? Did you bear him a child, too, Countess?"

When Margarite stood, too shocked by the sudden attack to move, Carlota screamed, "Get out! Get out of my sight!"

Her hand flung out, knocking the glass from Frau Kuhacsevich's hand, sending orange juice all over the front of Margarite's gown. Carlota's hands rose, clawed, as if ready to scratch at Margarite's face, when Frau Kuhacsevich almost pushed Margarite from the room and out into the hall.

"For God's sake, what have you done?" she said frantically. "It'll take hours for us to calm the empress down again."

Then she hurried back into the room, leaving Margarite standing, alone, shivering as if with a chill, out in the hall.

Chapter 25

ONCE again in her room, Margarite tore off her soiled gown. She felt sickened, remembering the wildness in Carlota's eyes and, especially devastating, that beautiful, porcelain face, usually so regal and self-controlled, destroyed by rage. More than rage, she thought, shivering. It was a madwoman who had tried to attack her.

She redressed quickly, with hands that trembled. She wouldn't wait any longer, she decided. She would go straight to Vienna, with or without a welcoming letter from her stepmother. Elissa might not greet her with open arms, but she could hardly turn her stepdaughter away from her door.

When the knock came at her door, she hesitated. What if it were Frau Kuhacsevich begging her to come back to the empress's suite? I can't, she thought, her heart thudding. I can't face her again. No matter her feeling of obligation to Maximilian, her sympathy for Carlota, she was terrified of lunacy with an almost primordial fear. When she had been a child, she had seen a barred wooden wagon pass by on the street, filled with gibbering men and women making obscene faces and gestures at the passersby on the street. Her father had hastily pulled her away, his voice sad. "Poor souls. They're being taken to the madhouse."

When she finally opened the door, though, it was the elderly *valet de chambre* standing there. "There is a gentleman in the lobby, *ma'm'selle*, a Baron Karl Von Friedrich. He wished to speak with you."

Margarite tried to remember. She couldn't recall ever meeting any Baron Von Friedrich. Well, she had to speak to the concierge in the lobby anyway about securing a railroad ticket to Vienna. And perhaps the baron was a friend of her father's.

As she descended the grand staircase into the lobby, there was a man waiting at the foot of the staircase. At the sight of Margarite, he stepped forward, bowing, with an almost soundless click of his heels. "Countess Von Melk, what a great pleasure that we should meet again."

At first Margarite stared blankly at the pleasantly distinguished face with the carefully tended waxed mustache over rather full, rosy lips. Then she remembered. Elissa's salon the day she and Paula had burst in and she had been wearing her first ball gown. There had been a gentleman with Elissa, a few years younger than her father, with something of her father's gentle mannerism.

The baron's amber eyes twinkled merrily, his voice filled with a mock despair. "How unflattering, Countess, that you should not remember me."

"Oh, but I do," she said quickly. "It's just that I hadn't expected to see you here in Paris, Baron."

He led her to a deserted corner of the lobby and two empty, somewhat frayed, damask chairs, then signaled imperiously. The hotel employees rushed to bring a silver pot of coffee, wafer-thin cups, and a plate of small iced tortes. Margarite was amused at the respectful glances the servants cast in her direction because she was with the baron, where before they had treated her, a single woman traveling alone, as someone of slightly inferior social status.

After she had poured the coffee for the both of them, she asked curiously, "How did you know I was staying here at the Grand?"

"Your stepmother told me when she asked me to come to Paris and bring you home." He glanced around the lobby, a look of distaste quivering across his aristocratic face. "I can't imagine how you could endure this wretched place for even a day."

"The empress Carlota and her party are staying here."

"So I've heard, and the fact that you were traveling with the empress is only another reason why I came as quickly as I could. The imperial family is shocked that

Maximilian should have allowed the empress Carlota to undertake such a foolhardy journey. Carlota is making herself the laughingstock of Paris with her wild accusations and mad behavior."

"The empress Carlota is not mad," Margarite protested bitterly, forgetting that only a few moments before she had thought much the same thing. "She's only trying to help her husband save the throne of Mexico after Napoleon and his own brother and brother-in-law deserted Maximilian. It took great courage for Her Majesty to make the trip without her husband beside her."

"That may be," the baron said, swallowing a chocolate torte in two bites, then wiping his fingers fastidiously on a white linen napkin. "But the empress is mad if she expects to get one sou or soldier from Napoleon. Louis knows only too well that he will need every man he can lay his hands on to fight off Bismarck. If Maximilian has any sense, he'll abdicate immediately." The full, rosy mouth tightened. "After all, Carlota and Maximilian are not the only ones who have lost in the Mexican debacle."

The baron himself had lost more than he cared to think about, investing in the Mexican bonds that had helped support Maximilian's cactus throne, money he could ill afford to lose. Pushing such troublesome thoughts from his mind, the baron said briskly, "Well, your connection with the ill-starred Maximilian and Carlota is finished now. I've already made our train reservations. We leave for Vienna in the morning." He smiled with an easy assurance at Margarite. "But tonight you must allow me the pleasure of showing you Paris."

Margarite wondered if the baron saw the traces of strain behind the rice powder she had hastily applied before she had come downstairs, because he added gently, "Unless, of course, you're too tired."

The thought of being with people, of being surrounded with music and gaiety suddenly seemed infinitely more appealing to Margarite than spending another lonely evening in her hotel room. And the baron turned out to be an amusing and attentive escort, as well as being very knowledgeable about the charms of Paris at night. The

restaurant to which he took her was aboard a floating
barge on the Seine. Tables above and below deck were
spread with snowy white tablecloths and silver cutlery,
candlelight glittering on the priceless diamonds and precious stones circling the throats of the expensively
gowned women at the tables. Violinists playing romantic melodies strolled between the tables as the boat
moved slowly down the river, the dark surface of the
water reflecting the moonlight like spangles on a black
velvet dress.

Perhaps it was the champagne, or the delicious meal,
or just a reaction to living for so long feeling half-dead
inside, whatever the reason, for the first time in weeks
Margarite felt herself relaxing. She even laughed at the
baron's anecdotes about his first visit to Paris as a
young man, fascinated by his witty, lightly malicious
gossip about the empress Elizabeth and her long absences from the Hapsburg court and Vienna, supposedly
for reasons of illness.

"Although the last time I saw the Kaiserin in Hungary,
she seemed as healthy as a horse," the baron said,
chuckling. "Frankly, I can't help wondering if it isn't
the constant presence of her mother-in-law, the archduchess Sophie, at Hofburg Palace that causes the
Kaiserin's mysterious illness!"

"I saw the empress Elizabeth once," Margarite said,
her face alight with the memory. "Only from a distance,
of course, one afternoon when she was riding in the
Prater. She wore a fur-trimmed, dark blue velvet riding
costume and she rode her horse magnificently. I'd never
seen anyone so beautiful. All the people cheered as she
rode by."

The baron grinned wickedly. "Our beautiful empress
works very hard at maintaining that legendary beauty
and stylish figure. Not only has she installed her own
personal gymnasium in the palace, but the stories are
she diets on raw milk and juice from raw beef and
covers her face with crushed strawberries at night to
preserve that lovely complexion." He made a comical
face. "Poor Franz Josef, one wonders if he knows if
he's going to dine or to bed!"

Margarite laughed at the picture he drew, even as she felt vaguely shocked that the baron should be aware of such intimate details about the empress Elizabeth. And then she wondered suddenly if the baron wasn't deliberately going out of his way to shock her, to make her forget whatever had put that look of unhappiness he must have seen on her face earlier. Although her dinner companion gave the impression of an amiable, rather dandified fop, there were moments, like now, when she glimpsed behind the amber eyes fastened upon her face a look of icy shrewdness.

Then she saw that his gaze wasn't upon her face but upon the emerald necklace and earrings that at the last moment she had decided to wear. The emeralds were only a shade darker than her sea green moiré gown shot with silver, one of her latest acquisitions from Worth's. As that gaze lowered, lingered on her gown, she wondered a little nervously if perhaps the bodice was cut too low, although she had been assured that such a daring décolletage was all the rage in Paris this year.

As if suddenly becoming aware of her discomfort, the baron smiled apologetically. "Forgive my staring, Countess, but that necklace is quite magnificent. I don't think I've ever seen another quite like it."

Margarite touched the cool green emeralds, unaware how in the candlelight their color deepened the shimmering green of her eyes and brought out the delicate creamy flesh tone of her neck and shoulders.

"The necklace belonged to my mother, or so my uncle told me."

The baron's face grew grave. "Ah, yes, I've been remiss in not offering my condolences. Your stepmother told me of the tragic deaths of your uncle and aunt, how you barely escaped death yourself." Then, as if sensing that his companion did not want to talk about that sad episode in her life, he said hastily, "But we won't dwell on unhappy memories tonight. Now you must finish your wine, for as soon as the boat docks, I plan to take you to a favorite little café of mine." He shook his finger roguishly at Margarite. "But you must never tell your stepmother I have taken you there. It is a place where a man takes his mistress, not an innocent *jeune fille*." He suddenly chuckled. "Although I suspect your sister, Paula, would find it entertaining."

"Paula is all right?" Margarite asked eagerly.

The baron looked surprised. "But of course. She is a lively young woman who causes her poor mother many headaches, but I'm sure that will change once she marries."

"Paula is to be married?"

"Didn't you know? I believe the wedding will take place within the month. I assumed that was why you were returning home, for your sister's wedding."

"No, no, I didn't know," Margarite said, her face thoughtful. "Who is she marrying?"

"I don't really know the gentleman. He is of the bourgeois." The baron smiled, softening the unconscious snobbery in his voice. "However, since Elissa chose him for her daughter, he must be eminently respectable and wealthy. I'm sure your sister feels very fortunate to have such an eligible suitor."

"I hate him, and I'll die before I marry him!" Paula exploded when Margarite arrived at the Von Melk home in Vienna two days later and was finally closeted alone with her sister in their old bedroom. The room hadn't changed a bit, she thought, although her stepsister certainly had. The baby fat had gone, leaving if not beauty, then a pert prettiness to her sister's rounded face and body that she suspected most men would find not only alluring but definitely inviting.

She gazed with fond amusement at Paula's face, a mask of high tragedy as her stepsister flung herself across the bed. "Don't you think that's a little drastic, killing yourself? Why don't you talk to Elissa?"

Paula sat up, scowling. "I have. She won't listen. Have you forgotten what she's like? All she's interested in is that I should marry someone wealthy enough to look after her too." She gazed pleadingly at Margarite. "Perhaps if you talked to her . . . That's why I wrote you. I was sure you could find a way to stop the marriage."

"I doubt if she'd listen to me either." Although Elissa's welcome had been effusive, almost embarrassingly so, Margarite had not been deceived. There was still no love lost between her stepmother and herself.

"Of course she'll listen to you," Paula said impatiently. "You're wealthy. All of Vienna is talking about the fabulous fortune you inherited from your Mexican relatives, silver mines and sugar and coffee plantations, and a king's ransom in jewelry. Please, Margarite. Please say you'll talk to her."

"All right," Margarite agreed reluctantly, but, as she had suspected, Elissa was no more willing to listen to her stepdaughter than to her daughter. Elissa was sweetly polite as she and Margarite shared coffee in the small drawing room the next day. The rose brocade covered furniture, Margarite couldn't help noticing, was shabbier than she remembered; the room had a dusty, untended air as if servants, as well as money, were in short supply in the household.

"I understand why Paula asked you to speak to me," Elissa said, smiling graciously. "And I'm sure you mean well, but the marriage is all arranged. The plans cannot possibly be changed at this late date." She sighed heavily. "Perhaps if your father had left me with more funds, but under the circumstances, and without a dowry, Paula is fortunate to marry a man of substantial means like Herr Ludwig."

"But he's old enough to be her father," Margarite protested, ignoring her stepmother's deliberate jibe at her father.

Elissa lifted one carefully arched eyebrow. "And what difference does that make? Your own father was twice my age. No, if anything, Paula needs an older, sensible husband." Then she added darkly, "And considering my daughter's irresponsible behavior of late, the wedding cannot be too soon for my peace of mind."

Margarite did not understand the reason for the last comment until the next morning when Paula, who was usually a late riser, insisted that Margarite and she take an early morning ride in the Prater. The dew still sparkled in the grass along the shady trails of the park, and the tables in the garden restaurants had not yet been set for the midmorning breakfast trade. There were no other horseback riders on the trail until suddenly a young Hussar rode out of the trees a short distance ahead of them. To Margarite's surprise, the man dismounted and almost immediately Paula slid off her horse and ran to meet the rider, who caught her in his arms in a fervent embrace.

When Margarite rode up, Paula, her arm still around the young officer's waist, turned to confront her sister, smiling proudly. "Now you see why I cannot possibly marry Herr Ludwig, Margarite. Louis and I are desperately in love and plan to be married just as soon as it can be arranged."

The officer gave Paula a fond, embarrassed smile, then turned to Margarite, nodding stiffly. "Lieutenant Louis Schaffner, Imperial Guard, Countess Von Melk. I hope you will excuse this little deception, but Paula was most eager for me to meet her sister, and since I am not permitted to pay my respects at her home . . ." He spread his hands helplessly.

Margarite dismounted slowly. There was something about the young officer, the proud way he wore his uniform, the eager, open smile and flowing mustache that reminded her painfully of Franz. She gave Paula a reproachful glance. "You might at least have told me."

"I wanted you to meet him first and see how wonderful he was," Paula said, her face so radiant with happiness as she looked at the lieutenant that for a moment she was truly beautiful.

"How long have you two known each other?" Margarite asked, tearing her gaze away from Paula and trying to look at the matter practically.

"Forever!" Paula exclaimed.

"Six months," Louis said, and then swiftly, "I can assure you, Countess, if it were at all possible, I would much prefer to have the blessing of Paula's mother."

"I assume you are not wealthy," Margarite said dryly.

The young man flushed. "I have a small income, and with my military pay, Paula will never be in want."

"As if that matters," Paula protested, outraged.

No, perhaps it didn't, not now, Margarite thought. And perhaps if the two were very much in love, it might never matter. But there was another consideration.

She thought of Franz, and those other young officers she had known, who now lay buried forever in the alien soil of Mexico. She spoke directly to the lieutenant. "You're a soldier, Lieutenant Schaffner, and often soldiers die in battle. What happens to Paula then?"

For a moment, humiliation flashed across the young face, as if he were remembering the recent crushing Austrian defeat at the hands of Prussia. "I make no apology for being a soldier," he said proudly. "I fought for the emperor at Königgrätz. We are at peace now, but I will fight again if the emperor orders his army into battle. Paula knows the risks I face."

Did she? Margarite wondered, unhappily looking into her sister's fresh young face, the guileless eyes wide with adoration as she gazed at the man beside her, so young and handsome in the gold-braided scarlet tunic and tight white trousers. How could Paula know, as she did, the pain of losing someone you loved, the terrible finality of death.

Paula suddenly tore herself away from the lieutenant and flung herself into Margarite's arms. "Please, Margarite. Louis is to be posted to Galicia within a few days, and I want to go with him. Please say you'll help us." Her face suddenly looked older than its years, her voice very sure. "Do you think whatever might happen to Louis, that we'll be sorry we found each other, or that we fell in love?"

Am I sorry? Margarite wondered. Would she rather never have met Patrick, never lain in his arms than go through the agony of these last weeks? No, she thought instantly. Dear God, no!

She forced her mind back to the present, to Paula waiting for her answer. She tucked one of the wayward curls back under her sister's riding hat and smiled faintly. "I'll help you if I can, although I don't know what I can do. You're under age and can't legally marry without Elissa's consent."

And Austrians, she knew, prided themselves on their

cumbersome bureaucracy. Any permission to marry required a great deal of official paperwork. Even if somehow Louis could secure that permission, it would take weeks. Unless. . . Baron Von Friedrich's face suddenly flashed into her mind. After he had delivered her to the Von Melk home, the baron had made her promise that if she ever needed anything, she must call upon him. A man like Baron Von Friedrich must know a lot of influential people. If she could somehow persuade him to help. . .

After she sent a message to the baron, though, asking him to call upon her on an afternoon when she knew Elissa would be away from the house, she began to have second thoughts. How did she know that his offer of assistance hadn't been only a polite gesture, not to be taken seriously. After all, wasn't it much more likely that an aristocrat like the baron would side with Elissa and her sensible choice of a husband for her daughter.

Still, when the baron did arrive, with flattering punctuality, he at least listened to her explaining the situation, his pleasant face revealing nothing until she had finished. Then he asked simply, "Is it what you want, that your sister should marry this young man?"

"I want what will make my sister happy."

"And you think marrying this no doubt handsome young officer will make her happy?"

The cynicism touched the baron's voice for only a moment, then he smiled broadly. "Well, then, if that's what you want, so be it."

Margarite leaned forward, a little startled at the man's quick capitulation. "You'll help Paula marry Lieutenant Schaffner?"

Her companion chuckled. "How could I refuse such a romantic undertaking? It's almost like one of Johann Strauss's romantic operettas, is it not?" He pursed his lips thoughtfully. "I do have two conditions. First, you allow me the honor of calling you Margarite, and you must call me Karl."

"And the second?"

He smiled mischievously. "The second, well, I'll tell you the second condition after we've finished joining the young lovers in holy matrimony." At Margarite's hesitation, the smile faded. "You cannot believe I would impose any dishonorable condition upon you," he said stiffly.

Margarite remembered the many kindnesses the baron had shown her in Paris and on the journey from Paris to Vienna. "No," she said, and then quickly, "No, of course not."

"Good!" the baron beamed. "Now we must put our heads together and make our plans. There is a small church not too far from here, off the Kärntnerstrasse. I will make arrangements for the priest there to perform the ceremony. Securing the necessary papers, that will take a few days longer. Say, Friday evening. I'll send my coach and driver to wait for you. He'll know where to take you. Can you and your sister and the lieutenant be ready by then?"

"Oh, yes, I'm sure we can," Margarite said eagerly. "But what of Elissa? How can we leave the house without my stepmother's knowing?"

The baron got to his feet, giving Margarite a roguish wink. "Let me worry about the fair Elissa."

Margarite was more nervous than the bride-to-be as the two young women hurried down the front steps into a waiting carriage in front of the house on Friday evening. As the baron had promised, Elissa was nowhere in sight, having left the house earlier, when the baron had arrived to take her to a reception at the Hofburg Palace.

Lieutenant Schaffner was waiting at the altar for his bride, a fellow officer standing beside him. The small, ancient church, candlelit and smelling of incense, reminded Margarite of the smaller, less ornate churches in Mexico, where the beauty of the church came from its simplicity, and not its lavish, gilded saints and jewel-coated altars. Margarite's hands trembled as she took the bridal bouquet from Paula's hands, but Paula's face was serene, her voice soft and firm at the same time as the vows were exchanged, while Lieutenant Schaffner seemed unable to tear his worshipping gaze from his bride's face.

It was only afterward, as Margarite pressed her wed-

ding gift, a diamond and ruby pendant necklace, into
Paula's hands, and said her good-byes to the happy
couple, that tears suddenly filled Paula's eyes and she
clung to her sister, whispering, "I hope and pray that
someday you'll be as happy as I am, Margarite."

Margarite lowered her eyelids quickly so that her
sister couldn't see the pain there, a desolation filling her
too deep for tears. The aching emptiness she felt remained with her even the next morning, when the maid
came to her bedroom, already so lonely without Paula's
laughing, eager presence, to tell her that she was wanted
in the small drawing room.

When she walked into the rose and cream brocade
room, she saw that not only Elissa was there waiting for
her, seated at the tea table, but Baron Von Friedrich
was standing behind her. Margarite braced herself for
her stepmother's wrath. Surely by now Elissa must have
guessed Margarite's role in her daughter's elopement.
To her surprise, however, her stepmother seemed to
have taken Paula's marriage in stride, dabbing at invisible tears as she murmured maternally, "Naturally, I'm
heartsick at not having been present at my only daughter's wedding, but the baron has very kindly volunteered
to talk to Herr Ludwig. Hopefully, the poor man will not
be too upset. How I will manage, though, without my
darling child, I'll never know."

Over Elissa's head Margarite saw again the faintly
cynical smile on the baron's face, and suddenly found
herself wondering if perhaps Karl hadn't made some
financial arrangement with her stepmother to ease her
pain, not so much at losing her daughter, but the money
that Paula's marriage to Herr Ludwig would have brought
to Elissa.

She cast a grateful glance to the baron, who lifted his
glass to her, amused, as if they were joint conspirators.
Intercepting the exchange, Elissa bridled, then forced a
set smile to her lips as she gazed at her stepdaughter and
said, her voice suddenly cold. "It seems that I have been
kept in the dark, not only about my daughter's activities,
but yours, too, Margarite. The baron has just informed
me that he plans to ask for your hand in marriage. . . ."

Chapter 26

AT the shocked look on Margarite's face, the baron put down his glass, his own face flushed with anger as he said sharply to his hostess, "May I speak to Margarite alone, Countess?"

Elissa glanced, flustered, up at the baron murmuring, "I'm not sure . . . under the circumstances . . ." But she got to her feet and withdrew quickly when the baron continued to stare at her without speaking.

After her stepmother had left the room, the baron turned with a sigh to the speechless girl. "I'm sorry, Margarite. I never meant for her to blurt it out that way, but with your father dead, and with your guardian, Don Francisco, so far away, I felt it only honorable that your stepmother should be aware of my intentions."

With one part of her mind Margarite wondered how the baron knew about Don Francisco, even as she stiffened indignantly and asked, "Is this the second condition for lending your assistance to my sister?"

The baron shrugged sheepishly. "I confess that from the first moment I saw you in Paris, I knew I wanted you for my wife. I have no wish, however, to force myself upon you. The only condition I make is that you do me the honor of sharing my company so that we may grow to know each other better. If in three months you still refuse my offer of marriage, nothing more will be said about the matter." He put a hand over his chest, sighing dramatically. "Although, naturally my heart will be broken forever."

Almost against her will, Margarite found herself smiling at her suitor. Of course, she had no intention of

marrying the baron. Still, what harm could it do to
spend some time with him? It would be lonely without
Paula, and she had no other close friends in Vienna.
And she had already discovered that Karl could be an
amusing companion. As long as he didn't force his attentions upon her, she thought, flinching at the idea of any
other man than Patrick touching her, making love to her.

Gradually, in the weeks that followed, the baron became her constant escort, calling at the Von Melk home
almost every afternoon. At first Margarite held herself
warily aloof when she was alone with him but, finally, as
Karl never gave her any cause for concern, treating her
more like a younger sister than a prospective wife, she
began to look forward to his visits, and, even, a little
guiltily, to enjoy them.

Although the newspapers were filled with the disastrous losses that Maximilian was suffering in Mexico,
and the looming shadow that Bismarck and the powerful
Prussian army were throwing over Europe, the coffee
houses and theaters and dance halls in Vienna were
filled to capacity with crowds of merrymakers who behaved as if they didn't have a care in the world.

Margarite accompanied Karl on horseback rides in the
Prater, or riding in the baron's black and silver carriage
as it joined the other splendid equipages that thronged
the new avenue called the Ringstrasse encircling the
city, where the ancient walls of Vienna had only recently been razed.

Always after these rides, they would stop at a pastry
shop for refreshment, with the baron insisting that Margarite must eat yet another deliciously rich sacher torte
and ordered more whipped cream for her coffee. "You
are much too thin," he said, frowning with mock
sternness.

One day they went for a long ride into the Vienna
woods, the trees ablaze with fall colors. Scarlets and
golds, like a luminous, medieval tapestry, shone amid the
rich green of pines. The carriage stopped for a midday
meal at a hunting lodge that Karl owned and seldom
used, he admitted with a wry smile. "I've always found
hunting rather dull, dozens of beaters driving the game

to within a few feet of the hunters' guns so they can't possibly miss." He took a hunting rifle from the wall near the huge stone fireplace, caressing its pearl and gold engraved stock. "Still, this is beautiful, is it not?"

Margarite looked quickly away, a picture flashing into her mind of Patrick in her arms, the blood from the gunshot wound staining his shirtfront, the acrid smell of the gunpowder in her nostrils, so that for a moment she thought she might be physically ill. Vaguely she was aware of Karl kneeling before her as she sat in a chair before the fireplace, coaxing her to drink some brandy, the look of anxiety in his face as he apologized, "What a *dumbkopf* I am to upset you with talks of guns, after the shocking experience you went through with your murdered aunt and uncle."

"You know how they died?" Margarite asked, startled.

Karl took her two small hands into his, his voice, kind. "Of course, child. Your stepmother told me. After we're married, we must make a sizable donation to the good Sisters at the Convent of the Cross in Querétaro for saving you from a similar, if not worse fate."

So he didn't really know the whole story, Margarite thought, relieved, and then felt a pang of remorse at deceiving someone who had been so kind to her. Almost, she opened her mouth to tell him the true facts, when she realized with a jolt what he had said. *After we're married.* Surely she had made it clear that she had no intention of accepting his proposal of marriage, hadn't she?

As she drew her hands hastily from his, Karl got to his feet, his stocky body braced as he gazed down at her. "Does the prospect of marrying me still seem so alarming, my dear?" For a moment, behind the brightly amused eyes, Margarite thought she saw something else, an anger, quickly hidden, as he reached down and pulled her to her feet. "You mustn't blame me for being an impatient suitor. Do you know how beautiful you look, with the firelight on your hair?" His voice was husky as his hand gently touched a pale cheek. "And your face so young and innocent, your skin firm, yet soft as a rose, not yet opened." Then abruptly the hand dropped away.

"Well, we'll talk no more about it, or I'll never get you back to Vienna before dark, and then," he chuckled, "I'm afraid the gossips would do nothing but talk!"

I must tell him that there is no possibility of a marriage, Margarite thought guiltily. It wasn't fair to let him believe that she might change her mind. Yet, somehow the right moment to tell him never seemed to come during the next weeks, as Vienna began to prepare for the Christmas season. Store windows were gaily garlanded with holly and ivy, a new Johann Strauss waltz celebrating the Danube filled the coffee houses and cafés, and fir trees glittered with gold and silver nuts, rosy apples, and tiny candles.

There was a special performance at the Spanish Riding School for the empress Elizabeth, whose birthday was on Christmas Eve, and whose fondness for horses was almost an obsession. The baron escorted Margarite to the performance, and she watched, fascinated, as the Lipizzaner stallions went through their paces before the imperial box. The Lipizzaners' white skin glowed, almost translucent white in the oval, candlelit riding hall, the horses seeming to float through the air in the difficult cabriole.

When they left the riding school, the first snow of the season was falling, large, dancing flakes drifting downward, making silver streaks in the light from Vienna's new street gas lamps. Laughing, Margarite reached up her hands to catch the flakes. Winter was the one season she had missed the most while she was in Mexico, with its eternal summer.

"They say it's cold enough that they're ice skating in the Prater," she said wistfully.

"Would you like to go skating?" Karl asked as his black and silver coach, with his baronial crest on the door, pulled up before them.

"Oh, could we?" Margarite asked eagerly. "You mean now?"

"Why not?" He studied her creamy satin gown, with its overlay of lace, the matching satin slippers, that she wore. "You'll have to change clothes, of course, something a bit warmer so you won't catch cold," he said firmly.

Margarite pushed back a feeling of annoyance. Did he think she was a child? Of course she knew she would have to change into warmer clothes for ice skating. Then she reminded herself how fortunate she was to have someone who cared enough to cosset her, even if Karl's constant fussing and fretting over her sometimes annoyed her to distraction.

At the Von Melk home she left Karl in the front parlor, then hurried up to her bedroom, meeting her stepmother coming down the stairs. Elissa was still in her morning clothes, and there was a coffee stain on the bodice of her gown, which barely covered breasts that had once been attractively eyecatching but were now heavy and pendulous.

"And where are you off to in such a hurry?" she asked Margarite, her voice slightly slurred, her hand clutching at the railing as if for support.

"Karl and I are going ice skating." And then, feeling a sudden pity for the older woman, who seldom left the house these days, asked, "Why don't you come with us?"

"I've never much enjoyed bucolic sports," Elissa said, a smile creasing the too plump cheeks, "but then, I suppose the baron would enjoy such childish pleasures." There was something slyly secretive about that smile and a deliberate spitefulness in Elissa's words, but before Margarite could question her stepmother, Elissa had continued on down the steps and into the front parlor.

Well, she shouldn't be surprised that her stepmother was jealous of the baron's attentions to her, Margarite thought as she undressed quickly in her room and pulled on warm woolen undergarments, a tawny brown velvet skirt and fur-collared jacket, a matching fur mantalet and huge fur muff. At one time she was sure that Elissa had hoped to snare the baron herself for a husband. Margarite had been surprised that her stepmother had accepted the situation between Karl and her as well as she had.

As she hurried back down the stairs with a pair of ice
skates tucked under her arm, she heard Elissa's voice
raised angrily through the partially opened parlor door.
"And I tell you I need more money, or would you prefer
I—" Her stepmother's voice broke off as she heard the
sound of Margarite's footsteps on the parquet floor.
When Margarite entered the room, Elissa was pouring
herself a drink from the brandy decanter and Karl was
standing by the window.

Elissa put down her drink and bustled forward to kiss
Margarite on the cheek. "Run along and have a good
time, child." She wagged a finger playfully at the baron.
"Now, you will look after my little girl? I don't want her
catching a chill."

He smiled graciously; only Margarite, who was beginning to recognize the baron's moods, realized how angry
he was as he bundled her into the carriage, making sure
the lap robe was tucked securely around her before
climbing in beside her.

"There's no need for you to give my stepmother
money," Margarite said, embarrassed. "We can manage
very well on what I have."

"So you overheard dear Elissa," the baron said, chuckling wryly. He slipped his hand into her fur muff and
gave Margarite's fingers a gentle squeeze. "You mustn't
concern yourself, child. I'm quite able to cope with your
stepmother, although I confess she could try the patience of a saint." His voice grew hard. "And the sooner
you're married and away from her pernicious influence,
the better."

But Margarite did not want to talk about marriage, not
on such a beautiful night. When they reached the Prater,
she saw that bonfires had been built along the frozen
streams and lakes and paper ribbons hanging in garlands
from the trees added to the gaiety of the scene. A few
snowflakes, like ballerinas, continued to pirouette through
the night while couples skated, locked arm in arm to the
music from a nearby café.

Margarite was not surprised that Karl skated as well
as he danced. For a large man, she had discovered that
he was surprisingly light on his feet. When she stumbled

over a rough patch of ice, his arm around her waist kept her from falling, then, laughing, he spun her around dizzily, until the stars reeled overhead and she clung to him breathlessly.

She hadn't even realized they had skated away from the others, the music faint now mingling with the whispering sound of the blades of their skates cutting smoothly over the ice, their breath rising and mixing in the moonlit night.

Then suddenly they were no longer skating. Karl had his arms around her and his lips were warm on hers. The shock that Margarite felt then was not from the kiss but the startled awareness that all the emotions and longings she had been so sure had died with Patrick had come suddenly alarmingly alive, like frostbitten flesh returning painfully to life.

With a gasp she tore herself free, but Karl's arms still rested around her waist as he smiled tenderly down at her. "Don't look so frightened, *Liebling*." he said. "After all, it's only natural that a man's caresses should shock and repulse you. How could it be otherwise for a gently reared young girl?"

He didn't understand, not at all, Margarite thought unhappily. The horror he saw in her eyes was her own sense of betrayal, because she had allowed herself to enjoy, even for a moment, Karl's embrace.

Karl held her face between his hands, his voice filled with pride. "How beautiful you are, *meine Liebchen*. All Vienna will envy me my prize."

Margarite shivered. It was snowing harder now, the flakes like little needles stinging her face. Instantly Karl was all solicitude, pulling her fur mantalet closer around her, fussing, worried, "You're trembling, child. I'll take you home at once. You don't want to catch a chill and miss the court ball."

To her relief, he did not attempt to kiss her again. But when the baron was called out of town on business and did not return until the night of the ball, she found she missed him, wandering around the house, feeling vaguely at loose ends. She hadn't realized how much she had come to depend upon Karl's company, how lonely she felt without him.

She found herself dressing with special care for the court ball in a new white velvet gown. The heart-shaped bodice with the fashionable narrow skirt and fan-shaped train were veiled with white silk gauze and embroidered with pearl-hearted margarites. Her lacy fan trimmed with ostrich plumes was embroidered with the same flower and she carried a nosegay of margarites and orange blossoms that Karl had sent her, tied with pearl-embroidered white streamers.

Then just before she left her room, she slipped the small diamond tiara she had brought with her from Mexico onto her dark hair which was piled on top of her head in a complex arrangement of coronets and curls. Taking a last critical look at herself in the mirror, she decided, pleased, that the new coiffure and tiara not only made her look inches taller but years older. She was getting tired of the baron treating her like a child fresh out of the nursery!

This was her first court ball and although the baron liked to poke fun at the rigid court rituals that ruled Viennese society and had made light of the invitation, pointing out, "After all, it's only a court ball, not a ball at court, where one must trace one's ancestry back through sixteen noble ancestors to be admitted." Yet she suspected that the baron was very proud of his noble ancestry and his distant relationship with the royal Wittelsbach family.

When she hurried down the staircase and into the front parlor where the baron was waiting, she dipped him a deep, graceful curtsy, then smiled up at him, waiting for his words of approval. Instead, to her surprise, his face darkened with anger as he demanded sharply, "What have you done to yourself?"

Before she realized what he was doing, he had removed the tiara, his hands swiftly removing her hairpins so that her hair tumbled down over her ears.

"What. . . . what are you doing?" she stammered, embarrassed.

Without speaking, the baron pinned the shining black

waves of hair to the back of her head, where they fell in a rich heavy mass over her shoulders. Then he took several orange blossoms from her nosegay and tucked them deftly into her hair. The darkness left his face as he stepped back and smiled approvingly at her changed appearance.

"Flowers are much more suitable than a tiara for a young, unmarried woman attending a court ball." As if to temper his criticism of her choice of hair ornamentation, he added warmly, "Untouched beauty such as yours, my dear, far outshines diamonds. You'll be the greatest beauty at the ball." He smiled teasingly. "With the possible exception of the empress Elizabeth, of course."

Margarite was still not mollified as he helped her into her ermine-lined cape. She coldly did not speak to her companion as the carriage drove through the narrow streets of the inner city to the Michaelerplatz, passing through the grand triple archway flanked by fountains that was the grand entranceway to the Hofburg Palace. But as their carriage took its place in the long line of carriages bringing guests to the ball, and she saw the usually dark and rather gloomy palace streaming with lights, a growing excitement dispelled her ill humor.

Karl escorted her through a gold and white ballroom, the parquet floor so highly polished, Margarite could see her reflection as if in a mirror. Crystal chandeliers with every taper lit glittered overhead, and the fragrance of hothouse flowers and perfume scented the air as if it were spring outside instead of January.

The guests were divided into various rooms according to their ranks, waiting in a breathless silence until the grand master of the ceremonies announced by rapidly striking the floor with his ivory wand of office that the emperor and empress were approaching. The royal party visited each room in turn, where the guests were introduced to them. It was all so much like the reception Margarite had attended at Chapultepec that she realized that Maximilian had deliberately copied the Hapsburg's court and strict rituals in his Mexican court.

When it came turn for Margarite to make her curtsy to

the royal pair, she saw that Franz Josef had a strong resemblance to his younger brother, but, loyally, Margarite could not help thinking that although Franz Josef had an air of authority, of command about him that Maximilian had lacked, the younger brother had more warmth and charm. As for Elizabeth, she was as exquisite close up as she had been from a distance, but it was a cool, touch-me-not beauty, the smile she gave to each guest in turn, remote, and, Margarite suspected, a trifle bored.

A short time later the emperor and his retinue appeared on a balcony and gave the signal for the first waltz to begin, the orchestra led by Kapellmeister Johann Strauss himself. As Margarite whirled around the floor in Karl's arms in a sea of brilliantly colored uniforms and gleaming white shoulders, Karl smiled down at her, "Are you still angry with me, *Liebling*?"

Margarite smiled and shook her head. She couldn't be angry with anyone tonight, she thought. She didn't even mind Karl's arm around her tiny waist holding her much too tightly or the revealing warmth in his eyes that never left her face. It was, after all, a comforting sort of warmth, she thought, like holding out one's hands to a cozy fire in a kitchen hearth, or nestling beneath a down-filled comforter in a chilly room. She could even close her eyes and imagine it was Patrick's arms holding her, his hard body so temptingly close to hers. . . .

"What are you thinking about, Margarite?"

Margarite's eyes flew open, the softly seductive smile that had teased at the corners of her mouth disappearing beneath Karl's narrowed stare.

"I think you are becoming overheated," Karl said thoughtfully. "I'll bring you a glass of punch."

The punch did make Margarite feel cooler but oddly giddy, or perhaps it was the gay polkas and quadrilles that followed the waltz, becoming even more frenzied after the emperor and his party left at ten o'clock. The dazzling colors of the uniforms and gowns, the glittering lights, spun around her in a dizzy kaleidoscope as she whirled faster and faster around in Karl's arms. All her senses seemed heightened sharply so that her flesh tin-

gled where Karl's hands touched her, while the rhythm
of the music pounded abnormally loud in her ears. She
felt her face growing hot while strangely, her hands felt
ice cold, and she was laughing much too loudly, she
sensed, for people were turning and staring but she
didn't care. They were jealous because she was having
such a good time.

When Karl insisted that it was time they leave, she
pouted and protested, but the next thing she knew she
was being bundled into the carriage, and Karl was wrapping her in the lap rug. How light-headed she felt, Margarite thought dreamily, almost the way she had felt that
night at Doña Soledad's hacienda when she'd had too
much to drink and Patrick had made love to her.

When she felt lips pressed against hers, for one intoxicating moment she thought it was Patrick, the warmth of
those lips sending familiar, quivering sensations of pleasure through her body as they left her mouth and moved
with deliberate, tantalizing slowness down her throat.
The hands at the bodice of her gown for one delirious
moment were Patrick's hands, Patrick's lips teasing at
the soft, warm peak of her breast.

Until Karl lifted his head and whispered hoarsely,
"Tell me, *Liebchen,* tell me you'll marry me. Now.
Tonight."

Even through the confusion clouding her mind, she
knew it wasn't Patrick. Yet, all at once, it didn't matter.
All that mattered was that it shouldn't end; her whole
body ached with the need for those lips and hands to
continue to caress her, to be held close in a man's arms
and feel alive and whole again.

She could not see Karl's face in the darkness of the
carriage, the wheels rumbling over the cobblestoned
streets, but she felt his breath warm against her flesh as
his coaxing hand replaced his lips at her breast, the
excitement racing through her at his touch, even as her
mind remained clouded, somehow remote from everything that was happening to her.

"Yes," she murmured with a sigh, her eyes closing,
her body surrendering as she lifted her arms, clinging to
Karl as if she were drowning.

She was only dimly aware that the carriage wasn't returning to the Von Melk house, but turning off onto a narrow side street, and stopping before a small, baroque palace. When she stumbled stepping out of the carriage, almost falling, her legs feeling oddly unable to hold her, Karl laughed, and scooping her up in his arms, carried her into the house.

When he put her down again, she saw she was in a small chapel, as baroque as the house itself, with a vaulted gold inlaid ceiling, and statues of saints in blue and gold robes standing in niches along the wall. The small, exquisite altar was inlaid with gold, the beautifully embroidered altar cloth snowy white in the candlelight. An elderly priest stood before the altar, his voice feeble as he turned to the baron and said, "There are papers that must be signed by the countess and yourself before I can perform the ceremony."

"Of course," Karl said smoothly, drawing Margarite to the refectory table, putting the pen into her hand, showing her where she must sign.

The priest watched the proceedings, frowning uneasily as he studied Margarite. "Perhaps the countess should consider more carefully . . . the hour is so late . . . no need for haste," he mumbled, with an unhappy sidelong glance at the baron.

Margarite saw Karl's face darken, then he smiled and slipped an arm around her waist. "The countess has no wish to reconsider, do you, *Liebling*?" he asked.

Through her gown she could feel her skin quiver in response to those pressing fingers. What she wanted, Margarite thought, shaking her head and leaning against that arm, was for all of this talk to be finished, and Karl to hold her in his arms again. Rotelike, she gave her responses to the priest, whose face seemed to swim oddly in front of her. As if they were all underwater, she thought, repressing a sudden impulse to giggle, her body curiously weightless as she held out her hand so that Karl could slip on a heavy gold ring.

Then the priest's face disappeared and she was once again being carried, this time up a narrow, carved staircase that never seemed to end, down a dark corridor into a dimly lit room. An enormous bed stood in the center of the room and although there was a fire in the porcelain stove in one corner of the room, its heat didn't reach the bed. She shivered as she stood like a wax doll and let Karl undress her, relieved to rid herself of her gown that felt so strangely heavy, hurting her flesh with its weight.

How cold she was, she thought, and welcomed the warmth of Karl's body as he joined her in the bed, shivering now not from cold but from excitement, as his mouth, no longer gentle, forced her lips apart. His hands suddenly pulled her beneath him, and forcing her legs apart, he entered her swiftly. When he just as swiftly withdrew with a muttered, furious curse, she stared up at him, her eyes confused and bewildered.

She saw his face then in the candlelight, no longer filled with passion. A lashing fury in the glittering amber eyes made her, suddenly frightened, pull away from him, trying to reach the safety of the far side of the bed. But she was not fast enough. His hand caught her shoulder, jerked her back toward him across the bed.

"Slut!" he snarled savagely. His arm lifted and the flat of his hand caught her full across the face, so that she felt her neck snap under the blow. "Whore!"

There was a roaring in her ears, the lamp beside the bed swung dizzily back and forth, and she was tumbling over and over again through a black tunnel into oblivion.

Chapter 27

WHAT a horrible nightmare! Wide awake, the terrors of the night still lingered with Margarite, but jumbled and confused in her mind, snatches only, that mistlike, drifted away as she clutched at them. Shuddering, Margarite opened her eyes. Not that she wanted to remember the frightening dreams that had pursued her through the night. It was the wine she drank at the ball. How foolish of her not to remember that she didn't have a head for wine. Her head ached abominably—she gasped and sat up in bed—her now cleared vision taking in the unfamiliar bedroom.

The ache in her head settled into a steady pounding. So it hadn't all been a nightmare, she thought, pushing back a feeling of nausea, sour-tasting in her throat. She remembered a priest and the small chapel and Karl slipping a ring on her finger and before that, how shamefully she had behaved in the carriage with Karl, as if her body hadn't belonged to her at all. And later, here in bed . . . but she couldn't bear to think about that. Humiliation washed over her in a red-hot wave, and the bile rising in her throat would not be pushed down. She made it to the wash basin just in time.

The fire had gone out in the stove and the room was bitterly cold. She crawled back beneath the covers, groaning, wishing she were dead. How could she ever face Karl? When she awoke again, the room was warmer. Someone had come in and started a fire. She sat up in bed, gazing wanly at her ball gown which still lay crumpled on the floor, when a knock came at the door. She was snatching the bedcover back around her when the baron walked into the room.

He smiled thinly at her attempting to cover herself. "It's a little late for maidenly modesty, isn't it?" he asked as he came to stand beside the bed. And he watched the pink of embarrassment that ran along her cheekbones as she clutched the coverlet to her.

What a practiced little slut she was, he thought, outraged. She even managed to blush on cue. And how cleverly she had managed to deceive him all these months, with her innocent, virginal airs, as if she were terrified of a man's touch. He had been surprised at the ardor of her response to his lovemaking in the carriage, but he had blamed it on the powders he had placed in her punch at the ball. The powders were to make sure she would be receptive to his marriage proposal. He had grown weary of her childish procrastination, and he thought grimly, his creditors had been growing even wearier.

The marriage would not have been simply one of convenience and financial necessity. It was time he sired a son to carry on the family name. Of course, the countess Von Melk's bloodline wasn't as illustrious as his own, and she was older than the bed partners he found desirable, but her tremendous fortune more than made up for these defects. He had even looked forward, with a certain relish, to their wedding night, initiating his bride's shocked and innocent young body to the conjugal bed and her marital duties. Instead, to his revulsion, she had been as practiced and eager as he was, and when he had taken possession, he had known at once by his ease of entry that he had not been the first to penetrate the trembling young body.

He stepped closer to the bed, feeling the anger pound in his temples as he glared at the girl. "Who was he?" Then, his glance raking her contemptuously, "Or should I ask, how many men were there before me?"

Margarite stiffened indignantly, then reminded herself that she couldn't blame Karl for being aggrieved, even furious with her. A man had the right to expect his bride to be a virgin. "There was only one," she said, her chin rising with unconscious pride. "His name was Patrick O'Malley."

Karl pulled up a chair beside the bed and sat down. "An Irishman?" His mouth curled scornfully. "You have a common taste in lovers. Just how did you manage to meet this O'Malley? I've always heard that the virtue of Mexican women was closely guarded."

Margarite looked away from the contempt in those amber eyes, and wished her head didn't hurt so much so that it was difficult to speak, much less think clearly. "After . . . after the bandits murdered my aunt and uncle, I was taken prisoner to their camp. I had lost my memory. Patrick . . . Patrick rescued me, looked after me."

"And you fell into his arms in gratitude. How touching,'' the baron sneered. His eyes narrowed speculatively. ''Or did he rape you?''

Not that it would make any difference. The countess was still used property, secondhand goods, unfit to bear the proud title of Baroness Von Friedrich, certainly unfit to bear his children. As for Karl himself, since his first sexual conquest, when he had seduced and then raped the child of one of the tenants on his father's estate, he had never been able to make love to a woman who had lain with other men. It was defiling innocence that excited him beyond control. Any other conquest was repugnant.

''I wasn't raped. I—I gave myself willingly.'' Impulsively, Margarite reached out a hand to her husband. ''I'm sorry, Karl. I never meant to deceive you.'' When her hand touched her husband's arm, she was shocked at his swift withdrawal from her touch, the icy stiffening of his face, as if she were unclean. She felt her face burn at the loathing she saw in his eyes. Pulling the coverlet more closely around her, as if she were clutching at the remnants of a tattered dignity, she said, ''I'll give you a divorce, of course.''

Or an annulment? she wondered. Surely what had happened in this bed last night could hardly be called the consummating of a marriage.

The baron got to his feet and walked to the door, turning at the last moment to face her, his voice cold. ''There will be no divorce. The dishonor of a divorce has never touched the Von Friedrich family. You are my wife and will remain my wife. In public, I expect you to conduct yourself as befitting the Baroness Von Friedrich.'' His glance traveled over her with icy indifference. ''How you conduct yourself in private is of no concern to me.'' He opened the door. ''Your clothes and personal possessions have arrived. I'll have them brought up.''

Margarite stared at the closed door. He didn't mean it, of course, she thought, trying to ignore the fluttering wings of panic in her stomach. For a moment she was afraid that she might be sick again. It was understandable that Karl should be angry with her at first, but he would get over his disappointment in time, she assured herself. She had only to be patient and wait and the old good-natured Karl would return.

A few minutes later a young servant girl came through the door, staggering under the weight of the portmanteaus she carried, then returned with a small wicker trunk that she pushed awkwardly ahead of her into the room.

Margarite, tripping over the coverlet still wrapped around her, rushed to assist her. "You should get another servant to help you," she scolded. The girl couldn't have been more than fourteen or fifteen, she thought, although she was large for her age. "What is your name?"

"Milli, Frau Baroness, Milli Novotny," the girl said, speaking slowly in a heavy Czech accent, her gaze cast downward to the floor, her large hands clutching nervously at her skirt as she made a clumsy curtsy. Margarite was not surprised at the accent. The streets of Vienna were filled with emigrants from the far-flung empire of the Hapsburgs, Bohemia, Moravia, Hungary, Galicia, all speaking a dozen different languages along with abominable German.

It was also quickly apparent that in addition to not speaking German well, Milli had no training as a lady's maid. She was almost pathetically eager to please, but Margarite finally ended up dressing herself, pulling on several warm woolen petticoats beneath a tartan skirt, slipping into a short black wool jacket decorated with braid. Although the room was warmer than when she had first awakened, it was still uncomfortably chill with only a small frugal log fire in the white porcelain stove.

Milli was, however, able to take care of the unpacking, while Margarite gratefully drank the hot coffee and ate the crullers the girl brought her, her new maid blushingly proud when she managed to pour the coffee without spilling a drop. The Viennese fork breakfast would come later in the morning, Margarite knew, but for now the coffee was exactly what she needed to help dull the throbbing in her head, at least enough so that, frowning, and glancing around her, she suddenly realized what had been missing from the unpacking of her belongings.

She quickly left her room and hurried down the long,

carved marble staircase, noticing that the carpeting on the staircase was threadbare. She found her husband sitting at a desk in a small room off the main entrance hall. "Karl, they're gone!" she said, rushing into the room. "All my jewelry that I brought with me from Mexico, even the few gold coins I had left."

The baron looked up, scowling, from the letter he was writing, obviously annoyed at the interruption. "Don't be foolish. Of course the jewelry's not gone. I've taken it into safekeeping. You don't suppose I'd leave valuable pieces like that lying around where anyone could steal them? As for the coins, what possible need do you have for money?"

But it's my jewelry, Margarite almost blurted out, then remembered suddenly that that was no longer true. She was a married woman now. Under the law, all the property of a wife belonged to her husband. Karl had the right to go through her portmaneaus before sending them to her room and remove anything of value. But why should he? she thought, mystified. Why should a man as wealthy as the baron bother about her few pieces of jewelry?

Karl waited impatiently for her to leave, then asked, "Was there something else?" He indicated the papers on his desk. "I'm very busy, as you can see. I have to notify your guardian, Don Francisco, of our marriage. I've already sent a message to Mexico over the Atlantic cable, but the legal documents certifying the marriage will have to be sent by sea."

For the first time, Margarite found herself wondering about that hurried marriage ceremony, the priest waiting so propitiously at the small chapel in the middle of the night. "You were very sure there would be a wedding, weren't you?" she asked slowly.

Karl tugged at a corner of his skewerlike mustache, his smile contemptuously amused. "Are you implying that I somehow tricked you into marriage? Have you forgotten how eager you were last night to share my caresses, how you could hardly wait to get me into your bed? Oh, no, one could hardly call you a reluctant bride." His glance roamed coldly over her. "Still, there was no need for the *Morgengabe,* now, was there?"

Margarite flushed, remembering that the "morning gift" was a traditional sum of money from a husband to his new bride to compensate for the loss of her virginity. She was aware of that glittering, amused amber gaze following her as she turned, and with as much dignity as she could muster, swept from the room.

Nevertheless, that evening, when Karl escorted her to a friend's home, where a party had been hastily arranged in honor of the baron and his new bride, she could not have asked for a more devoted or loving husband. Karl never left her side, accepting cheerfully the good-natured jibes of his friends, his voice warm and filled with pride as he lifted his own glass in a toast to his beautiful bride. It was only when they left the party in the small hours of the morning and entered their carriage that the baron immediately fell into a frigid silence. When they arrived at the Von Friedrich home, he stalked ahead of Margarite up the stairs to his own room, leaving his wife to trail along behind to her own quarters.

The following weeks fell into much the same pattern. When they were with his friends or at social occasions, Karl was attentive to his wife's every want, as thoughtful and considerate as any new doting husband. When they were alone, however, he was icily indifferent, speaking to Margarite only when absolutely necessary. Not that they saw each other that often. Several times the baron disappeared for days, visiting Baden-Baden "for the waters," he told Margarite, but she was not so naive that she didn't know of the luxurious gambling casinos at Baden-Baden. Did the baron's losses at gambling explain the frugalities practiced in the Von Friedrich household, she wondered, or was her husband just naturally parsimonious?

She almost welcomed her husband's absence from the house, though, for when he was home and they met accidentally in the hall or happened to eat a meal together, his glance looked straight through her, or he buried himself behind a newspaper.

As if she didn't exist for him at all, Margarite thought at breakfast one morning as she stared unhappily across the table at the newspaper propped before her husband. She was tearing absently at a hot buttered roll, feeling the beginnings of another one of her headaches, when the baron suddenly put aside his newspaper and asked abruptly, "Is your costume ready for the ball this evening?"

The roll crumbled in Margarite's hand. "Costume?" she asked blankly.

Karl tugged at a corner of his mustache, a habit she had discovered he had when he was annoyed with her. "I told you last week," he said sharply. "We're attending a carnival ball this evening at the Esterhazys'. Surely you haven't forgotten?"

She *had* forgotten, Margarite realized with a start of guilt. She couldn't even remember Karl's telling her about the ball. Well, at least it would be the last ball of the carnival season, she thought with relief. The beginning of Lent was only a few days away. She wasn't sure which was the more tiring, the continuous round of carnival balls Karl and she attended, lasting from early evening to early morning, or the exhaustion of maintaining the façade of the happy bride with Karl's friends. She pressed her fingers to her temples, feeling her headache grow worse, a steady pounding within her skull, her nerves pulled drum-tight. Thank God for the powders the doctor had left her, she thought gratefully.

When, shortly after her marriage, Margarite's headaches had begun to recur with alarming regularity, the baron had summoned a physician to treat his wife. The doctor, after examining Margarite, cleared his throat a little uncomfortably, then punctuating his words with paternal pats of her hand, he assured his patient as tactfully as possible that it was not at all uncommon for a young bride to develop vapors and headaches.

"The shock of the nuptial act to a young woman's delicate nervous system . . . hysteria of some sort is not at all unusual . . . almost to be expected . . . I've seen it countless times . . . not at all serious." He had left some powders for Margarite, smiling knowingly at the baron.

"At night, before you and your wife retire . . . you understand . . ."

Remembering the doctor's words, Margarite felt her face grow warm. Since Karl had not been near her bed since their disastrous wedding night, she could hardly blame her headaches on the nuptial act, she thought ruefully. The powders had helped, though, not only dulling the headaches but relaxing her taut nerves and helping her to sleep.

The only trouble was that the powders sometimes made her feel almost too lethargic, as if all she wanted to do was sleep, so that she was still in her dressing robe when the baron came by her room that evening.

"I'm sorry, Karl," she said, repressing a yawn, "I'm afraid I'm too tired to go out this evening."

'Nonsense!" he said brusquely. "A lady of your station never allows fatigue to keep her from her social duties." He studied his wife's pale face, annoyed. "What you need is a glass of wine," he announced. "It will make you feel better."

He turned to Milli, who was standing, her back pressed flat to the wall, as if trying to make herself invisible. Margarite had already noticed that her timid maid seemed to be terrified of the baron. "Fetch the baroness a glass of wine," he ordered. "There's a bottle opened in my bedroom."

When the girl stood frozen, he snapped, "*Trottel! Schnell!*" The girl turned and scuttled from the room.

"You shouldn't yell at Milli like that," Margarite protested.

Her husband's face flushed irritably. "The girl is an idiot."

'Why did you employ her, then?'

The baron shrugged. "A philanthropic impulse. She comes from some small village in Bohemia. There wasn't enough food to feed the family, so as such country people often do, her parents sent the child off to Vienna to make her own way. I found her walking the streets, starving. I thought she'd make a good chambermaid. Obviously it was a mistake, as such impulses usually are. I'll send her away."

"No!" Margarite said hastily. "I like her." She couldn't imagine poor, terrified Milli managing to find a job anywhere else.

She thought that Karl would resent her interference into household matters. He had already made it clear that she was to have no role in running the Von Friedrich household. An elderly, prune-faced housekeeper, Frau Wagner, dressed always in dull black, and who had been with the Von Friedrich family for over fifty years, had that honor. Instead of being annoyed, though, at her defying him, she was uneasily aware that her husband's amber eyes, watching her, held a secret amusement as he shrugged indifferently and said, "As you wish."

Although she was in no mood for wine, Margarite sipped obediently at the glass of sweet white wine Milli brought her, her husband watching her sternly until she had finished the glass. After drinking the wine, she did feel better, her tiredness slipping away from her like a discarded gown. She was all at once filled with a restless, nervous energy, and as Milli helped her dress, the maid's large, clumsy hands no longer quite so awkward, Margarite saw that in the dressing table mirror her eyes sparkled like green ice and there was an attractive rosy glow beneath the pallor of her skin.

Yet for all that her face felt flushed, the rest of her body was oddly chilled, and the Hungarian costume Karl had chosen for her to wear, the wide embroidered skirt, white apron of lace, scarlet velvet bodice, and fine muslin sleeves puffed at the shoulders, provided little warmth. Still, her husband was pleased with the costume, she saw as she presented herself to him, waiting impatiently at the bottom of the staircase.

His mouth twisted in a cynical smile. "The emperor and empress will undoubtedly make an appearance at the Esterhazy ball. Now that the Kaiserin has foolishly convinced Franz Josef that her beloved Hungary, with its wild, barbaric Magyars, is to be an equal partner with Austria, your costume should please the imperial family."

The Viennese newspapers had been filled for weeks with stories about Franz Josef's having granted rebellious Hungary its own parliament and constitution. There

was even to be a coronation that summer of Franz Josef
and Elizabeth as king and queen of Hungary and everything Hungarian was the fashion in Vienna these days.
The Esterhazys themselves were one of the oldest and
wealthiest of Hungarian families, Margarite knew. Part
of the inner circle of the Hapsburg court, their rococo
palace rivaled the Hofburg if not in size then in splendor,
and invitations to their balls were as eagerly sought after
as attendance at a court ball.

Unlike court balls, though, Margarite discovered when
she and Karl arrived at the Esterhazy palace, balls given
by the Esterhazys, especially carnival balls, were not
dull, formal occasions. There were no grim-faced chap-
erones seated in gilt chairs around the dance floor, making sure the guests were on their best behavior. In the
lavishly decorated Esterhazy palace, with treasures of
chinoiserie everywhere, roses and jasmines spreading
their fragrance in the air, the carnival spirit ruled. Mir-
rored walls reflected the light of hundreds of glittering
candles, while masked and costumed dancers whirled
with a joyous abandon to a constant stream of fast
waltzes and energetic polkas.

For the first time, at a social occasion Karl did not
stay close to his wife's side, but Margarite did not lack
for dancing partners. Stepping out onto the dance floor
was like flinging oneself into a maelstrom, but she was
quickly caught up in the carnival spirit, passing with
feverish gaiety from one pair of arms to another. She
had never, she thought, delighted, enjoyed dancing so
much. It was as if her body had turned into something
without bones, light as a feather in each man's arms, her
feet hardly seeming to touch the floor at all. How beautiful it all was, how alive and glowing she felt. She gave
her partner a ravishing smile, enjoying the admiring
warmth in his eyes, which only added to the intense
excitement building up inside of her as she let that
admiring gaze slide over her like warm, caressing hands.

Even catching a glimpse of Karl dancing with the
princess Kodosky, an aristocratic court beauty hardly
more than a child, couldn't spoil the euphoria she felt,
despite the fact that her husband was smiling at the girl

in his arms with the same tenderness she had once seen in his eyes when he smiled at her.

She knew she was flirting outrageously, but she couldn't seem to stop herself, not even when later in the evening, Count Ernst von Lindow, dashingly handsome in his white dress Hussar's uniform, pulled her into a discreetly darkened corridor away from the ballroom. She welcomed the warmth of his searching mouth on her lips and shoulders, the feel of his hard masculine body against hers, holding her close. Finally, breathlessly, she pulled a little away from her companion, leaning back in his arms, smiling seductively up into the black, moist eyes behind his mask.

"Your skin is on fire, *Liebchen*," the Hussar whispered. His hands slipping down her spine were skillfully, delicately, caressing. "I can see the passion burning in your eyes. Let me make you happy. Tomorrow in the afternoon. I'll be at the Hotel Goldener Hirsch. Promise me you'll be there."

He murmured the room number, as Margarite, laughing softly, stepped backward out of his arms and collided with a guest who had come up behind them. The man reached out a hand to catch her wrist and steady her. He was wearing a black domino costume and unlike most of the other male guests, his face, except for slitted openings for his eyes, was completely hidden by his mask. For one moment Margarite felt the hand tighten painfully on her wrist, and then abruptly, without a word, the man thrust her away from him, back into the arms of the Hussar.

Margarite twisted in the count's grasp, trying to catch a glimpse of the man in the domino, but he had disappeared. Suddenly, without knowing why, it was very important she find him. She pulled herself free of the count and rushed back into the ballroom, but she could see no guest in a black domino costume. Had she only imagined him? she wondered. How odd she felt, as if she wanted to cry when a moment before she had been so deliriously happy.

Then Karl was standing beside her, gazing down at

her, his voice sharply teasing. "What is it, Margarite? You look as if you've seen a ghost."

She shook her head, feeling all at once exhausted. And cold. Terribly cold. She began to shiver uncontrollably. "I'm tired. I want to go home, Karl," she whispered. "Take me home."

A frown marred the mask of the devoted husband. "It's still early," he objected.

"I want to go home!" She heard her voice raising shrilly, knew that guests were looking toward them and then tactfully, quickly away.

Karl's voice was soothing. "Of course, if you're not feeling well, my dear . . ."

In the carriage, despite the lap robe wrapped around her, Margarite could not seem to stop shivering. Tears rolled helplessly down her cheeks. When, as usual, her husband stalked ahead of her into the house and started up the stairs, she clutched at his sleeve. "Karl. Please wait. I want to talk to you."

He pulled himself free, went up a few steps, then turned, his voice coldly polite. "Can't it wait till morning? You said you were tired."

"No. No, it can't wait." If he would only hold her in his arms for a moment, she thought, shivering. She felt as if she would never be warm again. And there was only that cold, empty bed waiting for her upstairs. How long could they exist like this, two strangers living in the same house? "Karl, please," she blurted out. "We can't go on this way. It . . . it isn't natural."

She could not see his face clearly in the dim hall light, but she could hear the bored contempt in his voice flicking at her through the darkness. "My dear wife, I thought I made it clear. I have no desire to deprive you of your . . . natural rights. How you amuse yourself is your own business. All I ask is that you're discreet in your choice of lovers."

"You can't mean that!" she gasped.

But she was talking to the air, the only sound the echo of her husband's footsteps disappearing up the stairs, and finally, the sound of his bedroom door closing behind him.

Chapter 28

IT was noon the next day before the room bell summoned Milli to her mistress's bedroom. When she entered, she saw, surprised, that the baroness was already dressed in an afternoon frock of lilac cashmere with a fluff of lace between the velvet lapels at her throat. The *Frau* baroness was standing, staring out the window, and when she turned, there was a quality in her face that Milli had never seen before, a frozen stillness for all that the green eyes shone with a glassy brightness.

"Her ladyship is going out?" Milli asked, startled.

"Yes," Margarite went to her dressing table and lifted a plumed and beribboned hat from a box. "Would you fetch a fiacre for me, Milli?"

Margarite saw Milli's blue eyes widen. It wasn't done. A lady of quality using a hired coach. Margarite's mouth tightened. She was sure Karl would hardly consider it discreet for his wife to use the Von Friedrich equipage to visit her lover in a public hotel. And that was all her husband cared about, wasn't it, that she should be discreet? Certainly he could find no fault in her choice of lovers. Count von Lindow, although of only minor nobility, was a favorite of the empress Elizabeth, extremely wealthy, and, despite the rumors of his prowess with the ladies, noted for his discretion.

"Perhaps her ladyship would like a little breakfast before she leaves," Milli coaxed.

"Just coffee." She was too nervous to eat, her hand trembling so that she stuck herself with the hat pin as she adjusted the hat at the proper angle on her head. She gazed at herself in the mirror, saw how pale she looked,

and reached for her rouge pot. She seldom wore anything on her face except a dusting of rice powder, and
her hands applied the color uncertainly, unsure how
much to use. Would the count find her attractive? she
wondered. Suppose he hadn't meant his invitation. Suppose she went to the hotel and he wasn't there. And if
he were there, waiting for her, how could she possibly
go to bed with a man she hardly knew?

She felt a pounding in her head, her nerves wound so
tightly she jumped when Milli awkwardly deposited the
breakfast tray with a jarring crash on the table.

"Must you be so clumsy?" she snapped, and then
was instantly ashamed of her outburst. "I'm sorry, Milli."
She touched her hands to her forehead as if to smooth
away the pain.

Well, one of her headache powders should help the
pain, she thought, giving a sigh of relief as she found a
packet in her dressing table drawer. She swallowed the
powders along with the coffee. Within a few moments
she felt stronger, more relaxed, her headache almost
gone. What a fuss she was making over nothing, she
thought as she entered the hired carriage. After all, it
happened often enough among Karl's friends in the aristocracy, married women having affairs with the handsomely uniformed officers who strutted the streets of
Vienna. Why should she be any different? Since Karl
obviously didn't care to share her bed, why shouldn't
she turn to other men for the warmth he denied her?
Especially when her husband had practically given her
his permission to do so.

The Goldener Hirsch turned out to be a small, pleasant hotel sitting unobtrusively on a side street. The
fiacre man didn't seem to think it unusual that his fare
should debark there, nor did the hotel clerk at the desk
even glance at the fashionably dressed young woman
who crossed the lobby to the staircase.

It wasn't until Margarite stood, hand raised to knock
at the hotel room door, that the unshakable conviction
swept over her that she could not go through with it.
She could not force herself across that threshold, allow
a stranger to undress and make love to her through no

other motive than her hurt and anger at Karl, a childish desire for revenge.

She had half-turned away when the door suddenly swung open. Before she could open her mouth to scream, the man in the doorway had his hand around her wrist and she was pulled swiftly into the room. The curtains in the room were drawn. She heard the door slam shut behind her, a lock turning. Furious, rubbing at her throbbing wrist, she stared at the shadowy figure of a man, her voice, outraged. "Count von Lindow, I insist you open that door at once!"

"How quickly you've forgotten me, *poquita*." The softly mocking voice came at her through the darkness. Patrick's voice! But, of course, it couldn't be. It was all part of her illness, she thought, panic-stricken. Part of the headaches, her forgetfulness, the unreal, frightening dreams that tormented her at night—only now she was having them in the daytime. She swayed dizzily and would have fallen, except hands at her shoulders were forcing her to sit down on the edge of the bed.

Then the curtains at the window were being thrust apart and she lifted her head to stare at the man walking in the path of sunlight toward her. If it were a hallucination, how real he seemed, she thought, closing her eyes then opening them again quickly, as if afraid he would disappear. He looked exactly the same as he had that morning she had awakened in the cave and saw him for the first time. The copper-colored skin pulled taut over a stone-hard face, the same dark, unnerving, intense gaze. Only the mustache was gone.

"Patrick?" At first she only heard his name screaming in her mind. Then she managed to speak, although her voice sounded strangled. "Patrick . . . it can't be."

He looked down into her dazed eyes, the shock that made the rouge on her cheeks stand out, clownlike, in bold relief. "So you really did think I was dead," he said slowly. "I was beginning to wonder."

She could not take her eyes from his face, as if she were still afraid he might disappear if she turned away. Her senses drank in the sight and sound of him, his presence once more miraculously a part of her world, so that she felt drunk, delirious with happiness. Only gradually did it sink in that there was a curious flatness to his voice, and that instead of gathering her at once into his arms, he was standing, staring at her almost impersonally.

"Of course I thought you were dead," she said, bewildered. "I saw you die. What else was I to think?"

He shrugged. "My death was my mother's idea. She learned about Indian drugs while tending the vaqueros and their families when they were sick. The drug she gave me slowed my breathing to the point that even Father Alfredo thought I was dead. And with El Cuchillo gone, his men weren't too eager to stick around for my funeral."

"Star should have told me the truth," Margarite protested.

"She was afraid you'd give the show away. Anyway, I was near enough death so that it was weeks before she knew whether or not I'd survive. Then when she thought it was safe, she did send word to your home in Mexico, but there was no reply."

Don Francisco, Margarite thought. Her guardian would have stopped any mail from reaching her that would have interfered with the marriage he had carefully planned for her.

"She finally went to Mexico herself, only to discover that you'd gone running off to France with Carlota. It was my mother who insisted, when I was finally well enough to get around, that I must come to Vienna to find you. She had some romantic notion that you would pine away at my death." He lifted an amused eyebrow, but his voice was cold. "But you didn't grieve for me very long, did you, Baroness? You'd already been married for a month by the time I got here."

He walked to a small sideboard against the wall and poured himself a drink from one of the bottles. When he turned back and spoke again, his voice had lost its hard edge, but Margarite could see the anger still burning deep in the indigo eyes as he lifted his glass to her in a mock salute. "Still, the trip wasn't a complete waste. I discovered the gaming tables at Monte Carlo and Baden-Baden, and I always was lucky at gambling. It was at the casino at Baden-Baden that I met the archduke Ludwig Viktor." Patrick's smile flashed white against the deep-burnished face, his voice holding an ironic amusement. "It seems he'd never met an Indian before and was fascinated. So were his friends."

"You're the American Indian," Margarite said, startled. At the balls she had attended at the homes of Karl's friends she had heard stories about the man they called the American Indian. Introduced into society by the emperor's young, dissolute brother, the man had become the rage among the more debauched of the court circle, famous for his phenomenal success at gambling as well as his whispered successes with various, smitten ladies of the court. "It never occurred to me that . . ." She shrugged helplessly. "But then, I never heard your real name."

And, of course, she had been too wrapped up in her own misery these past months to give more than a cursory interest to court gossip. She stared at Patrick, her eyes flaring wide with pain. "You could have let me know you were alive," she whispered.

He finished the last of his drink. "Why bother? You had a new life, a new husband." He smiled thinly while his eyes traveled around the hotel room, then back to her. "Until I learned that your marriage meant very little to you. How often do you come to meet your lovers in rooms like this, Baroness, once a week, twice? Tell me, doesn't your husband satisfy you, or are you just bored?" His gaze traveled over her speculatively. "Not that you seemed very bored at the Esterhazys last night."

She remembered then the man in the black domino in the corridor, and felt a flush climb her face at the memory of that heated embrace. No wonder Patrick thought . . . No wonder he assumed that she and Ernst . . . And she felt the flush flow down her neck. All at once it occurred to her: Where was Ernst? She remembered, with a start of fear, Patrick's temper, the violence that could lay beneath that impassive exterior.

"Where is Count von Lindow? " she asked, frightened.

As if guessing what she was thinking, Patrick lifted an

amused eyebrow. "He's not dead. Nothing so dramatic. I admit there was some talk of a duel to settle who would have the honor of bedding the baroness Von Friedrich, but the Austrians are a practical people. We ended up cutting cards for you instead. The count lost, or won, depending on how you look at it."

Abruptly, he put down his drink, and crossing to the bed, reached down and jerked her to her feet, so that she fell against him. With one motion he had discarded her hat, her hair pins flying to the floor as his hands tumbled her hair down around her shoulders. "But I mustn't forget the reason why you're here this afternoon," he said harshly. "We can't disappoint a lady, now can we?"

His hand was tangled in her hair, pinioning her head, while his other arm circled her waist, lifting her, her body sliding over his hardness until her mouth was on a level with his. There was no first teasing, gentle exploration of her lips and mouth, only a bruising hardness as his mouth slanted demandingly back and forth over hers, until her lips parted under the onslaught of the kiss, his tongue plunging again and again within, deeper and deeper, like a small rape. When he finally released her, she was gasping for breath, her head spinning.

She felt his hands at her gown and feebly tried to push them away. "No, don't!"

He stepped back and cocked a quizzical eyebrow. "You prefer to undress yourself?" He grinned coldly. "I suppose a gown torn by an impatient lover would be hard to explain to your husband."

She could feel the anger then sweeping through her, making her forget the pounding in her head, forget everything but wanting to hurt him as he was hurting her. She flung herself at him, beating at his chest with her fists. "Shut up! Damn you, shut up!"

His hands caught her wrists, pinned them behind her. He laughed softly as she struggled fiercely against him. "Well, at least that hasn't changed. I'd forgotten what a little spitfire you were, Baroness." His hands tightened cruelly on her wrists until she gave a small cry of protest and grew quiet in his arms. At once he thrust her away from him, his eyes narrowed, pitiless. "We're wasting time, Baroness. And you may recall, I was never the most patient of men."

His hand reached out toward her gown again, brushing deliberately, slowly, against her breast. She closed her eyes, suddenly remembering their last time together, when she had hesitated to undress before him in the small gazebo, with the rain tapping at the roof. How gentle his voice had been then when he had asked, "Do you think anything you could do, *querida*, would shame me or yourself?"

But she had shamed herself, she thought, by marrying a man she knew now she had never loved, by coming here today to sleep with another man she didn't love. Perhaps Karl was right, she thought wearily. Perhaps she was no better than a whore. For she knew, even as she felt her hands move almost involuntarily to unbutton her gown and let it fall to her feet, that there was no way she could be in the same room with Patrick and not want him.

Her undergarments followed the dress to the floor, and she shivered for all that the room was overheated. She opened her eyes and saw that Patrick had already undressed and was pouring himself another drink. She stood quietly as his gaze traveled over her.

His voice was dispassionate. "You're thinner than I remember. I thought Austrians liked their women soft and plump." And he saw that that gamine quality he had loved was gone, the mischievous smile replaced by an almost nervous curving of her lips upward.

He came to stand before her, suddenly catching her chin in his hand and turning her face to the light. His thumb ran across her cheekbone. And since when, he wondered, did Margarite need rouge to put color in her face? Then he realized her flesh was chill to the touch, a faint bluish color beneath the pale skin.

Angry at himself for feeling concern, he abruptly picked her up in his arms and carried her to the bed. How light she was, he thought, surprised, like a bird caught in his hands. She made no protest as he lay down beside her on the bed, only sighing softly as his hands roamed over her, stroking and caressing, until he could see the beginnings of a faint flush of warmth beneath the almost translucent skin.

Damn it, what was the matter with her? He was half alarmed, half irritated. The Margarite he had known by now would be responding with joyous abandon to his caresses, her softness twining around him, her lips teasing, her arms pulling him close. Instead, she was lying passively, her eyes shut, as if she were somewhere he could not reach her.

She hadn't been so quiet in that Hussar's arms last night, he thought savagely. He would never forget how she had looked, the almost lewd way her body had moved within the man's embrace, her head thrown back to receive his kisses on her throat, the soft, moaning cry of pleasure coming from her lips, cries that he had been so sure he was the only one to hear. Nor would he forget the pain that like a dull knife had ripped through him.

He had come to the hotel today, his only purpose to take his revenge on her for having made a fool of him, to punish her for slipping past the guard of Patrick O'Malley and forcing him to feel love. Like any lovesick idiot, he had raced to her side as soon as he was strong enough to travel, stupidly sure she would be there, waiting for him. Instead, he had discovered she had not only quickly forgotten him, but had found herself a husband and a series of lovers. She had become like the other titled women he had met here in Vienna, playing at love and passion in forbidden affairs, but always in the end returning to their aristocratic husbands, their palaces, and safe, comfortable lives.

Yet gazing now into that beautiful patrician face, he knew irrationally that he still wanted her, that he had never stopped wanting her. Well, this time, he thought, furious as much with himself as with her, she would not forget him so quickly. His hands moving over the small silken body were no longer gently caressing, but roughly demanding, his mouth pulling at a soft nipple till he felt it harden, and heard her soft gasp of pain or pleasure, he didn't know and didn't care which.

When he abruptly entered her, without waiting to make sure she was ready for him, her eyelids flew open for a moment, and the blazing passion that he remembered was there. She was no longer somnolent, unresponsive in his arms. Her body moved in a sweet, driving rhythm with his as she opened herself completely to him. And it was almost as it was the last time they had lain together, as if neither were able to control the passion consuming them, exploding within them, so that afterward it was several seconds before Patrick found the energy to pull away from her.

Her eyes were closed, he saw as he turned toward Margarite. Her face was as white as the pillowcase and she hardly seemed to be breathing. That was different, too, he thought, studying the girl, trying to repress the vague anxiety he felt. Always afterward she had snuggled, smiling, in his arms, vibrantly warm and alive in the aftermath of passion. Now she looked exhausted.

He slipped quietly out of bed, made sure she was covered, then poured himself a drink and began to dress.

Margarite was aware that somebody was shaking her, but she was so deeply asleep, it was several minutes before she managed to drag her eyes open. It was the first good sleep she'd had in months, without the terrible, nightmarish dreams, and she protested sleepily, "Go away."

But the shaking irritatingly continued, a voice insisting, "Margarite! For God's sake, what's the matter with you? Wake up! You've been asleep for hours."

She frowned, annoyed, at Patrick standing at the side of the bed, scowling down at her. "Do you always sleep so heavily?" he demanded. "It's late. You should be getting home." His smile flashed mockingly. "Or doesn't the baron care what time you get home from your afternoons out?"

It *was* late, she thought, panic-stricken, seeing the darkness gathering at the window. She snatched up her clothes, and still groggy from the heavy sleep, pulled them on, her hands fumbling with buttons and sashes, thrusting her hair under her hat and stabbing hat pins home. Patrick did not offer to help, but stood watching her with an intense, curious gaze.

When she had finished, he strolled over to her, and before she could stop him, he had turned her face to the lamp he had lit, and forced her eyelids wide apart. "If I didn't know better," he said thoughtfully, "the way you slept, I'd say you'd been chewing peyote."

She jerked angrily away from him. "Don't be silly. I was tired, that's all." She turned away from that too searching gaze, her voice deliberately cool. "Too many late nights, I suppose."

Patrick insisted, over her objections, that he accompany her home in the fiacre he hired. She had felt merely groggy when she awoke, but now her head was beginning to ache, and she snapped, "I'm quite capable of getting home alone."

"I don't know about your other lovers," he drawled, trying to find a comfortable position for his long legs in the small hired carriage, "but I always make sure my women arrive home safely."

She flushed at the way he spoke of her, as if she were just another woman he had bedded in a casual afternoon of lovemaking. She put her fingers to her head. Already what had happened with Patrick in bed was taking on an unreal, dreamlike quality, as if it had happened to someone else, not her. If only she had brought some of her powders with her, she thought, feeling her nerves tightening, her hands like ice. She only hoped Karl wasn't waiting for her. Still, why should he? she thought hopefully. He paid very little attention to her comings and goings.

But when they reached the palace, and Patrick helped her from the carriage, Milli came flying out the front door as if she had been watching at the window, waiting for them. She gave Patrick a quick, curious glance, then turned to Margarite, her voice frightened. "His lordship has been asking for you."

Patrick frowned at the fear he saw in the servant's face. "Shall I go in with you, Baroness?" he asked, his voice holding a polite amusement. "I'm an old hand at soothing outraged husbands."

"I'm sure you are," Margarite said haughtily. "But there's no need."

He lifted her hand to his lips, then turned it over, and she could feel his lips warm against her palm, his tongue softly flicking at the sensitive flesh there. A shock wave of pleasure raced through her at the touch.

Their eyes met, hers wide and dilated, his holding a triumphant amusement, as if he knew he had only to beckon and she would be there again in his arms.

Margarite snatched her hand away. "Good-bye, Mr. O'Malley."

He stepped back, smiling. "*Auf Wiedersehn,* Baroness," he said.

Chapter 29

MARGARITE hurried up the stairs to her bedroom without, thankfully, seeing Karl in the hall or front parlor. However, the thought of sitting across the dinner table from her husband, after the afternoon she had spent with Patrick, made her head throb unbearably. She swallowed some of her headache powders and as soon as Milli had finished preparing her bath, she sent the servant to tell the baron that she was too ill to join him for dinner that evening.

The powders worked their magic, dulling her headache and relaxing her tense nerves and muscles. A pleasant drowsiness crept over her as she sat in the bathtub, the water delightfully warm and scented with her favorite rose fragrance. She wouldn't think about Patrick, she decided, the cold, hard anger she had seen in his eyes. Or how despite that anger, her body had melted at his touch, as if her bones had turned to candlewax. He was alive; that was all that mattered. She would think about the rest later, perhaps tomorrow, when she felt better. All she wanted now was to slip into bed, pull the covers over her, and sink into a sweet oblivion.

She had just stepped out of the bath and started to wrap a towel around her, when the door to her bedroom opened and her husband walked in. Startled, she tightened the towel around her, stammering, "What . . . what are you doing here?"

He chuckled, his amber eyes amused. "I'm your husband, remember? Surely I'm allowed to enter my wife's bedroom."

He came over to her, smiling, and taking the towel from her hand, began to dry her.

She felt embarrassed, as if a strange man had invaded her privacy. And yet for all the intimacy of those hands moving the towel over her body, there was something oddly sexless about the touch. "You needn't bother," she said hastily. "Milli will . . ."

"I've given Milli the night off. And it's no bother. You'll find I'm a very good lady's maid." After he had finished drying her, he took the white cambric nightgown stretched across her bed and slipped it over her head, deftly tying the ribbons at her throat and waist. "How charming you look," he said, smiling down at her. His hand moved lightly, caressingly, up her arm. "Your skin is as warm and fragrant as a field of roses in the sunshine."

When the hand slipped downward from her shoulder and lightly caressed her breast, she flinched, and said hastily, "I really do have the most terrible headache, Karl."

For a second the amber eyes narrowed, dangerously cold, but the next moment they were filled with concern as he helped her into bed and adjusted the pillows behind her. "Yes, I know. Your maid told me. I was distressed to hear that you were ill again." He sat comfortably on the side of the bed, taking her hand in his, playing with the fingers almost absently as he said, "Perhaps you shouldn't have gone out this afternoon." He made a moue of disapproval. "And in a fiacre! You know you have only to ask, my dear, and the coach is at your disposal.''

How had he known about the hired coach? Margarite wondered. Milli, of course. The girl was too frightened of the baron not to tell him the truth if he asked her.

"I had some shopping to do," she said, the lie sticking in her throat. "It took longer than I thought."

"You went shopping by yourself?" Again that concerned disapproval in his voice. "I really must insist that next time you take one of the servants with you. Was it a successful shopping expedition?"

It was the casual question a husband would ask his wife, but suddenly Margarite's throat tightened. He knows, she thought. He knows about Patrick and me and the hotel room. But how could he know? It wasn't possible. She fought to clear the powder-induced clouds gathering in her mind, making it difficult to think clearly. And she felt a faint stirring of anger. Why was he doing this, suddenly pretending tenderness and concern, after weeks of indifference? But she was too tired to feel any deep anger and her voice sounded merely sulky as she protested, "Why should you care?"

He smiled sadly, stroking her hand gently. "I can't blame you for being upset with me, *Liebling,* after the boorish way I've been behaving. Can you ever forgive me? I don't expect you to understand how a man's pride is crushed when he discovers that his bride is—" He broke off, shaking his head abruptly. "But we won't talk about that anymore, not even your rather, shall we say, bizarre behavior at the Esterhazys last night." He quirked an eyebrow, laughing softly. "As a matter of fact, it was seeing you enjoying yourself so thoroughly with those other men last night that made me realize what a jealous fool I've been. I know now I might have lost you because of my stupid pride and jealousy. If you'll only give me another chance to prove how much you mean to me. . . ."

His hand trailed up her arm, once again resting possessively over her breast. This time she managed not to flinch. She was too drowsy to feel anything, either guilt, fear, or desire. Only the wish that he would go away and let her alone so that she could sleep.

To her relief the hand was withdrawn, and Karl got to his feet, gazing down at her soberly. "My poor *Liebchen*. You aren't feeling well, are you? I believe Dr. Belasco is right. You do need a complete rest, away from the excitement and bad air of Vienna. I've decided we shall leave for the summer *schloss* at Friedrichsburg in the morning."

Dimly, Margarite remembered that the baron's ancestral home was in a small village near Baden in the Helenental Valley. "Usually I don't open the castle until June," Karl said. "But we should be comfortable enough there. I've wired Herr Braun to . . ."

But Margarite did not hear the rest. She was already asleep.

When she awoke the next morning, her first thought was: Patrick is alive! Tears of happiness filled her eyes. And this time he was real, not one of her cruel, tormenting dreams that dissolved in the light of day. She closed her eyes and could still feel his arms around her, feel his hardness thrusting deep inside of her, her body aching with remembered pleasure.

There was a knock at the door and Karl came in, followed by Milli, with her morning coffee. He came to the bed and dropped a swift kiss on her forehead, grinning teasingly down at her. "So you're finally awake, sleepyhead. I wanted to make an early start to Friedrichsburg. The coach is packed and ready."

She sat up slowly, and remembered, inevitably, the rest. Her husband coming to her room yesterday evening, the old Karl with the gentle smile and teasing laugh, begging her forgiveness, asking for a second chance.

The baron studied her face, his voice worried. "You look pale, my dear. Perhaps you should take one of those powders the doctor left you."

Margarite swung her legs over the side of the bed. A moment before she had felt elated; now she felt as if she were carrying a weight on her shoulders, too heavy to carry but impossible to put down. Perhaps it would be best, after all, for her to leave Vienna, she thought wearily. How could she bear to be in the same city with Patrick and never touch him, never hold him? Karl was her husband. Her first loyalty was to him.

"I'll feel better after my coffee," she said, forcing her stiff lips into a reassuring smile against the pain twisting through her at the thought of leaving Patrick again. It was the pain that made her reach for her headache powders, groping blindly for the blessed numbness they brought her.

She saw that Milli was hovering, uncertain, in the doorway, and asked, "May I take Milli with me?"

For one moment she thought Karl was going to refuse, then he shrugged. "Of course, whatever you wish. There's only a small staff of servants at the castle. The girl could prove useful."

It was a day's trip to Friedrichsburg from Vienna. The carriage was forced to stop occasionally for groups of pilgrims on the road on their way to worship at the shrine at Mariazell, where the statue of the Virgin supposedly performed miracles. Karl was impatient at the delays, but Margarite slept off and on most of the way, awakening only as the coach, followed by an open luggage cart on top of which Milli sat on a rough bench, rumbled up a gravel roadway through a copse of cedar and beech trees. As she stepped from the carriage, Margarite gazed at the castle, awestruck.

Although not much larger than the baroque palace in Vienna, the summer *schloss* of the Von Friedrich family was built in the medieval style. Round turrets flanked the four corners of the stone castle, with a pointed gray slate roof between. There was even the remains of a moat, no longer filled with water but weeds and stones.

"It looks like something out of a fairy tale," Margarite said, half to herself, wondering if it was just the dark, overcast March day that made the castle look so forbidding, or the dense woods that pressed so close to the crenellated walls.

Karl nodded proudly. "There is a story that Charles Perrault used Friedrichs Schloss as the setting for his fairy tale, 'The Sleeping Beauty.' Of course, it's just a legend. As far as I know, Perrault never visited the castle.''

He took Margarite's arm and escorted her through the great iron barred door into the large oval receiving hall. The wood-paneled walls were lined with battle axes, swords, halberds, and other ancient murderous weapons. But someone had tried to make the hall cheerful for the visitors. Candles were lit in the wall sconces and a fire blazed in the great stone hearth. The chill in the hall, though, still penetrated through the thin soles of Margarite's boots. She also couldn't help noticing that like the Von Friedrich home in Vienna, the *schloss*, too, had a rundown, neglected look. Paint flaked on the broad wooden staircase and the faded rug at the foot of the stairs was worn thin.

Karl looked around him, frowning. "There is much repair work that needs to be done. I had hoped—" He broke off, then in one of his lightning changes of mood, he was smiling jovially over his wife's shoulder at a man who had come silently into the hall and was standing, hat in hand, waiting to be noticed.

"This is my gamekeeper, Herr Braun," the baron said, gesturing toward the man. The gamekeeper was dressed in the country style. His gray jacket had a green collar and lapels; the felt hat he held in his hand was decorated with a brush made of chamois hairs. Karl smiled ruefully. "Herr Braun is my major-domo too. With the small staff we have at the *schloss,* I'd never be able to manage without him. You received my telegram then, Wilhelm? The baroness is ill and requires complete quiet."

"Yes, your lordship." Herr Braun was young and strongly built and would have been handsome, Margarite decided, if his blond hair had not been plastered to his skull with too much grease, and his smile, as he stared at her, had not had something too unctuous about it.

He nodded toward Margarite. "I am at the gracious lady's service, *gnädiger Herr* Baron. Perhaps the *gnädige Frau* baroness would like to see her room?"

"Yes, thank you," Margarite said, surprised at how tired she felt after she had slept practically all the way from Vienna. It must be the fresh country air, she decided. The room to which she was taken, with Milli trailing up the staircase behind her carrying several satchels, was as neglected-looking as the rest of the house. The canopy over the bed, the mattress, and the bedding had a moldy smell to them, as if there hadn't been time to air them out properly. Still, the room itself was clean, no cobwebs hanging from the ceiling or skeletons dangling in the wardrobe, she thought, smiling faintly, at her own fancy.

As Herr Braun carried in the rest of her satchels and her wicker portmanteau, she saw that Karl's luggage was not brought to her room. And then she felt a pang of guilt at her relief that she would not be sharing the room with her husband. Especially since Karl was once more the charming, good-natured man she had grown to like in Paris. He regaled her during dinner with stories of early Von Friedrichs who had lived in this castle, when his family had held a much higher position in the Hapsburg court of Maria Theresa.

"Now, there was a remarkable queen," the baron said, his amber eyes bright with amusement. "She was the mother of sixteen children, yet she still managed to turn Austria into the great power it is today."

After dinner he insisted Margarite must retire early and escorted her to her room. At the door he took her in his arms and whispered, "How I'd love to spend the whole night making love to you, *mein kleines Liebchen*." He sighed and stepped back regretfully. "But the doctor said it would be best if I restrained my ardor, at least until you're stronger. If you should need me, though, I'll be in the next room. Sleep well."

But Margarite didn't sleep well. At first it was thinking about Patrick that kept her tossing and turning, then it was the unfamiliar sounds of the old castle, creaking and groaning in the night. She imagined she heard footsteps on the stairs, someone tapping at the door of her bedroom, but of course when she went to the door, there was no one there. A cold draft from the hall wrapped around her ankles as she made a hasty retreat to her bed. Finally, her nerves screaming, she found the headache powders she had pushed to the rear of her dressing table drawer, hoping she wouldn't need them anymore. She swallowed the powders quickly, and waited, curled up in the fetal position in the middle of the bed, for sleep to rescue her from the terrors of the night.

In the daylight, Friedrichs Schloss looked much more cheerful, the terrors of the night disappearing with the sunshine pouring in through the arched leaded windows. After a hearty breakfast, she felt rested enough so that she would like to have taken a long walk through the countryside, but Karl insisted she must take only short strolls around the castle grounds.

"You mustn't overdo the walking, my dear," he warned, then smiled, his eyes twinkling. "You don't want to turn into a fanatic like the empress, now, do you?"

Margarite knew that the empress Elizabeth, to keep her trim, girlish figure, thought nothing of walking eight hours a day, with her ladies-in-waiting often falling, exhausted, along the way. Still, it would have been nice, she thought wistfully, to see outside the grounds of the *schloss,* although, to her dismay, she found that Karl was right. She did tire quickly, even from a short stroll through the castle gardens.

They had been at the *schloss* three weeks, when Karl took her into town in the carriage. She had been looking forward to seeing the village, but it was not at all what she expected. Friedrichsburg, for all its typical church with its bulbous Turkish tower and local *Gasthaüsers,* did not have the charming, scrubbed look of other Austrian villages she had visited. The shop fronts were dingy, the houses ill cared for, and the people on the street, although they doffed their hats respectfully enough as the baron drove by, had sullen looks on their faces, although a few gazed at her with an almost embarrassing curiosity in their eyes. Margarite was glad to return to the relative cheerfulness of the castle.

It was the night after the visit to the village that she began to have the nightmares again, frightening, hideous

dreams that drove her awake, gasping for breath, her
nightclothes soaked with perspiration. One night she
must have screamed in her sleep, for when she awoke,
the baron was beside her bed, his voice soothing as he
coaxed her into drinking a glass of the sweet white wine
she liked to drink at night to help her sleep.

"And what was this so terrible dream?" he asked
lightly, his hand pushing the damp hair back from her
forehead. "They say if you tell someone your dream, it
will go away."

Margarite shuddered. "My clothes were on fire. I was
burning alive!" She clutched at his arm, the horror of the
dream still too frighteningly real. "Please, stay with me,"
she begged. "Don't leave me alone."

"Nothing would bring me greater pleasure, my dear,"
her husband said unhappily. "I'm afraid, though, I'm
only human. If I were to share your bed . . ." He
shrugged ruefully. "You know what the doctor said.
You aren't strong enough yet . . . ."

No, Margarite thought, looking into those smiling yet
somehow remote amber eyes. It's not what the doctor
said that's stopping him. It's me. He can't bear to make
love to me. And then she was instantly ashamed, because Karl stayed by her bedside, talking to her softly,
soothingly, until she finally again fell asleep.

The next night the nightmare returned again, only
even more vivid, more frightening. She could smell the
acrid odor of smoke in her nostrils, choking her so that
she couldn't breathe, hear the crackling of fire, feel the
pain as the heat of the flames reached out closer and
closer toward her. And this time she couldn't even scream.
She could only stand, paralyzed, unable to move, watching the flames creep closer.

"Margarite!"

Her eyes, wide open, burned from the smoke all around
her. It *was* a dream, wasn't it? She coughed and choked
and coughed again. And she knew it wasn't a dream.
She was standing in her bedroom, the coverlet on the
bed still smoldering, the canopy half burned away. Milli
was tearing down the canopy, Karl was beating at ar-

rows of flame that were still racing up the wall near the bed.

Karl turned toward her, his voice furious. "For God's sake, what have you done?"

Why was he angry with her? she wondered bewildered. She stared at the smoldering bed. Her throat was raw from the smoke. She had to whisper as she stared, appalled, at the burns on Karl's hands. "What . . . what happened?"

"I smelled the smoke," he said. "When I came into the room, you were standing with a candle in your hand. You had set the canopy on fire. It was a miracle you didn't set yourself afire."

She was still clutching the candle holder, and she let it drop from a suddenly nerveless hand. "No," she whispered. "Oh, no!"

The rage disappeared from her husband's face to be replaced by a look of weariness. "Never mind. Thank God, Milli smelled the smoke too." He glanced around him. "We'll have to find you another room."

Karl brought a robe from his room and wrapped it around her. Then he picked her up and carried her down the hall. She could not see the darkened room into which he carried her, but she could feel the bed, a thick feather mattress, sinking beneath her. When Milli followed, carrying a candle which she started to place beside the bed, Karl whirled on her, snarling. "Idiot! Take that candle away. Do you want another fire?"

Then someone was pulling a coverlet over her; she heard the door close, and she was alone in the darkness.

When she awoke the next morning, she discovered she was in one of the round turret rooms. Faded tapestries hung on the paneled walls, more for warmth than beauty, and the bedding smelled even more strongly of mildew, as if the room had been long disused.

"Why are there bars at the windows?" she asked Karl when he came by to see her.

He frowned. "I believe this room used to be a nursery. I suppose the bars were to keep the children from falling out."

His hands were bandaged, and she winced, looking at

them. "Karl, what happened last night?" she asked,
swallowing hard around the lump of panic in her throat.
"How could I—"

"We won't talk about it," he said, interrupting her
brusquely. "It's finished."

But it wasn't finished, she thought. And not talking
about it, pretending nothing had happened, wouldn't
make the fire last night disappear.

When Milli brought her her breakfast, she asked, "Were
you in the room last night, Milli, when the fire started?"

Although the girl was much more at ease with her
mistress now than she had been in the beginning, this
morning her hands twisted in her apron, and she did not
meet Margarite's gaze. "No, your ladyship. The baron
was already beating out the flames when I smelled the
smoke and came in. You were standing, like a sleep-
walker, with the brass candlestick holder in your hand,
and the flames all around you." She gave her mistress
an imploring look. "Please, Frau baroness, may I go
now? I'm needed in the kitchen."

Margarite nodded and the girl flew from the room.
Margarite looked down at her breakfast tray, then pushed
it away. She had suddenly lost her appetite.

It was the next afternoon that the doctor Karl had
sent for arrived from Vienna. A small, fussy man with
pince-nez and a rather pompous manner, he insisted
firmly that the baron leave him alone with his patient.
His examination, however, was like none Margarite had
ever had. He sat beside the bed, asking her a seemingly
inexhaustible stream of questions about herself, about
her childhood, about the time she had spent in Mexico.
Karl must have told him about her having lost her memory for a short time after the bandit raid, for he kept
asking her questions about that period of her life.

"There's been no recurrences of these lapses of memory?" he asked, for the third time.

"I told you, no," Margarite said irritably, except she
suddenly realized there had been times these last months
when she had forgotten things Karl had asked her to do,
like ordering her costume for the Esterhazy ball.

"The fire in your bedroom your husband told me

about," the doctor said, his eyes behind the pince-nez studying Margarite's face rather as if she were a peculiarly interesting specimen, she thought, annoyed. "Do you remember setting the fire?"

"I didn't set the fire," she protested. "I'm sure I'd remember if I had."

He smiled soothingly. "Of course. But if you didn't start the fire, who do you suppose did? Do you fear that someone is trying to kill you, a servant, perhaps? Your husband?"

"No, of course not." Margarite frowned, for it suddenly occurred to her that Milli's sleeping quarters were in the attic. How could she have possibly smelled the smoke from the attic? Could Milli have crept down in the middle of the night and started the fire? But that was ridiculous. Milli wouldn't hurt her.

The doctor leaned forward; his glance seemed to bore through Margarite, his voice almost whiningly insistent. "You are afraid, aren't you, Baroness? There's no reason not to tell me. I want to help you. Is it the sexual act that frightens you? Is that why you set fire to the bed? Because you were afraid your husband might join you in the bed?"

Margarite felt her face burning with embarrassment. "No, of course not!" she blurted out, outraged, not only at the accusation but the relish with which the little man asked his questions, which were certainly none of his business.

"Ah!" The doctor made a steeple of his fingers and stared at Margarite over them, his eyes behind the pince-nez gleaming. "So you find the sexual act with a man enjoyable? With any man, Baroness, or only your husband? I've been told that you were very close to your father. Did you, as a child, perhaps want to sleep with your father?"

A fury such as she hadn't felt in months swept through Margarite, giving her a strength she thought she no longer possessed. She reached for the heavy, empty candlestick holder beside the bed, brandishing it at the obnoxious little man with his obscene insinuations. "Get out of here! Do you hear me? Get out of here before I. . ."

Karl must have been waiting right outside the door, for he hurried in, casting an anxious glance toward Margarite on the bed, then quickly ushering the doctor from the room. When he returned without the doctor, Margarite stared at him indignantly. "What sort of doctor is he?"

Karl pulled at his mustache, his voice uneasy. "He came very highly recommended. He was called in to treat the empress Carlota when she became . . . ill in Rome. It's all very new, of course, doctors who treat the mind and not the body, mental specialists they call themselves."

The newspapers in Vienna had been very discreet about the empress Carlota's illness during her visit to the Vatican, but Margarite had heard the stories that circulated through the cafés; that during a royal audience with the Pope, Carlota had attacked His Eminence, that while in Rome, she had refused to eat or drink anything and had sent away all the members of her loyal entourage, claiming they were poisoning her. An embarrassment to her brother, King Leopold II of Belgium, he had turned his back on his sister and would not let her stay in the family castle at Laeken, but sent her to stay in a private madhouse, Carlota's mind completely gone.

"Poor Carlota," Margarite said softly. She remembered the intelligence in that proud, lovely face. Did Carlota have moments of lucidity, she wondered, when she knew what was happening to her? How much better if the unhappy woman never knew how her dreams of glory for herself and her husband had ended.

"What of the emperor?" she asked. "What of Maximilian? Surely, he will abdicate and come home now."

Karl shrugged. "An Austrian frigate was sent to Vera Cruz to bring him back, but Maximilian refused to leave Mexico. He's evidently making some sort of last ditch stand in a town called Querétaro." Karl smiled mirthlessly. "But then, what has Maximilian to come home to, a failure with a mad wife."

How cold Karl's eyes were, Margarite thought suddenly, wondering why she had never noticed before how easily emotions slid over her husband's face, leaving no

lasting impression, like water over a stone, one moment
sparkling in the sunlight the next moment with no light
at all. And all at once with an odd stab of fear, she
wondered: How would Karl like being saddled with a
mad wife?

Chapter 30

*T*HE turret room became a prison. Oh, she was allowed to come and go as she pleased during the
day, but Margarite was always aware that the door was
locked each night and a candle was never left in her
room. Gradually she became aware of other things. The
cords disappeared from the curtains in her bedroom, her
food was served carefully cut up so she never needed or
was given a knife with her meals, and when she took her
daily strolls through the castle grounds, if Karl didn't
accompany her, she was sure that someone was always
watching her from a distance. Herr Braun no doubt
following the baron's orders that the baroness should
never be left alone.

Was it possible that the absurd little doctor had actually convinced Karl that she was losing her mind? she
thought as she took her daily afternoon stroll through
the garden, her paisley shawl flung over her shoulders.
Although May had long since arrived and she could see
the pale green running along the branches of the trees,
the sunshine was pale and watery, with little warmth to
it. Well, she couldn't really blame Karl, she thought
wryly, the fire in her bedroom, her outrageous conduct
with the doctor, even the strange way she had been
feeling and behaving these last months, constantly tired,

plagued with headaches, and unable to sleep. Sometimes she wondered herself if . . .

No! Her fingernails bit into her palms as if she had plunged to the edge of an abyss and had stopped herself just in time. She sank down onto a stone bench, staring bleakly into space. For if she didn't believe she was sane, how could she possibly hope to convince anyone else that she was not losing her mind?

She forced her thoughts to turn away from the abyss, to think of something else, another happier time. The weeks she had spent with the *arrieros,* sharing their hardships and their rough good humor, the sturdy little mustang beneath her, and the hot Mexican sun beating down upon her, with the air so clear around her she could see for miles. With no memory, and therefore no future and no past, she had existed only for the present, not realizing what a happy state that was. But thinking of the *arrieros* inevitably brought memories of Patrick rushing back, and she hugged her arms to her, rocking back and forth, trying to ease the pain inside of her.

"Are you warm enough, Margarite?"

She opened her eyes. Karl was staring down at her, wearing the perpetually worried look that never seemed to leave his face lately. "Perhaps you should go inside. You don't want to catch a chill."

"In a moment," she said.

"I'm driving into the village. Is there anything I can bring you back?"

How polite he sounded, she thought. They might be two acquaintances talking. She wondered what would happen if she screamed at him, Don't shut me out, Karl. I'm terrified that I might be going mad. Talk to me. She lowered her gaze to her hands clasped tightly in her lap. What would be the use? He would only look embarrassed and quickly change the subject. One didn't discuss madness in polite society. If you were unfortunate enough to have a lunatic for a wife, you shut her away, pretended she didn't exist. The way they had shut Carlota away.

She heard his footsteps move away, the small garden gate that always creaked closing behind him. She sat for

a while until the pale May sunshine disappeared behind
a cloud and the cold penetrated even through her shawl.
What she needed was a cup of hot chocolate, she decided as she got stiffly to her feet. She would ask the
cook to prepare a cup for her.

She had never been in the castle kitchen before, but it
wasn't difficult to find. The smell of past cooked meals
preceded her down a narrow flight of turning steps into a
cavernous, badly lit room. She had met the cook only
once, a country woman with gray hair that kept escaping
from a braid around her lined, weary face.

When Margarite came into the kitchen, the cook was
standing by a table serving food to a man Margarite had
never seen before. The woman dropped a hasty curtsy,
her voice startled. "Was there something you wanted,
your ladyship?"

The man said nothing; his face had the same sullen
look she had noticed on the faces in the village. No, not
sullenness, Margarite realized. Open hostility.

Uneasily, she looked away from the man, no doubt
the woman's husband, she decided, and, of course, the
cook should not have been feeding him from the castle
kitchen, but what difference did it make? She glanced
around the kitchen trying to think of something to say to
break the uncomfortable silence. And for the first time
she noticed there was a fourth person in the kitchen, a
blond-haired little girl crouched in a corner crooning to a
dirty, rag doll.

"What a pretty little . . ." Margarite began brightly,
and then the words died in her throat. For the girl
looked up and Margarite saw her face, a child's face on
a young woman's body. When she saw Margarite looking at her, the young woman smiled vacantly and held
up her doll, unintelligible gibberish coming from her lips.

Without thinking, Margarite took a step back, her
throat tightening with pity and horror. She started to
look away, when the man, with a low growl deep in his
throat, sprang to his feet.

He had Margarite by the arm, forcing her forward so
she had to look at the young woman. His hand pinched
at her flesh; he smelled of stale beer and unwashed

clothes and his voice hissed its venom into her ear. "Don't you find my daughter pleasant to look upon, Frau Baroness? Your husband did. She was not yet twelve when he took her to his bed. Such a pretty, sweet child, my Amalia. After that night she never spoke a word again."

The girl, frightened, began to cry. The woman, her face pasty gray with fear, tugged at her husband's arms, trying to free Margarite, her voice low, frightened. "You shouldn't have brought her here, Hans. I told you not to. You'll only cause trouble."

Margarite heard the sleeve of her gown rip as she managed to free herself. Somehow, she would never know how, she found herself in her bedroom, standing, shaking, in the middle of the room, as if with a fever. She put her hands to her ears, but she knew she would never shut out the sound of the man's words screaming in her head.

It did not occur to her to wonder why she had immediately accepted the man's terrible accusation as the truth. Had she always known somewhere deep inside of her that there was something wrong with Karl, even when he was courting her, the way he had always treated her as if she were a child, not a woman, as if it were the child he preferred, not the woman. And the way he couldn't bear to touch her, to make love to her, not because she hadn't been a virgin when she married him, but because she wasn't the child he preferred in his bed. How many others had there been before and after the cook's daughter, she wondered, sickened, girls, little more than children, who had served the baron's perverted need and then been discarded.

Milli! she thought, pacing back and forth now, unable to stand still. Hadn't Karl as much as told her he had found the young girl walking the streets and taken her home. Not just to his home, to his bed. And then when he tired of her, kept her on in his household as a servant. No wonder the girl was terrified of the baron.

All at once Margarite was terrified too. Her gaze flew wildly around the turret room. Oh, God, she couldn't stay here, not for another second. She had to get away.

Panic surged through her as she snatched up her shawl which had fallen to the floor at her nervous pacing and wrapped it around her. She hurried down the back stairs and out into the deserted garden. She wasn't sure whether the front door of the castle was locked, but she remembered Karl going through the garden gate and she didn't remember hearing it lock behind him.

There was a stable beyond the gate, she discovered as the garden door creaked shut behind her, but no horses in the stable. Karl must have taken the carriage and the horses into the village. Well, she would go on foot, she thought, but not into town. She didn't dare take the chance of running into Karl, nor could she count on the villagers to hide her. They might despise her husband, but they knew full well that their livelihood depended upon the Von Friedrichs, as their parents' had before them.

She turned instinctively toward the tangled darkness of the woods, at first rushing, stumbling through the brambles and thorny shrubs that snatched and tore at her gown. Then she realized she did not have the strength to keep up that pace. She could not even tell in which direction she was going. The sun was hidden behind dark clouds threatening rain. She walked more slowly, it seemed like hours, but she was sure it was not that long. Her legs trembled with fatigue, the skin on her arms was cut and bleeding from thrashing through underbrush, pushing aside branches blocking her way. She was breathing in gasps, a sharp pain knifing into her side, and she knew she must rest.

She slumped, exhausted, on a rock in a small clearing, resting her head on her knees.

"It will be raining soon, Frau Baroness. We'd better get back to the *schloss*."

She lifted her head and looked into the obsequious smile of Herr Braun. His hat was doffed, held deferentially in his hands as he stepped out into the clearing. He had been following her, she realized dully, probably ever since she had left the castle, wondering why he hadn't stopped her sooner. Except behind that obsequious smile, she sensed it was not the catching of game

Herr Braun enjoyed so much as the cruel pleasure he took in the tracking of game, pursuing his quarries until they were too exhausted to run any farther, and could only wait, helplessly, hearts pounding, for their deaths.

She glanced toward the woods and the man shook his head, still smiling. "I know these woods like my own hand, Frau Baroness. There's nowhere you could hide that I wouldn't find you." His smile became insufferably smug as he bragged. "Not even a red Indian can come into my woods and I wouldn't find him." He reached for her arm, pulling her to her feet, his voice scolding, as if she were a fractious child. "Come along now. You don't want to worry Herr Baron, now, do you?"

Back in her bedroom, Milli's eyes widened with dismay when she saw the cuts and bruises on her mistress's arms and legs, the baroness's dark hair hanging disheveled around a face that was strangely blank and pale. Without a word she brought hot water and cloths, her hands gentle as she removed Margarite's gown and coaxed her into bed.

Only once during her ministrations did her mistress stir from her odd lethargy, reaching out and grabbing Milli's hand in a death grip, her voice frantic. "You must leave here, Milli. You mustn't stay!"

Milli glanced toward the bedroom door that was slightly ajar. She reached for the hairbrush and ran it carefully through the dark, tangled curls, her voice soothing. "Why should I want to leave you, my ladyship? Where would I go?" She slipped a fresh nightgown over Margarite's unresistant body, tied the now smooth dark hair back from the oval face with a satin ribbon. Then, taking the candle in her hand, she said softly, "Try and rest, my ladyship."

Margarite heard the girl's footsteps leave the room, the door close, the lock slip into place. And the darkness of the turret room closed in around her. If only she could rest, she thought, curling into a ball in the center of the bed. If only she could close her eyes and forget the blond-haired young woman crouching in the corner of the kitchen with a child's vacant face, forget that she was married to a monster who could do that to a child.

She should have asked Milli to give her some of her powders, she thought, feeling hysteria rise like bile in her throat. She would never make it through the night without her powders. She groped her way through the darkness until she found the table beside the bed, and opened the drawer where the powders were always kept. Her hand fumbled inside the empty drawer disbelievingly. She was sure there were several packets left. Where were they?

Tears of frustration stung her eyes as she sank back against the pillows. She wanted to scream but knew if she started, she would not be able to stop. The darkness in the room pressed in upon her like a feathery black pillow, suffocating her. She gasped for breath. She could hear her heart pounding against her ribs so that her whole body shook. And then slowly, breath by cautious breath, she discovered she had reached a place where the terror was still there, curled inside of her, but no longer with the power to hurt her. She had reached a point beyond fear.

She was lying quietly, waiting, when she heard the door to her bedroom open. Karl came in, carrying a candle, its flame bobbing before him as he approached the bed. The candlelight played across his features, touching first the amber eyes, the distinguished nose, the strong chin, the good-natured set to his features that could so quickly dissolve into a winning smile. How strange that he should look exactly the same, Margarite thought, surprised.

Even his voice sounded the same, kind and concerned, as he said, "I was afraid you might still be awake. I've brought some of your favorite wine. Would you like a glass to help you sleep?"

She watched as he set the candlestick holder on the table and poured the white wine into a small ruby-red goblet. When he handed the glass to her, she stared at him coldly. "What did you put in the wine this time?"

He lifted a shocked eyebrow. "My dear child, what are you saying? You can't believe that I—" He broke off unhappily. "But then, the doctor warned me that it was part of your illness that you'd have these illusions, the same as poor Carlota, that someone was trying to poison you.''

"Not poison, a drug of some kind," Margarite said slowly. For the first time in months, it seemed, she was thinking with a crystal clarity, as if the shocking truth she had learned that day, the fear she had endured at being imprisoned in the darkness of this room, had jolted her free of the drug-induced confusions and uncertainties that had clouded her mind for so long. "The first time was the night of the court ball, wasn't it? I thought I behaved so badly because I'd had too much wine, but that wasn't it, was it? It was what you had put in my wine, to make sure that I would go along with the hasty marriage you'd already planned.''

Unexpectedly, he chuckled, his amber eyes bright with amusement. "There's no reason to look so vindictive, my dear. I'm sure our marriage would have been as satisfying as most. I've always considered marriage a vastly overrated institution anyway.''

He sat down on the edge of the bed. "As for the hastiness of the wedding ceremony, you can thank your dear stepmother, Elissa, for that. Somehow she found out about my, shall we say, private pleasures. She threatened to tell you if I didn't pay for her silence. But she became too greedy, and I simply couldn't afford to keep paying her. Of course, once we were married, it really didn't matter what she told you, did it?'' He frowned thoughtfully. "Frankly, I'm surprised she didn't tell you even after the marriage, from pure spite.''

Margarite winced. "I didn't know," she said. "Not until today. Do you think I'd have stayed with you for a moment, if I had known?''

Her husband nodded almost indifferently. "Yes, I rather thought you'd seen the cook's brat, that that's what set you haring off into the woods this afternoon. Herr Braun told me what happened." His voice was faintly condescending. "You mustn't be so provincial, my dear. One of the emperor's brothers has a fondness for boys. I happen to like young girls. I can assure you I'm not alone in my preference." The amber eyes hardened with anger. "And, after all, you brought your own little surprise to our wedding bed, didn't you? Can you imagine the revulsion I felt when I discovered that another man had used your body before me? And not even a white man, a red savage!"

At Margarite's start of surprise, he smiled derisively. "Oh, yes, I know about the American Indian—isn't that what they call him? How you had no sooner met him again at the Esterhazys, than like a bitch in heat you had to crawl back into his bed." He shook his head with mock sadness. "But then the good doctor from Vienna assured me that these unnatural sexual cravings of yours are all part of the pattern of your illness, the same as your bizarre behavior, your headaches and nightmares and forgetfulness, even setting fire to your bedroom."

He smiled smugly. "I thought the fire was particularly clever on my part, don't you? I got the idea from your nightmare, you know. Although I must admit it's been simpler all along than I thought it would be, convincing everyone that the baroness Von Friedrich is quite mad."

"Why?" Margarite stared with an almost horrified fascination at her husband. "Why are you doing this? If it's my inheritance, you already have that . . ."

Then she shrank back against the pillows, as if physically shoved by the burning rage that distorted her husband's face. "You have no inheritance!" he spat. "Salvador Ortiz is the sole inheritor of his father's estate."

"I don't understand. My cousin was disinherited, and, anyway, he's dead."

"Salvador Ortiz is very much alive. And disinherited or not, with Juárez back in power, the Mexican courts have accepted his claim for his father's estate, a natural son, and a supporter of Juárez over that of a foreigner and a woman who served in the court of Maximilian."

Karl jerked to his feet, his face livid. "Not only have I tied myself to a wife with the morals of a prostitute, but one who has even less money than I have. If it weren't for those jewels you ran off with, my creditors would have had me in court long before this."

"I'm . . . I'm sorry," Margarite said, not even knowing why she was apologizing, but well able to imagine the devastating shock the baron must have felt when he learned that his carefully planned marriage to a wealthy heiress to recoup the Von Friedrich fortune had all been for nothing. "There's still divorce," she said desperately. "I know the church doesn't approve, but it's still possible."

"There'll be no divorce," Karl said coldly. "I told you that before. The scandal of a divorce would stand in the way of my marrying the princess Kodosky." He smiled cruelly. "You remember the princess? You saw me with her at the Esterhazys, much younger and much wealthier than you, my dear. Her father would never allow her to marry a divorced man, but a grief-stricken widower whose lunatic wife committed suicide, after a proper mourning period, yes, I'm sure his sympathy would be with me."

"You're insane!" Margarite gasped. But the fear curled deep inside of her began to stir, squeezing with icy fingers at her stomach and heart. For looking into Karl's face, she saw it wasn't madness she glimpsed in the cool amber eyes. It was the arrogance, the self-possession of the aristocrat who'd always felt himself superior to others, who lived his life by his own rules, and an inconvenient wife standing in the way of a more suitable marriage, was just that—an inconvenience to be disposed of in any way necessary.

The fear was clutching at her throat now; she spoke in a whisper. "You can't believe I'll commit suicide just to please you."

"No, I don't suppose so," the baron said regretfully. "Still, I believe you would find death preferable to being locked up like poor Carlota. I could do that, you know. I'm sure the doctor would sign any necessary papers. Most unpleasant places, madhouses," he said thoughtfully. "I've no doubt that in a year or two you'd much prefer a quick, merciful death."

He sighed. "But I don't have a year or two, unfortunately. The princess Kodosky might grow impatient and find another suitor." He frowned, his voice growing irritable as he gazed down at her. "We've wasted enough time talking." He nodded impatiently toward the goblet. "Drink the wine, my dear. It's for your own good."

"No!" Terrified, she saw in the cold amber eyes what he intended, had undoubtedly intended, all along. Her body twisted, trying to free itself of the encircling bed covers, but she was too slow. His hand pinched cruelly at the soft flesh just below her jaws, her mouth opening in an involuntary scream of pain. The wine splashed into her mouth, some of it spilling down over her breasts, but the rest, as he suddenly released his hold on her throat, she swallowed convulsively.

Karl got briskly to his feet, taking out a snowy white handkerchief and wiping his hands fastidiously where the wine had spilled on them. "I am sorry that this couldn't all be handled in a much more civilized fashion. But I simply can't afford to wait any longer. You've caused me enough problems, slipping away the way you did this afternoon, and, of course, your Indian lover showing up unexpectedly."

She thought that she was past feeling any new blows Karl could deal her, but now she gazed at him, stunned. "Patrick here? I don't believe you!"

"Oh, didn't Herr Braun tell you? It seems the man showed up in the village several days ago, looking for you. Then the gamekeeper found him skulking in the woods near the castle yesterday." The baron chuckled complacently. "Wilhelm has had a lot of experience catching and punishing poachers. You have only to ask the men in the village."

Margarite dug her nails into the soft flesh of her palms; the pain and her terrible racking fear for Patrick helped drive back a little the cold numb feeling in her legs, the drowsiness that was filling her mind like a fog. If she could keep Karl talking, she thought desperately, hold off that deadly sleep for a little while longer.

But whatever drug he had given her was acting differently on her body than the other times. She felt as if she were choking. It was a tremendous effort just to force air in and out of her lungs. A smoky haze seemed to float before her eyes. She struggled to get to her feet, swaying dizzily. If she could get to the door, call for help. Perhaps Milli would hear her. She had to find Patrick!

Karl watched her efforts, a mocking smile on his face. "Such touching devotion, my dear, but at the moment your Patrick is unharmed. Wilhelm is watching him. Of course, it could be embarrassing to have your lover around afterward, questioning your suicide. No doubt Herr Braun can arrange something, a hunting accident, perhaps, in the woods."

"No." The word came out a whisper of anguish and rage. Her eyes fastened on the brass candlestick holder next to the bed. She had it clutched in her hand and flung it at Karl. She heard him grunt as it struck him in the face, the candle falling free, rolling over the rug. She was almost at the door when she felt arms around her, lifting her roughly, pinioning her, so that she couldn't move, her face held, smothered against Karl's jacket, the heavy buttons bruising her skin.

She could hear him cursing, furious, but he wasn't carrying her back into the bedroom, she realized. He was carrying her toward the narrow wooden steps that ran up to the crenellated roof of the turret. What better place for a suicide, she thought, a mad young wife flinging herself to her death from the turret of the castle to the stones below. And what a properly grief-stricken widower Karl would make. But her thoughts slipped through her mind like silk. She couldn't seem to hold on to them. And the gray haze she had noticed in the bedroom was heavier out here in the hall, making her eyes and throat burn. Not haze, she thought, faintly surprised. Smoke.

The arms around her suddenly loosened and she fell on her knees to the floor. She heard Karl's frightened, indrawn whistling breath. It *was* smoke, she thought, confused, gazing around her at the thick layers of blackness pouring up the staircase and into the upstairs hall.

And stalking through the swirling smoke, like an apparition from the dead, she imagined she saw Patrick, a Patrick whose eyes, fastened upon Karl, held death in their depths.

Karl must have seen death staring at him too. With a strangled cry he ran for the turret steps. But there was no way he could escape. Crouched on the floor, Marga-

rite watched, unable to tear her eyes away as Patrick
swung the man around and smashed his fist into Karl's
chest. As the baron fell forward, another fist caught him
on the chin, snapping his head back against the wall.
The death's-head mask that was Patrick's face never
changed as his fists methodically hammered at Karl's
face. She could hear the sound of crushing bone. There
was blood on the wall, and Karl was making an odd,
keening sound of agony.

She stumbled to her feet. She could not bear it. Not
even Karl should die this way.

"Patrick! Stop, for God's sake!" She was reaching
ineffectually to try to hold back those murderous fists,
and then she screamed when she saw golden tongues of
flame racing up the dry wooden staircase, setting the
hall carpeting on fire.

Her scream did what nothing else could have done to
penetrate Patrick's blind fury. He swung on the balls of
his feet away from his victim. His arms swept Margarite
up, away from the floor and the flames. "Let's get the
hell out of here, *poquita*," he growled.

Even with his arms around her, sheltering her, Margarite could feel the heat singeing the hairs on her skin.
The smoke stabbed into her throat and lungs as Patrick
plunged down the staircase. The smoke was thicker on
the first floor, the noise of the flames louder. Behind her
she heard a crash as parts of the staircase fell. Then they
were outside the house, and she was on her hands and
knees on the ground, coughing and choking. Nothing,
she was sure, would ever taste so good as that first
breath of cool, fresh air sliding down her raw throat.

Still on her knees, she watched as Patrick beat out the
flames that had blackened his shirt. Then, dazed, disoriented, she turned to stare at the burning castle. She
could see flames at almost every window now. How
quickly the old dry wood burned, she thought, amazed.

She was aware that there were people, villagers, gathered quietly at the edge of the woods, gazing up at the
burning castle. Not just at the castle, she saw, but at a
dark figure silhouetted against the flames on one of the
round turrets of the castle.

She heard as if from a nightmare, a nightmare she would remember all her life, Karl screaming in outraged fury down to the villagers. "Help me! For God's sake, help me!"

As if she thought, shivering at the sound, he still could not believe it possible that the baron Von Friedrich should be left to die this way, with no hand lifted to save him. A rising wind carried the flames higher around the silhouette, outlined it for one last moment. A scream of agony rendered the night air. Then the only sound was the roar of flames and the exploding of windows, wooden walls, and stairs crashing inward into the burning castle. When Margarite looked again, the woods were deserted. The villagers were gone.

She shivered again convulsively. How could she be so cold, she wondered absently, after going through flames?

Patrick pulled Margarite to her feet, his eyes traveling quickly over her face. Her brows and lashes were singed, but the rest of her face and her body was untouched, he saw, relieved. But it was the contraction of the pupils of her eyes, the coldness of her skin to his touch that struck a sudden terrible fear in his heart.

"What is it?" he asked fiercely, shaking her shoulders as if trying to shake that look of deadly drowsiness from her face.

"I—I can't feel my legs," Margarite murmured sleepily. "Karl made me drink . . . something. Am I going to die?" Then Patrick's face disappeared and she pitched forward into his arms.

Chapter 31

DURING the next hours . . . or was it days . . . she would never be sure, Margarite wished she were dead. She wanted nothing so much as to put her head down and drift off into the tempting, peaceful darkness surrounding her, pulling at her. Instead, rough hands forced her to her feet, struck her across the face, then forced some vile-tasting concoction down her throat. She was immediately violently sick to her stomach.

Once more she was jerked erect and hands were propelling her back and forth in a tortuous treadmill without end. Her legs felt heavy as lead; her body screamed in protest. She staggered and fell, but always the hands ruthlessly pushed her forward again. Why? she wondered helplessly. Why didn't they let her sleep? Why were they tormenting her this way?

She weakly cried out at the indignities she was suffering. Where was Patrick? Why was he allowing this torture? But shockingly it was Patrick's voice shouting at her. "Walk, damn it, walk!" Whenever she was allowed to rest for a moment, coffee, hot and bitter, was poured down her throat.

Vaguely she became aware that there was another person, Milli, in the room, but the girl was equally relentless. Her strong young arms forced the treadmill to continue, although her voice was gentler, coaxing, "One more step, Frau Baroness, just one more step," ignoring Margarite's mumbled pleas to be allowed to sleep, to leave her in peace. Finally, she no longer questioned. It was futile. She simply put one trembling leg before the other, stumbling, staggering, while the darkness lapped at her mind and the pitiless arms forced her to keep walking.

And when she was, at last, allowed to rest, it was not to sleep. Someone was removing her bedraggled, stained nightgown and other clothes were being placed on her. Then she was being bundled into a carriage that bounced and jolted over rough back roads, so that her sleep was fitful, her head pillowed against Patrick's shoulder. When she was awake, her head ached abominably. Finally, she slipped into a blessed limbo that was neither consciousness nor unconsciousness, completely indifferent to what was happening around her.

She wasn't sure what drove her, at last, to full wakefulness. Perhaps it was the unsteady movement of the bed beneath her or the gnawing feeling in her stomach, as if she hadn't eaten in days. Her eyelids felt as if they were weighted. When she forced them apart, the glaring morning light pouring through a small round window made her close them again quickly. Had it all been just another of the nightmares she had been having lately, she wondered, the scenes flashing through her mind, Karl trying to kill her, the fire sweeping through the summer *schloss*. And Patrick. Had she only imagined that Patrick had been there at the castle with her?

"How are you feeling, Baroness?"

She opened her eyes and for a moment felt weak with the rush of happiness that surged through her. Patrick was standing beside her bed, his face behind a growth of beard, lined with weariness. Still not quite believing her good fortune, she reached out a hand and touched him.

For a moment she thought the hand was going to grasp hers, but instead, disappointed, she watched as Patrick pulled up a chair and sat down beside the bed. She pushed herself up to a sitting position, her gaze flying to the small porthole, recognizing, then, the slight swaying of the bed beneath her. "We're aboard a ship, aren't we?" she asked, surprised.

"An Italian ship, two days out of Trieste," he answered. "I decided not to take a chance trying to cross Austria with you to a French port. The Austrian police might have caught up with us before we reached the western border.''

''The police?'' She gazed at him, startled, for a moment forgetting the odd constraint between them.

He shrugged. ''It wouldn't take the Austrian authorities long to discover that the baroness Von Friedrich hadn't died in the fire with her husband. And since the baron went to a great deal of trouble to convince everyone his wife was mad, how long do you think it'd be before they'd decide that the baron's lunatic wife had burned down the castle and murdered her husband?''

''You could have told them the truth, told them what really happened,'' she protested.

He lifted a skeptical eyebrow. ''The Austrian police are very thorough. They'd have no trouble finding out that you and I had been lovers. They might even think that I had conspired with you to kill your husband.'' He shrugged impatiently. ''In any case, you were in no condition to be questioned. I decided the best thing to do was get us both out of Austria as quickly as possible.''

''I did throw the candle at Karl,'' she said, suddenly remembering, her voice dismayed. ''Was that what started the fire?''

Patrick shook his head, frowning. ''The fire started in the kitchen. It was already spreading when Milli got me away from Wilhelm.'' He rubbed ruefully a portion of his skull that was still tender. ''I didn't even hear him come up behind me in the woods. The next thing I knew I was in a room in the cellar of the castle where the gamekeeper evidently kept poachers.''

Margarite's eyes widened incredulously. Milli! Her terrorized, frightened Milli? She had no doubt that the servant girl would have known about the man kept prisoner in the cellar of the castle, might even have recognized Patrick from that day in Vienna when he had brought her home from the hotel. But she couldn't imagine Milli having the nerve or strength to overpower the burly Herr Braun. ''How did she manage it?'' she asked, amazed.

''A very clever girl, your Milli.'' Patrick grinned. ''She took some powders you had in your room and put them in a glass of wine that she gave to Herr Braun. When he was sleeping peacefully, she found the key and unlocked the door. She told me that she was sure your husband was trying to kill you. By then we both smelled smoke. I went upstairs to find you while Milli dragged the game-keeper from the cellar. Too bad she didn't leave him in the cellar,'' Patrick added grimly. ''The bastard's proba-bly telling the police all about the mad antics of the baroness and her lover, who escaped just before the fire started. The rest you probably remember.''

Yes, Margarite thought with a shudder, knowing she would never forget the horror of those last moments in the bedroom with Karl, the lack of any warmth or pity in those cold amber eyes, that bland, indifferent face. How easy it would have been for the baron to drop her unconscious body over the parapet, an apparent suicide. Certainly he had made sure that enough people in Vi-enna, and no doubt, even the people in the village, had been made aware of the erratic behavior of his wife. There had even been times when she had begun to doubt her own sanity. If it hadn't been for Milli's courage and Patrick, and, of course, the fire . . .''

Her gaze returned to Patrick, puzzled. ''Who did set the fire? Was it an accident?''

But even as she asked, she knew that the fire had not been an accident. The fire had begun in the kitchen, and she remembered only too well the frustrated pain and murderous fury she had seen in the face of the cook's husband. Had he, at last, found the courage to take his revenge on the man who had raped and destroyed his child?

''I don't suppose we'll ever know,'' Patrick said, study-ing Margarite's face thoughtfully. ''And you can be sure the police won't learn anything from the villagers. Milli talked them into hiding us for the night, but they couldn't wait to send us on our way the next morning.''

Margarite remembered, then, that Milli had been with her afterward, remembered the young servant girl coax-ing her into that endless walking that had saved her life. Her eyes roamed around the cabin, then back to Patrick. ''Where is Milli? Isn't she with us?''

"I left her behind in Baden with enough money to get her back to her village in Bohemia, and more than enough to furnish her with a handsome dowry," Patrick explained. "Apparently, there's a young man in her village that she wants to marry. But she refused to leave you until she was sure you were out of danger. Fortunately, whatever it was your husband gave you wasn't enough to kill you, although it came close enough."

A watchfulness touched the dark indigo eyes resting on Margarite's face. "I met the baron once at a casino in Baden. He was one of those men who couldn't stop gambling, no matter his losses, but he seemed pleasant enough. Somehow I would never have pegged him as a wife-killer." Patrick lifted a quizzical eyebrow, his voice hardening. "Or did your husband find out about your visits to the Goldener Hirsch?"

Did that explain it? Margarite wondered, the wariness she had sensed in Patrick toward her from the moment she had awakened, the way he was sitting so carefully away from her, not touching her. Was he remembering that small, discreet hotel room where unfaithful wives met their lovers?

She didn't want to think, much less talk about her marriage, but she knew she owed Patrick some sort of explanation, even if he didn't believe her story. "Until that afternoon with you, I was never unfaithful to Karl," she said, and then, bitterly, "Not that it would have mattered to my husband, if I had been. The marriage was a . . . a mistake, from the beginning. And at the end, there was somebody else my husband wanted to marry."

"Is that why you took opium, to help you forget your marriage?" Patrick asked. At Margarite's puzzled look, he added, scowling, "Milli told me about the powders you took. She even had one packet left that she showed me."

Margarite straightened indignantly. "That's ridiculous. I never took opium. The headache powders were given to me by a reputable doctor. There wouldn't have been anything harmful in them." As a matter of fact, she thought, pressing a hand to her forehead, feeling the beginnings of one of her headaches, she wished she had some of her powders now

That flat, expressionless Indian look was back on Patrick's face as he drawled, "The powders the doctor gave you might have been harmless, but your husband wouldn't have had any trouble replacing them with opium. I suppose a half-drugged wife would be easier to control, and the opium would cause bizarre behavior at times. That afternoon in the hotel room, when you passed out on me and the way your eyes looked, I was sure that you were taking some sort of drug. That's why I followed you when you left Vienna."

"You make me sound like some sort of drug addict!" Margarite protested. She rubbed her arms, feeling suddenly uncomfortably chill. "It's just that I haven't been feeling well. The powders help when I have these headaches and can't sleep. I take them only when necessary."

"No more dream powders, Baroness." For a moment compassion flicked at those indigo eyes and then was gone. "And without those powders, I promise you, you're going to feel a hell of a lot worse, before very long. . . ."

Always afterward, Margarite tried to put the memory of the next weeks out of her mind, as if they could not have happened to her but to someone else, some other woman who screamed and cajoled and begged abjectly, who fought against Patrick even as he coaxed her into drinking the overly sweet tea, into eating if only a little food each day, then held her tightly in his arms while she shivered as if her body were encased in ice, and the painful muscular cramps racked her body.

The day she was finally able to dress herself, and climbed the companionway to the deck alone, the ship had reached warmer waters. She stood at the railing, delighting in the white-tipped waves, the tangy scent of the sea air, the warmth of the sun against her face. For the first time in months, she felt as if her mind were whole and free of nightmares.

"Are you feeling better, *Signorina*?" The cabin steward had come up beside her, his face sympathetic. "The seasickness is a terrible thing."

So that was how Patrick had explained her staying

closeted in her cabin all this time, Margarite thought. "Much better, thank you," she said, smiling at the young Italian boy.

He smiled back, pleased. "If you are feeling well enough, the captain asks that you and the *signore* join him for dinner this evening."

When she returned to her cabin, Margarite looked at herself in the mirror for the first time in weeks and was shocked at what she saw. Her face was pale and lifeless, her hair, dry and limp, and she had lost so much weight, she could see the sharp edge of her collarbones. Quickly, she made what repairs she could, scrubbing herself with hot water until her skin burned and there was a faint glow of color in her face. The cabin steward happily brought her some olive oil, and after she had washed her hair, she soaked it in warm olive oil, then washed it again, and brushed it dry until it shone. There was no time for an elaborate coiffure. Instead, she parted her hair and pulled it loosely into a chignon at the nape of her neck, allowing a few stray curls to escape at her temples.

There was nothing she could do about her much too thin body except hide it as best she could beneath one of the gowns she found in the clothes chest in the cabin. She chose a pale lavender-colored moiré, with long tight sleeves, and a heart-shaped neckline. Unfortunately the bodice was too large and gaped at the neck. Well, she'd just have to wear a scarf, she decided as she struggled to fasten the back of the gown. She was still trying to fasten the tiny hooks, when there was a knock at the door and Patrick stepped inside.

He had shaved the stubble of beard she was accustomed to seeing on his face these last weeks while he had practically lived in the cabin with her, and she noticed a faint scratch on one cheek, not yet completely healed. Had she done that? she wondered, turning away quickly, feeling suddenly ill at ease, remembering, embarrassed, what had passed between them these past weeks.

How could he look at her, she wondered, her face warm, and not see that other woman, wild-eyed, shaking and sobbing uncontrollably, remember the names she had screamed at him, how she had clawed at him and fought against him, because he would not bring her her precious powders.

If he was aware of her embarrassment, his voice did not show it as he said, "I thought you might need some help with your gown, Baroness." Then she felt his hands at the back of her gown, fastening the hooks, the hands dropping quickly away as they finished. She recalled with a sharp pang when those hands would have lingered to caress her skin. But, of course, there was a time, too, she thought bleakly, when he would not have called her baroness in that cool tone of voice.

When she turned toward him again, her face showed no sign of her inner turmoil as she gestured toward her gown and said, "I haven't thanked you for the clothes. Where did you manage to find them?"

"Oh, Trieste has a great many fashionable shops, Baroness." The indigo gaze held a hint of amusement as it fastened upon the too loose bodice of her frock. "Though Italian women are perhaps more liberally endowed," he said, smiling.

Margarite flushed, and reaching for her shawl, wrapped it around her shoulders, her voice cold. "You must give me the bills for the gowns so that I can repay you, and, of course, for the cost of the trip."

For a moment Patrick's eyes narrowed, then he nodded indifferently. "As you wish, Baroness."

And just how was she going to repay him? Margarite wondered. She was no longer the heiress to the Ortiz fortune and whatever little was left in the Von Friedrich estate, Karl's creditors would undoubtedly claim, even if she could somehow return to Austria and not face a murder charge. Then she forgot her worries about the deplorable state of her finances as Patrick escorted her to the captain's table in the ship's saloon and she became aware of passengers at the other tables, turning to stare with open curiosity at her.

The captain, however, couldn't have been more gracious. A handsome, heavyset man with large soulful black eyes, he commiserated with Margarite over her *mal de mer,* and apologized profusely that his ship should have been the cause of discomfort to one so *bellissima*.

Then he winked broadly at Patrick. "But perhaps it is you to whom I should apologize, *Signore*? How you must have suffered, having your sweetheart snatched from your arms into a sick bed." The black eyes gazed appreciatively at Margarite across the table, although the captain couldn't help thinking that for himself, the *signorina* was too small and skinny. Still, she had those remarkable green eyes and there was something about her, a way she had of looking directly at a man, that made him wonder if she might not be a formidable woman to love.

The captain sighed gustily. "And after all you have already suffered, *Signore*, fighting a duel to the death in the lady's honor, and spiriting her away in the dead of night from a cold-hearted father."

Margarite gave Patrick a startled glance, but he avoided her gaze, although she noticed he choked a little on the wine he was drinking.

"What did you tell the captain about us?" she demanded later that evening as they left the saloon and stood on deck for a few moments while Patrick lighted a long, thin cigar.

"Well, I might have embellished the story a little," he admitted sheepishly. "But, after all, I did want passage at the last minute, with very little luggage and a half-unconscious woman on my hands. Fortunately, the captain is a born romantic with a soft spot in his heart for young lovers. I told him you had been badly mistreated by your cruel father, who was forcing you into a loveless marriage, and that I had killed your faithless fiancé in a duel. Forced to flee Austria, we were eloping to America."

No wonder the passengers had stared at her, Margarite thought, amused, then gave her companion a startled glance. "America? Isn't this ship going to Vera Cruz?"

Patrick shook his head. "What gave you that idea? We should be arriving in New York in two days."

"New York!" Margarite was unable to keep the dismay from her voice. What would she do in New York? She knew no one there.

"Sorry if the travel arrangements don't meet with your approval, Baroness," Patrick said dryly, "but I didn't have too much choice. This was the first ship leaving Trieste, and I had no intention of waiting around for the police to show up and arrest us." He drew carefully on his cigar till it glowed red in the darkness, his voice thoughtful. "And America suits me well enough."

At her continued silence, Patrick scowled, wishing that he could see her face. There was a full moon washing its pale light across the deck, but Margarite was standing in the shadow of a smokestack, her face hidden from him. He could barely make out the outline of her figure, stiffly erect in the silvery-lilac dress. Did it mean so much to her, then, returning to Mexico, to the Ortiz wealth waiting for her there? Had he been a fool to think that none of that mattered to her, only being with him, wherever that might be?

He had almost forgotten, until he had walked into her cabin earlier, how aristocratic she could look, the haughty reserve she could wrap around herself, reminding him without a word who she was and who he was. When she spoke, her voice was so soft he had to strain to hear her. "What will you do in New York?"

"I don't plan to stay in New York. I thought I'd make my way to Texas and visit my ranch. It's probably nothing more than sagebrush and tumbleweeds, but with my gambling winnings, I might try to turn it into a working ranch. Don Miguel had been experimenting with some new, hardier range cattle that I'd like to try in Texas."

Patrick had no illusions that the spread in Texas would compare in size or luxury with the Ortiz or Cordoba ranchos. And, no doubt, building up the ranch would be hard, backbreaking work. Not the sort of life to offer a baroness with silver mines and vast acres of rich ranchland of her own, he thought grimly.

"Star and Don Miguel will be disappointed that you

aren't returning to Mexico,'' Margarite said, forcing herself to hide her own sense of despair.

The faces of his foster parents flashed into Patrick's mind, the way they had stood arm in arm the last time he had seen them as he rode away from the ranch, Star, smiling through her tears, Don Miguel, scowling, the way he did to hide his feelings. Oh, he knew they would always welcome him back, but it wasn't enough. A man needed land of his own beneath his feet. He could no more continue to accept Don Miguel's generosity than he could consider accepting a peso of Margarite's fortune. Surely, she could understand that, he thought, then remembered with a sharp jab of anger how she had haughtily insisted upon paying for the clothes he had bought her, as if he were a servant who must, of course, be paid for his services.

"You needn't concern yourself about your return trip to Mexico,'' he said. "Once we reach New York, you can get in touch with your estate agents. I'm sure they'll arrange for your transportation to Mexico.''

Margarite turned, startled. It hadn't occurred to her that Patrick didn't know that the Ortiz estate was no longer hers. Impulsively, she almost blurted out the truth but stopped herself in time. She was sure Patrick would give her whatever money she needed to return to Mexico. Because he felt sorry for her. She would see the same pity that had been in his eyes those days locked in her cabin with her, when he had helped her through that hellish time. And pity was no substitute for love. Her head lifted proudly. *Kopf hoch, Liebchen.* Her father's words echoed in her ears. Whatever else might happen to her, she was still a Von Melk. She would manage somehow.

"If you're worried about your safety in Mexico, Baroness, you needn't be,'' Patrick said. "I'll write a letter to General Diaz, Juárez's second in command. Diaz owes me a favor and I'm sure he'll give you safe passage to your home in Mexico.''

"Is the war finished, then?'' she asked, forgetting her own unhappiness in her surprise at the news. "Has Maximilian abdicated?''

"The war is ended but Maximilian never abdicated," Patrick said quietly. "I heard the news just before we left Trieste. The imperial forces surrendered at Querétaro. Maximilian was captured and executed on the Hill of the Bells. They say he died well. He had more courage than I would have thought, your Maximilian."

He heard Margarite's sharp indrawn breath. When she spoke, her voice was suddenly unutterably weary. "It's late. I think I'll return to my cabin." Patrick reached out his arm to escort her, but she stepped back. "No, stay and finish your cigar."

The desire to forget his pride, forget everything but his need to hold her close in his arms, feel her mouth part, warm and yielding, beneath his, almost overwhelmed Patrick as he watched Margarite walk toward the companionway, her back very straight, her small head held imperiously high. Only just for a moment he had glimpsed her face in the moonlight before she had turned away from him and knew he was the one who had put that look of pain there. Moodily, he turned back to the railing, cursing his own stupidity. He should have remembered how Margarite felt about Maximilian.

His mouth suddenly curved in a faint smile, remembering that day when he and his men had been waiting on the hillside for Maximilian's carriage on the road to Cuernavaca. And how Margarite had defied him, as if with her own small body she would stop him from capturing the emperor. And afterward, when he had held her in his arms, as if he could not hold her tightly enough, and she had whispered triumphantly, "No one can stop us from being together now."

Scowling darkly, he flicked his cigar away, watching its red glow arch through the night, then disappear. Other memories came rushing back. Margarite in that ridiculous boy's outfit riding the mustang with the other *arrieros* as if she had been born on a horse, always managing somehow to defy him, but never complaining of the hardships of the trail. After Juan Heras's attack, how she had begged to stay with him, her eyes bright with unshed tears as bewildered as a child who is being punished without knowing why. And he had sent her away although it felt as if his heart were being ripped from his body.

Even more vividly he remembered that first night he had taken her in the hotel room in Querétaro, the soft cries of rapture he had coaxed from her lips, and the *niña* had turned into a woman in his arms.

Still scowling, Patrick began to pace back and forth on the deck. Like a sluice gate opening, more and more memories flooded back, battering at the wall of his pride. . . .

In her cabin Margarite sat, staring, without seeing, at the bulkhead. She remembered Maximilian as she had seen him last that early morning at Chapultepec, his face tired and worn, but taking the time to speak to her with kindness, the blue eyes warm and concerned. She had never doubted his courage, but was it courage, she wondered, that had held Maximilian in Mexico and refused to let him abdicate, or pride? The pride of a Hapsburg unwilling to return to Europe a failure. The same pride that had driven Carlota from Mexico to Paris and Rome and, finally, madness. Was even pride worth so much suffering, so many sacrifices?

She frowned uncertainly. For wasn't it pride that was stopping her from asking Patrick to take her to Texas with him, pride that made her wait for him to make the first move, the first gesture that would break down the invisible wall that had grown between them. She couldn't believe he didn't care for her, not after he had crossed an ocean to come to her. And not after the way he made her feel in his arms. What did it really matter who took the first step as long as the step was taken?

She had risen to her feet, half-turned to the door, when the door suddenly crashed open. Patrick filled the doorway, scowling blackly at her, his voice fierce. "You're not going to Mexico, Margarite. You're coming to Texas with me."

He crossed to her side, his hands at her shoulders, pulling her roughly into his arms. "There'll be no argument, do you understand? The captain can marry us. . . ."

His voice fell away, as he stared, alarmed, down at the top of the dark smooth hair, heard the strangled sounds coming from Margarite, her shoulders shaking beneath his hands as if with sobs.

"*Querida,* please," he whispered. "Don't cry. You'll see. You'll like Texas." His hand slipped beneath the heavy coil of hair to caress the smooth nape of her neck.

Her head all at once fell back and he saw the tears streaming down her face were tears of joy, her glorious green eyes shining with happiness. She was laughing, bursts of laughter, so that it was several seconds before she was able to speak, shaking her head, and still laughing as she gasped, "Of course I'm going to Texas with you. Just try and stop me."

She stood on tiptoe, straining to reach his lips. His arms lifted her, carried her to the bed, where he sat, cradling her in his arms. She had no difficulty then in reaching his lips, his own mouth tenderly caressing hers, his hands gently stroking her dark hair. Until she murmured protestingly, her hands locking behind his head, pulling him closer, her lips burning, moving insistently over his, her hands slipping beneath his shirt as if it were only their flesh touching that could satisfy the compelling need growing within her.

Patrick drew back, studying, concerned, the pale oval of her face, the shadows that still remained from the ordeal of the past weeks, like bruises above the fragile cheekbones. She weighed so little in his arms, he thought, as if a strong wind would blow her away. How could he expect her to stand the hardships of the life he was offering her, he thought, groaning to himself. *"Mi amor,"* he murmured brokenly. "I have no right to deprive you selfishly of the comforts your uncle's fortune can give you."

She snuggled closer in his arms, then smiled and shook her head. "I have no fortune, not in Mexico, nor anywhere else. My cousin, Salvador, is very much alive and has inherited Uncle Manuel's estate." She sighed in mock resignation. "But now that you know I'm only a poor widow, without a peso to my name, you will no longer want to marry me."

There was nothing gentle about his kiss this time. When he finally released her, her eyes shone with a green fire, and her mouth was still half parted and trembling. A pulse beat in her throat and he could see the rosy flush from her face flow down beneath the bodice of her dress. With the gaping neckline he could look down at her small, upthrust breasts, see the gleaming softness of flesh that he knew would feel like satin beneath his hands, the pink tips hardening at his touch.

Abruptly, he got up from the bed, swinging Margarite to her feet before him as he cocked an amused eyebrow. "If I don't find the captain right away, there won't be any marriage, not tonight anyway."

The wedding ceremony, at the bride's request, was held on the deck of the ship beneath a sky where stars made a milky haze overhead and the moon spread a silver, phosphorescent path over the ocean. The captain beamed happily as he performed the ceremony before the hastily assembled passengers. Afterward, he insisted the bride and groom must be toasted with champagne, and the cabin boy brought up his accordion and began playing for the wedding guests. But when the captain looked for the bride so that he could have the first dance, he discovered the bride and groom had quietly slipped away.

The captain smiled nostalgically, remembering the pleasures of his own wedding night as he strolled to the railing and surveyed the night sky approvingly. It was going to be a fine day tomorrow, he decided.

About the Author

Although Marcella Thum is the author of several award-winning non-fiction and juvenile books, she finds particular delight in writing historical romances. She is able to combine her love of historical research and the weaving of suspenseful plots around beautiful, courageous heroines and dashing, handsome heroes.

The author has visited and lived in many fascinating parts of the world including Hawaii and Mexico, the setting for her most recent novel, MARGARITE. Her other books for Fawcett Gold Medal include BLAZING STAR, JASMINE and WILD LAUREL.

Romance Returns...
with
MARCELLA THUM

HER VOLUPTUOUSNESS WAS BOTH HER ENEMY—AND HER SAVING GRACE

It was Margarite's dark haired beauty that made her jealous stepmother banish her from the Austrian court, to the exotic climes of Mexico.

And it was her curvaceousness that captured the eye of the maniacal bandit, El Cuchillo, who vowed he would have his fill of Margarite before he was done.

But it was Margarite's bold beauty that brought the handsome, enigmatic Patrick O'Malley to her rescue. A captain in the Union Army, he was secretly working for the United States in Mexico. Even as he fought the very people she supported, Margarite found love in Patrick's embrace as, again and again, he took her to the peaks of passion—and beyond.

Her all-consuming love would take her through the terrifying days of Mexico's fight for independence, into the court of the mad Carlota and her emperor husband Maxmilian, and back to her Austrian home where Margarite literally battles for her life—and the love of the man she can never forget....

ISBN 0-449-